The Memory Stones

Forgiveness is a Journey in Time
(Book 1)

By
Lewis Pennington

Silver Lining
PUBLISHING

Silver Lining
PUBLISHING
622 Brush Creek Road
Fairview, NC 28730

Note To Readers
Please know that many of the locations as well
as military elements, names, dates, etc., mentioned
in *The Memory Stones* are purely fictional. Its
purpose is not to educate you with exact Civil War era
information but rather to inspire you with a message
on the power of forgiveness.

For mom,
who gave me the wings to fly.

Chapter 1
(1861)

"Fetch the thunder stick!" said the old man, stretching his bony arm toward the pond. His splotchy, paper-thin palm unfolded a knobby finger that pointed across the shimmering surface to the silhouette of a large house hovering above the far bank.

Mase stood frozen in front of the smokehouse squeezing his crucifix, its edges digging into his palm. He looked into the black abyss of the man's eyes with a plea of forgiveness. There was none to be given.

"I said fetch me the thunder," the man roared, blood vessels bulging along his temples. He turned to an ogre of a man pacing in circles beside him. "*Now!*"

Mase jumped back, dodging the massive man who had been commanded to fulfill the task. Out of the corner of his eye, he watched him disappear into the darkness while he remained toe to toe with the old man bent on an act of revenge that would have devastating consequences.

Several breathless minutes later the ogre reappeared, huffing his way toward them and carrying a double-barreled shotgun.

"What're you going to do?" Mase asked.

The man snatched the weapon and hobbled to the front door.

He moved with him. "What're you planning?"

"Delivering justice!" he said, pounding the entrance with the butt of the gun.

The door swung open, revealing a small, dark, windowless room filled with a half-dozen ham shanks, plucked fowl, and other assorted meats hanging from the ceiling's large oak beams. Cutting knives, saws, and butcher cleavers hung from the walls. With a solitary candle lighting the room, one could barely make out the black man standing with his face against the opposite wall. His shackled hands were raised above his head, attached to chains running into the ceiling trusses. From a distance, he could have been mistaken for just another side of meat about to be processed.

The old man walked inside, slamming the door behind him.

Mase stared into the hardwood planks. He muttered to himself, dropped the crucifix, and barged inside to find the man holding the firearm against the back of the black man's head.

"Nooooo," he yelled as he grabbed the gun.

"By God, boy, if you don't let—"

"No, please—you can't!"

The man glared at him, his chest heaving.

Mase pressed the gun barrel downward. "If it's going to be done, I'm the one who has to do it."

The man stepped back, panting, struggling to remain stable. "You shouldn't even be here."

"If justice has to be served, it *has* to come from me."

The old man gritted his teeth, holding back the urge to finish what he had set out to do. "Here!" He rammed the weapon into Mase's chest. "Do what you have to," he said, slamming the door behind him.

The words echoed in Mase's ears. *Do what you have to.*

Chapter 2
(12 Years Earlier - 1849)

Click, clack, clickety, clack, clack, clickety, clickety…
back and forth, from knee to knee, the silver flashed.
Faster, then slower, then faster still, the cadence of his
instruments danced in rhythm with the masterful movements of a true artist.

An enormous, barreled-chested black man and an
equally robust black woman watched from their rocking
chairs in amazement as the young boy tapped, slapped,
and patted his spoons feverishly between his palms, across
his chest, and over the rope belt barely holding up his
pants. The warm glow of the midday sun shone into the
cabin and onto his spoons, sending flashes of light dancing
across its tiny walls.

"Oooohhh wheeee," the man bellowed. "He sho can
play them silvers."

The lady's eyes crinkled. "Ain't that the truth."

The boy stopped, let out an exaggerated wheeze, then
laid the utensils on the dirt floor while wiping his forehead
with a ragged sleeve. "I's plum tuckered, Maudie. Mind if
I rest a spell?"

Maudie sat in her rocking chair next to a rickety crib. Her doughy face was full of cheer. With rounded features and an overweight but sturdy frame, she was an adoring figure in the young man's life. Out of all the orphans on the plantation, she had chosen him to raise as her own. Inside the crib was her baby girl, sound asleep upon a small tuft of hay covered with a thin cotton blanket.

She smiled at him, appreciative of the entertainment he had provided.

"I reckon you deserve a squat," she said, fidgeting with the ever-present kerchief on her head. "Only one thing you gotta do, though, before Cluc turns you loose."

The boy looked to the mountainous man. Cluc tilted his head with a mischievous grin, revealing a large gap between his front teeth that greatly lessened the intimidation of his Herculean frame. With a wink, he bent down with both arms stretched toward him. "Bring it here, Mr. Spoon," he bellowed.

The boy smiled ear to ear. At the age of seven, he felt special whenever Cluc or anyone put the word "mister" in front of his nickname.

"Well, what's ya waitin' for?" Cluc said.

Spoon tucked his head and sprinted straight into his arms.

A second later the big man had him above his head, twirling him about like a sparrow on a blustery day.

At six feet, four inches and close to three hundred pounds, Cluc was a dominating figure on the plantation. *Rock-solid, steady, and loyal as the day is long* was written on the bill of goods that accompanied him on his purchase at the slave auction. These traits, along with his towering presence, made him a natural choice as a slave foreman.

"Remember to give Sissy a kiss when you land," Maudie shouted above their raucous laughter.

No quicker than Cluc had lowered him to the floor, than he was hovering over the little girl who had slept through his performance. As he leaned over the crib's railing, his feet dangled off the ground. With a single *umph* and a shift of his weight over the edge, Spoon kissed his palm, then gently touched it to her forehead. "Here ya go, Sissy girl," he whispered.

Back on the floor, he proceeded to amuse his two onlookers with an exaggerated display of tiptoeing to the opposite corner, where he pulled out a small parcel from under his bed.

Maudie and Cluc gave each other a knowing look indicating their knowledge of its contents.

"Where you headin'?" Cluc asked him, his tone more than curious.

"Gotta get to the creek," he said. "I'll be back on time—I promise."

Like many other Sundays, the day was bright and full of wonder for the young boy. Normally he would meander his way along the winding path through the slave quarters, yelling greetings to the inhabitants of each of the fifteen tiny, one-room cabins. But today was different. He was on a mission.

Although a far cry from the row houses of Charleston, these shanties were better than those on other plantations. Each had a proper chimney with a fireplace large enough to cook a chicken while boiling a side pot of water. Some even had small holly bushes adorning the sides of the front door, and while most others did not have any windows, these had two.

The order in which the cabins were occupied was strategic. Cluc resided in the first one. As the slave foreman, the plantation's owner liked to have his gentle giant as near as possible to the big house. Next to him was the house mother's cabin, which was where Maudie, Sissy, and Spoon lived. From that point on, a cabin lined the path every twenty-five yards until they came to the edge of the woods.

As Spoon bounded outside, he stopped to make sure he was ahead of schedule. Turning back, he looked past Cluc's cabin, past the smokehouse, and around the giant wall of cedars that separated the slave quarters from the big house.

He peered across the seven-acre pond and up the hill to where the great house sat overlooking the plantation's eleven hundred acres of cotton, soybean, corn, and cattle. With its huge weeping willows overhanging the water's edge and the swans and ducklings paddling about, visitors easily fell under its charm. Coupled with the backdrop of the third-largest mansion in South Carolina, Willow Creek Plantation was beyond breathtaking.

A few seconds later he spotted his target coming out the front door, a tiny speck racing down the hill toward the pond. Spoon bounced. He knew it would only take him fifteen minutes to reach his destination, arriving in plenty of time ahead of the speck that was growing larger by the second. Rather than chancing it, he tucked his package under his arm and started toward the creek. As he passed the last cabin and entered the woods, he chuckled at the thought of what lay ahead.

Within a few minutes, he was off the trail and standing

next to the creek he loved so much. The sun's rays penetrated the surface, giving its rocky bottom a look of gold. This was a sacred place for him. Even at such a tender age, he knew he would always rely on its crystal-clear waters for refuge. Maudie would often tell him it represented his life—the present, future, and past. He didn't understand it, but he knew it to be true.

Sitting on a small grassy knoll, he scooped out some undergrowth from behind a fern and stashed his parcel inside. Then he crossed his legs, patted his knees, and waited, proud of accomplishing the first piece of his master plan.

His brief respite ended as a lanky young boy with a mop of sandy-brown hair came running through the woods.

Mase, the plantation owner's only son and Spoon's best friend, had run the entire distance from the big house to the creek. With several long breaths he managed to push out, "I thought—I'd beaten you—for sure."

"Ain't ever gonna happen," Spoon responded with glee. "You knows I'm always punktool."

Still bent over, Mase slapped him on the back. "You mean punct—u—al."

Spoon looked at his friend with fake disgust. "What day is it?"

"Sunday. Why?"

"No, what—*day*—is it?" he said, stretching out the word.

Mase's green eyes gleamed. "Ohhh, is it Thanksgiving? No, it's Christmas. Wait, I know—it's the day before tomorrow."

Spoon skewed his lips then pounced on him, pinning

him to the ground. "No it ain't, you knucklehead—it's your *birthday!*"

Mase lay affixed to the ground as the two busted into laughter.

"Close your eyes."

"Do I have to get up?"

"Not yet." He leaned over, pulled his secret package from the fern, and laid it next to his head. "Okay, go on, open it."

As he picked up the bundle, Spoon pulled him to his feet. "Aw, really? You got me somethin'?"

"Why sure! We're best buddies, ain't we?"

"Course we are," Mase replied, digging into the brown wrapping paper.

Spoon leaned forward as he watched him rip the last piece away, exposing a pine box about the size of a thick book. He nudged him. "Go on. Open it!"

Mase lifted the lid. Inside was just that, a black leather book. Carved into the cover was the word *DIARY.*

Spoon beamed with pride. "I made the cover with Cluc's old bowie knife." He started bouncing. "Open it. Open it."

Mase pulled it out and flipped the cover. "I can't believe this. You really got me a diary!"

Spoon bobbed his head in rhythm with his bouncing. "Look on the last page."

On the inside back cover, written in jagged letters, was *To Mase. Yor best frend. Jeziah C.*

"Wow! I still can't believe you got me a diary!"

"I know how much ya like scribblin' on stuff," he said, spinning around. "I've been savin' for near a year. Maudie and Cluc even pitched in."

"This is the nicest thing I've ever got for my birthday. Daddy got me a genuine pocket watch, but it ain't near as nice as this." He wrapped his arms around his friend. "This is the best gift of my entire life."

"What ya gonna write in it?"

"Don't know yet. Daddy says there's a war coming one day. Maybe I'll write about that."

"There's a what a comin'?"

"A war. You know what a war is, don't ya?"

Spoon scratched his head. "I reckon not."

"It's when two people, or a lot of people, don't like each other and they kill one another."

"Hmmm, I reckon that's something to write about."

Mase held his new possession over his head as they danced in a circle, basking in their friendship.

"Come on, let's go show Maudie," Spoon said, running into the woods. "Last one there's a rotten egg."

By the time they were out of the woods, they were drenched in sweat. As they raced past the stretch of cabins, they dodged in and out of a long line of slaves marching down the winding path in the direction of Cluc's cabin.

"Where're they going?" Mase asked. "Church is already over."

"Don't know," Spoon said, speeding by his friend.

Plopping up onto Maudie's front step, they had barely caught their breath when the door swung open. "You boys get in here now," Maudie demanded.

Mase looked at Spoon. "We in trouble?"

He shrugged, eyes wide with uncertainty.

Sheepishly they stepped inside, the door slamming behind them. The two small windows on the front of the house were closed, leaving them alone in the dark with Maudie.

Mase reached out, waving his hand, hoping to find his friend next to him. But nothing. "Spoon," he whispered, "where are you?" There was no reply. "Maudie, where'd you go?" Something shuffled about from across the room. "Come on, Spoon. Where are you?" he urged, circling around aimlessly. "This ain't funny."

Inching his way back in the direction where he thought he'd find the door, he toppled over something on the floor. Something wet slapped against his cheek, followed by a whimper. "That you, Bo?" Another sloppy lick across his chin indicated his rambunctious mutt was with them.

A muffled snicker was followed by a tiny whisper. "One—two—three!" On three, the door and both windows flew open, instantly transforming the cabin into a sun-filled room of friends and family. "Happy birthday!" they all shouted.

Mase rubbed his eyes as the room erupted in cheers, songs, hoots and hollers. He couldn't believe such a tiny space could hold so many people. Maudie was there holding Sissy. Cluc and three friends were there, along with Mase's older sister, Annabelle, and his father. Standing next to him was Spoon, singing the loudest of everyone.

"Show 'em what I got you," he said, bouncing about on the balls of his feet.

Mase hoisted his gift above his head. "I got a genuine leather diary!"

The crowd oohed and awed.

"What you gonna write in it, Mr. Mase?" someone asked.

"Don't rightly know yet."

11

"He's gonna write about that war his daddy told him was comin'," Spoon blurted out.

"War?" Cluc said.

A tall, solidly built, grey-bearded man with a kindly face shuffled next to Mase. "Now, now son," he said, patting him on the shoulder. "That's all hearsay."

The crowd went silent.

"What's you mean hearsay, Mr. Brax?" said one of the slaves.

"Well, what it means is—hmmm—hearsay is when... I'll tell you what it means." He dropped to one knee and gave his son a big hug. "It means it's time for cake!" he crowed.

Annabelle rushed to her brother's side, pulled back her long black pigtails, and gave him a quick hug and kiss. "Happy birthday," she said, handing him a small silver crucifix. "Daddy helped me pick it out." She spun around. "Follow me!" she squealed, rushing out of the cabin.

As they walked outside, Mase realized all the slaves they had passed on the path were standing in front of the cabin. Annabelle appeared in front of him again, this time with a small white-frosting cake with eight candles stuck randomly on top.

"Three cheers for Mr. Mase," a slave in the back yelled.

The crowd erupted in the joyous chant.

Cluc leaned over to Mase's father. "War, Mr. Brax?" he said, barely audible over the merriment.

Mr. Winslow patted him on the shoulder. "Don't worry none. Everything's fine."

Annabelle held the cake out to her brother. "Go on. Make a wish!"

As he was taking a deep breath, a sudden gust of cold

air blew in from the direction of the creek, snuffing out the candles.

"There," he exclaimed, "I got my wish!"

While waving his diary in one hand and holding Spoon's hand with the other, they danced around Annabelle. Still holding the cake, she spun in the opposite direction, laughing as her pigtails flew out beside her.

The sudden change in temperature ran a chill up Maudie's spine. She folded her arms and began to shiver as she watched the three youngsters rejoicing in the innocence of the day. What she witnessed brought a smile to her face, but the premonition that swept over her stole it away. She closed her eyes and silently prayed.

Chapter 3

The sun from the previous day rolled over to the next, and all the slaves proceeded about their chores in the fields, with Cluc overseeing their progress and leading them in endless rounds of gospel songs.

Spoon followed Maudie and Sissy to the big house. Although he was often underfoot, he always managed to help by making her laugh with whatever antics he could muster. Mase and Annabelle had their own set of chores that included periodically pitching in to help them.

Mase's father adored his children, but he was a firm believer that hard work built character and that working alongside others, especially his slaves, was the best way to promote harmony.

Although he was highly respected within the community, his leniency toward his slaves often brought ridicule and at times rebuke. On such occasions, he would do his best to brush aside the offending comment or deed by deflecting to a brighter subject. If pressed, he would diffuse the situation with a healthy dose of wit or wisdom.

Braxton Winslow was indeed a different breed of man. Unlike many other plantation owners who built their fortunes by breaking the backs of their slaves, he made his by understanding human nature and the power of kindness. He had never abused any of them. For whatever reason he refused to follow suit with the atrocities practiced by so many others. In fact, the only whips on the property were the ones the horse trainers used.

Maudie often said most of his kindness came from his wife who was known for loving everyone, no matter of race or religion. After losing her to typhoid when Mase was two, Braxton came to rely heavily on Maudie. Even after learning of her secret rituals at the creek, he entrusted her entirely with the safety of both his children.

If he had any shortcoming at all, it was the fact that he was the brother to Judge Joseph Winslow. The Judge, as folks referred to him, was a sickly man with a temperament in stark contrast to Braxton's.

"Polio is the culprit to his demeanor," Mr. Winslow would say when defending his brother's sour attitude. As a young boy, he had contracted the disease in his left leg, leaving him with a limp that required the use a cane for the rest of his life. During this time, he learned the plantation would ultimately be given to his brother. As much as the cane allowed him to walk, it also served as a daily reminder of his father's bias.

Although Braxton was four years his senior, the Judge looked fifteen years older. His frame was also much smaller, which furthered his envy of Braxton or anyone of stature. The only positive thing that could be said about the Judge was he was wickedly smart. After graduating at the top of his law school class, he went on to have a successful career defending several prominent politicians on various ethics charges. Those relationships were why people speculated he had been appointed judge of Beaufort County at the young age of twenty-nine.

When Mase learned his uncle had been detained in court on the day of his birthday, he was far from upset. Upon finding out the Judge would be making up for his absence by arriving that afternoon, Mase simply wanted to know when he'd be leaving.

Maudie thumped his ear. "Mind yourself, young man. Kinfolk is to be welcomed," she said. "No matter who they is," she continued under her breath.

Just before noon, the Judge's black carriage trotted across the half-mile entrance leading to the pond and around to the big house. A massive man on horseback wearing a long, weathered trench coat and broad-brimmed hat pulled down to his eyes trailed behind. With a raven's feather pinned to the side of the hat and his long, crusty beard and jet-black hair, he resembled a pirate awaiting to board the unsuspecting carriage that preceded him.

"Poppa," Annabelle yelled from the upstairs balcony where she'd been playing with Spoon, "I think Uncle Joseph's coming."

Mr. Winslow emerged from his study with Mase. "Run outside, children. Let's give your uncle a proper welcome."

From the parlor, Maudie peered out the window, pursed her lips, inhaled deeply, then walked to the front door.

Mr. Winslow, Mase, Annabelle, Spoon, and two other house slaves stood on the front lawn awaiting the carriage. Unbeknown to anyone, Bo was digging holes under the porch. As soon as the carriage rolled up, the temptation got the best of him. With his healthy affection for visitors, he ran out to eagerly greet the new arrivals, sending the horses into a tizzy. The carriage lurched back violently, tilted left and right, and almost sent its driver over the side.

Maudie snickered at the thought of how its occupant must be dealing with being tussled about.

As Mr. Winslow's slaves subdued the horses, an awful swearing commenced from within the carriage, followed by a shrill, "Silas!"

The horseman who had been following immediately galloped up, taking charge. "Step back," he barked while opening the carriage door. The end of a shaky cane appeared out of the opening to which the large man took hold. With a carefully practiced pull, he withdrew the frail man on the other end out and onto the road.

"Brother!" Braxton said, coming up to greet him. "How are you?"

"If I had my derringer, you'd be less one mangy dog." He managed a crooked smile as they shook hands. "I'm alright, I reckon."

"Kids, come greet your uncle."

Mase and Annabelle rushed to their father but stopped short of delivering any welcoming hugs.

"Go on now," he said, motioning them forward.

One at a time, each suffered a halfhearted embrace for the Judge.

"Sorry I missed your big day, boy." He jerked his head toward the man in the trench coat. "Silas!"

In an instant, the man appeared with a small felt box, which the Judge pushed toward Mase with the end of his cane. "Happy birthday," he croaked.

Mase began to flip the lid.

"It's a pocketknife," the Judge blurted. "Every ten-year-old boy needs a good knife."

"But I'm actually—"

"Excited to get it," Braxton interjected. "What a great gift. I bet it'll be good cutting into the ham Maudie's prepared for dinner or—better yet—good for whittling."

His son frowned. "Sure, Daddy."

"Why don't y'all go help with the table while we get Uncle Joseph squared away."

As the children scurried into the house, the Judge whacked his companion's forearm, causing him to drop the armful of baggage he was dutifully preparing to carry inside. "Braxton, let me introduce you to my man, Silas Dagon."

"Glad to meet you, sir," Braxton said, offering his hand.

"Howdy," he grunted, ignoring the gesture as he reached down to gather the baggage.

Braxton withdrew his hand and started to help pick up some of the scattered items.

"I got it," the burly man said in a gravely baritone.

"For Pete's sake, either shake the man's hand or let him help you, Silas."

"Sorry." He turned and looked up at Braxton from under his hat, revealing a pair of deep-set eyes. The left one was clear and blue, but the other bore a thin line of bare skin, parting the eyebrow and leading to a hazy displaced pupil that had been pushed permanently to the lower corner.

Braxton winced as the man clutched his hand, squeezing it beyond the cordial grip of a gentleman.

"Silas is my new associate. He handles many of my— well, let's just say my affairs requiring a special ability to persuade." The Judge gave the man a wink. "You'd be wise to bring on a fellow with his skills, big brother. He'd get that bunch of lazy no goods to be more productive. With a man like mine, I guarantee you could increase productivity tenfold."

"Oh, I believe Cluc's got everything under control just fine," Braxton said.

"I still can't believe you've got a slave in place of where a white man ought to be. You need to start treating these darkies the way they're supposed to be treated. They don't even call you Master. It's a wonder nobody's strung *you* up yet."

Braxton chuckled.

"Mark my words," the Judge said, "the day's coming when all hell's going to break loose, and you'll wish you had the right arm of a man like Silas."

After dinner, the two men retired to the back porch for cigars and brandy while Mase and Spoon ran to the creek to catch crawfish. With dusk approaching, Mase stood proudly along the creek bank, giggling and holding a wooden bucket full of their catch.

"What's so funny?" Spoon asked.

"I was thinkin'—what if we turn some of these critters loose in Uncle Joseph's bed tonight?"

"You crazy? I ain't gonna rile that old man for nothin'. He'll sic his big grizzly fella on us."

"We'll just have to let Maudie fry 'em up then."

Spoon licked his lips at the thought of downing their delicacy. "Wait, what's that?" he said, turning his head downstream. "You hear it?"

Mase cupped his hand around his ear. "Yeah, sounds like singing. Come on, let's check it out."

Moving closer to the noise, they struggled through the thicket, ducking in and out of brush so as not to be noticed.

"Ouch!" Spoon said, tugging his shirt sleeve out of a briar patch.

"Shush! You'll give us away."

"Look yonder." Spoon pointed to a small shallow turn in the creek.

On the opposite bank, a lady in a long white dress was bending over the embankment, splashing water onto herself.

"She takin' a bath?"

"Let's get closer," Mase said, crawling underneath a large Magnolia bush directly across from her.

As the lady crouched over the water's edge, she shook her head once, then slowly stepped into the stream. Reaching into the water, she pulled up a handful of mud and placed it in a small box sitting on the bank.

Spoon giggled. "What the heck she doin?"

Mase put his finger to his lips. "Shhh."

She stood and raised the box above her head. Arching backwards, she looked past her outstretched arms and began moving her lips as if talking with someone hovering directly above it.

"Well, I'll be. Is that Maudie?" Spoon whispered in Mase's ear.

"Shore is," he said, staring in wonder. "Never seen her without her kerchief."

Out of nowhere, Silas crept from the woods. Standing on the opposite bank, he looked on, motionless, like a tiger stalking his prey. Meanwhile Maudie proceeded, ignorant of his presence.

His head pitched to the side as he tried surmising the

ritual before him. "What witchery you brewin' here?" he blurted, causing her to stumble back onto the bank.

Steadying herself, she gathered her kerchief and wrapped it around the box. "Nothing, sir. Just heading back to the big house."

"Then what you got in that there box?" he said, stepping into the creek. "Let's have a look-see, shall we?" He treaded his way toward her until he was within an arm's length.

"No, sir!" she said, backing up.

"I said, I want to see what's in the box," he growled. With catlike reflexes, he snatched it from her, throwing the kerchief to the ground. His eyes narrowed as he gazed inside. "What in the world…"

Mase heard the swoosh of his friend's arm pass inches from his head.

With a solid whop, Spoon's rock landed squarely on Silas's forehead, sending him toppling backward into the water.

As he fumbled and splashed around, trying to regain his footing, Maudie grabbed her box and slipped away with Mase and Spoon following behind her unnoticed.

When the boys reached the big house, they were exhausted but thrilled with their adventure. Annabelle, hearing them thumping their way up the front steps, came out to meet them in her nightgown, followed a moment later by Mr. Winslow.

"Mase, time for bed, son. And, Spoon, you best get on back to Maudie."

Just then, Silas came trudging along behind them. Soaked from head to toe, the scowl on his face conveyed the anger and embarrassment of his failed attempt at the creek.

Spoon gulped, and Mase put his hand on his shoulder, discreetly shaking his head, hoping to calm his friend's nerves.

With his sopping-wet hat in hand, minus the raven's feather, Silas puffed his chest and marched past Mr. Winslow.

"Wellll—good evening, Silas." He glanced at the boys and winked. "Out for an evening swim, are we?"

"Hmmph," he grunted. Stopping for a second, he plopped his hat onto his head. Water streamed down his face and through his beard. He snarled then proceeded onward as if on parade.

Mase snickered, causing him to stop again. After what seemed an eternity, he proceeded toward Annabelle. Pulling off his hat, he bowed as if part of a royal procession. The scar over his eye arched upward as he raised a lustful eyebrow. Licking his lips, he moved the gaze of his one good eye from her slender neck to her waist, then down to her bare feet and back to her breasts, where they remained for a long moment.

"Excuse me, Mr. Dagon," Braxton said, positioning his fist on his hip, "your room—*sir*—is around the corner in the guest house. I highly recommend you go *now* before you catch your death."

Silas slowly turned his head back in Braxton's direction, cleared his throat, then spit, barely missing Annabelle's foot. With a smile that lingered into a gruesome frown, he disappeared into the night.

Chapter 4

The next morning, Mase awoke to his favorite smell. Bacon was sizzling downstairs in a cast-iron skillet, filling the house with its enticing aroma. Many a morning started this way for the young heir to the Willow Creek Plantation. The only difference today was the inclusion of a fierce debate emanating from the end of the hall. As much as he wanted to avoid whatever had now turned into an outright argument, the appeal of scarfing down a half-dozen slices of crispy bacon was too much.

Still in his nightclothes, he cracked the door and stuck his head out to see his father and uncle standing at the top of the stairs, engaged in a heated conversation. For the time being, he would have to wait to get to his savory delight until the passage cleared.

"For God's sake, brother, you don't understand the economics of the situation," the Judge said.

"I know it all too well," Mase's father retorted.

"How's that?"

"I have my family and fifty-three other souls in my care, and I aim to make sure every one of them is taken care of."

"Oh, come off it, Braxton. I know you want the best for your boy and girl, but those fifty-three slaves of yours are just that—slaves! They only exist to serve you and your family. And by the look of your books, you better have a plan that takes care of your kin, not your slaves."

Braxton didn't say a word as he let his frustration simmer. "What then would you have me do, brother?"

The Judge pounded his cane on the floor, delighted to feel he was coming closer to making his point. "Sell at least ten of them, diversify the capital, and bring on a bonified team to increase the return on the remaining ones."

"So, to keep Willow Creek solvent, you're telling me to sell ten slaves and take the money and do what again?"

"When the time comes, put the money into bonds."

"What type of bonds?"

The Judge rolled his eyes. "Do I have to spoon-feed you? You know war is inevitable. When the Southern states secede from the Union, they'll have to issue bonds to support the effort, and those bonds will yield a handsome return after the war ends."

"And what 'bonified team' are you talking about that will increase the return on—" he could barely muster the words, "the others."

The Judge tapped the end of his cane with his finger. "Why, that would be Mr. Dagon and myself."

Even from the other end of the hall, Mase could see his father's face turn bloodred as his voice rose with every syllable. "First of all, none of these slaves will ever—I repeat ever—be sold. Half of them are orphans I purchased to give them some sense of family. The other half were purchased from owners who would have beaten them to death." His brow furrowed as he glowered at the Judge. "Believe it or not, little brother…" His face suddenly lost its color as he slapped his hand to his forehead and his voice faded. "Believe it or not—this—is…"

Suddenly his right leg buckled, then his entire right side went limp and he stumbled forward. Unable to grab the railing, he tumbled down the steps.

"Daddy!" Mase yelled, running past his uncle to the bottom of the stairwell. His father's body lay contorted on the floor. "Daddy, are you alright?" He cradled his father's face. "Talk to me."

His left eyelid fluttered open.

"Daddy, please!"

His father tried raising his hand but failed. He blinked, then spoke in a slow, slurred voice. "What happened?"

"You fell," the Judge said, finally making his way down the stairs. He leaned over Mase. "You all right?" he asked flatly.

He lay motionless, looking up in bewilderment. "Brother…"

The Judge leaned closer.

Shaking, Braxton touched him on the sleeve as saliva dripped from the corners of his mouth. "I'm sorry, dear brother," he slurred before his head rolled to the side and his eyelids slowly fell.

For the next few hours, the family waited anxiously outside his bedroom. Cluc stood by the door, firm on protecting his master, while Maudie sat with a Bible in her lap, and Annabelle lay curled up in the corner. Mase paced frantically in front of his father's door, stopping every few minutes, begging Maudie to let him in.

"Not yet, child," she said tenderly. "Doc's still taking

care of things."

Meanwhile, Judge Joseph sat in Braxton's downstairs office, having his noonday brandy, periodically sending Silas to inquire about his brother's well-being. Upon returning, he would look around, making sure no one was nearby, then whisper his findings in the Judge's ear. Every time he passed her, Maudie's face registered a deeper level of contempt.

"Sure you don't want me to keep that fool away?" Cluc would say.

And every time she would shake her head and simply reply, "Wish we could."

An hour later, the doctor emerged from the room. Besides Maudie, everyone, including Cluc, lay asleep on the floor.

Doc Parkin was a beloved figure throughout the county. With a grandfather's demeanor and a penchant for pipe smoking, he possessed a soul that was equally kind to all living things. He had been both the slaves' and family's practitioner since Maudie first came to the plantation as a baby. Malnourished and near death, he had nursed her back to health.

Taking her by the arm, he walked her down the hallway. "Maudie, my dear," he whispered, "I'm afraid Braxton has suffered a severe case of apoplexy."

She clutched her Bible to her chest. "Oh Lord, how bad?"

"He's been in and out of consciousness for the past four hours. He's resting now." He sighed. "I just don't know."

"Know what, Doc?" she said, looking toward the children.

"I don't know the extent of the damage. He's strong as

an ox, but the apoplexy may have been stronger. The fall certainly didn't help matters."

Maudie's eyes welled with tears.

He placed his hand on her shoulder. "Don't you worry, I'm going to stay with him for the rest of the evening. You try and get some sleep." He turned and went back inside the room.

The next morning came quickly. Maudie had just fallen asleep when Mase tugged at her sleeve. "Can I see Daddy now?"

She rubbed her eyes while Cluc remained slumped in his chair, snoring.

"Come on, Maudie. Can I see him? Pleeease."

Just then, the door cracked open. Mase seized the opportunity and started to rush in only to run smack-dab into Doc Parkin. "Mase, my boy—you can't go in yet."

"But why?" he pleaded.

Maudie was awake now and equally anxious to hear his reply.

"Because he's sleeping," the doctor said, kneeling in front of him. "Master Mase, your daddy's been through a lot. You've got to promise me something."

He nodded quickly.

"You have to be very quiet today. Will you promise me that?"

"Yes, yes. But when can I see him?"

"One other thing. You must be patient too, which means waiting until it's time. I'll be back shortly, and we'll see then, okay?"

He stuck out his lower lip. "Okay." He lowered his head and walked away.

"Maudie," he said, packing his pipe with tobacco, "I have to see the Carrington's youngest daughter. She was expecting yesterday, and I need to check on her progress." He took out his pocket watch. "Let's see, it's ten after six now. I'll try and be back by eleven." He pulled her next to Cluc, who was just waking.

"How's he doing, Doc?" the big man asked, blinking the sleep from his eyes.

"Better, but he's not out of the woods yet." He looked at Maudie. "I want you to check on him every ten minutes. Make sure he's comfortable and give him water if he needs it." He turned to Cluc. "And most of all, make sure the house is extra quiet."

As he walked down the stairs, Doc passed Silas stomping his way up. "Excuse me, sir. Can you be so kind as to walk a little more lightly? Mr. Winslow is sleeping and shouldn't be awakened."

"I'll walk as I please," he grumbled as he passed. When he approached the top, he came to a halt.

Standing with his arms crossed was Cluc, his immense frame blocking his path. "No, sir," he said, straight-faced.

Although Silas was a big man, he appeared much smaller than the slave foreman, given his lower position on the steps. For a moment, the two did not move. Silas looked up into Cluc's resolute gaze and knew any attempt to pass would have undesirable consequences. Without a word, he walked back to the kitchen where he reported the results to the Judge, who sat with his feet propped on Braxton's desk, reading the newspaper and smoking a cigar.

"Must be worse than I expected," he muttered, the edges of his mouth curling upward as he tapped his cane.

Just before noon, Dr. Parkin returned to find the family crowded silently outside Braxton's door. "I'm sorry I'm a little late."

"How's young Mrs. Carrington?" asked Maudie.

"A healthy baby girl," he said, entering the bedroom.

Maudie followed behind, holding a small pine box she had retrieved from her cabin. Each time she went in to check on him, she had it with her. Braxton lay immobile, his arms straight by his sides.

"How's he been?"

"Maybe better, maybe the same." She shrugged. "Honestly, Doc, I don't know. Two of the times I went in, he was awake but didn't say anything. The second time I thought he wanted water, but when I put the glass to his mouth, it ran out the sides."

As they continued talking, she felt a small tug on her dress causing her to turn to the bed. "He's awake, Doc!"

The doctor bent over, pulling his patient's eyelids open, examining the size of his pupils. "Braxton, can you hear me?"

He dipped his head. "Yessss." His voice was more robust, but the word rolled out like molasses.

After several minutes of examination, Braxton raised his left arm and tried pointing to the door. "The children."

"You want to see the children?" Maudie asked.

He returned a shallow nod.

She looked at Dr. Parkin for the appropriate response.

Taking her by the arm, he walked her into the hall where the children were anxiously waiting. "Mase, Annabelle, you can go in now. But before you do, you have to know he's not well, but he's going to be okay. Your daddy's a strong man." He wanted to explain further but stopped. "Remember to be calm and quiet as possible."

"We will," they said in unison. As requested, they slowly entered the room.

When the door had closed, the doctor motioned for Cluc to join him and Maudie at the top of the stairs. "Braxton's apoplexy is more severe than I thought. He has almost complete paralysis on his right side."

Maudie gasped.

"What's paralysis, Doc?" Cluc asked.

"He can't move his arm," she said.

"And his right leg is partially paralyzed," the doctor added.

"But he's gonna be alright, ain't he?" Cluc asked.

"I'm hoping, but only time will tell."

The Judge stood at the foot of the stairs, out of sight from those above. His eyes were closed in concentration as he eavesdropped on their conversation.

The doctor put a hand on each of their shoulders. "Cluc, you'll be his rock. And, Maudie, you'll be his light."

The two looked at each other, their concern for their embattled master evident in their eyes.

"Of course we will," she said.

"I know. But you're going to need help."

Downstairs the Judge rapidly tapped his cane.

"What kind of help?" Maudie asked.

"Someone to take charge of the place or at least assist in running it. Someone like a family member."

Maudie grimaced.

"What is it?" the doctor asked.

"The only kin he's got is downstairs," she said flatly.

"You mean Judge Joseph?" he said, straightening up. "I didn't realize he was here. Why that's good news. He can manage things for sure."

Maudie grabbed for Cluc's forearm as if about to faint. Dr. Parkin put his arm around her waist and helped her to a chair. "My dear, I'm afraid all this stress is taking a toll on you as well. Why don't you rest here a spell? Cluc, would you get her some water?" He patted her on the leg. "Now, don't you worry. Now that I know the Judge is here, everything's going to be better."

Maudie held the pine box she had been carrying tightly in her lap. She rubbed the top.

"Trust me," he said. "Everything's going to be *just* fine."

Chapter 5

Over the next twelve years, the plantation's condition diminished as the war grew from hearsay—as Mase had been told it was on his eighth birthday—into reality. As Willow Creek slowly fell into disrepair, so did its owner's health with his mobility failing him more each day.

Although Braxton did not see it, the Judge and his henchman had been systematically taking control of the estate. Initially, they managed its affairs from town, coming in once or twice a month to oversee its operations. Of late, they were there every week. Sometimes they would even stay for the entire month.

During these periods, the slaves' anxiety ran high as Silas would often patrol the fields brandishing a large bowie knife. If Cluc wasn't around and he saw a slave he thought was loafing, he would throw the blade as close to their feet as possible, roaring with laughter as he watched his target jump out of the way. Braxton had never whipped a slave, but it was apparent, had the Judge been in charge, he most assuredly would have employed the tactic. Luckily, Braxton still made all final decisions, especially regarding the slaves.

True to their word, Maudie and Cluc had taken care of him. Maudie used a wheelchair to move Braxton about the big house since he was unable to walk without assistance. Cluc would also routinely come in from the fields, carry him to his carriage, and drive him around the property so he could wave to everyone. As his speech grew more difficult to produce, he wore a chalkboard around his neck in case he couldn't fully form his words.

Out of both love and fear of what might happen if he became completely disabled, they remained determined to keep him in charge. Multiple times the Judge tried to sell some of his slaves, and every time Braxton prevented it. With no one to turn to for the plantation's operations, he had to rely on his brother until Mase could take charge.

The one constant during these years was the friendship between his son and Spoon. As Braxton had come to rely on Maudie, Mase had grown to rely on Spoon in his own way. He loved his father dearly, but due to his physical condition, he was increasingly less present in Mase's life. Spoon, however, was there for him every day, providing support and comfort.

Although he was a year younger, Spoon was instrumental in building Mase's character through example. Never once had Mase seen Spoon get mad or talk poorly of someone, especially when it came to Silas, whom all the slaves had grown to despise. Just as Braxton had always defended his brother, Spoon defended the weak and intolerable. He believed they must have had it bad growing up or something had happened that made them that way. Instead of getting mad or seeking revenge, he always chose forgiveness.

In return, Mase was his guardian. Outside the plantation, those who knew him only saw a slave, oblivious to how close they were. On multiple occasions, when Spoon was taunted, ridiculed, and even beaten, Mase was always there to save him.

Now approaching his twentieth birthday, the young Mr. Winslow was a handsome image of his father's earlier years, complete with a strong jaw, green eyes, and tightly trimmed beard. He was lean and sturdy, just as Spoon was. In fact, from behind, they could have easily been mistaken for twins had it not been for Mase's sandy-brown hair. Similar still, they both enjoyed the same sense of humor and adventure. Maudie marveled at how adept they were at completing each other's sentences. "Sure you two aren't brothers?" she would often say.

When they weren't together, they continued to hone their individual talents. Spoon worked on playing the utensil for which he was nicknamed, and Mase constantly wrote, often in the diary Spoon had given him long ago. Over the years, Mase had also become an accomplished teacher. As illegal as it was, and at the risk of being punished himself, every day he would sit with Sissy and Maudie, teaching them how to read and write. To his credit the results were remarkable. Time and again visitors to the plantation remarked on how articulate they were, only to turn around and chide Braxton on how unnatural it was. The only times they ever faltered was when they were tired or flustered.

Cluc joked, "There weren't a pair of more proper-speakin' plantation ladies anywhere in the county unless they was ornery then their colored talk would jump back in 'em."

During this time, the only two girls in Mase's life were also transforming. Sissy was now a cute, bubbly teenager with doe eyes and a magnetic smile. At the same time, Annabelle had blossomed from a freckle-faced tomboy into the belle of the county. With a slender build and porcelain complexion accented by waist-length, silky black hair, she was continually being courted by all the heirs to the neighboring plantations.

The effects of Annabelle's beauty were most evident during special events at the estate. Dozens of suitors would flock around her, trying to make an impression with a witty remark or special gesture. Often the competing bucks ended up arm wrestling in their attempts at winning her affection.

Although Braxton's health was failing, he still enjoyed displaying his love for his friends and family by throwing elaborate parties, like his upcoming July Fourth barbeque. He was especially excited about this year's event as Annabelle had been discussing the possibilities of marriage. He knew all she had to do was provide even the smallest amount of interest in a beau, and the wedding date would soon follow.

He also knew, with times being what they were and with the plantation's uncertainty, securing her future meant she needed to wed. It was, therefore, essential for this event to be the grandest of all. The larger the pot of honey, the more bees it would attract, and his daughter, he said, deserved the largest pot he could fill.

On the day before the event, it was all hands on deck. Everyone pitched in. Even the Judge and Silas provided a marginal effort by securing additional kegs of rum from a nearby distillery. Work had been suspended in the fields and refocused on bringing back the plantation's old charm. The half-mile entrance to the estate was lined with streamers, flags, and balloons. Extra swans and ducklings were brought in to accent the pond, which had been painstakingly manicured for two full days. The front of the house received a thorough whitewashing, and red-white-and-blue banners, along with the Confederate flag, hung from every window, ledge, and balcony. Southern charm was on full display.

Around nine that morning, Mase and Spoon prepped a wagon and headed into town to pick up tablecloths, potatoes, and feed for the swans. For most of the hour-long journey, Spoon played a pair of prized silver spoons Mr. Winslow had given him in appreciation for playing at previous events.

"Wow, everybody in the county must be here today," Mase said as they pulled in front of the mercantile store.

A tall man tipped his beaver-skin top hat to him as he went by. "Looking forward to tomorrow," he said.

"See you at the barbeque," said an elderly lady, peeking out from behind her parasol.

As they were getting out of the wagon, a couple of Mase's acquaintances galloped up. The bigger, more dashing of the two spoke first. "Tell Ms. Annabelle I'm looking forward to seeing her tomorrow."

The smaller, more ordinary one stuttered his intensions immediately after the first, "Tell her Le-Le-Levi Johnston will b-be there too."

"Hey, Levi." Mase chuckled, not in response to the boy's speech impediment but at the realization of how absurd tomorrow was going to be, given all the potential suitors heading his sister's way.

After they finished loading their purchases, he handed the reins to Spoon. "Mind meeting me next to Franklin's blacksmith shop? I need to run one more errand."

"Sure you don't want me to come too?"

"No, I promise I won't be long." He tossed him a large strap of licorice. "Got this for ya while you weren't looking."

Spoon jammed the candy into his mouth. "Take your time," he said, grinning.

Mase waited a moment for the wagon to pull away then rushed across the street to stand in line behind several other young men about his age. Patiently they waited to enter a tiny, nondescript building. Momentarily a young man, probably two years younger than he, walked out the door, his chest puffed up. His chin held high, he ambled by Mase with an air of accomplishment.

"Good luck," he said as he passed.

About forty-five minutes later, Mase reappeared on the street to a commotion coming from the direction of the blacksmith shop. As he got closer, he saw two men appearing to take control of his wagon. One kept the horse still by holding its harness while the other chased Spoon around, chunking potatoes at him out of a bag. As he was about to launch another one, Mase tackled him, planting him face-first into the dirt, sending potatoes rolling in every direction. The crowd that had gathered booed him for ending the fun. As he stood over the assailant, out of the corner of his eye, he spotted the other man running toward him.

"Watch out!" Spoon yelled, then all went black.

A few minutes later, he woke up in the back of the wagon between a stack of tablecloths and a pile of potatoes. With a groan he worked his way onto the bench seat next to his friend, holding the side of his head. There was no blood, only a slight swelling below his cheek.

"Daggone white trash," he said, swiveling his jaw back and forth.

Spoon stared at the reins, biting his lip as tears glistened down his cheeks.

"Well," Mase said somberly, "I guess some folks have an odd way of mashing their potatoes." He leaned into his friend, hoping his lame joke would produce at least a snicker.

Spoon continued his gaze downward. Suddenly, his cheeks puffed up. "You know, I love me some mashed taters," he blurted.

Mase doubled over laughing. "Another one for the diary." He put his arm around Spoon's shoulder, content in knowing their friendship would last forever and fulfilled that he had been there for him again.

Along the way, his thoughts reflected on his last errand of the day. The moment he became a man. A smile crossed his face then faded as suddenly as it had appeared.

Chapter 6

At seven thirty the next morning, the front lawn was abuzz with the final preparations for the big day. In every direction, people were rushing about, setting up tents, chairs, and tables. Maudie danced about while directing her helpers in the correct ways to set a banquet table while Cluc managed the firepit where two huge pigs lay roasting. Mase and Spoon sat cutting potatoes, regaling everyone in earshot about how they had battled to save their prized vegetables during the previous day's skirmish.

From the front step, Braxton sat in his wheelchair, overseeing it all. Periodically, Annabelle would appear on the balcony wearing a different dress. "What about this one, Daddy?" she said, spinning around.

Each time he would either clap his hands or give her a thumbs-up. The third time she came out, she was wearing a simple, pristine, white gown with lace accents around the neck, shoulders, and hemline. Sissy appeared from behind her with a large yellow silk ribbon. She wrapped it around her waist, tying it off to the side with a bow that brought a sparkle to his eye. He held his chalkboard toward her. It read, *Perfect, my angel.*

Four hours later, the first partygoers arrived, followed by Dr. Parkin. Immediately after that, three carriages of the Henthorn family pulled up. For the next hour, Willow Creek's long, winding entrance transformed into a parade of guests.

With Mase's help, Braxton managed to stand and meet each of them. He had saved all his energy for this one spectacular day. His voice was also the strongest it had been in years. His guests who knew him best were surprised by how well he was speaking, often citing it as a miracle.

Leaning into his father, Mase motioned discreetly toward a circle of a dozen young men already laying siege to the gazebo down by the pond.

Braxton's eyes brightened when he caught a glimpse of his daughter's yellow ribbon. "My precious baby girl." He peered into the cluster. "Any front-runners yet?" he asked.

Mase stroked his beard. "Hmmm, can't tell. Too many to sort out this early."

On the opposite side of the yard from Annabelle and her throng of admirers, Spoon sat clicking and clacking his silver instruments to the delight of a handful of children.

All the while, the two hundred guests enjoyed what many regarded as the best pig in the county, and beer, wine, and rum flowed smoothly throughout the day. Spoon's performances ultimately gave way to an eight-piece band stationed on the edge of the pinewood dance floor that had been erected for the occasion.

Mase, who had not left his father's side, nudged his elbow, noting the emergence of his sister from the gazebo. As the band began to play the Virginia reel, a square-jawed young Confederate officer escorted her to the dance floor. Father and son smiled their approval at one another. Unfortunately for the remaining hopefuls, the gazebo was left vacant for the remainder of the event as they conceded to the captain's victory.

Braxton beamed as he watched his daughter sashay joyfully across the pine flooring. He turned to Mase and touched him on the cheek. "And how about you, my son? Anyone caught your eye yet?"

"Well," he said, averting his eyes downward, "actually there—"

Just then, a shell burst overhead, causing everyone to duck. A second later, another exploded, then another three in rapid succession. Dozens of screaming streaks of fire rocketed across the darkening sky, all ending in brilliant flashes of cascading colors. The crowd howled in excitement as plumes of smoke trailed the rainbows of sparkles and streamers falling from the sky.

"Happy birthday, America," yelled one of the guests.

"Happy birthday, Dixie," yelled another.

As the fireworks built to a climax, the crowd erupted into a glorious version of the "Battle Cry of Freedom." By the song's end, the smell of gunpowder had faded. A light breeze drifted over the pond and across the backyard, replacing it with the sweet scent of honeysuckle.

As the sun continued its descent, torches peppered the grounds.

For the first time, Braxton sat. "Son, can you fetch your uncle for me?" His speech was starting to slow.

"You okay, Dad?"

"Yes," he said, rubbing his temple, "go fetch your uncle."

After several minutes, he returned with the Judge hobbling

along with his constant companions, a glass of brandy in one hand and his cane in the other.

Unable to be heard over the crowd, Braxton motioned him to his wheelchair. "I don't think I can manage it, little brother. Can you?"

His brother swayed as the effects of a full day of drink took their toll. "I'm not sure I can either," he snickered.

Braxton furrowed his brow at him.

"Alright, alright," he said, leaning on his cane and straightening his bow tie. "Ahhmm—ladies and gentlemen. May, uh, may I have…" The crowd continued, unaware of the sloppy introduction. "Attention, everybody! Hey—listen, ladies and gentlemen," he screeched.

Still no response.

Braxton looked at Mase while motioning the band to stop playing.

"Ladies and gentlemen," Mase called out with authority, "may I please have your attention?"

The crowd went silent, as all eyes turned to him.

"On behalf of my father and the rest of the Winslow family, we want to thank you for coming today and being part of this special occasion."

His father started to stand. Mase pulled him up while the Judge withdrew off to the side, straining to stay vertical.

Braxton summoned all his strength as he scanned the crowd. "This has been an exceptional day." He paused as he collected his next breath. "Over the years, friendships have been forged, bonds have been made, and the prosperity we've enjoyed is a result of these. Our relationships"—his voice wavered—"and how we treat one another are the cornerstone of all that is dear."

"God bless you, Braxton Winslow," yelled one of the guests.

"God bless the Confederacy," came another.

"Three cheers for Braxton and Mase!" The crowd erupted. "Hip, hip, hooray! Hip, hip, hooray..."

Feeling his father's energy leaving his body, Mase helped him back to his chair as the crowd cheered on.

He patted his son on the hand, confident the timing was right to pass the plantation to him.

By nine o'clock all but two guests had left. Dr. Parkin remained behind to check on Braxton while the young Confederate captain continued strolling the estate with Annabelle.

After checking Braxton's pulse and reflexes, the doctor declared him to be healthy but highly overexerted.

Mase lit a cigar and handed it to him. "Thanks, Doc. I keep telling him he has to slow down."

His father whacked him on the leg. "I'm slow alright, but not as slow as him," he said, tilting his head to the Judge who sat slouched in a rocking chair, snoring away.

The doctor puffed out a cloud of smoke and slapped his knee. "Brax—you're as stubborn as that blue-ribbon ox of yours."

Braxton winked. "But smart as the fox that's been stealing my hens."

"How's that, Dad?"

"As of noon tomorrow, you, my boy, will be the sole owner of the Willow Creek Plantation!" He examined his son's reaction. "How's that for taking it slow?" he crowed.

Mase stood dumbfounded.

"Excellent!" Doc Parkin slapped him on the back. "Just excellent!"

"What in tarnation..." the Judge babbled, awakened

by the jubilation.

"Congratulate your nephew, Judge."

"Why would I want to do that?" he grumbled.

"Your brother just passed the proverbial torch to him, that's why."

"He did what?"

"Braxton is passing ownership of Willow Creek to Mase."

The Judge grabbed his cane, standing faster than he had in twenty years. "You mean to tell me—"

"Nooo," Mase interrupted, staring at his father. "You can't."

"You're right about *that*, boy." The Judge slammed his cane on the table, sending his brandy crashing to the floor. He stood seething, staring at the broken glass, fist clenched.

"For heaven's sake, man, calm yourself," the doctor said.

Braxton ignored his brother's outburst. "Why sure I can," he said, laying his hand on Mase's forearm. "You're a man now. You know everything about this place, and more importantly"—he tapped him on the chest—"I know your heart. You'll take care of everyone on it."

"Well, sure I will, but—but you don't understand."

"Of course I do."

"No, you don't." He turned away. "I wanted to tell you this earlier, but there was too much going on, and… well—"

"Well what?"

"I enlisted in the army," he blurted.

"You did *what?*" Braxton and Doc Parkin said in unison.

The Judge slowly lifted his head, his scowl transforming into the knowing grin of a man whose fortunes had suddenly gone from nothing to everything.

"I enlisted. I thought you'd be proud of me."

"Why, I've always been proud of you, son, but enlisting in the army? When?"

"Yesterday, when we went to town for supplies."

"How soon do you head out?" the Judge asked.

"Day after tomorrow."

"The day after tomorrow!" Doc Parkin said, looking at Braxton in anticipation of his reaction. "You okay, Brax?"

"Come here, son," he whispered.

As Mase knelt beside him, his father placed his hand on his cheek.

Mase lowered his head. "I'm sorry, Dad."

"Why on earth would you be sorry?" His voice, although weak, was soft and warm.

"I'm leaving you—the plantation and Annabelle. Who'll take care of everything?"

Taking Mase's face in his hands, he stared into his son's eyes with the unconditional love of a father. "You could never disappoint me."

Mase fell into his father's embrace.

Doc Parkin put his arm around the Judge's shoulders. "Now that's love."

Judge Joseph smirked. He scanned the dark horizon, visualizing the enormous estate that would soon be his to govern. "Yes indeed—the power of love," he muttered.

As he started to grasp the magnitude of this turn of events and how it was going to affect his life, he heard a faint whimper from across the pond. Subtle as a newborn's plea for milk, it gradually grew into weeping. Above the water's farthest bank, he saw the silhouette of a man run past one of the few remaining torches.

"Mr. Brax!" yelled the man.

The weeping grew louder.

"Mr. Brax!" he continued shouting as he rounded the corner of the pond and up the hill. His voice was strained and filled with distress.

Dr. Parkin turned. "It's Cluc."

"What's the matter?" Mase yelled.

The big man chugged his way to the steps then stooped over, gasping for air. "Oh my Lord—Mr. Brax—you gotta come." He started back in the direction he had come. "It's Annabelle!"

Mase jumped up. "What's wrong?"

He gulped. "Can't say. You just gotta come."

"Everybody, stay put," Mase commanded.

Cluc yelled over his shoulder as they ran off. "You gotta come too, Doc!"

Braxton slapped the side of his wheelchair. "Get me over there!"

The Judge threw his cane onto his brother's lap, grabbed the handles, and heaved him into motion. Within seconds Mase, Cluc, and the doctor had vanished into the night, leaving Mr. Winslow and the Judge behind.

"Faster!" Braxton ordered.

The Judge leaned into the chair with all his weight. "I'm trying, brother, I swear."

A moment later, they arrived at a small grove of dogwood trees on the farthest edge of the pond. A tiny oil lamp hung from a branch of the largest tree, at the base of which was Annabelle, curled into a shivering ball. Her dress was ripped at the neckline and pulled down to her waist, revealing her naked breast. Her yellow ribbon lay spread out next to her.

Mase dropped to his knees and wrapped his arms around her as her body convulsed in waves of uncontrollable sobs. Tears rolled down her face and onto his neck. "Annabelle," he said, pulling her hair back from her face, "what happened?"

Her eyes twitched. "Where is it?" she screamed. She jerked away, looking left then right. "Where is it?"

"Where's what?" Mase asked, reaching out to her.

She brushed his hand aside and crawled across the dirt, first in one direction then the other. "Where is it?" she cried.

Mase looked at the doctor, his mouth agape, clueless as to what to ask or do next. When he turned back, she was gone.

Cluc pointed to a holly bush. Mase slowly walked over and knelt in front of her.

She continued weeping, clutching her yellow ribbon the breeze had almost stolen from her. She rocked back and forth, holding it to her half-naked body.

Cluc wrapped his shirt around her, and Mase stroked her hair until he heard his father and uncle coming. Running out in front of them, Mase prevented them from seeing her condition while giving Dr. Parkin time to diagnose her.

"What happened?" asked Braxton.

"First of all, she's okay..." He looked down. "Well, she's not injured."

Braxton winced at his word choices. "But what happened?"

"I'm not sure. Doc is with her."

Braxton pounded the armrest with his palm then lunged forward before falling back into the chair.

"Dad, no. It's better if you wait."

"My daughter needs me," he said, struggling to rise again.

"Dad, just wait—please."

From out of the grove of trees, Dr. Parkin emerged with the oil lamp. Cluc followed, carrying Annabelle in his arms, her head resting on his shoulder. Her eyes were closed.

"My baby!" Braxton took two steps toward them before his legs gave way. Mase caught him and placed him back in his chair. Too drained to sit upright, he slumped in the wheelchair and watched helplessly as his trusted foreman carried his daughter into the darkness. The sounds of crickets and croaking toads filled the night air, but he heard none of it.

"*What* exactly happened?" the Judge demanded.

Mase turned to the doctor, his heart beating faster as he waited for his answer.

"I got 'em," rang out a voice from behind them.

"Who's there?" Mase yelled.

The sound of rustling leaves came from the direction of the dogwoods.

"I said, who's there?"

Ten yards away, Silas appeared from out of the blackness pulling an unconscious man facedown through the thicket. "Me!" he huffed. "By God, I got 'em!" He dropped the man's leg with a thud. "He's the one who done it," he panted.

"Done what?" Mase asked.

Silas slapped his hands together, beating the dirt from them. "Why deflowered your sis, of course."

"Oh no!" Braxton looked at Dr. Parkin, praying for

him to differ. "She was—

He nodded.

Mase's eyes flashed to Braxton then back to the man on the ground. His fingers curled inward until his nails felt the tendons of his inner palms. Torn between waiting for his father's order and exacting immediate vengeance, he stood transfixed as a vortex of emotions swept over him. Oblivious to his own decision, he grabbed his uncle's cane and leaped onto the man's back. With his weapon raised, he jerked the man's head to the side and prepared to strike.

The small glow from the lamp illuminated the man's face, causing his heart to skip a beat. He dropped the cane. "No!" he cried, staggering back from the body. "Nooo. This can't be."

The Judge grabbed the lamp and dangled it next to the man's head, gasping as the light revealed his beaten face. One eye was swollen shut, blood oozed from his nose, and his jaw was several inches out of alignment with his skull. With the little light available, his identity was still apparent.

The Judge looked back at Mase then turned to Braxton. "Why—it's your boy, Spoon."

Mase swung his head back and forth. "This isn't possible. It can't be. It just can't." He grabbed Silas by the collar. "How do you know it was him?"

"Because," he said with the edges of his mouth slowly inching upward, "I was making sure the young lady was being courted proper-like by that captain fella. I seen it happen. I seen it all." He lifted his chin. "Now take yer filthy paws off me," he growled.

Mase turned to his father with his hands opened out.

"I had to, son. I hadn't met the man, so I wanted to make sure he was honorable."

"I still don't believe it was Spoon," Mase said, glaring back at the accuser.

"I'll be honest. I'd been drinkin' some," Silas said with a corroborating slur, "but I weren't alone. Ezra was with me. He'll tell ya the same."

"Who's Ezra?" asked Dr. Parkin.

"Just another lowbrow darky," the Judge said.

"No, Uncle. He's a shy ten-year-old boy—*that's* who he is." He turned to Silas. "Why would he even be with you?"

"Cause nobody else was hankering to tag along to watch a pair of lovebirds canoodle all day. Besides, I needed somebody to fetch me food and drink."

Mase's eyes narrowed on him.

"After her beau left, I figgurd it was alright fer Ezra and me to leave too. As we was roundin' the pond back to the house is when I heard the commotion. We run back, and that's when I found him on top of her. He done pulled—"

"That's enough," Mase said, holding up his hand and taking a long, deep breath. "And Ezra was right there too? He saw everything?"

"Shore did."

"Where's he now?"

"He run off whilst I was throwing the hammer down on 'em."

Braxton grabbed his brother's arm. "Go find Ezra and bring him to the smokehouse." He turned to Silas. "You come with us."

Mase hoisted Spoon's limp body over his back, and they set off back to the plantation.

The usual fifteen-minute walk took almost an hour with

Spoon being transferred back and forth between Dr. Parkin and Mase. When they finally arrived, they found the Judge standing in the middle of the small cabin holding a young boy by the scruff of the neck. The room's single candle dappled quivering waves of light onto the walls, giving the hanging meats and butchering tools a sense of motion.

"Stop shaking so dang much," the Judge commanded him.

The doctor laid Spoon out on the dirt floor. "He's in bad shape. His nose should be okay, but he may lose the eye and his jaw's broken. Even if he wakes, you won't be getting much out of him anytime soon."

"That's just great. Now we've got two mutes," the Judge said.

"What do you mean?" asked the doctor.

"Ezra's a mute, Doc," Mase interjected upon entering the cabin. "Dad bought him from a slave owner who had cut out his tongue."

"How can people be so barbaric?"

"For Christ's sake, let's get on with it," the Judge fumed. He turned to Braxton. "He can still nod or shake his head, can't he? I'm a lawyer. I'll handle this."

The overall stress of the day compounded by the horrific last two hours weighed heavily on Braxton. He could barely move and was starting to sweat profusely. He motioned for the Judge to begin his line of questioning, Ezra's eyes bulging like an animal being pulled to the slaughterhouse.

The Judge bent down and squared him up with a quick jerk of the shoulders. "I want you to nod for yes and shake your head for no when I ask you something. You understand me?"

There was no response.

The Judge grabbed him back by his shirt sleeve. "Do—you—understand?" he yelled into his ear.

The boy fidgeted with his rope belt while bobbing his head up and down.

"Were you with Silas today?"

He nodded once.

"Were you with him all day?"

He nodded again.

"Did you see something happen that should *not* have happened?

Ezra gulped, then slowly moved his head up and down.

"Did you see the soldier leave Ms. Annabelle?"

He replied with a series of three quick nods.

"After that, you and Silas left and headed back to the house. Is that correct?"

Ezra glanced at Silas, then twisted his head back to the door. Sweat beaded on his forehead. He nodded.

"While you were walking back to the plantation, did you hear a scream and then rush back to where Annabelle was?"

A line of sweat ran past Ezra's temple as he shifted from side to side. He looked at Silas, who stood stone-faced. Ezra's lips became a thin line as he nodded once again.

The Judge's tone grew harsh. "And what did you find? I—I mean, that's when you found Spoon on top of Annabelle. Isn't that correct? Isn't that what you saw?"

The boy's eyes darted from the Judge to Spoon then back to Silas as sweat poured down his face. His baggy shirt was shaking. He opened his mouth, but nothing came out. He lowered his head, paused, then slowly his head rose and fell.

"Guilty!" the Judge barked.

Mase threw up his hand. "Wait. Hold on." He turned to Dr. Parkin. "Doc, you examined Annabelle. Did you ask her who had"— he couldn't say the word—"well, did you ask her anything?"

"She was in a state of shock—I couldn't."

Mase looked at him hopefully. "But—"

"She kept repeating one word and crying."

"What was the word?" he asked.

Regret filled the doctor's eyes. "Spoon."

"That's it! Everybody out," the Judge commanded.

"But he's still unconscious," the doctor said.

"Good. String him up!"

Dr. Parkin turned to Braxton and waited.

"Do as he says," Braxton whispered just before his head dropped forward, and he passed out.

"I need to get him to bed before he has another fit of apoplexy," the doctor said.

Mase stood in disbelief as he watched his father being taken from the room while Silas shackled his best friend's wrists to the pulley system they used for hanging meat.

"Help me outside," the Judge said, grabbing Mase's hand.

Dutifully he led the old man out into the darkness, leaving Silas to hoist the accused upright.

"Now listen to me, boy," said the Judge, "what happens tonight is justice—plain and simple."

Momentarily, Silas stepped outside, closing the door behind him. He bent over with his hands on his knees. "That boy's heavier than he looks," he panted. "What now?"

Chapter 7

Mase stood outside the smokehouse alongside the two men, squeezing the crucifix Annabelle had given him, its edges digging into his palm.

"Fetch me the thunder stick!" the Judge barked.

Mase looked into his eyes with a plea of forgiveness, but there was none to be given. He stood frozen.

"I said fetch me the thunder," he roared, blood vessels bulging along his temples. "Now!"

Silas bolted into action, almost knocking Mase over as he ran into the night. When he returned minutes later, he was carrying a double-barreled shotgun.

"What're you going to do?" Mase asked.

His uncle snatched the gun and walked to the front door.

Mase moved with him. "What're you planning?"

"Delivering justice!" he said as he pounded the door open with the butt of the gun.

On the opposite wall, Spoon was hanging by his wrists from chains that ran into the ceiling. The Judge walked inside and slammed the door behind him.

Mase stared into the hardwood planks. He muttered to

himself, dropped the crucifix, and barged inside to find the Judge with the shotgun raised against the back of Spoon's head. "Nooo!" he yelled as he grabbed the gun.

"By God, boy, if you don't let—"

"No, please—you can't!"

His uncle glared at him, his chest heaving.

Mase put his hand on the gun barrel and moved it downward. "If it's going to be done, I'm the one who has to do it."

The Judge stepped back, panting, struggling to remain erect. "You shouldn't even be here."

"If justice has to be exacted, it *has* to come from me."

The Judge gritted his teeth, holding back the urge to finish what he had set out to do. "Here!" He rammed the gun into Mase's chest. "Do what you have to," he said, slamming the door behind him.

The words echoed in his ears. *Do what you have to.* Too many emotions flooded his mind, colliding, conflicting, all maddening. His sister's emotional health was shattered, and her future with any man dashed. His lifelong companion and confidant had been tried and found guilty. Revenge or forgiveness—punishment or leniency. If he did not act in line with his uncle's prescribed level of justice, then either he or Silas would deliver the final blow. Grabbing the sides of his head, Mase tried to silence the conflict raging within. Revenge—forgiveness—punishment—leniency. The voices grew louder and louder. The vision of Spoon pinning his sister to the ground tipped the scales.

He dropped the shotgun, picked up a thin, jagged metal rod, and struck Spoon across the back, ripping through his shirt and skin. A leather strap would have been a more humane weapon. The rod broke ribs and tore the flesh with ease. Blood splattered across his face. As the scene of his sister's ordeal played out in his mind, he struck him again and again as thoughts of Spoon violating his sister clashed with his love for him.

Drawing back for another blow, Cluc's enormous hand suddenly wrapped around his, suspending the rod in midair. "Stop!" he said.

Mase spun around, his eyes still wild with vengeance. "Turn me loose!" he commanded. He wiped the blood and sweat from his eyes and glared up at him as if he had never seen the man before.

Cluc pulled the rod out of his hand. "Mr. Mase. You gots to stop."

Mase gnashed his teeth.

"You gonna kill 'em. Please stop."

Mase turned back to Spoon. His shirt was shredded into a hundred pieces, the white cotton now crimson-red. His back was crisscrossed with gaping wounds exposing his ribs, spine, and torn muscle. Had he not already been unconscious, such torture would easily have induced it.

By degrees, Mase's emotions subsided as the realization of his actions came into focus. He dropped to his knees and buried his head in his hands.

Cluc knelt next to him and placed his arm over his shoulder. For the next few minutes, they sat without saying anything as Mase began struggling with the consequences of his revenge while still envisioning his sister's suffering.

"My God!"

Cluc looked over his shoulder to find Dr. Parkin standing in the doorway carrying a medicine bag and a large bedsheet. He rushed toward them but stopped short, not knowing where to place his hands on the mangled body. Dropping his bag along with the sheet, he checked Spoon's pulse.

"He's still alive. Cluc, help me get him down and onto his stomach."

Mase eyed the men as they lowered him to the ground. "But he's a criminal," he said in a soft, detached voice, his gaze moving past them out of the smokehouse and into the night. He sat affixed to the ground, trying to silently free himself of the horrible reality around him.

The doctor pulled out a bottle of alcohol, laid it to the side, then feverishly tore the sheet into small strips. Cluc cradled Spoon's head in his lap while the doctor applied the alcohol and bandages across his back.

"Turn him to the side. I need to stop the bleeding on the ribs."

Cluc gently rolled him over then watched as Doc Parkin worked to keep him alive.

After an hour on his hands and knees, the doctor leaned back to survey his efforts. He let out a long sigh, wiped his forehead, and proceeded to take the one advantage of Spoon's unconscious state by realigning his broken jaw.

"Well," he said, wiping the blood from his hands, "he might just make it."

Cluc placed his hand against Spoon's swollen cheek. "You think he did it?"

The doctor turned his head from side to side. "Come on. We need to get him to the house. Can you carry him?"

Cluc wiped his eyes. "Course I can."

As he was bending down to pick him up, he heard someone shouting from a distance.

"Wait—don't do anything!" It was Maudie, her words

laden with stress. "Don't do anything! Spoon's not—"

"What'd she say 'bout Spoon?" Cluc asked.

Dr. Parkin dropped his bag. "Stay here." In an instant, he was out the door in hopes of reaching her before she could witness the atrocity inside the smokehouse.

Fifty yards away, he ran into her.

"I—I..." she couldn't catch her breath to form the words. All she could do was shake her head and wave her hands.

"Take your time," he said, putting his hand to her back. "Just breathe."

"But—but—I..." She pulled a square piece of slate to her chest. After a few moments she was able to say she was okay.

"Are you sure?" he said.

"Yes, yes. I've got to stop it! He's not the one." She started again toward the smokehouse.

"Wait!" He pulled at her arm.

"Turn me loose!" she screamed. "*He didn't do it!*"

He grabbed her other arm, forcing her around toward him. "He's *alive!*"

Her eyes grew large, and she placed her hand to her head. "Oh, praise the Lord. Thank you, Lord. Thank you, thank you, thank you." With her other hand, she raised the black piece of slate to her lips and kissed it. "Praise Jesus. Praise Jesus."

The doctor continued holding her in fear she might run to the smokehouse. Instead, she calmly bowed her head and said a prayer of thanks.

Upon finishing, she launched into her jubilant news of acquittal. "He didn't do it. Spoon's not the one. It was all a mistake—a big, ugly mistake."

"Are you sure?"

"Sure as sure can be!" She held up the slate. "Spoon *did not* touch Annabelle!"

"Is that Mr. Winslow's chalkboard?"

"Yes, sir. And it's the proof. Read it!" she said, holding it out to him.

Four simple words scribbled in chalk exonerated Spoon. *I'm sorry I lied.* He drew the board closer. "Who wrote this?"

"Ezra!" she said, clapping her hands.

"Was it Ezra who violated—"

"No, No! While y'all were at the smokehouse, he confessed he'd lied for that low-down, evil, no good—"

"Who?!"

"Mr. Silas," she said through clenched teeth. "Poor Ezra scratched everything out on the board. He was too afraid to go against him because he threatened to kill him if he did. Ezra saw everything!"

"What about Spoon?"

"He saw everything too. He came up on them and tried to stop it." She paused. "My little Spoon against Goliath…" Her voice faded then launched back. "That's when Silas tried to beat him to death. He surely would have too if he hadn't heard you and the others coming."

"Where's Silas now?"

"He took off. There's a posse getting ready to go after him."

Sissy came running up.

"Honey, I told you to stay put."

"Sorry, Maudie, but Mr. Brax wants everybody back to the house with Silas being on the loose. Poor Mr. Brax is barely able to give orders cause he's so weak, the Judge is drinking himself into a terrible state and Ms. Annabelle… well, thankfully she's asleep, but I'm afraid of what she might do if she wakes."

"I understand, child." Maudie's voice settled into a calming tone as she dispensed her wishes. "Why don't you and the doc go check on her."

"Yes ma'am," Sissy replied.

"But Maudie, you need—"

"Doc, listen to me. I know what you're going to say, but I don't want to hear it."

He looked at her, straining to understand her logic for wanting to witness what she knew awaited within the log building behind them.

"I know you've done all you can, but those boys need me." She handed him the chalkboard. "Besides, you gotta go see about Annabelle and Mr. Brax."

He wanted to argue but knew she was right. Her tone was that of a resolute mother intent on dispensing her love no matter what the cost was to her. Steadfast, she stood ready to walk through him if necessary.

"Okay then," he said, "I'll see you in just a little while."

With a deep breath she adjusted her kerchief and headed to the smokehouse. As she approached the entrance, she reached into her pocket, making sure the contents were there, then she quietly entered to find Cluc with his arms still around Mase. Beside them, Spoon lay motionless on his stomach.

Cluc gave a sigh of relief when he saw her, though all he could do was shake his head.

She bit her knuckle as she looked upon the carnage that was Spoon's body. His face was almost unrecognizable, and his back was lined with strips of blood-soaked linen.

Falling to her knees, she stretched her hands over him and prayed. When she finished, she reached into her pocket and pulled out a rusty grey stone a quarter the size of her fist. With her other hand, she reached over and opened his palm. She was folding his fingers around it when, suddenly, he jerked.

"He's awake! Did you see that? He's awake!"

Cluc rushed to his side. "Praise be," he said, putting his arm around Maudie.

Spoon slid his hand across the floor until his fingers touched hers. "Mau—die." The word was barely there, but it was still a word. He rolled his head to the side. "Cluc."

"Shush, no more chatter," she said, gently stroking his hair. "You save your strength now." She leaned over and kissed him tenderly on the forehead.

He winced as he came back into consciousness. "Where's Mase?" he groaned. As quickly as he had awoken, he slipped back into his dreamless state.

"Did you hear that?" She turned. "Mase, he was asking for you." The room was silent.

The space where Mase had been kneeling was vacant. "Where'd he go?"

Cluc looked around. "I don't know."

"Mase!" she called out. "Spoon was—"

"Oh no—the thunder—it's gone!" he said.

"What thunder?"

Cluc ran to the opposite side of the cabin, then from one corner to the next. He grabbed the candle, dropped to his hands and knees, and began looking under the huge chopping-block table in the middle of the room. He jumped to his feet.

"What are you doing?" she asked.

He scanned the room again then stopped. It was the first time she had seen him look panicked. "He's done took the *thunder stick*."

Chapter 8

Maudie took the stone she had placed in Spoon's hand and pulled Cluc toward him. "Take him to the big house. I think I know where to find Mase."

With a sliver of moonlight illuminating the path, she was able to run almost the entire way to the creek. As she ran, she looked in every direction, hoping to find him hiding behind one of the cabins or tucked in behind a tree or bush.

Seventy-five yards from the clearing where he and Spoon spent so much of their youth, she stopped to catch her breath, putting her hands on her knees and drawing in the cool night air. Looking up, she noticed the vague outline of a man standing on the edge of the creek.

"Mase!" she shouted, running toward him.

The figure didn't move. In his right hand, he held what appeared to be a long object, thicker than a broom but shorter.

"It's me, Maudie!" She ran faster.

Within fifty yards, he raised the object to his chest, placing one end under his chin.

As her pace quickened, she lost her balance, tripping

over a root. Twenty-five yards away, she lay spread out on the dirt. She looked up in time to see a thin flash of moonlight streak across the gun's barrel.

"Noooo!" she screamed, scrambling to her feet.

At ten yards away, she heard the click of the hammer being pulled back into the firing position.

"Noooo!" she screamed again. With all her remaining strength, she lunged, knocking him to the ground and the gun out of his hand.

As if nothing had happened Mase stood, brushed himself off, and remained motionless, staring out into the darkness.

Pulling herself up to her hands and knees, she reached out and grabbed his leg. "What were you thinking?"

He remained rooted to the bank.

Using her weight for leverage, she took his arm and pulled him down next to her. She stared into his vacant eyes while tears welled in hers. "Why?" she said, throwing her arms around him. "There was no way you could have known." She pulled back and looked at him.

His eyes were no longer void of emotion. Instead they were sad and full of regret. His lip quivered.

"Spoon's not dead. He's *alive*," she said, wanting to purge his soul of the anguish building inside him.

He let his head fall into her embrace. For the next twenty minutes, the regret and grief of the night poured out onto her shoulder.

"Is he going to be alright?" he eked out.

"I believe so."

Maudie had brought Mase back from the brink of his own destruction—at least for the time being. The healing process, however, was far from complete. His scars would remain for life, just as Spoon's would.

"I want to give you something." She reached into her pocket and pulled out the stone she had placed in Spoon's hand earlier. The moonlight shone on it, creating a halo effect. "This here is a memory stone." For a moment she began to drift off as she held it out, admiring the powers she knew it possessed. "It represents your bond with Spoon. It symbolizes a powerful connection you'll have with him for the rest of your life. Nothing and no one can ever break that." She took his hand and placed it in his.

He slowly turned it from side to side, examining its curves while running his fingers over its smooth surface.

"Come on," Maudie said, leading him to the embankment. "We have to go a little further." Methodically placing one foot in front of the other, she guided him into the creek then took his hand with the stone and pulled it below the surface.

There he stood, transfixed, as he watched her arch her head back and close her eyes. The rush of the water, the toads, and the cicadas all fell silent

Ever so slowly her lips began moving with nothing coming out. Suddenly her eyes flashed open—her gaze boring through him, out into the distance. Her hands vibrated around his. An energy surged from beneath the water flowing around the stone, into his hand, up his arm, and through his chest. All at once it stopped, her hands grew still, and the cicadas and toads resumed their nightly chatter. The rush of the water filled the air again. He stood rigid, his pulse rising in time with the current below him.

"Come with me," she said, leading him up the bank to a grassy landing where he and Spoon used to play.

"It's okay," she said, patting his trembling hands.

"We'll just sit a spell and listen to the cicadas talk to one another."

A few minutes later he let out a long sigh as he regained some of his composure.

"Better?" she asked.

He nodded.

"Mase, you know I'm—well—different." She tilted her head down at him and smiled. "You knew that, right?"

"Yes," he said softly.

"Well, when we were in the creek, I was able to see something about your life—a path that diverges unlike any I've ever known. There's a path of adventure with trials and tribulations and one of despair and destruction. Which one you take, I can't tell."

"I don't understand," he said.

"We all have a journey. I can't see yours entirely. It fades out like morning fog rolling through the creek. What I do know is you'll have to draw upon your wisdom and heart to bring it back into focus."

He sat riveted to her every word. He had heard tales before of her visions but had never witnessed it for himself until now. "Where will this journey lead me?"

She shrugged. "I don't know, but what's certain is your memories will carry you either into the light or into the darkness. It's up to you to decide on the path." She squeezed his hand. "I'm giving you this memory stone for you to carry with you. You *cannot* let it out of your possession. A time may come when you'll need it."

He wanted to delve deeper into her mystics and learn more about what life might have in store for him. In two days, he would be wearing a Confederate uniform and in harm's way as never before. Would he make it through the war? Would he be captured or wounded? He wanted to know more, but the horrors of the previous hours were creeping back. The edges of his mouth fell, and his eyes glazed over.

Observing his transformation, she jumped up, hoping to break the oncoming melancholy. "I think it's time we head back."

He blinked, then ran his hand through his hair, swallowing hard as he tried to find the words. "I'm—I'm sorry, Maudie. I—I just—"

She tugged on his sleeve. "Come on. Let's go home."

He slid the stone into his pocket, his fist wrapped around it, squeezing it as they walked. "Do you think," he paused, "do you think he can ever forgive me?"

She stopped and turned to him. "This is Spoon—your best friend. You and me both know that boy's heart. What do you think?"

"But he didn't deserve to be—"

"Neither did Jesus." She stopped and smiled. "But he forgave—he forgave 'em all."

For a fleeting moment, his faith and everything he had learned in church about forgiveness and grace provided solace. As quick as it came, though, it left, and guilt, despair, and shame took its place.

On their way back, they passed a dozen men riding off on horseback, wielding rifles and torches.

"We'll find him!" yelled one of them.

"He's gonna pay!" shouted another.

Sissy was sitting on the front porch, biting her nails. When she saw them coming up the hill, she ran onto the lawn, hugging and kissing him, her eyes red and swollen, traces of tears staining her cheeks. "You had all us worried to death."

"I'm sorry," he said flatly.

The smell of brandy preceded the Judge as he came stumbling out the front door. "Well, well—if it ain't the ole slave master himself. You sure spanked the tar out of that boy tonight. 'Bout time someone put the fear of God in them darkies."

Maudie's eyes blazed.

The old man staggered toward them. He held out his cane, pointing it directly into Mase's face, then waved it aimlessly into the darkness. "My man is out there somewhere," he said, drawing closer. "You know what I think… I don't think Silas did it at all—do you?"

Maudie jumped in front of him, ripping her kerchief off her head and flinging it at his feet.

Before she could unleash a response, Mase pulled her back while Sissy grabbed her around the waist. Together they brushed past the Judge, refusing to acknowledge the rest of his drunken rants as he followed them up the steps. Once inside, Sissy slammed the door in his face, turned, and bolted it shut.

"Well done, Miss Sissy," Dr. Parkin said, stepping out of the parlor. His pipe was clenched between his teeth, and he was still wearing the same bloody shirt he had on while attending to Spoon. When he saw Mase, his faced beamed. "Oh, my heavens," he said in a whisper. He laid his pipe to the side and rushed over and hugged him. Still in a hushed voice, he said, "Come in the parlor. I'm sure your daddy's going to be happy to see you."

As they were about to enter, the doctor continued his low tone. "We need to be as calm as possible. He's been through a lot tonight."

"Everyone's been through a lot tonight," came a weak voice from the other side of the room where Braxton lay with a wet towel across his eyes. He pulled it off, letting it drop to the floor, and reached out his hand. "My boy." His voice was frail and hoarse. "Come here."

Mase walked over and knelt beside him. "Daddy, I—I..." He put his head onto his chest and sobbed.

Wrapping his arm over his son, Braxton gently patted his back then drifted asleep.

"He needs his rest now," Doc Parkin said. "The sun will be up in a few hours, and it's best we all do the same. Don't worry, I'll stay with him."

Maudie pulled Mase to his feet, and together with Sissy, they went upstairs.

"Which room is Spoon in?" he asked. "I'd like to see him."

Maudie glanced at Sissy, then back to him. "Not tonight, Mr. Mase," she said gently. "Tonight, the angels are watching over him."

Chapter 9

Along with the arrival of the morning sun over the plantation's easternmost fields came the thundering of horse hoofs down the entrance.

Mase awoke to the clomping of boots against the hardwood planks of the front porch. Three loud knocks resonated throughout the house, followed by the muffled tones of men's voices. Unable to hear what they were saying, he rushed downstairs in time to see Dr. Parkin closing the door.

"Who was that?"

"Fletcher Cartright. The man heading up the posse to find Silas."

"And—" he said hopefully.

"Nothing. They can't even find a trail."

Mase pounded his leg with his fist, then looked back at the entrance to the parlor. "What about Dad?"

"Still asleep, thank goodness. He needs continued rest. Same with Spoon. I don't think—" He stopped as Mase's face flushed at the mention of his name. "You need to try and get more rest too. If you're leaving tomorrow to defend this great land of ours, you need to be well rested.

She'll tell you the same."

Still in her nightgown, Maudie stepped into the foyer, wrapping her kerchief around her head. "He's right. You're gonna need all the energy you can muster. I hear those Yankees are getting better at fighting."

He turned to the doctor with a blank stare. "I'm not going."

"What?!"

Maudie dropped her kerchief. "But, Mr. Mase—"

"I can't go. Not *now*. Not with Spoon like he is. And not with Annabelle being like she is."

The doctor motioned them to keep their voices down. "But you *have* to go. Do you know what they'll do to you if you don't?"

"I don't care," he said flatly.

"But you took an oath. If you don't go, they'll throw you in jail for breaking your contract. You'll be branded a coward." Dr. Parkin's voice grew louder. "The *entire* county will cut you off. You'll be ridiculed and shunned from society." Catching himself, he lowered his voice to an intense whisper. "And what's worse is the reputation of your family will be ruined. Everything Braxton has worked so hard for—how he's managed to build this place more on love and kindness than the whip—will all be tarnished."

Mase stared past him. "I'm sorry, I can't," he said, walking back up the stairs.

"Maudie, will you talk some sense into him?"

"You need to listen to him. You know he's right," she pleaded.

Mase continued walking.

"I'll talk to him later," she said, "but we've got more

important things right now. I went in to check on Spoon—he's not doing well."

Without a word, the doctor grabbed his bag and ran up the stairs in time to block Mase from entering Spoon's room. "Wait!" He reached across the door. "You can't go in. Not yet."

Mase grabbed his arm and pulled. "Let me in, Doc, or I'll have to—"

"Stop it now, child!" Maudie said, coming up behind him. "If you want to see him, you'll need to wait. Plain and simple."

As they had always done, Maudie's words convicted him to oblige. He let loose of the doctor's arm. "But I want to see how he is. Why can't I do that?"

"Not just yet, my boy," the doctor said. "I need some time with him first."

Mase tucked his chin and walked to Annabelle's room. The doctor watched as he tried opening the door to no avail, jiggling the handle then looking back.

"I'm sorry, Mase. We have to give her time too."

Mase's chin dropped to his chest again as he quietly headed back to his room. As soon as he was out of sight, the doctor entered Spoon's room with Maudie in tow.

Heavy curtains covered the shuttered windows, preventing even a fraction of light from coming into the room. The smell of medicinal alcohol tinged with blood permeated the air. Maudie quietly parted the curtains. Crevices of light between the shutters spread across the room in a crosshatched pattern, revealing the outline of the motionless body.

Taken aback at the scene, he jumped into action. "Why's he on his back? His wounds can't heal that way."

"I—I—came in, and he was coughing horribly. I

thought rolling him to his back would help."

"Come help me roll him over."

In a second, Maudie was at his side.

"On three, we pull the sheet to us while I turn him. Ready? One—two—three."

With no moaning or the slightest reaction from the patient, he was on his stomach once again.

She fell next to him, placed her hand on his head, and sobbed. "I'm sorry, Doc. I didn't know."

"I know you were just trying to help," he said.

For the next several minutes, she continued to weep while he examined Spoon.

"You were right," he said, placing his stethoscope back into his bag. "His condition has worsened. There's nothing else I can do for him." He sighed. "You know I'm not a praying man."

"No, I didn't know that," she said, wiping her eyes.

He placed his hand on hers. "Maybe now's a good time I started."

As the morning faded into the afternoon, the house remained silent as Maudie and the doctor held vigil over Spoon. While the Judge skulked off somewhere to sleep off his hangover, Mase stayed in his room alone to battle the demons of guilt while his father slept in the parlor, recovering from the stress of the previous twenty-four hours. Cluc and Sissy took turns checking on each of them except for Annabelle, who remained locked in her room.

Before dinner, the doctor retrieved Maudie from Spoon's room by convincing her that sitting in the dark with him wasn't going to have any effect on his recovery. "Maybe now's a good time to check in on Mase. You could talk to him about going through with his enlistment."

"But it's Mr. Brax he'll come around to."

"That's true, but you know he still listens to you."

A moment later she was knocking on his door. When Mase didn't answer, she slowly creaked the door open to find him sitting in a chair, staring out the window.

"Come to talk me into going?" he said without turning.

"I'm here to see how you're doing."

"Cluc and Sissy have been doing that all day." His voice remained as bland and distant as the day before.

"What are those?" she asked, referring to the two books he was holding in his lap. Both had black covers and were roughly the same size. The only difference was one was more weathered.

He passed them to her while still looking out the window. The newer one was the Bible. The other was the diary Spoon had given him. Its edges were frayed, and the binding was starting to crack, but considering it was twelve years old, it was in pretty good shape.

She placed the Bible aside and began leafing through the diary. There were snippets and notes about birthdays, weddings, all sorts of events on the plantation, and endless adventures he had had with Spoon. Every piece and parcel of thought was chronologically labeled.

"My, my… you sure do love to write." She thumbed to the last entry dated July 4, 1862: *Big day today – Annual 4th of July BBQ. Looking forward to telling Dad about enlisting!*

"You know you're not supposed to read other people's diaries."

"Oh my—you're absolutely right." She pulled a chair up next to him. For a moment she sat staring down at the book in her lap. "Mase, I don't have the words for what's happened. No one does. But you *can't* quit living. Your daddy doesn't want that, Annabelle doesn't, and you know Spoon doesn't either."

A tear rolled down onto his chin. "Why'd it have to go so wrong?" he muttered. "I *curse* the day my uncle brought that monster into our home. And I *curse* my uncle for being the deceitful, warped, hateful creation he is." He grabbed her arm. "You know what'll happen if I go off and fight, don't you? He'll-he'll take over!"

"The Judge?"

"Of course!"

"Now, now," she said, patting him on the hand, "as long as Braxton Winslow has breath in his lungs, he'll be in charge. Besides, he's got Cluc to keep things together. And what's more, the war will be over before you know it, and you'll be home. Crops will be coming in twice as much, cattle will be multiplying, and there'll be barbeques every week. Won't that be something?" She rolled her head toward him, looking for some sign of relief from his troubled heart.

"You know what else I think?" she said, clasping her hands together. "I think another entry into your book would be a good idea." When she stood to get a quill pen from his desk, the diary fell onto the floor with the stone falling out beside it.

"Where'd that come from?"

A glint of a smile appeared on his face as he picked up the book and began flipping the pages. About two thirds of the way through he stopped, revealing a hole he had carved in the remaining pages.

She handed him the stone, smiling as she watched him

wedge it into place.

"Well, you said I should keep it with me all the time."

"Clever boy." She dipped the quill pen into the ink well. "May I?" she said, tilting her head to the diary. "Don't worry, I just have one thing to add."

After a brief hesitation, he passed her the book.

Her eyebrows drew together as she scribbled out her single line. "Aren't you glad you taught me how to write?" she said, handing it back.

He looked at it for a moment, cocking his head. *"Like our memories, the river's water can never return home, but the stones it smooths and polishes over time are ours to be taken anyway.* I don't understand," he said.

She looked about the room as if searching for someone to help guide her words. "I would've told you this earlier, but it wasn't the right time."

His quizzical look indicated he needed more.

She hesitated, wanting to make every word count. "This stone is more than it appears. It's not just a rock— not just a piece of hardened earth. It's a powerful force of nature that, when the time comes, it can—"

The door flew open. Dr. Parkin stood in the entrance, his forehead moist with sweat.

"Maudie, can you please come with me?" His voice cracked with an uncharacteristic uneasiness.

Noting his desire for her to remain calm, she dutifully played her part and gently placed the diary back in Mase's lap. "I'll be back shortly."

Closing the door behind them, the doctor led her to Annabelle's room. The door was open, allowing a cool breeze to float in from the window across the room. He pulled her inside then quietly locked it behind them.

She looked around. "Where's Annabelle?"

"She's gone," he whispered.

"Gone!"

"Shhh—you *have* to be quiet." He pulled her across the room to the open window. Out of the corner of her eye, she noticed the bed. The sheets were missing, and the covers lay crumpled next to it. The scent of jasmine rolled through the curtains as they gently waved across the opening. He pulled them back, causing her to squint as the light flooded the room.

"She's run away," he said.

Tied to a wrought-iron flower box under her window were the sheets that should have been on her bed, bound one to the other, along with a nightgown and a robe. Together they proved to be the exact length from the window to the lawn.

Chapter 10

Maudie clasped her hands to the sides of her face. "How can things get any worse?" she moaned.

"I don't know," the doctor said, "but one thing's for sure—Masen Winslow is the last person who needs to find out his sister has run away."

She fought to keep her composure, knowing now was not a time to crumble. She and the doctor had to figure out how to keep things from continuing to spiral out of control. "How long do you think she's been gone?"

"No idea. It could've been as early as when we first brought her back or right before I jimmied the lock open ten minutes ago. Regardless, she's gone, and we have to send somebody looking for her without Mase knowing it."

"Mr. Brax sure can't find out either. Lord knows he'll be seized by apoplexy again."

"You're right about that." With his head down, he paced and pondered the situation, occasionally stopping to look out the window. "Hmmm—what time are all the recruits supposed to leave the station tomorrow morning."

"Eight o'clock, why?"

He began pacing again. "Is he anywhere near wanting

to join them?"

In her mind, she replayed all their recent conversations. "No, I don't think so. There's been some glimmer of hope, but he keeps slipping back."

He pursed his lips. "Before proceeding, I want to make sure you understand whatever we do is for *Mase's* own good and the best for Willow Creek *and* everybody here. Do you understand?"

She rocked back on her heels. "I most certainly do!"

"I'm sorry, I knew you did. I had to make sure."

"Doc, I've raised that boy since he was a pup. All I want is his well-being."

"Of course you do." He took a breath. "Well then, we're going to have to act fast today. Here's what we're going to do…"

For the next several minutes, she listened intently to his plan of deception and lies, all aimed at keeping a young man's future—and the future of his family and friends—intact.

"Are you sure this will work?" she asked.

"There's only one way to find out."

Several minutes later, they emerged from the room, locking it behind them. Doc Parkin went to see how Spoon was progressing then downstairs to check on Braxton while Maudie went to enlist the help of Cluc and Sissy.

As the doctor entered the parlor, he was pleased to see Braxton awake and sitting erect. "How're you feeling?"

"Better," said Braxton, his voice still weak but crisper. "How's my family? How's Spoon?

"Spoon is still the same. He keeps fading in and out of consciousness. Annabelle is resting peacefully. I spoke with her, and I believe she's doing better. She wants to be left alone. I'd give her another day, at least."

"And Mase?"

"Mase is still grieving for Annabelle and is beating himself up over Spoon. Braxton, you have to talk to him about his enlistment."

"In what way?"

"He doesn't want to go—he thinks he's needed here more than on the front lines. He's harboring so much guilt it's crippling him. We all love him, but you know what the consequences are if he doesn't fulfill his obligation."

"His obligation?"

"To his country, to the oath he took, to—"

"Yes, Yes! I know." He slammed his fist on the side table next to him, then motioned to the corner. "Hand me my cane."

"What're you going to do?"

"What you told me to do—talk to him."

The doctor called for one of the house slaves, and together they walked him up to Mase's room. Dr. Parkin slowly opened the door, allowing Braxton to shuffle his way inside. With a nod, he pulled the door shut.

Mase had not moved. He remained seated, staring out the window. He didn't even notice when his father placed his hand on his shoulder.

"Mase?" he said, struggling into the chair next to him. "Son, do you hear me?"

Mase's eyes were empty.

Braxton squeezed his arm. "Son, we need to talk."

Still nothing.

"Mase, please…" He started to stand, but his hand slipped on the armrest, sending him crashing to the floor.

Mase swooped him up and placed him back in the chair as quickly as he had hit the floor. "Are you okay?"

He cleared his throat. "I'm alright," he said, brushing himself off. "I'll have to remember that's what it takes to get your attention." He looked into his eyes. "I'm worried about you."

"I'm not the one you should be worried about."

"I'm worried about all of us, son."

"I know you are. That's why I can't go. I have to stay here and take care of things." His eyebrows lifted. "That's why you're here. You're going to try and talk me into going, aren't you?"

"Son, I want—"

"I know what you want." He suddenly became bent on persuading his father that reneging on the oath he had taken days earlier was the right thing to do. "I'm sorry, Dad, but Annabelle and Spoon need me—the plantation needs me! *You* need me!"

"I've spoken with Doc Parkin. He said Annabelle just needs more time and Spoon—" Braxton had never been prone to lies. "Well... Spoon... he needs time too."

"And what about you?"

"I'm fine, and so is the rest of Willow Creek."

Mase slapped his palms on his armrests. "No, you're not, and neither is the plantation. Dad, you're a good man. You're the most generous, honest, loving man I've ever known, but you're the most naïve too. Your health is not good. And somewhere lurking out there is that wicked brother of yours waiting to take control of the place."

"Now, that's enough!" he said. "I know he's cantankerous at times but look at the hand he's been dealt. We weren't the ones who had our legs stolen by polio. We didn't have to suffer the ridicule of other kids growing up or feel the loneliness of being isolated in a defective body. He's family, and that's that. Besides, he's a smart man, and I'm going to need that while you're away."

"Awwhhh!" Mase spun away from his father. "I've already told you *I'm not going!*"

With no more rebuttals left, Braxton played the last card he was sure would sway his son. "If you stay, I'll have no choice but to hand over the plantation to your uncle because you'll be in jail, and I'll have had a heart attack—of *that,* I'm sure!"

Mase rubbed the side of his head, his mind churning through his father's ultimatum. "You'd do that?"

Braxton cupped his hand around the back of his son's neck and pressed his head to his. "Son," he said, his voice wavering, "I love you more than you can imagine. You're right, I might be naïve about a lot of things, but this is one thing I know for certain. If you don't honor your commitment, your life *will* crumble."

Mase looked deep into Braxton's eyes. He had always known his father to be a logical man, one who understood the dynamics of every situation he confronted. His reasoning was beyond reproach.

He nodded. "You're right, Dad. You're right about everything." He turned back to the window. "But you're wrong about this."

For the next half hour, Braxton pleaded with him to reconsider, to no avail. Every word drained him until finally, he conceded. "Alright, if that's your decision, then we'll all have to live with it." Grabbing his cane, he pulled himself up and made his way to the door. As he was leaving, he turned. "I'll do what I can to rectify this with the enlistment office, but the rest will be on you."

As the door closed behind him, Dr. Parkin grabbed him by the arm. He had been waiting in the hallway, knowing he would need to assist him back downstairs. The dejected look upon his face conveyed the outcome of his discussion.

"He's not going, is he?"

Braxton shook his head. "I told him I would talk to the enlistment people."

"You know you can bribe them?"

He stopped as he weighed out the consequences of such an angle. "Doc, I can't even do that. Word would be bound to get out. His life and Annabelle's would be ruined."

Dr. Parkin realized he would have to implement the riskiest part of his plan. "Well, maybe he'll change his mind."

"Maybe," he said softly. "Do you mind helping me to Annabelle's room?"

"I'm not sure that's a good idea," he said. "She wants to be alone."

"I have to, Doc. My heart's breaking."

"But, Brax—"

"She's *my* daughter. I'll go with or without your help."

"Alright then," he sighed. "Remember her wishes though." They stopped just before entering. "Now, if she's asleep, we shouldn't wake her. Promise me, Brax."

"Yes, yes. I promise."

The room was dark and heavy with the scent of the perfume he had given her on her last birthday. A thin ray of light crept across the floor. As it made its way to the bed and onto the covers, it rose then fell, revealing the curves of what appeared to be a body beneath it. A sizeable pillow was atop the supposed slumbering head with the intent of barring any light from creeping underneath. Annabelle's yellow ribbon hung on the corner of the four-poster bed, like a sorrowful banner of the happiness that once was.

Braxton took a step toward the foot of the bed. He reached out his hand and touched the covers, hoping his daughter would suddenly pull them back and jump into his arms. He closed his eyes and uttered the faintest of prayers.

"Okay, Doc," he whispered a moment later. "I'm ready to go back now."

After successfully executing the first part of his plan and getting Braxton back into his room, the doctor went looking for Cluc.

Within several minutes he found him where they had agreed and with the target securely bound. Still sleeping off his hangover, the Judge lay spread out on the smokehouse floor, shackled to the same chains that had subdued Spoon.

Cluc stood over him. "Easy as puddin'," he said, his gap-tooth grin shining brightly.

"Was he asleep when you found him?"

He chuckled. "Yep. He ain't woke nary once since I hauled him in here."

"Well done, well done indeed."

Suddenly the Judge jerked, causing them to jump across the room, trying to get out without being detected. After a couple snorts and grunts, he rolled to his side and continued snoozing away.

Outside, Doc Parkin asked Cluc to bar the door shut then alert the rest of the slaves they were not to go inside for any reason. If they heard him screaming for help or yelling to let him out, they were not to assist him in any way.

"Trust me, Doc, you ain't gonna have no problem with that."

As the doctor walked back to the house, he met Sissy on the front porch. "Dr. Parkin, Maudie's got all Mase's stuff and is sitting outside his door like you asked. And Mr. Brax is still in his room. I think I heard him crying.

"And Spoon..." Her eyes welled up. "Is-is-he going to be okay?" she said, bursting into tears.

"You poor thing. With all this madness going on around here, you've been left to fend on your own."

"Th-that's okay," she sobbed.

He pressed the back of his hand to her cheek. "Everything's going to be alright." He wrapped an arm around her. "I promise."

"You do?"

"Sure." He took his handkerchief and patted her cheeks. "Now, can you do me a favor and relieve Maudie? And remember to watch the doors and let us know if Mase or Mr. Winslow comes out."

"Yes, sir—just like the plan," she whimpered as she headed back inside.

Moments later, Maudie appeared on the front porch with his medicine bag.

"No movement from either one?" he asked.

"None."

"And Spoon?"

"Still out."

He rummaged through his bag. "All we have to do now is wait it out until morning. Phewww—there it is," he said, pulling out a small brown bottle marked *chloroform*. He placed it back inside.

For the rest of the day, Maudie and Sissy took turns sitting in the upstairs hallway monitoring Mase's and Braxton's rooms while Dr. Parkin stayed with Spoon. If either came out and attempted to see Annabelle, they had been directed to divert them by whatever means possible until he could arrive. Into the evening, the house remained a silent fortress of tension.

As midnight spilled over into the small hours of the next day, both Maudie and Sissy succumbed to the ordeals of the day and fell asleep.

Maudie awakened to the grandfather clock in the parlor chiming six times, accompanied by the sounds of horses and wagon wheels rolling up to the front of the house. Wiping her eyes, she tiptoed into Spoon's room.

"Doc, it's time," she whispered with a nudge to his arm.

"What time is it?" he muttered.

"Six. Cluc's downstairs with the wagon."

"Okay." He stood and stretched. "He's right on time." He grabbed his medicine bag and headed out the door. "I'm going to go help Cluc. Watch Spoon until I'm back."

The stench of Spoon's rotting flesh was starting to make her sick, so she opened the window to cleanse the air. As the hazy morning light slowly filled the room, Maudie sat next to him with his hand in hers. Seconds later, she felt a twitch, then a squeeze.

"Is—that—you—Maudie?" he said through gritted teeth.

"Yes, yes, it's me," she whispered into his ear. "My dear. You're going to be better. I know it."

He tried to part his lips again, but the pain of his mending jawbone was too much. All he could do was moan.

"Hush now," she said, placing her finger to his lips. "Don't try to say anything."

Not wanting to venture another word, he held one palm face up and pantomimed writing on it with the other hand.

"You wanna write something?"

He angled his chin down then raised it with a painful exhale.

She looked around but could not find either paper or pen when suddenly it came to her. "I'll be right back."

In a moment, she was by his side, holding a small jar of ink with a quill pen sticking out of it. In her other hand was Mase's diary.

As he reached for the items, he let out a horrific scream. She turned to the door, waiting to hear the unwanted clamor of feet rushing in to see what was wrong. "Spoon—baby, you've got to take it easy."

With a half nod he scribbled, *what happened,* onto a blank page.

For the next twenty minutes, she recounted the horrific events of the past forty-eight hours, occasionally having to stop. Spoon would pat her on the hand and manage a smile as best he could.

"Look at me," she said. "Here I am playing the pitiful one while you're lying there in pain."

When she finished telling the story, he lifted the pen

in his trembling hand. She quickly thumbed to the page of Mase's last entry and held it out to him. With her helping to hold his hand steady, he scratched out a single line.

Her eyes glistened at the page. She knelt next to him, leaning her forehead against his. "You truly are a miracle," she whispered.

A thud against the door caused her to jump to her feet just before the door swung open. Mase stood in the entrance, his eyes fixated on Spoon.

Before he could take a step forward, a hand, wrapped in cloth, whipped around from behind his head and covered his mouth and nose. The unknown assailant pulled him back into the hall, and the door slammed shut.

Maudie rushed outside to find Dr. Parkin gently lowering him to the floor while Cluc kept a lookout for Braxton.

"How long will the chloroform last?" she asked.

"No way to tell," he grunted as he reached under Mase's arms and started to lift. "Everybody's different."

Cluc ran over and took Mase's limp body over his shoulder, then hurried downstairs and out to the wagon where he laid him out on a bed of hay.

"You going to be okay?" Dr. Parkin asked her as he dusted himself off.

"We'll be fine. You boys best be heading out now."

In a blink, he was hopping onto the driver's bench alongside Cluc. "Okay, big fella, let's get going. We got one hour to get to that depot."

Cluc snapped the reins. "Giddup," he barked. The horses jumped into motion.

"Wait!" Maudie came yelling after them.

Cluc pulled the horses back to a standstill.

"He needs this." She reached up and handed the doctor

Mase's diary.

"He most certainly will," he said. He grabbed the book, and on they went with their cargo resting peacefully atop the bed of hay Cluc had carefully prepared.

It had not rained in nearly two weeks, so the road into town was more comfortable than usual. Dr. Parkin pulled out his pipe and lit it. After a long draw, he looked at his pocket watch. "Right on schedule. Fifteen more minutes and young Mr. Winslow will be on his way."

At ten till eight, they had almost reached the train depot, where all the recruits were loading, when Mase began to stir. Dr. Parkin motioned Cluc's attention to the back of the wagon. "He just couldn't wait," he said as he reached into his bag.

"Ohhh, my head," he moaned.

The doctor scrambled to wrap a cloth around his hand. As he began to pour the chloroform onto it, the wagon hit a bump, and the bottle jostled around his lap and onto the floorboard.

"Where am I?" Mase mumbled, struggling to sit up.

Before the doctor could grab the bottle, another bump sent it bobbling out onto the road.

"Stop!" The doctor jumped out and seized the precious vessel as it was about to be run over by an oncoming carriage. Meanwhile Cluc was struggling with the reins as Mase staggered onto the street.

"Grab him!" Dr. Parkin yelled as he tilted the bottle against the cloth. Nothing came out.

Mase jerked his head back and forth as the effects of the anesthetic wore off. "What's going on?" He looked down the block. Still in a haze, he could barely make out the line of recruits waiting to board the train. "Is this... Oh no—nooo! I don't know what you did, but I told you, I'm *not* going!" As he turned to run in the opposite direction, Cluc uncoiled a right hook to his temple that sent him flying onto his back and into unconsciousness.

"I'm sorry, Mr. Mase," he said, hoisting his limp body back onto the wagon.

Dr. Parkin patted the big man on the shoulder. "Not exactly your standard anesthetic, but just as effective."

Dozens of fresh-faced new soldiers packed the station, all accompanied by family and friends taking turns bidding them farewell with hugs and kisses. As they pulled next to the platform, a rugged young lieutenant with a clipboard walked up to the doctor. "Are you Mase Winslow?" he asked.

"No sir, there's your man," he said, pointing to the back of the wagon.

"Is he okay?"

"Couldn't be better. His folks threw him a going-away bash last night, and he's still—well, how do you say—sleeping it off."

The lieutenant grinned. "I pretty much did the same thing." He handed him the clipboard and pencil. "If you'll sign next to his name and have your big guy toss him on board, we'll take it from here.

Like a sack of potatoes, Cluc toted him under his arm to one of the open cattle cars being used to transport the recruits to toward the front lines. Dr. Parkin followed close behind.

"I'll help ya," said a gangly, bucktooth, freckle-faced boy with bushy red hair. He reached down from the car and helped to lift Mase onto the dirty wooden planks. "Big night huh? I'll watch out for him 'til he sobers up."

"Much obliged," Cluc said. He rubbed Mase's arm and whispered into his ear, "You come back to us, ya hear?"

"Young fella, can you make sure he gets this?" Dr. Parkin asked as he tossed in a pillowcase containing a change of clothes and his diary. "Oh, and this too." He pulled his pipe from his breast pocket and stuffed it in the bag.

"All accounted for," yelled the lieutenant.

"All accounted for," yelled another soldier two cars away.

The train whistle blasted three times in quick succession then chugged into motion.

The doctor waved to the freckle-faced boy sitting cross-legged next to Mase's motionless body. "Good luck, boys!" he shouted.

"They'll be needing more than that," said a man in a tattered grey uniform standing next to him. In place of his missing leg, he used a single crutch to balance himself.

Dr. Parkin turned to him and asked, "Why's that?"

The man stared past him, watching as the train puffed its way out of sight. "The lieutenant didn't tell you where they're headed?"

"I believe it's Fort Donelson in Tennessee."

"Into the hornets' nest they're going." The man turned his head to the doctor. "All them boys—barely old enough to be called men—are being sent to the 8th Brigade under Brigadier General Thaddeus McCain." He shifted his weight to his good leg. "His claim to fame—some of the highest casualty rates in the war." He looked to where his leg had been. "That's *our* casualties," he said through clenched teeth. "In two days, ole Thaddeus is heading into another ruckus in a little town called Platsville." He looked at the doctor with hollow eyes then hobbled off the platform and onto the street. "Into the hornets' nest... Into the hornets' nest..." he kept muttering as he disappeared into the crowd.

Chapter 11

A half hour after leaving the station, Mase woke from the knockout punch he had received from his friend. The clackety-clack of the locomotive's wheels upon the track, combined with the stench of hardened cow manure, made for a rough re-entry into consciousness.

"Ohhh, my aching head." He touched his temple. "Ouch!" he said, recoiling his hand. "What happened?"

"Welcome aboard the USS cow patty," said the freckle-faced boy. "Private Timothy McCarthy at your service." He snapped off a salute followed by a toothy grin equally as silly as his over-the-top attempt at military correctness.

Mase pulled himself up on his side with a moan. "Who'd you say you were?"

"Timothy McCarthy. Your fellow companions, who I failed to gain name recognition, asked me to take care of you—and that I will." He jumped to attention with a repeat of his first salute. "'To protect and serve' is my motto."

Mase jiggled his jaw, making sure it wasn't broken. "You're a tad on the different side, aren't you?"

"That I am, or at least I've been told, sir." His grin grew wider.

Mase couldn't help but chuckle at such animated enthusiasm. "How old are you?'

"Nineteen and then some, sir." He bent over and whispered, "Actually, seventeen and three quarters—don't tell anybody though."

"Didn't they explain how you had to be over eighteen?"

"Course they did. I wrote the word *eighteen* on some paper, stuffed it inside my shoe, then when they asked if I was over eighteen, I told 'em sure—I'm *over* eighteen."

One corner of Mase's mouth rose as he visualized the underaged boy pulling off his scheme. "Good for you," he said as he scanned the boxcar.

Every five feet, a recruit was stretched out, staring at the ceiling, contemplating what lay ahead. Some played cards while others chatted with their new Confederate countrymen. Their patriotic zeal filled the fly-infested space as they shouted out phrases like, "We're gonna whip them Yanks good" or "We're coming for you, Abe."

The same feelings began to rise in Mase only to be dashed by the memories of the recent past. Visions of him ripping open the back of an innocent man leaped into his mind like a wolf ravishing its prey, and his sister's ordeal at the hands of his uncle's henchman made his blood boil. The waves of despair heightened as he heard his father telling him he *had to go* to battle. Instead of feeling the pride of volunteering, he felt the disgrace of being pushed away by the one man he loved the most. With each new mile, he slipped farther and farther away.

"Sir, are you alright? Sir!"

He blinked. The warmth of Timothy's hand resting on his shoulder brought him back.

"Sir, are you okay?"

He rubbed his face. "Yes, yes. I'm fine. I was—I was thinking about home."

"I've been doing the same thing, sir."

"You don't have to keep calling me 'sir.' The name's Mase."

"Pleasure to meet you, Mister—?"

"Winslow. But I told you, you can call me Mase."

"Well, Mr. Mase Winslow, why don't you have a smoke?"

"No—it's *just* Mase."

"Well then, *Just Mase*, how's about a smoke to make you feel better?"

"You're a stitch," he chuckled.

"Ah! I knew I could coax a laugh out of that gloomy puss of yours. So how about that smoke? When I start feeling low, I sneak into Pa's tobacci stash and light one up."

"What in tarnation are you talking about?"

"Your uncle, or whoever that gentleman was who dropped you off, left you a present in this here high-dollar cotton satchel." Timothy handed him the pillowcase Dr. Parkin had given him.

Mase parted the opening to find the doctor's pipe lying on the change of clothing Maudie had packed. He held it in front of him, rotating it back and forth, admiring it as if he had never seen it before.

"He's not my uncle, you know. I wish he were. My real uncle's a—well—never mind."

"Any tobacci in there?"

"Hmmm, let's see." He pulled out the change of clothes. "Nope, I don't have…" His eyes gleamed as they landed on the one remaining item within the pillowcase.

"What'd they put in there—gold?"

"You might say that," he said as he pulled out the one book that meant everything to him.

"What's that?"

"My diary," he said, inspecting its condition.

"How about ripping out a page? We'll shred it and use it in place of tobacci."

He gave him a sideways glance. "No, *Just Tim*, let's not." He paused. "Maybe we'll chop up a dried cow patty—how about that?"

Timothy rolled over, laughing. "And you think *I'm* a little different!"

By the time the train rolled into Fort Donelson, the sun was setting. Like the cattle that formally occupied the box-cars, the recruits filed out into a line leading to a table where one soldier was giving out supplies and another assigning tent mates.

Mase counted out the number of men ahead of him and Timothy. "Sir," he said to the man behind Timothy, "would you like to jump ahead of me?"

"Sure, why not."

When Mase stepped up to the table, he provided his name. In return, he received his uniform, musket, saber, canteen, cartridge box, and burlap pack complete with fifty pounds of other soldering gear.

"Private Winslow, your tent mate is…" He looked behind him. "What's your name, soldier?"

"Private Timothy McCarthy—sir!" he said with more gusto than a hopped-up West Point cadet.

The two officers grinned at one another. "You boys get a good night's sleep," said the soldier, plopping Timothy's gear into his skinny, outstretched arms. "Drills are at six o'clock sharp."

As they came upon their tent, Timothy stopped. His exuberant tone faded. "Thanks."

"For what?" Mase asked.

"For wanting to bunk with me. Most people would... well, you know—not."

Mase slapped him on the arm. "Can't imagine why."

The sound of reveille at five the next morning blasted the camp awake, and a hundred eager privates piled out of two rows of tents like ants coming out at night for a drop of sugar water.

A beefy sergeant with fluffy sideburns named Quintin Hamilton paced up and down the corridor of tents. He held a torch as the men stood in their underwear, slumped shouldered and fidgeting next to their new canvas homes. "Attention!" he barked.

The men randomly popped their shoulders back, some tucked their necks, and others sucked in their guts. All stared straight ahead, anxiously awaiting their next command.

"You've got thirty minutes to eat and put your uniforms on. At exactly six o'clock, you'll rally to the red flag next to the torch on top of the hill behind me. And, ladies—you *will* bring your packs fully loaded. Is that understood?"

The men replied in peppered responses of "Yes, sir," "Yes," and "Yes, sergeant."

"At ease."

The men relaxed.

"Pathetic," he growled. "Now go!"

Precisely thirty minutes later, Mase and Timothy were standing side by side in formation with the other ninety-eight men of their company. For an hour, they marched over the open field as Sergeant Hamilton ordered them about with unfamiliar terms like *ketch step*, *dress to the left*, and *close ranks*. All the while Mase grew to appreciate the officer's relentless instructions as it kept his mind from wandering back to the plantation.

For another two hours, they learned to maneuver from marching formations to fighting formations. He later wrote in his diary, *For the most part, the men were enthusiastic about learning these new skills, especially my new friend, who I've dubbed 'Just Tim.'*

That afternoon they repeated the same drills from the morning followed by thirty minutes of target practice.

"Wish we could do more shootin'," Timothy said.

"We're Southerners," Mase replied. "We're supposed to know how to shoot, hunt, and track."

"I've plowed fields and primed tobacci my whole life. Only shot a gun a handful of times."

"Don't worry," Mase said. "I'll teach you."

The next day the sun came up quickly with the temperature rising just as fast. By noon it was pushing ninety degrees. More marching and other drills comprised the day, only with fewer breaks as the word went out the rest of their training would be taking place on the battlefield.

"That's all?" exclaimed Timothy as he lay in his cot that evening. "I-I don't think I'm ready."

Mase rinsed his socks in a bucket and hung them over his pack to dry. "We've got a two-day march ahead of us. Most likely, we'll still be training along the way."

"But you haven't even taught me how to shoot proper."

Mase balled up a damp sock and bopped him in the

head with it. "Where's that 'Just Tim' spirit?" He pulled out his diary. "I'm gonna have to write you up." As he flipped it open in mock disgust, he fell upon a page that contained only one line, the letters strung together with long, craggy scratches. His index finger quivered as he slid it slowly across the words.

"Are you okay?" Timothy asked.

Tears fell to the page, causing the letters to spread like water coloring.

"Mase?"

He glanced up while continuing to run his finger back and forth over the sentence.

Timothy knelt beside him and tilted his head as he read the jagged text. *I forgive you, brother.* He looked at him. "You've got a brother?"

Mase nodded, still concentrating on the entry.

"What's his name?"

"Jeziah." He tucked the book under his pillow then lay down, staring up at the canvas ceiling. "But I call him Spoon."

Reveille came an hour early the next morning. At the top of the hill, sitting on a silky grey mare, company commander Captain Francis Dalton fired off a dozen orders to his first and second lieutenants. In turn, they split the responsibilities among the four sergeants in charge of their platoons. By the time the orders filtered to the company's eight corporals, the camp was already breaking down tents and preparing for the march to Platsville. There they were to fall in with the 28th Regiment and then into General McCain's 8th Brigade.

By sunup, the company was on the move. Spirits ran

high with the new Confederates feeling their two days of drills had prepared them well enough to whip anything the Federals threw at them.

Mase kept step with the rest of his fellow troops as they moved toward their destination. At times, the revelation of Spoon's diary entry helped ease his ever-present angst, at other times, it heightened it by emphasizing his imperfect character as compared to the purity and goodness of his friend's. Still gnawing at him was how truthful those four words were—had Spoon truly forgiven him? If he had, how could he have done it so easily? Such mercy ignited a slow burn from within, illuminating his unworthiness even to exist. Regardless, this single thought provided the fuel that propelled him forward over the day's twenty-mile march.

The next morning the company woke and prepared for a short three-mile trek to the outskirts of Platsville, where they joined up with the 28th Regiment. With the sun yet to rise, they fell in behind four columns of soldiers that stretched into the early-morning darkness.

"How many are there, Mase?" Timothy asked.

"Can't tell," he said, standing on his toes, trying to calculate the endless grey lines of men ahead of them.

"Quiet in the ranks," shouted Sergeant Hamilton.

"Forrrrrward!" came the order from a commander in the distance.

The clomping of boots suddenly filled the air as the regiment lumbered its way through the quiet little town, across a freshly cut cornfield, and down a narrow road to a covered bridge that crossed into a stand of giant hardwoods. The pink and yellow sunrise filtered through the hundred-foot trees, painting an inviting picture of serenity.

"Halt!" came the order from the front of the lines.

Ten minutes passed as they stood rigid while the officers convened in a discussion, the sounds of their voices mingling with the birds and the flow of water beneath the bridge. The heat had not arrived yet, and the day was still pleasant, still inviting—still innocent.

The sound of Captain Dalton's mare preceded him as he came galloping out of the bridge. He stopped momentarily, bending over to conference with his subordinates. Then spinning his horse around, he pulled his saber, raised it out in front of him, and rode down the lines.

"Gentlemen, soldiers, brothers—prepare your hearts," he shouted. "For today we honor our right to be free of tyranny!"

A roar went up from the ranks. The men stomped their feet, hooting and hollering.

Timothy shifted from side to side. "I gotta pee."

"Not now, Tim."

"What're we gonna do, Mase?"

"We'll know soon enough."

Officers began barking off orders. Sergeant Hamilton stepped off the road next to Timothy. He looked right then left, then said, "In ten minutes, we'll be crossing through that bridge and down a short road. On the other side there's a large field where we'll be falling in between two other regiments of General McCain's brigade. Our objective is to cross that field and secure the farmhouse that stands in the center. There's a stone wall in front of it. To gain the advantage, we *have* to reach it before the Federals. The regiments to our left and right will be performing flanking maneuvers and providing covering fire."

"Mase," Timothy whispered. "Psst... Mase!"

"Quiet now. Listen."

"Any questions?" the sergeant asked. "Good luck, boys. It's going to be a lively day indeed."

Mase stared into the covered bridge. His heartbeat was steady, his palms dry and secure around his weapon. Whatever was on the other side, he had prepared himself for it since being taken against his will from the plantation. The moment of resolve was at hand, and he was more than willing to release the tempest from within.

"Forrrward," came the order. Through the bridge, the troops marched into the towering forest and out into the opening where two full regiments of Confederate soldiers awaited them. As they approached, the regiments shifted to the left and right, leaving space in the middle for their company.

Once settled into position, the battlefield unfolded. A thousand acres of plowed farmland and gently rolling pastures stretched out before them. On the farthest left edge of the opening, another brigade of men in grey stretched out in two long rows. Directly ahead, less than a hundred yards away, was the farmhouse they had been ordered to take. Beyond it, running the full length of the field, was another immense forest.

For twenty minutes, General McCain's brigade of 7,800 men occupied the battlefield unopposed. Only a handful of Union troops could be spotted hustling back and forth along the faraway tree line.

Timothy rocked back and forth. "May-may-maybe they aren't comin' today."

"Shhh. Ya don't wanna wake 'em, do ya?" whispered a soldier to his left.

"Both of you, hush." Mase's criticism was reflected in

his rigid posture, his jaw muscles bulging from the pressure of his bite, his knuckles white from the tension of the grip on his musket. Stone-faced, he stared at the farmhouse. The only vision of victory was the image of Silas standing in the doorway as he ran his saber through him. Anyone in his way would pay the price of his revenge.

The blast of a distant cannon caused most of the men to jump. A half second later, its projectile exploded in the treetops behind them, sending branches and bark cascading onto the drummer boys stationed in the rear.

Suddenly the blue skies were ablaze with cannon fire, shells bursting every fifty feet—some behind the lines, some in front, and some directly within their ranks, killing three or four men at a time.

Mase started forward.

"Hold, soldier!" shouted Sergeant Hamilton, who was standing with his sword above his head. "Wait for the call, boys!"

Just then, five shrill bugle notes pierced the air, followed by the pounding of drums.

"March!" he yelled, still holding his saber aloft.

Simultaneously the regiments to the left and right veered off while Mase's company quick-stepped straight ahead.

From out of the woods on the opposite side of the field, soldiers in blue emerged in numbers twice as many as theirs.

A volley of musket fire ripped through Mase's regiment, dropping a tenth of the men.

Sergeant Hamilton waved his sword in the air. "Charge!"

Every soldier dropped his weapon to his side and raced toward the cover of the stones, yelling and shouting horrific noises. Fifty yards from the wall, the Union lines delivered a second round of fire, decimating another tenth of the regiment, including the flag bearer whose arm was blown off a few yards ahead of Mase.

As he ran past the fallen soldier, he grabbed the flag. He lowered his head and sprinted past the sergeant and the rest of the regiment who were hunkered to the ground, fearful of moving any closer to the next hell-storm sure to follow.

Within seconds he reached the stone wall, but instead of using it as protection, he jumped on top and heaved the banner as high as he could. At the same time, the Union unleashed another wave of lead. Dozens of minnie balls zipped through the flag, one through his jacket, and another grazed his cheek.

"Come on!" he screamed above the roar of battle.

"Rally to Mase," yelled Sergeant Hamilton.

"To Winslow and the colors," shouted another.

Within moments the regiment was on its feet, rushing to the wall.

As the troops fell in behind the granite stones, the sergeant grabbed Mase's leg and pulled him to the ground. "Get your cotton-pickin' tail down before you get your cotton-pickin' tail shot off."

Mase dropped to his knees and planted the flag in a crack in the wall.

"Fix bayonets!" barked the sergeant. "Not you," he said, patting Mase on the shoulder. "You're our color-bearer now, son."

As the rest of the men scrambled to modify their weapons for close-quarter combat, Mase surveyed the killing field behind them. "Where's Spoon?"

"Where's who?" asked the sergeant, sliding the blade onto the end of his musket.

"I-I mean, where's Tim McCarthy?"

Something ricocheted off his shirt's top button. He spun around and caught Timothy about to toss another pebble at him from five soldiers away. The grin he wore was one-part joy, two-parts fear. "We made it," he mouthed.

Mase nodded. "Now get ready," he mouthed back.

"Listen up, boys," Sergeant Hamilton yelled. "Wait for my command, then take your best shot. Understood?"

"Yes, sir!" the men yelled as the battle raged about them.

The sergeant raised his hand while aiming with the other. "Hollld!" He squinted, waiting for them to come close enough to make out the image of their belt buckle. "Hollld." At sixty yards, he dropped his hand. "Fire!"

Immediately a quarter of the approaching horde fell. The remainder clashed into the Confederates, creating a deadly whirlwind of muskets being used as clubs and bayonets as butcher knives. Swords clanged, metal against metal with the victor wielding metal against flesh.

Mase stood defiantly transfixed to the wall with the Confederate flag in one hand and a saber in the other. For fifteen minutes, he fended off attack after attack while not once letting the flag touch the ground. At one point, he dropped his saber to use the pole to knock out a Union soldier bearing down on Sergeant Hamilton with a knife.

After twenty minutes, Union bugles blew retreat. Seizing the moment, Mase rushed toward the farmhouse, waving the flag as the entire regiment followed. Breathless and bloodied, he pounded the pole onto each of the wooden steps leading to the front porch, his vision of Silas in the doorway and his chance at redemption fading with each step.

McCain's men cheered as they watched their defeated foes flee into the woods from which they came.

Exhausted, Mase stumbled to the steps and into the arms of Sergeant Hamilton. Another soldier grabbed the flag while the sergeant eased him onto the porch. "Get me a canteen for this man." He patted him on the knee. "We'll talk later, young man. Right now, I need to tend to our brothers."

As he rested, soldiers filed by, thanking him for his inspiration—everyone except Timothy McCarthy. Mase turned his head from side to side, filtering through the swarm of men working to fortify the farmhouse for a possible counterattack.

"Has anyone seen Tim McCarthy?" he yelled out. Another soldier thanked him for his courage. "Have you seen Tim McCarthy?"

"No, sir, but thank you again for getting us here."

Mase walked the perimeter of the house, looking in every direction, yelling Tim's name. He turned back toward the battlefield and the stone wall and ran. Every ten feet, a body lay motionless, crawling, or reaching for help. The agony of the wounded swelled into a terrifying harmony of moans.

As he got closer, he slowed his pace for fear of stepping on bodies until he came to the crack where he had lodged the flag. Dozens of dead men were sprawled over the giant pieces of granite, and rivers of blood ran through the crevices into crimson puddles. One by one, he slowly turned over the bodies.

Through the growing pleas for help, a whisper managed its way to him. "Maaassse."

He jerked his head left.

"Maaassse."

He turned right. "Where are you?"

Twenty feet past the wall, he saw a bloody hand rise. Mase rushed to him and fell to his knees. "Oh, Tim... nooo." He watched Tim fold his hands across the pool of red in the middle of his stomach.

Blood gurgled from his mouth. "Never did get that t-t-target p-p-practice."

Mase searched the battlefield. "Medic!"

"No. It's okay..." Tim said softly.

Mase bent over and stroked his hair. "I'm sooo sorry," he said, watching Tim's chest rise and fall for the last time.

Mase hung his head and closed his eyes as scenes from the battle flashed through his mind, mingling with images of Annabelle curled up crying, his father lecturing him about having to go to war—Silas laughing at him. When he opened them, Spoon was lying where Timothy had been, eyes closed, hands folded in the same bloody spot on his stomach.

Suddenly Spoon's eyes flashed open, and his lips slowly parted. "You should have protected him." His deathly gaze bore into him. "He was just a boy—just a boy..."

Mase slapped his palms against his face and rubbed his eyes. When he opened them, Spoon was gone. Timothy lay beside him once again.

Mase stared at his face—so serene, so tranquil. He envied the peace Tim had found. Reaching inside his boot, he pulled out a small knife and raised it to his face. Turning it side to side, he recalled how effectively he had used it to skin rabbits. He ran his thumb across it, drawing a thin line of blood. He watched as it ran into his palm.

Placing the blade's tip just above where a Yankee bullet had grazed his cheek, he pushed it through the skin into bone then slowly pulled downward. For the first time that day, he felt real physical pain while experiencing the temporary relief from the anguish that continued to build inside.

"Mase, you gotta get back."

He looked over his shoulder to find a lieutenant running up behind him. "There's a counterattack on the way. Come on! The men need you."

He looked back at his friend's lifeless body while running his finger across his new wound. Dropping the knife, he followed the lieutenant back to the farmhouse.

Chapter 12

The counterattack on the farmhouse never occurred that day. Instead, the Union forces regrouped for an attack the following morning. Once again, Mase carried the flag, and again, the Confederates prevailed. As a result of his bravery, he was promoted to corporal and went on to fight unscathed in several major battles over the following two months.

During this time, he had received only one letter from home, which was from his father but in his uncle's handwriting. According to the Judge, due to his father's declining health, it was easier for him to dictate than write, even so, the letter was less than a page long, sterile, and cold. Everything was fine, and the plantation was doing well. No mention of Annabelle or Spoon and nothing of Braxton's love for his son.

The following week a division of Union troops had McCain's brigade under siege near a little town on the Tennessee-Georgia line. A Confederate courier was able to sneak through and deliver a small bundle of mail.

To Mase's surprise, he received a package from Maudie. Settling on his cot, he carefully unwrapped it. Its contents consisted of a jar of his favorite blackstrap molasses along with a bag of her special cornmeal. Underneath was a thick envelope containing three meticulously written pages revealing the truth of what was really happening at the plantation.

He cringed when he read her description of how the Judge had taken over. Cluc had been replaced by a foul-mouthed goon who was running roughshod over everyone. His stomach churned, and his face flushed with rage to learn—unbeknown to his father—several of the slaves had been whipped for no good reason. The one consistency with his uncle's letter was his father's failing health. Still, Braxton missed Mase and, along with everyone else, prayed for his safe return.

The last two pages were the most devastating. Maudie was never one to mince words and, as such, explained in detail about Annabelle's disappearance. She prayed he would forgive her for the deception she and Doc Parkin had used on him and his father.

He clenched his fist when reading how Silas was still on the loose and how more evidence had come out about his past, including burglary, assault and battery, and several accusations of rape. Allegedly, his milky eye was the result of one victim's attempt to stab him with a hairpin.

As for Spoon, he had recovered well enough but was blind in his left eye. What proved worse was he had been taken from the plantation. Mase's uncle had offered him up to serve as a valet to his old friend Colonel Johnathon Reynolds of the 103rd Georgia Brigade. He had rationalized that Spoon's presence would only remind Braxton of the assault on Annabelle and her subsequent disappearance.

Maudie believed the real reason was he was payment for a gambling debt. As for herself, she was heartbroken. The letter's tear-stained pages provided testament to those feelings.

Mase held the pages in his hand, thankful he had taught her how to read and write while simultaneously wishing he hadn't. A sense of helplessness now compounded the guilt he bore for leaving. He couldn't help his father, there was no way to search for his sister, and Spoon was most likely gone forever.

Grabbing the letter with his other hand, he ripped it to shreds, pacing back and forth in the tent like a caged tiger, wanting revenge on his captors. He gnashed his teeth and paced faster, his thoughts swirling incoherently through his head as he tried to solve the unsolvable.

He dropped to his knees and hid his face in his hands, hoping when he removed them, he'd be sitting on the front porch with his father and sister while his best friend entertained them with his spoons. He could hear all their voices at once, including Maudie's, who grew louder as she pieced together his name—Reynolds—Johnathon Reynolds—Colonel Johnathon Reynolds.

He pulled his hands away and began desperately searching through the bits of the letter for the needed information. A minute later he found the answer among three small fragments, Colonel Johnathon—Reynolds—*103rd Georgia Brigade.*

He ran out of his tent and straight into Sergeant Hamilton. "Whoa. What's the hurry, Corporal?"

"Sarge, do you know the name of the private who was transferred here from the 103rd?"

"Yeah, Calvin Middleton. Why?"

"Which tent is he in?"

"He's not."

"What?"

"He was wounded—pretty bad—earlier today on a scouting expedition. He's in that makeshift hospital in town."

"How far is it?"

"Not too far through the woods. Maybe an hour's walk by the path we took the other day. Why?"

"What about the road?"

"Yanks got it blocked. Say, you're not thinking of—"

"No, sir," he said, turning and heading back to his tent.

"Be careful 'round here, Mase," he yelled after him. "It'll be dark in an hour, and those Yankee snipers don't sleep. *That's* why Middleton's where he is."

Mase went back into his tent. As he waited for the sergeant to leave, he pulled his diary and pencil from his pack and shoved them into his jacket's oversized pocket.

As soon as Hamilton was out of sight, Mase stole away into the fading light of the woods and down the path to the hospital. During his time with McCain's Brigade, he had become adept at skillfully navigating his way through treacherous territory. This, however, was a different situation. His thoughts were not about himself and his safety. He was obsessed with finding out if the wounded soldier had met his friend, what his condition was, and how he could help him escape.

Within an hour, the path led him to a small clearing. On the other side, it resumed through a small thicket and out onto the street where the hospital was.

As he stepped into the opening, he heard what sounded like a musket's firing hammer being pulled into place. Stepping back, he revised his route and pushed through the safety of the dense brush surrounding the clearing's perimeter.

By the time he made it to the other side, it was dark, making it hard to locate the hospital. His only sense of direction was to follow the moans of its patients. As he came closer, the crates of books beside the front door indicated the building had once been a library. The pile of bloody bandages and detached limbs in the back confirmed he was in the right place.

He took off his hat as he entered. A long corridor of wounded soldiers lay groaning in beds, pleading for help, some begging for mercy. An elderly lady in a blood-splattered apron walked toward him.

"Nurse, can you tell me where Calvin Middleton is?"

"Come with me," she said. Halfway down the hall, she stopped and pointed to a priest hovering over a patient at the last bed.

"Calvin?"

She nodded.

"Has he passed?"

"I don't know, but—"

"Thank you, ma'am," he said, quickening his pace.

As he approached the bed, the priest turned. "Are you here for Calvin?"

"Yes, sir—I mean, yes, Father. I'm Corporal Masen Winslow and—"

"I'm sorry, son," he said, shaking his head. "I'm afraid he's gone." With no time to offer any condolences, he walked across the aisle and started administering last rights to another one of the war's unfortunate victims.

"You a friend of Calvin's?" asked the soldier in the bed behind him. His head was bandaged, and his arm was in a blood-soaked sling.

Mase turned. "Well, I wasn't actually—"

"Hey, are you that corporal?"

"Well, I'm a corporal—"

"The flag bearer. Winslow, Mase Winslow?"

"That's right. I'm Corporal Winslow."

"Calvin and me heard a lot about you. It's an honor to meet you, sir."

"You actually knew him?"

"Yes, sir. He and me transferred in together three days ago. Yes, sir, we heard you—"

"You were with Colonel Reynold's 103rd Brigade?"

"Yes, sir. I'd shake your hand but—"

"Did you ever meet the colonel?" Mase couldn't help interrupting the soldier's attempts at admiration, his excitement to get information about Spoon was too great. Sitting next to the wounded man, Mase pulled out his diary, eager to take notes.

"'Bout every day," he said. "I's his courier."

Mase's face lit up. "Did you happen to meet his valet?"

"Which one? He had three. The colonel was pretty much a dandy if you ask me."

"A young fellow about my age. About my same size too. Big smile."

"Hmmm, honestly, sir, I didn't pay much attention to 'em. I just delivered messages. I was always in and out."

"His name was Jeziah, but everybody called him Spoon."

He shook his head. "Afraid I don't remember any of their names."

The elderly nurse approached him. "I'm sorry, sir. I'm afraid visiting hours are over. You can come back tomorrow though."

"One more minute, please." He turned to the soldier. "He was blind in one eye. Does that help?"

"Sir, I'm sorry, it's getting late," the nurse said. "I'm going to have to ask—"

"Yeah—I do recall one of them boys being blind now. Colored boy they called 'cyclops.' They was always making fun of him."

"But he's okay, right?"

"Well…"

"Well, what?"

The soldier's tone turned somber. "Two days after we were transferred in, we heard our boys faced off against General Sherman. They were outnumbered three to one— three to one, can you imagine? I don't know if it's true, but we heard they had about forty-five percent casualties and another thirty percent captured—including the colonel."

"Where'd they take them?"

"Most likely up the road to Pointer's Cove—the town the Yanks took control of before the battle. After that, God only knows."

Mase ground his pencil into the pages of his diary, snapping it in two, as visions of him finding his friend faded away.

He composed himself, then thanked the soldier and wished him a speedy recovery. As he stepped outside, the night had almost turned into day. Whatever clouds were in the sky before had vanished. In their place was a full moon, illuminating every cobblestone on the street, every blade of grass in the fields. It was the type of night snipers dreamed of.

Mase looked across the clearing to the path that had brought him in. As beautiful as it appeared, it was just as deadly. He would have to take a more challenging route back to camp, one that would take him deep into the woods. He put his diary back into his jacket and headed off the road to the densest part of the woods he could find.

After fifteen minutes, he turned into some heavy brush and began his journey. Luckily, the new route opened up, allowing him to move along a bit more quickly. Because the tops of the trees were extremely overgrown, they created a nice canopy of darkness below. His only real challenges were the twigs, leaves, and underbrush he stepped on, each crunch and crackle alerting any snipers a target was in their midst.

After an hour of trudging through the forest, he estimated he was about halfway to camp. The backs of his hands were raw from thorns raking across them, and his face was scratched and scraped from random branches whiplashing back on him. The long slog was exhausting and painful, and without a canteen, he was more than parched.

He sat with his back against a large hickory tree to rest and contemplate whether to stay the course or reroute to a small stream that he could hear off in the distance. He concluded the stream option to be the better choice. He could quench his thirst, and the sound of the water would muffle his steps. It would take him more time, but that was one thing he had plenty of.

As he was about to stand, he heard something rustling behind him—a short crinkling of leaves, then silence. He opened his mouth wide and inhaled slowly, a stealth technique his drill instructor had taught him for conditions such as these. Another crinkle, this time closer, a pop of a twig, then silence again.

Reaching inside his boot, he searched for the knife he had used on his cheek. It wasn't there. A branch snapped even closer, now five or six feet away. He had to find something—anything—for protection. Creeping his hand along the ground, he found a jagged rock. Inch by inch, he slid his way up with his back against the tree.

Holding his weapon to his chest, he waited. Seconds later, another twig cracked directly behind him. Without hesitation, he jumped out, holding the rock above his head, ready to pound it into the skull of the would-be assailant. Other than the possum nibbling away at the tree's bark, there was nothing. He let out a sigh as he watched the furry creature scurry into the darkness. He stood for another moment, collecting his emotions.

When his pulse returned to normal, he started toward the stream. He took one step forward and heard another stirring off in the distance. At that moment he became aware of the difference between the sounds of a human's woodland movements and an animal's. He turned just in time to see the ignition of gunpowder accompanied by the crack of thunder.

Chapter 13

The early morning fog lifted through the trees and disappeared into the heavens, leaving a fine mist on the underbrush, rotting leaves, and decaying tree trunks of the forest floor. Mase's body was wet with dew and blood. He lay facedown, left to die from a sniper's bullet, his breathing shallow and growing thinner by the minute.

He had been conscious for less than two minutes from the time the bullet entered his body until that morning when he was yanked by the leg and dragged to a clearing where he was flung onto a mule and carried farther into the woods. For the next two days, his tortured soul suffered a painful respite, occasionally waking for several blurry minutes only to fall back into unconsciousness.

On the third day, he awoke to the smell of bacon and thoughts of home until a searing pain in his stomach jarred him back to reality. He tried to sit up, but from out of nowhere, a small, bony hand pushed him back onto a mound of animal fur.

"No, child. Ya gots to be still. Ya gots to enjoy da death," said a petite, wrinkled woman. Her shoulders were hunched, and she wore a sprig of sage in a rat's nest of grey hair with several strands of beads and trinkets dangling down the other side.

He grabbed his side and moaned. "Where am I?"

"Ya with me. Ya in Juana's house," she said in a crackling yet chipper voice.

An oil lamp and several candles dimly lit the room as incense mixed with burning pork clouded the tiny space. Through the haze, he could see animal skulls hanging from the cabin's sagging walls alongside wooden masks and assorted amulets. A pile of small bones and a straw doll occupied a rickety table in the middle of the dirt floor.

"How'd I get here?" he said, pressing his trembling lips together.

"Why, I brung ya."

He tried to get up again but fell back. The pain and fatigue were too much.

"I fixed ya—until ya go, that is."

"What do you mean *fixed* me?"

"Go on, feel dem stitches," she said, pointing to his stomach.

He pulled his jacket back and lifted his shirt to his chin while straining his head downward. Slightly to the right of his belly button was a three-inch line of heavy thread running in and out of his skin, blood trickling out of it. His head fell back onto the bed.

"Good job, huh?" she said.

His lips were chapped and cracking. "I'm awful thirsty. Can I get some water?"

She held a clay mug to his mouth while he swallowed. "Ahhh, that's awful. It tastes like—"

"Blood?"

"Kinda," he groaned.

"Cuz it is yur blood."

"What!" he said, wincing in more pain.

"Ya bleedin' from da inside."

"How long have I been—"

"Tree days."

"Three days! I've got to get back to my regiment." He tried to get up again but couldn't manage to lift his head this time.

"Juana done told ya, ya *gots to settle*."

"You don't understand. They'll think I've deserted."

"Dat's true," she said, milling about the room, searching for something.

"Can you—"

"Take ya back? No, sir. Besides, dem others already gone. Gone two days now." She poured a syrupy liquid into a cup and crushed in flakes of something from a tiny leather pouch. "Ya deserted. But it don't much matter now, do it?"

"I'm not a—" He contracted into a painful ball, unable to continue.

"Here, drink dis," she said, lifting his head and pouring the concoction into his mouth. Half went in, half spilled down the sides of his face. "Dis'll make da pain go away. Den ya can enjoy da passin'."

"What was that?" he groaned.

She placed a damp rag across his eyes and forehead. "Shhhh."

Off in the distance, he heard a crow cawing mixed in with the soft shuffling of the old woman as she moved about. The wind whistled around the cabin then slowly subsided. He thought about pulling the rag from his face, but its warmth became a source of comfort. He relaxed as sounds—and the pain—faded away. He drifted off to sleep.

An hour later, a tug at his arm drew him back. The crow returned. The sounds of the wind grew louder.

"Wake up. Ya don't wanna miss him now, do ya?"

He squinted. The room was hazier and blurrier than before. He rubbed his eyes. Things came into focus, but the increased amount of burning incense kept the room in a cloud. He felt different—he felt better. The pain had gone away completely. The only difference was his arms and legs felt like cannon barrels. Maybe he had been dreaming. He looked down. The makeshift sutures weaving in and out of his stomach indicated otherwise.

"Why, I do feel better but I can't move—what've you done to me?" He gritted his teeth and tried lunging his body upward but couldn't.

"What did Juana tell ya? Ya gots ta stay put."

"But I feel better. Seriously, if I could stand up, I can get back to the camp—I swear!"

"No, child. Ya only feels da way ya duz cuz Juana got the pain hid. He's still comin'."

"Who's coming? A doctor?"

"No, child. Ain't no doctor."

"Who's coming then?" he pleaded, hoping for an answer that would result in him getting back to his company.

"Death's uh comin'," she said, sprinkling purple-colored dust over his head, causing him to cough.

"*Death?*"

"Dat's right." She sprinkled more dust. "Ya feels better, but ya be dyin' inside." She paused. "Ya dyin' inside in more dan one wayz. Ya been dyin' long afore ya wuz shot."

"How bad am I?"

She pulled a small mirror off the wall and held it in front of him.

The reflection staring back at him was that of a ghost. His skin was a dull grey. The only color he had was the pinkish rims around his eyes. His hair had become brittle and ashen. He closed his eyes. "I'm bleeding to death, aren't I?"

"Yuz gut shot. Gut shot's da wurst t'ing. Takes a loooong time for him da come."

"You can't stop the bleeding?"

She quickly turned her head side to side. "No, only t'ing Juana can stop is da pain. Just a matta uh time."

"Can you help me sit up?"

"Shore t'ing," she said, reaching under his arms. "Ya gots to help Juana now." Together they managed to skootch him upright.

"Thank you," he said softly.

"Don't ya worry now. Just uh matta uh time."

Mase looked around, wondering how it had all come to this. His life's journey had taken him from the loving embrace of Willow Creek to the battlefields of the South and now... to a slow death inside a remote cabin where he would leave the world as another unknown soldier, the victim of man's inhumanity.

He turned to Juana. "I'm sorry, I never told you my name. I'm Mase Winslow."

She rolled her head to the side as if examining him. "Juana, wants ya ta do uh favor. Will ya tro da bonez?"

His eyes fluttered as his body began shutting down. "I-I don't know what you mean."

She reached over and picked up the small pile of bones from the table and placed them in his hand. "Just tro 'em on da floor."

He gave a shallow nod then slowly drew them to his chest.

"Dat's it. Now jus tro 'em."

He swung his hand downward, releasing them out across the floor.

She dropped to her hands and knees and inspected each bone at eye level. After a couple minutes, she stood staring at him in the same way Maudie had done at the creek the day she gave him the memory stone. He could feel the same gaze passing through him and out into some far-off place.

"I was right," she said, "Youz dyin' inside in bunch uh ways."

He began to wheeze. "What do you mean?"

"Ya gots to let go of dat past. Darz only one way ta meet him and dat's with da past in da past."

He sighed as he resigned himself to the inevitable death that was moments away. "Can you get my diary, please?"

"Diary?"

"I think it's in my right pocket."

She dove her hand inside, then pulled it back out, empty.

"Try the other."

She reached into his left pocket. "Juana's sorry. Deez some big pockets but ain't noth'n in—wait—I t'ink I feelz someteen." She reached farther down, her arm disappearing to the elbow. "Ya gots a hole in dis side. I can feelz it in da bottom of…" With one quick yank, out it came. "Dis it?" she said holding it out to him.

"Yes, thank you."

"Whatz ya wantz me ta do wid it now?"

"Can you write something in it for me?"

"Sorry, Juana cain't write."

His eyes grew heavy. His skin turned from grey to white as the last of his blood oozed from his body. "Then, can you get the stone?"

"Da stone?"

"It—it's… in the back." He began coughing.

"Go on close dem eyes. Soon ya be—"

"Please, it's—in—the—back."

She laid the diary on his chest, opened it to the middle, then flipped to the back when suddenly her finger punched through a page into something hard on the other side. "Wass dis here?" she said as she turned the sheet of paper.

He tried muttering a reply, but his voice was gone.

Tilting her head in wonder, she rubbed her finger over the stone's smooth surface. Her eyes grew big as she frantically tried prying it out with her fingernails. With the diary in her grasp, she dropped to the floor and grabbed one of the bones. She jabbed it in between the stone and the pages and, with a quick twist, popped it out onto the floor.

For a second, she hesitated to touch it, looking at him then back to the stone. With both hands she scooped it up and held it out in front of her. Her body went stiff, and her eyes flashed wide as the power surged through her. She gasped as she let it fall to the floor. She stood motionless, looking at it, her eyes tightening around the edges.

"Ohhh, child!" she said, holding her hand over her heart. "Ya knowz what ya gots here?" She glanced at him. "Ya gots da memory stone! Ya hear what I say?" She stood and danced in a circle. "Ya gots da *memory stone!*" She looked at his chest—but there was no movement.

Grabbing the tiny mirror she had held in front of him earlier, she put it under his nose. A few seconds later, a faint mist appeared upon its surface. She tossed it to the side then shoved his diary back into his left coat pocket, through the hole and into the lining from where she had retrieved it. "Yuz gonna need dat for da trip," she said, patting him on the head.

In one quick motion she slapped the stone into his palm, folded his fingers around it, then pulled a small leather strap from the wall and wrapped it around his hand, keeping his fingers tight around the stone.

"Juana gonna help ya keep da past in da past. Time ta be risin' new." Closing her eyes, she began to rock back and forth, chanting, "River and time, water and wine, blessed be da fruits uh mine. Gone da past, tru da age, seek da soul where yuz iz cast…"

The only other sounds Mase could hear were his heartbeat fading away and the faint cawing of the crow as he flew off to another place in the wilderness—to a place he had never been before.

Chapter 14

The soft, rhythmic droning of geese high above gently broke the silence, their calling to one another growing louder. Their melodic honking suddenly gave way to the blaring sounds of angry horns from self-propelled vehicles blaring through crowded streets.

Mase gasped for air as if ascending from some dark, watery abyss, and he sat up from the hardpan of dirt and gravel. His hair was matted, and his clothes were as filthy as the dingy man lying on the bench next to him, snoring. The only difference between them was the cheap polyester blanket the man had wrapped around him and a cardboard sign hanging from his neck that read *Homeless. Any help appreciated.*

"Watch out!"

He turned just in time to jump out of the way of a man running at him along a hard, black path.

"Excuse me!" yelled a girl flying across the same path on some type of two-wheeled vehicle.

Suddenly there were people with strange-looking haircuts, wearing strange clothes, coming at him from both directions. Most of them were not talking to one another but staring down at little black boxes in their hands. Many appeared to be talking to themselves. The air was full of sound—horrible, irritating noises he had never heard before. He clasped his hands over his ears.

"Get out of the way, ya bum!" a man yelled seconds before pushing him to the ground.

Mase looked up to see him zigzagging his way through the endless stream of people as if he was on ice skates.

Mase grabbed the edge of the snoring man's blanket. "Mister—mister, wake up."

The man wiped his face with a dirty hand. His eyes bulged with huge red veins occupying where white had once been.

"Where am I?" Mase asked him.

"Go away," the man growled.

"Mister, please! Where am I?" he said, continuing to tug on the blanket.

"I said, go away." The man yanked the blanket out of his hand and rolled back asleep.

Mase backed away from the black path and stumbled toward an opening in a stone wall. Beyond it, hundreds of people were rushing by, all in a hurry to get somewhere. As he walked through it, he was instantly caught up in an onslaught of men, women, and children, all pushing and shoving their way alongside a road that was black and hard like the path he had fled. People on bicycles that weren't being pedaled zoomed through the streets. Vehicles of all shapes and colors, mostly yellow, stopped and started. They were frightening beasts that blew foul-smelling smoke from their tails. People jumped in and out of the yellow ones. Like cattle, he was forced to continue moving for fear of being trampled.

As he was about to be swept out into the street, he reached out and grabbed a pole. Clinging to it, he caught his reflection in one of the vehicles that had stopped in front of him. The cross-shaped scar on his cheek confirmed his identity. While the raging mass of humanity rushed past, he stood, his heart pounding as he tried to comprehend the bizarre nature of his situation.

A young couple stopped in front of him and pulled out a map. "It's even more magnificent than I imagined," the girl cooed.

He turned and followed her gaze to the hundred-story building. For a moment, all the noise and chaos came to a standstill as he stood slack-jawed, looking up at the mountainous structure before him. In every direction, granite and concrete buildings reached into the clouds.

Something tapped his leg, causing the madness to begin whirling back around him.

"For you, sir."

He looked down at a little boy who couldn't have been more than five or six. His tiny hand stretched out to him, holding a folded piece of paper.

"You-you can b-buy some food," he said. A friendly-looking lady standing a few feet behind the boy edged him on with a smile.

Puzzled by the gesture but feeling obligated by the giver's youth and sincerity, he thanked him and took the paper. The boy turned and scampered off into the lady's arms.

Still confused by the transaction, he unfolded the paper and saw that it was a five-dollar piece of currency. Why would a boy, especially so young, give a stranger so much money? Five dollars could buy food for a week. The picture on it confused him even more. The five-dollar bill he was accustomed to seeing had Alexander Hamilton's face on it, *not* Abraham Lincoln's. Of all people, *he* most certainly did not deserve the honor currency like this bestowed.

What was this place? Where had his world gone? Was he *dead*? As he stood on the corner with his senses being bombarded from every angle, he realized the most obvious of clues—where was his pain? Had Juana's medicine been that powerful, or was he indeed—?

He frantically pulled back the edges of his tattered jacket and looked down on his bloody shirt. Pitching his hand under it, he felt for the wound that had most assuredly ended his life and sent him into this purgatory. But there was no wound—no rough, makeshift stitches—only smooth, warm skin. He ripped open his shirt, revealing what his touch had found—nothing. All his transgressions and guilt came flooding back. Whatever hell this was or whatever witchery the old lady had placed upon him, he knew he had deserved it.

His head spun as the spectacle of this unfamiliar place swirled about him. Suddenly his head grew light, and his balance became unstable, causing his legs to give way. Losing his grip on the pole, he staggered out into the street.

The last thing he remembered before being struck by the cab was seeing the little boy pointing at him over the lady's shoulder.

Seven hours later, Mase woke to another kind of pain. Instead of waking to animal bones, wooden masks, and potions in a hazy, run-down cabin, he was wrapped in clean cotton sheets in a sterile bedroom surrounded by heart monitors, blood-pressure gauges, and a slew of other devices designed to take the place of throwing *da bones.*

The murmuring of people in the room almost lulled him back to sleep, but the pain in his leg kept him awake. "Where am I?" he squeezed out in a labored breath.

"He's coming to," said a young lady dressed in a blue one-piece outfit.

A stumpy man dressed the same way hovered over him with a clipboard. "Welcome back, Mr.—umm…"

"He's a John Doe—probably homeless," the lady whispered.

"Welcome back, young fella," the man said, putting a stethoscope to Mase's chest. "How do you feel?"

"Confused," he slurred, stroking the bandage wrapped around the top of his head.

"And your leg—how's the pain on a one to ten?"

"I'm not sure what you mean."

"If there's no pain say it's a one. If it's unbearable say it's a ten.

Mase looked down. His right leg was in a cast from his knee to ankle. "Can I say seven?" he grunted.

A slender, clean-shaven, middle-aged black man wearing a white jacket over a dress shirt and tie walked in. "So how's our patient?"

"Vitals look good," said the man in the blue outfit. "Pain level is a seven, the head contusion has stopped swelling, and his cast has set nicely. He also just woke up. Said he was confused."

Using a metal device with a light shining out one end, the black man pulled up Mase's left eyelid and shined it into his pupil.

"I'm not surprised you're confused, young fella," he

said, repeating the process with his other eye. "You took a pretty good hit out there today. Can you follow this light for me?" Mase's eyes tracked the light as the man moved it back and forth. "Good," he said, flicking the light off and reaching out his hand. "My name's Dr. Nichols."

"You're a doctor?"

"Sure am," he said.

Mase shook his hand. "But—you're—"

"I'm what?" the doctor asked.

"Oh—oh, nothing," he said.

The doctor tilted his head. "Do you remember the cab hitting you?"

"No." He flinched from a surge of pain in his leg.

"Your leg?"

He nodded, pursing his lips.

The lady leaned over and tucked a pillow under his knee.

"Let's give him 25 milligrams of morphine." The doctor turned to Mase. "What we've got is a broken tibia just below your knee. You'll be in the cast for about eight weeks. Luckily, the cab wasn't going that fast, any higher on the leg or pelvis, and things could've been dramatically different. What concerns me more is your head," he said while unwrapping the bandage. "You've got a large contusion on your left side from where you hit the ground. You were unconscious when they brought you in. We took a CAT scan and everything—"

"Wait, wait, wait," Mase said, throwing up his hands. "What are you talking about—CAT scan—contusion—I'm not following—"

"Oh, I'm sorry. I'm going too fast. Simply put, you have a big bruise on the side of your head, and we want to make sure there's no damage to your brain, which leads me to some questions I need to ask. Are you okay to answer a few for me?"

"Sure," Mase groaned.

"Great. First, can you tell me your full name?"

"Masen James Winslow."

"Where do you live?"

"Currently?"

"Yes, please."

"Currently, I'm in the ACSA in the 8th Brigade under Brigadier General McCain."

"Oh, you're in the military. My brother is too. Did you say ACSA?"

"Yes, sir."

"What's that stand for?"

"Army of the Confederate States of America. I've been in for around four months."

The doctor glanced over at the others in the room, both of whom stared at Mase with raised eyebrows.

"Mr. Winslow," the doctor proceeded with concern, "do you have any relatives we can contact?"

"My father, Braxton Winslow. He lives on the Willow Creek Plantation in Beaufort, South Carolina."

"Is there a way we can contact him? Does he have a cell number?"

"I have no idea what you mean by *cell number,* but you can contact him by mail or telegraph."

The doctor cleared his throat. "We noted all the blood on your shirt and some on your coat as well. There was a lot of it, but you didn't have any wounds in that area. Can you explain how it got there and whose it is?"

"I was shot. No, I mean, I-I... don't remember."

Dr. Nichols stood. "Can you excuse me a second?" he asked Mase, motioning with his eyes for the man and woman to follow him out of the room.

"We obviously have a psych patient here, or there's been a brain injury the CAT scan didn't detect. Roger, will you order a brain MRI and find out who the psychiatrist is on duty and have them schedule an exam later today? Danielle, would you contact the police and have them check their missing persons and have them send a homicide detective as well?"

The doctor returned to find Mase fidgeting with a blood-pressure cuff.

"Ever seen one of those, Mr. Winslow?"

"I've never seen anything like it." He looked around. "I've never seen anything like any of this." His voice softened. "Doctor, this is going to sound crazy, but I have to ask—*where* am I?"

"You're in Mount Sinai Hospital in New York City."

Mase looked out the window. "I've never seen buildings like what's out there or heard the horrible sounds like I have… and the people—everybody's so different. And there's sooo many of them. Putting his hands over his face and hanging his head, he muttered into his palms, "I'm losing my mind."

The doctor looked at his tormented patient, then stuck his head out the door and caught the attention of the lady in blue. "Pssst—Danielle," he whispered, "can you call security and have them on hand—just in case?"

Over the next several hours, Mase underwent a barrage of tests, including the MRI and a two-hour session with Dr. Dannenberg, the on-staff psychiatrist.

"I'm not sure what to make of this," the psychiatrist told Dr. Nichols. "He appears sane in terms of relative competency—in fact, he's rather intelligent. However, his perception of reality is off the charts. He thinks he's a corporal in the Confederate army. He's an expert in life during the Civil War era, or at least halfway through it. But from that point to today, he doesn't have any understanding of the world. He doesn't know what a phone is, what cars are, how buildings can be so tall, why Lincoln is on a five-dollar bill—nothing. On another note, I also saw definite signs of post-traumatic stress disorder."

"What's your recommendation?"

"Obviously, we need more sessions. The one thing that would help more than anything is talking to family members."

"I'm afraid that's out. We found out he doesn't exist."

"Doesn't exist?"

"I'm sorry, what I meant was the name he gave us is bogus," said Dr. Nichols. "There're no records of a Masen James Winslow or Braxton Winslow in the Beaufort, South Carolina, area."

"Well, that kind of fits with delusional characteristics. What about the blood on his shirt the report mentioned?"

"We ran a DNA test. It turns out it's his. What we can't figure out is why there was so much of it."

"And the MRI?"

"Checked out fine."

"Hmmm, well, the blow he took to the head could still be a contributing factor," said the psychiatrist.

"Why's that?"

"He said he's starting to forget things from the past. In fact, during the first five minutes, he told me he had a sister, but when I asked him about her later, he didn't remember having one. He also had a hard time remembering the name of the plantation where he said he lived."

"Amnesia?"

Dr. Dannenberg stroked his chin. "It's certainly a possibility. Only time will tell. By the way, don't pressure him for any more details. Stressing him could have negative results." He handed Dr. Nichols a sheet of paper. "Here're my notes for his records. I'll follow up tomorrow morning. You do plan on keeping him overnight, don't you?"

"Oh yeah, he'll be here for a couple days at a minimum. We're not even sure how to begin to discharge him."

As the doctor left to finish his rounds, he overheard one of the orderlies asking for a notepad for the John Doe in room 306.

"Excuse me, the John Doe you mentioned—can you tell me why he requested the notepad?"

"I'm not sure. He just said he enjoys writing."

He tilted his head. "Here, I'll take that for you." A few minutes later, he was tapping on the door to room 306. "Mase, it's Dr. Nichols."

"Come on in."

"How are you feeling?"

"Better. The morphine seems to help."

"Pain?"

"About a six."

"Well, that's better than a seven. I have something for you." He handed him the notebook.

"Oh, thank you."

"You write?"

"I love to write. I've been writing since I was a boy. A friend of mine gave me a diary when I was little because I loved it so much."

"What was his name?"

"Jeziah, but we called him…" He put his hand to his temple, and his face scrunched up. "Umm, his nickname was—dang it—I can't think of it now."

"That's okay," Dr. Nichols said on his way out. "By the way, there should be pens in the drawer unless you'd rather use a pencil."

"A pen's fine. I usually dictate on my phone when I'm without either, but I guess I lost it in the accident."

"Wait, you had—" The doctor stopped short of finishing his question, remembering the instructions to keep Mase's stress low. "Never mind, I'll check in on you tomorrow."

The next day, on his way to see Mase, the doctor shared the elevator with a young female nurse.

"Have you heard about our gallant Confederate corporal?" she said.

"John Doe in room 306?" he replied.

"Yeah, the cute Mr. 306 with the rugged beard," she giggled. "He's on his way back."

"He's what?"

Just then, the elevator door opened. "Sorry, gotta run." As it started to shut, she yelled back, "Tell Paul, Nurse Becca said hi."

What did she mean by *Paul*, and *who* was on their way back? Whatever it was, one thing was for sure, someone had made an impact on the young girl.

As the doctor approached the cracked door of room 306, he could see his patient scribbling away in his notebook.

"Good day, Mase," he said as he entered. The greeting had no impact. Mase continued scribbling. "How're you feeling today, Mr. Winslow?"

"Are you talking to me?" he said, looking up from his writing.

"Uh, yes, I was, but I guess you've got something more interesting happening on those pages."

"Kinda." He continued writing. "I'm trying to get this dream written out before I forget it."

"Can we talk a minute?"

"Sure." Mase put the pen into the notebook and closed it. "I'm sorry, Dr. Nichols, but it's fading, and I have to record what I can before I forget."

"No problem. So I talked to some of my colleagues, and they believe the young Mr. Winslow is doing well and you—"

"I'm sorry, who did you say?"

Dr. Nichols looked at him quizzically. "You—Masen Winslow."

"My name's not Masen Winslow. It's Paul Talbert."

He blinked. "Oh… Ohhh, I'm sorry, Paul. I was thinking about the patient in 308. Go on back to your writing. I-I actually need to check on him first. I'll be right back."

Nichols hurried out the door and trotted over to the nurses' station. "Is Danielle here today?"

"I'm here," she said, coming up behind him.

"Can you tell me what's going on with John Doe in 306? He said his name is Paul Talbert, *and* earlier he mentioned having a cell phone. Is his memory coming back?"

"It's amazing," she said. "He's been blabbering on about his job here in the city, his lost cell phone, this weird dream he had—"

"Hmmm, it could also be schizophrenia."

"I don't believe so."

"Why?" Nichols asked.

"I went ahead and did the research. There *is* a Paul Talbert who lives in the city."

"That's a pretty common name in a city as big as New York."

She turned to a laptop on the counter and began typing. "That's true." She swiveled the screen to him. "But how many Paul Talberts are an editor for the *NYC Chronicle* and look like this?"

"Well I'll be," he said, staring at the editorial staff page of the *NYC Chronicle* website. Second to the left, bottom row was none other than his patient in room 306.

"What would you like me to do?" she asked.

"Contact Dr. Dannenberg and give him an update. I'll wait to do my checkup until after he meets with him this morning. In the meantime, check his pain level and administer morphine as needed."

Shortly after lunch, Dr. Nichols was about to complete his rounds, saving his most interesting patient for last. As he entered room 306, he found him once again engrossed in his notebook. "Good afternoon, Mr. *Talbert.*"

"Hello, Doc," he said as he put the final strokes on a sentence before laying his notebook to the side. "I'm sorry, I had to get that last line in before I tapped out."

"What do you mean *tapped out*?"

"My dream. The sentence I just wrote is the last thing I can remember."

"Oh, I see. Well, maybe you can write about it for the *NYC Chronicle.*"

"Yeah, maybe."

"I've talked to Dr. Dannenberg, and it looks like you've had an incredible recovery. Evidently, you had some form of amnesia."

"It was like walking out of a fog bank into a clear, blue summer day. I've never experienced anything like it. I had to get as much of it on paper as possible."

"Well, we're glad you're better. We do want to keep you in for another night though. We always want to play it safe with head injuries. In the meantime, we need to get some information to discharge you. Danielle will be in shortly to get the process started." He slapped him on the back. "Glad to have you back, Mr. Talbert."

As he approached the nurses' station, Danielle was still working on the computer.

"Can you have Mr. Talbert processed for discharging tomorrow? Oh, and can you also make sure the outpatient social worker assigned to him knows about his post-traumatic stress disorder?"

"Absolutely—but I thought he was fine," she said.

"He is, in regard to his memory, but there may be something else going on with him that's deeper, something that'll need addressing at some point." He looked down the hall. "The last thing we want to see is the Confederate corporal marching through those doors again."

Chapter 15

By noon the next day, Paul Talbert was officially ready to go home, to the only home he now remembered. His past, as Juana had said it should be, was in *da past*.

While patiently waiting in his medical gown for the discharge nurse to officially release him, he folded his jacket and laid it next to the crutches that would be his support system for the coming months. He stared at his grey jacket, his only remaining article of clothing, and had a hard time imagining why he would have ever purchased such a drab, weathered garment.

The door cracked open, and a nurse stuck her head inside. "I have a friend to see you. Can I—"

"Hey, hey!" chirped a bouncy young lady rolling her way into his room in a wheelchair. With choppy black hair featuring a pink stripe dyed down the side and dozens of colorful tattoos running up and down her arms and shoulders, she was all Goth gal on the outside. On the inside, she was pure flower child. The daisy sticking out from behind her ear was the tip of the complex iceberg that was Zoey Antonelli.

"Ohhh, I'm sorry," she said, grabbing the nurse by the

hand. "I didn't mean to barge in like that. It's just that I haven't seen—holy cannoli!" she said, spinning toward Paul. "What truck with a kitchen sink landed on you?" She jumped out of the chair and grabbed his cheeks. "Wow—coool scar!" She threw her arms around him. "Pauly, you look like you got hit by a cab." She took a step back for dramatic effect. "Oh wait, you did!" She giggled as she wrapped him into an extended hug.

Her vivacious whirlwind of happiness was why he had requested the hospital call her to pick him up—that plus she was his only friend and the one person he could depend on. She had always been there for him ever since he hired her as his fact-checker at the *Chronicle* when no one else wanted to. She was the misfit yin to his troubled yang.

"Funny as a crutch, Zo. Speaking of which, can you hand me those over there?"

"Oh no, Mr. Talbert, this is your ride out of here," the nurse said, pointing to the wheelchair.

"Can I push him out? Can I, can I, can I?" Zoey asked, jumping around.

"Sure, I'll be right outside when you're ready."

"Here," Zoey said, throwing him a brown bag. "Put these on, and let's blow this popsicle stand before I get sick and have to be admitted." She twirled away from him. "This is for you." She pulled her daisy from her hair and tossed it over her shoulder like a bouquet.

"Why, thanks," he said, placing it behind his ear.

"Now that's a funky look," she said, eyeing his jacket." Where'd you get it?"

"What—the jacket?"

"Yeah, I'm diggin' it. It's so retro."

"Well then, consider it yours."

"Really? Are you sure?"

"Absolutely. Beware though, the thing weighs a ton."

She threw it over her head and spun around, blindly holding her hands out in front of her. "Thank you. I'm never taking it off."

"You might wanna wash it first."

"Point taken," she said, feigning a cough.

"All right, I'm ready."

She peeked out from under her newly acquired garment to find him sitting in the chair fully dressed. "Well, what're we waiting for?"

After finishing the discharge process, Dr. Dannenberg came by to say farewell while Zoey brought the car around. "I still can't believe how well you've done."

"Thanks, Doc. I do appreciate everything."

"Remember, a social worker will be coming by in the next couple days."

"Do I have to?"

"Sorry, it's policy, plus she can help you with those other issues we discussed."

"I guess," he said as Zoey pulled up in her yellow Volkswagen Beetle, complete with peace-symbol stickers and painted eyelashes over the headlights.

After helping him into the car, the doctor bent over and handed him a business card. "If you need me, call." He stepped onto the curb. "And remember—social worker—two days."

"I will, I will." He closed the door and waved goodbye, then turned to Zoey. "Get me out here and to the nearest bar—fast."

She didn't respond, remembering how emphatic Dr. Nichols had been about his staying sober.

"So?" he said.

"So—what?"

"Can we get that drink?"

"I'm sorry, Pauly. I've gotta run back to the office and help Greg fact-check his *Forbes 500* article. How about I do a run-through at Smoothie Town and get us two veggie-carrot-kale supremes?"

"Ughh. The air in my mouth tastes better. I'll just hop over to the Molly Mart and grab a six-pack."

"Paul, no! You heard the doctor say you shouldn't be drinking while you're on these meds, plus you're liable to—"

"What? Spiral out of control and blow my brains out. Did he say that—did he?"

Her bottom lip stuck out, her sunny disposition turning cold and distant. "I still can't get the other time out of my mind. And when you didn't call in last week and no one could get a hold of you... I-I thought you might have done something."

"Dang it. I'm such a jerk. I'm sorry, Zo," he said softly. "I'm just tired. I wouldn't do that—blow my brains out, that is. I might drink myself to death but—"

"Seriously, Paul."

"Just kidding, for goodness' sake. I promise not to drink either. Just drop me off at the apartment. I'll be okay."

"Yay!" she said, bouncing in her seat as they arrived in front of a worn-out brownstone sandwiched between a filthy pawnshop and out-of-date laundromat. "I'll be back this evening and make you ramen noodles."

"Oh joy, that'll kick my taste buds back into action after all that hospital food."

"Beggars can't be—"

"Ah, don't you dare cliché me, *Miss Soon-to-Be Copy Editor*," he said. "Oh—before you go, how about work? Have they missed me, or am I in trouble for leaving somebody in the lurch?"

"Don't worry. I called Greg and told him about the accident and that you'd be out another week. He said it's cool. But you'll need the cast and crutches to convince him you weren't faking it. You know him."

"Unfortunately, I do."

That evening she showed up on his stoop with a bag of Chinese takeout instead of her promised ramen noodles. "Thanks, Zo. I love anything takeout from Chang's Garden."

"You shouldn't have," she said, walking inside the studio apartment.

"What do you mean?"

"Cleaning up for me. You know I'm a guest, don't you?" Piles of clothes lay randomly on the floor, mingled with old bubble-gum wrappers, balls of paper, and discarded popcorn bags. A half-eaten slice of cheesecake sat on the kitchen counter along with more empty popcorn bags and a sorry-looking ukulele next to a strung-out spool of dental floss.

"I bet if you'd let me clean this place, you could actually get a girl to stick around, maybe even snag a wife."

"Marriage? Bah—the concept's archaic."

"Sounds more like sour grapes to me," she said, flicking

his hair with her finger.

He swatted her hand away as if it were a pesky gnat.

She pulled up a small stool from his kitchen and sat directly in front of him, her eyes roving over his face.

"What're you looking at?" he said, rearing his head back.

"I bet if we did something with this," she said, pointing at him with her chopsticks, "you might have a chance."

"Did something with what?"

"This—this look of yours," she said, using the chopsticks again to draw an imaginary circle around his face. "This whole literary Sasquatch thing."

"You don't like what I got going on?"

She puckered her lips and squinted. "The new cheek scar's kinda cute, but the beard that grew out so fast and the rest…" she said, shaking her head, "well, let's put it this way, unless you're looking for a lady plumber from Anchorage, it might be time for a change."

"Hmmm, and all this time, I was sure you thought I was hot."

As they dove into their chicken chow mein, Zoey broached a subject that always made him uneasy—his job. Although his writing was flawless, he'd been fired from his past two positions for missing deadlines, and the rumor was he might be laid off again for the same reason.

She was the only one who had any clue the problem revolved around his family—or rather the lack of a family. Paul was orphaned at the age of three after his father committed suicide and his mother mysteriously disappeared. When no relatives stepped up to take him in, he became a ward of the state, rotating in and out of orphanages and foster homes until he came of legal age. As a coping mechanism against the demons of a crappy childhood, he would often escape through alcohol or sleep, both of which usually resulted in missed deadlines.

"Pauly, who's your biggest fan?"

"You are," he said, fiddling with his chopsticks.

"And who's always got your back and tells you the truth?"

"Hmmm. I guess that'd be… you."

"Then don't freak out when I tell you this, but I think you need to make sure you get that article on governmental budget cuts completed by the deadline."

"I got ran over by a car! How do they expect me to finish a piece like that in four days?"

"I don't know, but when I was in the office today, I overheard Greg telling Maryanne Montgomery he was expecting you to finish. His comment was you had broken your leg, not your fingers."

"Oh, for the love of… These guys have no compassion. I bust my friggin' tail month in and month out, writing on all these boring subjects, and they have the—it's mind-numbing."

"I understand," she said, biting her fingernails. "I'm saying this because… well, you've kinda missed some deadlines in the past, you know."

"Yeah, but this is different."

"I know, I know, but they don't see it that way. Pauly—you've *got* to deliver."

After several more attempts to persuade him his job was in jeopardy, she left with a hug, along with a recommendation for him to go on to bed so he could wake up early and work on the article.

As soon as the door shut behind her, he reached into a

kitchen cabinet and pulled out a full bottle of rum. He took a long, hard gulp, followed by another, then another.

The next morning at ten o'clock, his doorbell rang. After several attempts to sit up, he managed to swing his cast off the pullout couch and hobble the few feet across the room. "Can I help you?" he said through the door.

"If this is the home of Paul Talbert, you sure can," an attractive brunette said, smiling into the peephole.

"Hold on." He reached over, pulled a bathrobe off a hook on the wall, then cracked the door open and squinted, filtering out the harsh morning sun. "Who'd you say you were?"

"I didn't. I'm Maria Gisela Mercado," she said, flashing him a sunny grin. She tapped the face of her watch. "We had a ten o'clock appointment."

"Ohhh, right—the social worker," he said, still trying to shake the cobwebs from the night before. He pulled the door open, then walked over and plopped onto his fold-out couch. "Come on in," he said, waving her toward the only other chair in the cramped apartment. "Have a seat."

She surveyed the room. "Hmmm, nice place."

He grabbed a half-empty box of Tums and tossed two into his mouth. "Really? I don't hear that from too many people."

"You should see some of the things I've seen. Trust me, you're living in style, Mr. Talbert. Mind if I call you 'Paul'?"

"Sure," he said, holding out the box of Tums to her. "No, thank you."

"I detect an accent," he said.

"I'm Puerto Rican."

"Ah, that explains all the names."

"There's only three," she said with a grin.

"Must be all the syllables. Just sounds long." He grabbed a bag of stale popcorn and began eating from it. "Like some?"

"Uh, no, thank you. So, Mr. Talbert—I mean Paul. I want to assure you my visit's one of good intent. Our social department and the hospital want to make sure your transition back into the community is a healthy one."

"Peanuts?" he said.

"No, I'm fine. As I was saying, the purpose of my—"

He reached over, grabbed the bottle of rum from the night before, and took a long swig. "Oh snap," he giggled. "Guess it's not a good call to drink in front of the social worker."

Her lips skewed with a raised eyebrow. "Yeah, you're probably right."

"You know it's from Puerto Rico—the rum, that is. Yep, all good things come from Puerto Rico." He slapped his palm onto the coffee table. "Alrighty then, let's get on with it."

"Wellll, maybe we need to reschedule. I believe last night might still be hanging around some. What if we shoot for—"

He held up his hand. "Hold on a minute." A moment passed as he collected his thoughts. "I'm sorry. I'm-I'm a little stressed out and last night—"

"No need to explain, I understand. But it might still be better if I did come back."

"No, please. You've come all the way here, and to be honest, it'd be great to get this out of the way."

"I'm sure it would, but I don't—"

"Please, I-I just tend to get this way when—as I said—when I get stressed out. I promise I'm good."

She hesitated. "Are you sure?"

"Yeah, yeah, I'm sure."

"Well, okay. Let's start again…"

For the next hour, she listened as he told her many of the same things he had already discussed with Dr. Dannenberg, including how he turned to the bottle when his anxiety grew too heavy. As the effects of the previous night's alcohol wore off, they were replaced with a self-loathing and observable fear of some unknown trauma.

"I don't know what it is, Ms. Mercado, but for some reason, there's something else—something I can't explain. I don't remember anything about the accident, but since my memory returned, I've felt more like I wanted to…" He looked away.

"Do you want to harm yourself?"

He dipped his head, wiping away a tear before it had a chance to appear. "I-I don't know how to put it into words. I don't know where it's coming from, and I don't know what's causing it." He hung his head as tears fell into his palms. "I just *hate* myself—now more than ever."

She put her hand on his shoulder. "Will you do something for me?"

He wiped his face with the back of his hands. "Sure."

She handed him a card. "I'd like for you to go see this gentleman. His name is Peter Atwell."

"Is he a shrink?"

"He's a psychiatrist, a very good one who specializes in cases like yours." She paused, gauging his acceptance of her suggestion. "It's going to be alright, Paul. I promise."

He stared at the card for a moment. "You really think he can help?"

"I do. *Please* call him, okay?"

"Alright."

"In the meantime, there're things you can do to help. You're a writer, aren't you?"

"Yeah."

"Then you understand how therapeutic it can be."

He managed a chuckle. "Not when you have to write about the beige things I have to."

"I don't mean work-related stuff. Focus on something you enjoy, something you're passionate about." She slapped him on the shoulder. "Come on, this is Writing 101."

"Yeah, you're right." He looked around the room then paused his gaze beside his couch. "Hmm, maybe this could help." He squatted and began rummaging through a stack of papers. A moment later he pulled out the notebook he'd been using while in the hospital. "Yeah, maybe I'll use this."

"Great, anything you're passionate about will work. Paul, I'm sorry but I have another appointment across town, but I'm not going to leave until you promise you're going to call Dr. Atwell."

"I promise."

"Tomorrow—okay?"

"Yes, yes. I promise," he said.

After she left, he sat, contemplating his next move. A notebook to his left. His budgetary article to his right. An almost empty bottle of rum in the middle. Decisions, decisions. The critical path to success suddenly crystallized into three easy steps. First, replenish the booze, second, start writing his novel, and coming in a distant third, finish off the budget article.

For the rest of the afternoon, he executed steps one and two to perfection. He was well into his first chapter and halfway into a new bottle of rum. By nightfall, he had completed the chapter and polished off the rum. Maybe he didn't need the help of a shrink after all. Maria's recommendations were holding the demons at bay. A Hemingway kind of life (minus his demise) could be the course best suited for him.

The next morning, he woke to a splitting headache and the realization that he'd never touched step three. The solution? Rinse and repeat the previous day, but work on the budget article instead of his book.

After an hour of writing, only two paragraphs had emerged. His rum intake, however, was right on pace with the day before. Frustrated at his production level, he turned back to his novel and churned out his prose.

On the third day, he woke even later than the previous day. The first thing he saw upon opening his eyes was a meager half page of a proposed three-page budget article. The anxiety he had managed to stave off for the past two days gnawed at him, and his frustrations with himself crept back. No ifs, ands, or buts, he had to complete the article by the end of the day.

After lunch, Zoey stopped by. "Hey, hey," she said, knocking on the door.

"It's open," he yelled without looking up.

She bounded in with her signature zest and a commitment to make sure he was on track to finish the *Chronicle* article. "Is that what I think it is?" she said, pointing to a small stack of papers on the kitchen table.

"Hi, Zo," he said, continuing to type.

She took the pages and started to read. "Hey, this isn't bad." After fifteen minutes, she laid them back on the table. "I'm not sure when you had time to write this, but—wow! Seriously, those are some of the most interesting first two chapters I've read in a long time. Is there more? Gimme, gimme, gimme—Zoey wants more," she said, mimicking a two-year-old begging for ice cream.

He stopped to take a swig of rum. "I'm flattered, but you're a tad bit over-the-top."

"I know, but seriously, it's terrific. Where'd you get the idea?"

He went back to typing. "Got it while in the hospital. Morphine makes for an intoxicating muse."

"Well, keep it going. Hold off on the morphine but keep the writing going." She crossed her fingers as she turned her attention to her main objective. "So did you finish the budget article?"

"Mmmm, not quite." He pointed to a bunch of crumpled pieces of papers on the coffee table.

"Where?"

"Underneath."

"Oh, for a minute, I thought you hadn't—" She pulled out a single rum-stained page. "Is *this* it?" She held the paper between two fingers as if it were contaminated. "Oh, Paul, please tell me there's more."

"Nope."

"Pauly, come on now! Greg's going to kill you. No,

he'll fire you, then kill you."

He turned and lifted his glass of rum. "Calm yourself, m'lady. It's all in here," he said, tapping his glass against his forehead.

"What?"

"I'm in a zone. My mind is like a fountain of creativity. Ideas are flowing like water—pure, wonderful, life-sustaining water."

"The only thing flowing is cheap liquor!" She snatched his glass. "After you finish the article, then you can go back to your book idea, but for your job's sake, you *have to finish* the budget piece first. It's due tomorrow morning."

"You don't understand," he said, patting her on the cheek. "I've gotta write what I'm passionate about or they'll come for me. They came for Hemingway too, you know."

"What're you talking about?"

"The passion police. There's no passion in a budget article."

"No, there's not. There's a paycheck in it though! Now snap out of it, Pauly," she said, pulling his laptop from him.

Bemused, he tilted his head at her uncommonly tense reaction. "Arrr, what dare ya be doing, missy?"

She rolled her eyes. "For Pete's sake, drinking rum doesn't make you a pirate." She slapped his sparsely written budget article down in front of him. "Please, Paul, I'm begging you to finish this. If you get fired, I'm going to quit, and neither one of us can afford to be unemployed. Besides, you're the only one in the office that helps me keep my own sanity. You're the only person more screwed up than me."

"I beg your pardon," he said, lazily raising one eyebrow and moving the paper to the side. "Now may I please have my laptop?" His eyelids grew thick and heavy as his head tipped downward.

"No, no, no! Do *not* fall asleep." She pulled her chair close to him. "I'm staying here until you finish this, so let's get started. The passion police will have to wait."

The sun blasting through the kitchen window at seven the next morning bolted her awake. Beside her, Paul's head lay flat on the table, his hand still clutching his computer mouse.

She nudged him. "Pauly, wake up."

"Ummph. Go to bed," he said, pushing her away with his other hand.

"It's time to get going. We have to be in the office in an hour."

"You go," he mumbled.

"You've got to deliver the article."

He pointed to his laptop, his head still affixed to the table.

She wiped her eyes and gazed at the screen. His email app was opened full screen. The last entry read, *To Greg Eniss, sent at 5:33 a.m.* A document was attached titled *Budgetary Cuts: How America Will React.*

She patted him on the head. "Good job, Mr. Hemingway," she whispered in his ear.

Chapter 16

When Zoey reached the office, there was a sticky note on her computer screen that read, *See Me – Greg.*

As she made her way through the sea of monochrome cubicles, she could hear the obscenities flowing out of his office. Employees averted their eyes as she walked past.

"You wanted to see me?" she said.

"I thought you were going to keep him on track." The thin strands of his comb-over shook from the tension running through his portly frame, and his pudgy face was plump with rage. "This is what you let him submit?" he said, spinning his computer monitor around to her.

As she scanned the first page of Paul's article, she failed to see anything but excellent writing. It was the other pages that caused her jaw to drop. Beginning at the top of the second page, the word "Spoon" was repeated over and over until the last sentence, which simply read, "No more, No less."

"I-I don't know what to say, Greg. I'm—"

"Embarrassed, ashamed—how about feeling guilty for letting this loon waste the company's time and cost us money?"

"But it's not been released yet—has it?"

"Of course not," he said, slamming his hand on his desk. "But we don't have squat to fill that space. I want you to take this piece of garbage and add the following two words at the end—*You're fired*! Seriously, I want you to print it and hand-deliver it to that maniac, get his laptop, confiscate his access card to the building, and report back to me. Am I clear?"

"Ye-yes, sir, Mr. Ennis." She started to walk away and then turned back to him. "Am I—"

"Fired too? Not yet, but you will be if you don't take care of all this today. Now go! I have to pull a rabbit out of my hat to fill this space."

On the way to Paul's apartment, she received a text message from him that read, *Sorry about article. Do me a favor. Greg will want all company assets. They're in a tote bag on kitchen table with envelope to him. Do NOT open! Give it to him immediately. Keys to apartment are under doormat.*

Immediately, every horrible thought ran through her head. She tried calling and texting him but got no response. All she could do was fulfill his wishes and pray.

Within less than an hour, she was back in Greg's office with the tote bag in hand. He motioned her to sit while he continued to chew out an editor over the phone who couldn't pitch in and finish Paul's disastrous article.

"Well, Bob, if you're not capable of pulling it off, then I guess you're not capable of that raise either." He slammed the phone down.

She held out the envelope Paul had instructed her to deliver. Before she could blink, he plucked it from her, tore it open, and began reading. His eyes narrowed as he processed the page. "Hmmm..." His eyebrows rose. He reached in, pulled the laptop out, and booted it as he reread the contents of the envelope, tapping his fingers rapidly on the table as the computer screen lit up.

"What's going—"

He raised his hand. "Quiet!"

After several minutes he snapped the cover shut and picked up the phone. "Bob, pack your stuff. You're moving down the hall, end cubicle next to the storage room. Be out in forty-five minutes."

"But, Greg, that's *my* cubicle," she whimpered. "Am I being fired?"

"No. You're moving into Bob's office."

"Why would I be doing that?"

"Maybe I should reconsider. I don't know if I need a new editor with so much modesty." His tone turned syrupy. "Zoey, this article is well written. For such a milk-toast subject, the arc is compelling, plus a line editor won't even have to touch it. Thanks to you, we've got our space filled!"

"But I don't understand."

"Thank your crazy friend for retaining enough sanity to give credit where credit's due. Now don't waste any more of my time. Go kick Bob out and get situated. We've got a copy meeting in an hour. Oh, and take Mr. Crazy's laptop. You're going to need something you can take home at night. Being an editor's more than a nine-to-five job, you know."

As soon as the meeting was over, she called Paul. Again, no answer. She texted him, nothing. At precisely five o'clock, she was out the door and on her way to his apartment when he called.

"Where are you?" she blurted. "I've been worried sick."

"I'm okay. I'll be home in five minutes if you want to meet me there."

"I'll see you in a few."

When Zoey arrived, she bombarded him with questions. "Where've you been all day? What did you tell Greg? Why'd you submit that crazy article? What—"

"Whoa! Take a breath, Zo. First of all, everything's okay. I went to see someone today. I can't believe I'm saying this, but—I saw a shrink."

"What's wrong with that? I'm proud of you. I realize it was hard, but given everything you've been through and now that you've been—"

"Fired. Yeah, I was counting on that."

"I know you were, but still. So did he or she help?"

"His name's Dr. Atwell."

"Dr. *Peter* Atwell?" she gleamed.

"Yeah, why?"

"He's the one I've been seeing all these years. He's great!"

"Oh, good. As I was saying, I was there for almost two hours, and to be honest—yes—I do feel better, but there are some things I need to do. He'd also like to talk with you if that's okay."

"Just tell me when."

He handed her a business card.

"Don't need it. I've got him on speed dial. I'll call to-morrow. So what did he say?"

"I can't tell you. He needs to speak with you first.

However, the one thing he did mention is I need to reconnect with my family."

"But you told me you've never been able to locate any of them—not even one."

"That's where I need your help. I know you're a big-shot editor now, but if you could use some of your fact-finding skills, I'd appreciate it."

"You know I will, but before I do, you have to tell me why you submitted the article the way you did."

"I wish I could explain it, Zo." His voice fell. "I truly do. But the fact is I-I honestly don't know."

"Well, where'd the word 'Spoon' come from?"

"It popped in my head, and I just started typing. I didn't even realize I was doing it."

"Well, how'd I get promoted? I know you know that."

He put his hand on her shoulder. "Zo, don't worry about it. You're in that position now, and you're going to do great." He turned and grabbed a notebook and pen. "Now if you'll excuse me, I've got some writing to do."

She tugged on his sleeve. "Tell me you're not going to be drinking tonight."

He shook his head. "No, not tonight."

When she got back to her apartment, she pulled out Paul's old laptop that was now hers and found the desktop to be as much a mess as his apartment. One by one, she dragged items to the trash icon. Before hitting the delete key, she scanned all the files to make sure she wasn't getting rid of anything important. The two most recent items immediately jumped out at her. Both were Word documents, one titled "Zoey's article" and one titled "Greg."

The "Zoey's article" proved to be the budget article Paul

had gotten fired over. However, this one had no gibberish and no repetitive words, it was simply a well-written piece with no grammatical errors. The one thing that caught her eye was the byline, which included her name, not his.

The other document titled "Greg" was a short paragraph that simply read,

Dear Greg, I'm afraid I have nothing left to offer the Chronicle *except Zoey Antonelli. She's a major talent who can easily pick up where I have left off. The document titled "Zoey's Article" is what she finished for me when I could not. If you're looking for another great editor, look no further. She will shine for you. Regards, Paul.*

She pulled the computer to her chest and sobbed.

At exactly eight the next morning, Zoey called Dr. Atwell.

"This is Dr. Atwell, may I help you?"

"Hello, Doctor, this is Zoey Antonelli."

"Why hello, Zoey, how are you?"

"Fine, Doctor. My friend, Paul Talbert, said I needed to call you."

"That's right. What a small world. Paul said I'd probably hear from you this morning. I hate to ask, but could you come by the office today?"

"I started a new position and can only get away during lunch. I'm only two blocks away, so I could probably be there a few minutes after twelve. Would that work?"

"That'll be fine. See you then."

When noon rolled around, she practically ran the entire two blocks then sprinted up three flights of stairs to the doctor's office. As she was catching her wind, a voice came from down the hall. "Hi, Zoey."

"Hi, Doc," she panted.

"Would you like to continue your jog into my office," said a stocky, grey-haired man in round glasses.

"Thanks for seeing me," she panted.

"My, my, your energy has always amazed me."

"So, how's my Pauly?"

He closed the front door and motioned her to another room a few feet away. Instead of sitting behind his large mahogany desk, he pulled a chair next to her. "I'm going to get straight to the point, Zoey. The reason I wanted to see you so soon is... well, Paul is in a difficult spot." He paused. "Actually, an extremely difficult spot."

"Is he in trouble? Sick? I can tell he—"

The doctor held up his hand. "Zoey, Paul's experiencing delusional characteristics accompanied by suicidal inclinations so strong he could act upon those thoughts sooner than later."

The room fell silent as she looked him in the eyes without blinking. "Paul's had thoughts of killing himself?"

"That's why I needed you to come in so soon."

"Are they as bad as—"

"Yours?"

She looked down then nodded slowly.

"We shouldn't compare, my dear, but the bottom line is... they're troubling. From what I understand, you're his only friend, and he apparently doesn't have any relatives, at least from what I can ascertain. From what he told me, he was put in an orphanage when he was three, and no relative has ever reached out to him. This poor man has gone through life virtually alone.

"If there're any you know of, then you need to help him reconnect with them if possible." He paused. "There's also something else. I won't go into the details, but I did an hour-long session of hypnotherapy with him. Evidently, he had an abusive childhood."

She smirked. "Anything like my charming upbringing?"

He pursed his lips with a shrug. "All I can tell you is that his feelings are deep-rooted and extremely strong. He has debilitating feelings of being judged, which are part of the reason he's struggled at work so much. This is often the case with orphans who've been through what he has."

Zoey squeezed the plastic water bottle she'd brought with her, causing it to overflow onto her hand. "Yes, that's something I've seen firsthand from him."

"There's one last thing. I've never observed this with any of my other patients, but under hypnosis, he can recall aspects of another life with details as vivid as what you and I are experiencing right now. Unfortunately, parts of these memories—or delusions—are even more horrific than what he experienced in his real childhood. As a way of coping, I can only surmise his subconscious is projecting his troubled youth onto a fantasy one. Unfortunately, it's compounding the problem."

"Do you think the accident had anything to do with this?" she asked.

"I'm glad you mentioned that. In your mind, how would you compare his mental state before and after he was hit?"

"Well, he's always been a little gloomy, but he's always had a heart of gold too. He got me my job." She looked out the window and paused. "And he just helped me get promoted."

"Did he ever try to commit suicide?"

"I can't say for sure, but there was one time when his

boss chewed him out for no good reason. He got so bent out of shape he ran off to a cabin in the woods. No one even knew where he was. He left work and didn't tell anyone. I couldn't get a hold of him. No one could. A couple days later, he showed up as if nothing had happened. He didn't say anything about suicide, but I'm sure he must have thought about it."

"Since the accident, what've you noticed that's different?"

"He's more detached, more distant. There's something different—it's like he's carrying a heavier burden now or something. I-I can't explain it." Her eyes welled up. "Can you help him?"

He handed her a tissue. "I've already prescribed medication that will help dull the anxiety and reduce the self-loathing, but he's going to need a lot of therapy. As I mentioned earlier, reconnecting with someone from his past, preferably a relative, will help. Do you think you'll be able to help with that?"

"I don't even know where to begin, but yes, I'll try."

"One last thing. Does the name 'Spoon' mean anything to you?"

Her brow furrowed. "No, not as a name. The word by itself does."

"What do you mean?"

"He repeated it over and over in an article he submitted to our boss. Probably more than three hundred times—all in a row too. Why?"

"Interesting." He stroked his beard. "During the hypnotherapy, he kept mentioning a friend."

"A friend?"

"Yes. He called him 'Spoon.'"

Chapter 17

Over the next couple months, Paul's weekly visits to see Dr. Atwell, along with his medication, kept him emotionally stable. Zoey provided additional support by either calling him or dropping by every day. Overall, things seemed to be moving in a positive direction, except for the fact she had not come close to locating any living relatives. One day Dr. Atwell called to inquire about her progress and to give her his weekly status report on how well Paul was doing.

"Any luck this week locating any Talbert relatives?"

"Unfortunately, no. I've checked every ancestry and friend-finder website, and I can't find a single living relative. I've never seen a family tree with fewer branches. However, a detective friend did do an exhaustive investigation and said there's a slight possibility of a connection down south."

A long moment passed.

"Doc, are you still there?"

"Yes."

"What's wrong?"

"Zoey, I'm afraid things might be getting worse."

"Oh no! what happened?"

"It's not what happened, it's what *might* happen. Paul's insurance has expired due to his termination, and without insurance, I can't refer him to anyone."

"Why would you need to refer him to someone?"

"I have to go out of the country on a research project, and I'll be gone for five months. Continuing with the meds will help, but he's in dire need of the therapy sessions. Without insurance, I'm sure he won't be able to afford them. Even paying for his medication will be tough."

"Don't worry about the meds. I'll cover those."

"That's sweet of you, Zoey. They're important, but it's the sessions he needs more than anything—that and finding any relatives. So you said your detective friend might have found something."

"He didn't have a lot of details, but the potential connections are with a plantation in South Carolina that went into ruins after the Civil War and never recovered."

"Where in South Carolina was this plantation?"

"Someplace called Beaufort. An hour or so south of Charleston."

"Hmmm."

"What're you thinking, Doc?"

"People didn't usually travel too far from home during those times. It's a long shot, but it might be worth taking a trip to check it out. Who knows, maybe the family tree does branch out there."

"I'd go, but I still don't have any time off."

"I wasn't thinking about you. I was thinking about Paul. It'll give him a purpose that will keep his mind occupied. He'll be motivated to do the search. Plus, without a job, he's got the time."

"That makes sense," she said.

"One other thing. How are you doing? Will you be okay with me being gone this long?"

"I'm fine." Her voice faded away then sprang back. "You know me—chipper, chipper, always sunny-side up."

"Seriously, Zoey, how are you?"

"I'll be okay, Doc."

"Have you talked to your mom and dad lately?"

"Nope," she said flatly.

"And no more tattoos?"

She managed a smile. "Nothing left to cover—I got 'em all."

"Okay. Just checking. If you need me, you have my cell, okay?"

"Thanks, Doc. I appreciate it."

When Zoey told Paul about her call with Dr. Atwell, he laughed. "I can't believe this. I knew my insurance was running out, so I traded my car for an old junkie van so I could continue paying for the sessions."

"Well, that sounds kinda logical," she said. "How's the job search going?"

"Still looking every day. But with my employment record, I'm a leper in the job market. To be honest, I don't want to go back into the corporate world. It's too cutthroat. There's so much backstabbing, in-fighting, and lack of compassion. I'd love to find something where my mood is based on *my mood*—not my boss's."

"Then why don't you write?"

"That's what I *was* doing."

"No—for yourself. You could write novels or even screenplays. Become a freelancer."

"I've thought about that, but I wouldn't be able to support myself. It takes years to build an audience large enough to make the kind of money you need to survive."

"Then drive a cab and write at night or on your lunch hour or between fares. You could even take a night-shift job or anything that would give you time to write. You know you can do it!"

"This is actually sounding better. I could even give up the apartment and live out of the van."

She flashed him a disapproving frown.

"You've seen my apartment. It'd be an improvement."

"Well, you got a point there. It's about the same size, that's for sure." Suddenly her eyes lit up. "All this *does* make sense—at least for the time being."

"What does?"

"Your van, your writing, Beaufort."

"Beaufort! Where'd that come in?"

"A detective friend of mine discovered you may have had some sort of connection in a town called Beaufort, South Carolina."

He stood. "Really?"

"Oh, yeah! And get this—it involves a plantation. They may have even been rich!"

"He found relatives?"

"Unfortunately, no. Something happened that ultimately caused the family who owned the plantation to fade out—at least on paper."

"What do you mean *on paper*?"

"There aren't any records of descendants after the Civil War era."

"So why'd you say this makes sense?"

"Because Dr. Atwell thinks you should go there and

have a look for yourself. He thinks it's possible some may still be living there but they don't show up in any of the searches we've done. At a minimum, it'd be interesting for you to visit."

Paul scratched his beard as he mulled over the endeavor. "Wanna see my luxurious new van?"

"Don't you want to consider the plantation idea?"

"I have. I just want you to look at the van and tell me if you think it'll make it all the way to South Carolina."

"Yay!" she said, jumping up and down, clapping her hands. "What an awesome road trip it'll be. I'll check your mail and dust off your silk plants. And if you promise to call me every day, I might even give your place a cleaning."

"I'll settle for the correct coordinates."

"What?"

"Directions, knucklehead," he said, laughing. For the first time in months, he felt a sliver of hope.

The next day, Paul packed his van and drove by the *Chronicle* to say goodbye to Zoey. "Come on out," he texted her. "I'm in the loading zone in front of the building."

A minute later, she came bouncing out the front door to an empty sidewalk. "Paul, where are you?" she said, turning in a circle. From behind a bush, a handsome man in khakis and a white T-shirt came walking toward her, his arms opened to his sides.

"Well?" he said.

She stepped back. "I'm sorry, can I help you?"

"How about a goodbye hug?" he said, extending his arms wider.

She threw her hands over her mouth. "Oh my gosh!"

she squealed. "Paul—is that you?"

"Uh, yeah," he said with a smile.

"You shaved… and you cut your hair. You look *totally* different. You look amazing—absolutely amazing!"

"Well, when someone calls you a Sasquatch, what's a guy to do? Plus, it's hotter in the South, so I thought it best to cool things down."

"On the contrary—I think you heated them up!"

Never comfortable with compliments, he redirected. "Enough about me." He turned toward the curb and pointed to the only vehicle in the loading zone. "What do you think of my new van?"

"Oh my word. You're certainly using the word 'new' lightly, aren't you?" she laughed.

He beamed with a sense of pride in knowing he'd purchased the most hideous vehicle he could find. "It's me, don't you think?" he said, positioning his fist on his hip in a triumphant pose.

She couldn't help but find the truth in what he said. The faded lime-green body with the multiple dents, the duct-taped rearview mirror, the dangling bumper… it was all a perfect reflection of how she knew he saw himself.

"Why… I-I love it! I bet it gets great gas mileage," was the only compliment she could come up with.

"That's the best you can do?" he said, handing her the keys to his apartment. "I'll call you when I get there. Now you better get back to work, or else Greg, is liable to come looking for you."

"I guess." She hugged him again then kissed him on his freshly shaven cheek. On her way inside, she turned back and yelled, "Paul Talbert, may the road rise up to meet you. May the wind always be at your back. May the sun shine warm upon your face, and rains fall soft upon your fields. And until we meet again, may God hold you in the palm of His hand."

"Nice! One of my favorite toasts." He pulled a flask from the glove compartment and raised it to his lips.

"Nooo! You said you wouldn't."

He belted out a hearty laugh at his childish prank. "Don't worry, it's sweet iced tea. I'm still prepping for Dixie." He blew her a kiss, and off he went.

After work, Zoey went to his apartment to fulfill her promise of caring for his apartment and checking mail. When she had completed both tasks, she set out to tidy up the place. As she went to empty his trash, she noticed a large stack of papers, bound together by a black binder clip, tucked under a copy of the *New York Times*. The cover sheet contained Paul's name along with one sentence that read "Title To Be Determined."

Curious by nature, she flipped to the first page. Immediately she recognized it as the continuation of the piece he had been working on when he should have been writing the budget article. She quickly read the second page, then the third and fourth. Fifteen minutes later, she was flipping to the twentieth page. Thirty minutes later, she was still reading. Two hours later, she turned the last page. She laid her hand on top and sighed. Looking around, as if making sure no hidden cameras or spies were watching, she rolled up the pages and stuffed them into her purse.

Chapter 18

Through the night, Paul and his green junker clanked and chugged their way down the East Coast toward Port Royal Island, one of South Carolina's coastal sea islands and the home of the scenic little town of Beaufort. There, he would begin his ancestral exploration.

He knew he shouldn't, but his mind wouldn't let loose of the vision of him finding a sprawling estate with a household of distant relatives waiting with open arms to welcome him into their fold.

An hour outside the city, he pulled off the side of the road to take advantage of the remaining darkness for a quick nap.

Several hours later, he awoke to the sounds of seagulls and a warm breeze. After several turns through tobacco and cotton fields, as well as a swamp, his GPS led him to the winding, historic antebellum streets of the city.

He could feel the city's slow, steady pulse as shop-keepers hung out their signs and opened their doors to the sprinkling of early-bird tourists eager to take advantage of the city's morning charm. Despite the picturesque welcoming, his anxiety grew.

Stopping in front of the Shiny Diner, he pulled out his medication along with the flask of rum he had hidden from Zoey. A few sips later, he sat waiting for the medicine and booze to kick in when the smell of bacon wafted through the van. It wasn't long before he was inside ordering the "Hungry Man's Special" accompanied by all the fixin's.

"Excuse me," he said to the pimple-faced teenager pouring his tea, "do you happen to know where the Willow Creek Plantation is?"

"Umm, it kinda sounds familiar, but to be honest, sir, I can't say for sure. I've only lived here for less than two months." He turned his head and yelled over the pass-through window into the kitchen. "Hey, Manny, you know where the Willow Creek Plantation is?"

"Willow Creek, yeah. Plantation, no," came a husky reply.

The waiter turned to a middle-aged waitress cleaning a booth across the counter. "How 'bout you, Darlene? You know where Willow Creek Plantation is?"

She turned to the boy, her attention pausing on Paul with a long, lustful blush. "Why, no, but I'm always open for guided tours."

The boy smirked. "Guess that's a no."

For the next several hours, Paul enjoyed exploring the beautiful little town. From the cobblestone streets of the historic district all the way to the shoreline, he took in all he could. He meandered in and out of quaint little shops and markets. He talked with the locals and communed with the pigeons in the park. He found himself drawn to it in a way he hadn't expected. He had never truly been comfortable in the city, but for some reason, he felt oddly connected to this place.

As he passed by another park, he stopped for a quick hit from his flask and to play fetch with a random cocker spaniel. Sitting on a bench and taking several more swigs, his mission of finding the plantation slowly became blurred as the effects of the medication combined with the alcohol slowed his senses to a crawl. He leaned back onto a park bench, closed his eyes, and drifted off to sleep.

An hour later, something tugging at his arm stirred him awake. The same cocker spaniel was nipping at his shirt sleeve, urging him on for another game of fetch.

"I'm sorry," said an elderly man in a power wheelchair, rolling up to him. "I tried to get to him in time, but the General's four legs are faster than my four wheels." His voice was strong and proud, but his Vietnam veteran hat and missing leg denoted a hard, determined life.

"Oh, no problem," Paul said, stretching his arms out for a big yawn. "Me and ole General got acquainted a little earlier."

"Well, I'm sorry he woke you." He patted the side of his chair and began to whiz along a dirt path, his furry companion trotting behind.

"Excuse me, sir," Paul called after him. "Are you from here?"

The old man spun his chair around. "Born and raised."

"Do you happen to know of a place around these parts called Willow Creek Plantation?"

The old man leaned forward and wheeled closer. "Come again?"

"Have you heard of Willow Creek Plantation?"

The man motored his way back to within a few feet of

him. "As a matter of fact, I do."

Paul lit up. "Can you tell me where it is? Is it close? Are there—"

"Hollld on, sonny. Slow down. I remember it because me and my buddy Tommy Drolet would play in the creek that used to run next to it." He turned his head. "Those sure were the days..." he said, fading off in a memory.

"I'm sorry," Paul said, holding out his hand. "I'm afraid I didn't introduce myself. My name's Paul Talbert."

"Please to meet you. I'm Bert," he said, grabbing his hand.

"You said you used to play in the creek there."

"Oh, we had a big time. That was back when kids were outside all day—no cell phones, no computer games, just rompin' around the woods and having good, honest fun. Why I recall—"

"I'm sorry, Bert, but when you said the creek *used* to run through the plantation, does that mean it's no longer there?"

"The creek's still there, just not the plantation."

Paul's shoulders slumped as he dropped his head and sighed.

"You okay, young fella?"

He straightened himself. "Oh yeah, yeah, I'm fine. I was just hoping to find—well, never mind."

"Where you from, Paul?"

"New York City."

"I didn't think you were from around here. You on vacation, visiting friends, family?"

"I-I don't know."

The old man gave him a sideways look. "You don't know *why* you're here?"

"Oh, no—I'm sorry. I know why I'm here. It's just that it's kinda complicated. You see, I thought I might have some distant relatives who lived on the plantation and they might still be there, and I was hoping—"

"Well, if you do, then they're ghosts." Bert stared at him for a moment. "What do you know about that place?"

"Nothing, why?"

"I don't believe anyone else does either. It's one of the mysteries around here. When we were kids, there were still a couple old cabins, parts of a smokehouse, and the foundation of what I guess was the main house, but it's all been bulldozed over and made into a mall. Rumor back when I was little was it was haunted."

"Why would it be haunted?"

Bert rubbed his chin. "Gosh, it's been such a long time. All I remember is something bad happened there during the Civil War."

Paul reached into his pocket, pulled out his flask, and took a quick swallow. He held it out to the old man.

"No thanks. Quit about twenty years ago."

"Mind if I—"

"No, no, by all means."

Paul took another long drink. "Do you remember any of the stories?"

Bert's lips puckered as he tried reaching back to his youth. "Sorry," he said, placing his fingers to his temple. "I'm afraid Vietnam stole most of my childhood." He paused. "But I do remember how pretty that creek was."

"Well, Bert, I don't wanna take up any more of your and the General's time."

"Sorry I couldn't help you more." He spun his wheelchair around and started to motor off, then stopped. "It won't be much of a treat to see, but the Willow Creek Mall is where the plantation used to be. Be careful if you go though—it's not a nice part of town."

As he watched the old man and his dog disappear through the park gate, an emptiness overcame him. His idyllic vision of finding the estate he had been hoping for was gone.

Over the next couple days, Paul continued, in vain, to uncover anything connecting him to the area. After speaking to Zoey, they agreed one more day was enough, and then he should head home. As much as he had fallen in love with the city, the failure to discover anything was becoming another source of anxiety they knew could overtake him.

Still with high hopes, he combed the city the next day, asking the locals about their knowledge of the Willow Creek Plantation. With no leads coming from his efforts, he decided to have a late dinner then hit the road for an all-night drive back to New York. As he was preparing to leave, the obvious struck him. He had not visited the mall where the man from the park said the plantation had originally been located. With no rush to get back, he decided to swing by on his way out of town.

As the man had said, the area was indeed a major eye sore. Rows of trailers and condemned houses lined the streets, while their downtrodden tenants—slumped in plastic, thrift-store rocking chairs on their front porches—stared aimlessly into nowhere.

Fifty yards past a set of railroad tracks, a neon sign reading "Willow Creek Mall" sporadically blinked on and off. An almost vacant parking lot circled a beige square building with a stained awning over the main entrance. Off in the distance, the creek for which the mall was named ran parallel to the tracks. Its banks were overgrown with more dilapidated trailers above the flood line.

Finding anything of value here was a shot in the dark. He contemplated passing it by, but his flask of rum was dry, and the allure of a small sign next to the entrance that read "Tony's Tiki Bar and Grill" sounded like a logical pit stop.

A dull silence met him at the mall's front door—no music, no teenagers laughing as they hung around crowded kiosks, trying on sunglasses or playing with the latest mobile gadgetry. He couldn't help but feel the despair the handful of shop owners must be feeling as they slowly watched their dreams dashed by their poor investments. Somehow, he felt a kinship with them in the way this desolate complex had robbed them of their hopes for a brighter future.

His only mission now was a stiff drink from a guy named Tony. Not surprisingly, the mood of the Tiki Bar and Grill matched the rest of the mall. Its only redeeming exception was the reggae music coming from the jukebox in the distant corner. Behind the bar, a large man in a tie-dyed shirt with long grey hair pulled into a ponytail stood drying shot glasses while yelling obscenities into his cell phone. At the far end of the bar, a robust, middle-aged African American lady sat nursing a cocktail.

After slinging several more expletives at the person on the other end of the line, the bartender slammed his phone onto the counter. "Women—can't live with 'em, can't live without 'em." The tired cliché made Paul's skin crawl, but how appropriate it was, given the source. "How can I help ya?" the big man said, throwing his towel onto his shoulder.

"Rum, please."

"Rum and…" he asked.

"Just rum. A shot will do."

"Arrrhhh, a true pirate, I sees!"

Paul smiled at the spot-on impersonation. "Would you happen to be Tony?"

"Yep. Proprietor and entrepreneur extraordinaire. Believe it or not, this is a side gig. I've got an app in the works that's gonna make millions."

The lady at the end of the bar snickered. The bartender flashed a frown her way and continued. "You ever go into a grocery store, and it takes you two hours to get five things?"

"Uh, yeah," he replied obligingly.

"With my app, you type in everything you want, and when you get to the store, it shows you where it's all at." He held out his hands. "Ta da. In and out."

"That's a great idea. Grocery stores are like jungles to me. I can never find anything." He chugged his shot. "How about another?" He was pleased with his new friendship, especially given it came with access to his favorite beverage.

Tony poured him another, which he immediately threw back.

"I gotta find a backer to get it done." He squinted one eye. "You wouldn't happen to be a rich investor, would you?"

"Me? The only investing I can do is in another shot!"

The bartender laughed. "I believe I like you."

Paul swallowed his drink.

"You live around here?" Tony asked.

"No. Just visiting." He thought about dropping his

response at that point but decided he should give his fact-finding efforts one last shot. "I came looking for some of my past." The effects of his shots had started to take effect. "I mean, I'm here looking for some relatives who used to live around here... or maybe still do."

"Oh, where exactly?"

Paul spun his finger around in the air, accompanied by the whistling sound of a bomb dropping, then landed it on the bar as if aiming for a bull's-eye. "Right here!"

"In this godforsaken neck of the woods?"

"No." He tapped the bar with three solid thumps. "I mean *right here*. Like in the *Wizard of Oz*, your lovely mall landed on top of them."

The lady at the end of the bar coughed.

"You okay down there?" Tony asked. When she didn't respond, he turned back. "You mean to tell me your relatives owned the Willow Creek Plantation?"

Paul's eyes lit up, as did the lady's. "Honestly, I'm not sure. Do you know anything about the place?"

"Only that it was cursed. Not one single business that's been in or around this property has ever done well. Ain't that right, Hanna?" he shouted toward the lady at the end of the bar. "Cursed, cursed, cursed!" He stared at her, waiting for a response he was sure would come.

She chugged her drink then slammed it upside down onto the bar. For a lady who looked to be in her mid-fifties, she had a stout frame with strong shoulders. Her plump face would have been a pleasant one had it not been for the scowl she wore as she glared at the bartender.

"The only thing cursed around here is your foul mouth and over-breaded chicken wings," she said, walking toward Paul. "Son, don't you listen to a word this over-the-hill hippie is telling you. The only thing cursed about the Willow Creek Plantation was the same thing that cursed the rest of the South during those times—the Civil War." She tilted her head toward him. "Did I overhear you say you *had* relatives at the plantation?"

"Yes, ma'am—well, no, ma'am—I mean, I'm not sure."

She stepped back from the bar, looking him over. "How many shots have you had?"

"It's not the shots," he said, fumbling with his glass. "Well, maybe a little… it's-it's complicated."

Her tone grew serious. "Well, what's so complicated about it? You either do or don't."

Tony stopped drying glasses and leaned forward, intrigued by the pending confrontation.

"It's kind of private, actually."

She narrowed her gaze on him. "Where'd you say you were from?"

"New York City."

"Uh-huh," she exclaimed, as if discovering the missing piece to a puzzle. "You're here with that other fellow that's been snooping 'round, aren't you?"

Paul looked at Tony then back at her. "I'm sorry, I'm not sure what you mean. I've only been here three days."

"Three days is a long time. A man can get a lot of information in that amount of time, especially in a town this small."

"I-I guess you're right." He paused, trying to understand her concern about his wanting to learn more about the plantation. "I'm sorry, ma'am, but am I missing something here? I'm trying to uncover—"

"Something about the plantation!" Her voice grew louder.

"You and that other fellow. You wanna get some—"

"Whoa! Hold on. Give the boy some air." Tony handed her a drink. "Here. Chill, would ya?" He turned to Paul. "Sorry about Miss Hanna's passion for the place. She's kind of protective of it."

"Hush, Tony!"

"Sorry, I thought—"

"You thought nothing is what you did." She reached into her purse and threw a twenty-dollar bill onto the bar. "Here." She turned to Paul, gave him another once-over, then marched out the door.

"Don't you want your change?"

"Nope," she said as the door closed behind her.

"I'm real sorry about that. Here—this one's on me." Tony pushed him another shot across the bar.

"Did I do something wrong?"

"Nah. She's a regular in here, so I know her well enough to know she's got something on her mind. She can get pretty dark sometimes, but all in all, she's sweet as molasses. We all have our baggage."

Paul sipped his complimentary rum. "You can say that again."

Just then, the front door swung open, and two attractive young girls fell in, holding onto one another, laughing at some obvious joke they shared from outside. The cheap electronic tiki torches zip-tied beside the door revealed one to be a tall Scandinavian blond and the other an African American, girl-next-door type. Both appeared to be in their early twenties.

"Customers! Must be *my* lucky night," Tony said, leaving Paul to himself as he rushed to the end of the bar where his newest patrons resided.

Paul continued sipping his rum, still baffled by his previous encounter.

A couple minutes later, Tony reappeared in front of him with a big grin and a snazzy tropical drink, complete with a miniature umbrella sticking out of it. "Must be *your* lucky night. The two young maidens at yonder bar bought you our house specialty."

He looked to his left to find the tall blond waving at him with a sheepish, come-hither smile while the other girl stared into her drink.

The clock above the jukebox told his sensible self if he left now, he could drive all night and be home by sunup. The lonely guy with nothing better to do convinced him otherwise. Striking up a conversation with two attractive females was a no-brainer, plus, the only polite thing to do was to thank them for the drink. With his previous rum intake bolstering his confidence, he walked over and introduced himself.

"Hi, my name's Paul. I wanted to thank you for the cocktail."

The blond batted her eyes and giggled. "I'm Brandy. Do you like the drink?"

"Oh yeah, it's great. The umbrella keeps poking me in the eye, but other than that, it's pretty good."

She laughed while the other girl continued examining the bar.

"I'm sorry, I didn't get your name," he said, leaning past the blond to catch her attention.

"Oh, hi—sorry—I'm Elisabeth."

"She's shy," the blond mouthed to him.

Paul had been the third wheel too many times in his life and always hated seeing others left out. "What do you two do here in charming Beaufort?"

"I'm studying cosmetology," said the blond. She turned to her friend. "I can't wait to do a makeover on this one."

"But why?" he asked.

Elisabeth looked away, as if the compliment had been meant for someone else.

"What do you do, Elisabeth?"

"I'm studying to be a journalist," she said, making brief eye contact before turning her gaze back to her drink.

"Really! That's what I do—I'm a writer."

She pushed her drink to the side. "No kidding. Where do you work?"

"The *NYC Chronicle*."

"Shut up!" she said, perking up. "I *love* the *Chronicle*. Did you have anything to do with last month's article on the budget?"

"What? You actually read that boring thing?"

"Boring my hiney," she laughed. "That piece helped me get an A in my mass media law class. I used it for examples of effectively citing sources."

"Be still my beating heart. You can't imagine how great that makes me feel. I wrote—I mean, I *helped* someone write something that made a difference."

"That's exactly what I want to do. I want to write things that impact people, that make them think or change their lives. I want to leave the world a better place through my writing. Does that make sense?"

Paul was mesmerized. "Absolutely."

Unable to contribute to the conversation, Brandy faked receiving a text message. "Oh snap, looks like I've got to bug out." She turned to Elisabeth. "Looks like Bobby's having a conniption to see me. That's my boyfriend," she said, directing her comment to Paul. "Sorry, I have to go."

"Oh, okay," Elisabeth said. "Let me pay up, and we'll get going."

"No, no, I'm going in the opposite direction. Can't Mr. Steinbeck here drive you home?" Brandy looked down her nose at him. "That's right, I've read a book or two from ole Jim Steinbeck—*The Mouse and Man, The Grape Raft*—all his classics."

Paul glanced at Elisabeth, who was stifling a laugh.

"I'd be more than happy to drop you off, Elisabeth."

"Well…" she looked over at Brandy, who was winking her approval. "But we just met, literally a few minutes ago."

"Go on, girl, seriously. I gotta go see Bobby before he freaks out. Mr. Steinbeck looks okay to me."

"Well… I guess. You aren't a serial killer, are you?"

"Hmmm, let me see. Uh, nope—not a convicted one anyway."

The corners of her mouth turned up slightly. "Well, I guess. Let me see if there's anyone else around first. There was someone I was supposed to meet here." After doing a quick search, she was back. Nobody here, guess we can go."

As they walked outside, she immediately pointed to his van. "Is that yours?"

"I'm sorry. I told you I'm a writer, just not a very successful one."

"Don't be silly! It's got sooo much character—along with a lot of rust, but hey, the character's what it's all about."

He tried opening her door, but it wouldn't budge. "Daggone it. I just bought this thing, and I never even thought to check to see if it would actually open."

Her cheeks puffed out in preparation for an internal combustion.

"I'm so sorry," he said fumbling with the handle. "You can, uh, let's see—oh, I got it. You can climb across the driver's seat."

Her lip quivered, then she doubled over laughing.

"Are you okay?"

She straightened up, holding her side. "Absolutely," she sighed. "I haven't laughed that hard in a long time."

"Thanks—I guess."

"Seriously, it's awesome. I love the green machine."

He smiled.

For the entire twenty-minute trip to her house, they chatted freely. When they pulled up to her house, they remained in the van, talking for another hour and a half about their love of writing as well as dozens of other random topics ranging from football to fashion. Whatever popped into their heads, they were comfortable with sharing, so when the subject got around to why he was in Beaufort, she was beyond excited.

"I can't believe you may have relatives from the plantation. Are you serious?"

"It's a long shot, but who knows? It's possible."

"Mama's gonna freak out."

"What? Why?"

"Paul, will you do something for me?"

"Sure."

"Will you please not go home tonight? Pleeease."

"Are you asking me to—"

She whacked him on the shoulder. "Nooo, Casanova—

we just met. You said earlier you were on your way back to New York. I wanted to invite you over for dinner tomorrow night."

"Oh—Ohhh!" He blushed at his misinterpretation. "I'm sorry. I-I don't know what I was thinking. Yes. I'll stay."

After helping her navigate past the console and over the driver's seat, he ushered her to the curb. For a moment, they nervously hemmed and hawed before she took him by the hand. "I really enjoyed meeting you tonight."

He started to move closer but hesitated. He wanted to say more, but all he could come up with was, "What time do you want me here?"

"Seven thirty," she said, skipping back a step. "And don't be late. You're going to be in a for a huge treat!"

Chapter 19

Paul spent most of the next day exploring the city, but instead of trying to uncover information about the plantation, he looked for interesting things to discuss that evening with Elisabeth. He visited the shops along Bay Street as well as Hunting Island Lighthouse, and he even hopped on a buggy tour. And unlike the other days, he did it all without the need for alcohol.

As the evening approached, his only anxious moment came when he realized he hadn't bathed in two days. The solution came quickly as he remembered an outdoor shower next to one of the oceanside hotels.

After a quick rinse, he headed to Elisabeth's house, stopping at a park to pick a handful of gardenias and geraniums. The fact that he didn't know which was which made no difference to him. They were both beautiful, as was everything about the drive to her house. Their engaging conversation from the night before had blinded him to the magnificent antebellum homes and canvas of Spanish moss crisscrossing over the streets that led to her two-story colonial house.

Pulling into her driveway, he couldn't help but notice how

heinous his van was amid the rows of Mercedes, Porsches, Bentleys, and other luxury cars lining the street. Character—that's what she said his van had. He took a deep breath and rang the doorbell. As he waited, he looked at his cell phone. Seven thirty exactly. Flowers, character, *and* punctuality would surely win the day.

"Hello there, Mr. Steinbeck," she laughed, swinging the screen door open. "Any trouble getting here?" she said with a hug.

"Not at all—oh, these are for you," he said, pulling the flowers from behind his back.

"Oh, they're so pretty. Thank you." She kissed him on the cheek. "Come on back. Momma's in the courtyard finishing up."

As she led him through the hall, he was astonished by the elegant furnishings and the well-appointed details, down to the lace doilies under each lamp. What caught his eye most were the dozens of old black-and-white pictures that adorned the hallway and adjacent rooms. Only a few appeared to be in color.

The house's backyard charm equally matched the elegance displayed throughout the house. The cobblestone patio with its ivy-covered pergola cast a romantic atmosphere that enhanced its host's beauty. In the middle of the courtyard was a wrought-iron table already set for three. Covered dishes laid out reflected a page from *Southern Living Magazine*.

"Momma? Are you out here?" she said, looking about the yard.

"I'll be out in a minute, honey," came a voice from inside.

"I can't wait for you to meet her. You're going to—"

"Here I am." Walking through the back door was a large lady whose eyes were locked on the plate she was carrying. When she reached the bottom step, she stopped to look up and greet their guest. "You must be—"

Paul gulped.

She blinked. "Why, you're—" She stopped again and narrowed her eyes.

"Momma, this is Paul Talbert. Are you okay?"

Although his share of rum from the night before had been substantial, he could still remember the lady who had raked him over the coals at the Tiki Bar. Her awkward entrance was a sure indication she recognized him as well.

"Oh, I'm sorry, honey," she said. "I had two things on my mind at the same time—your mister Talbert here and the pie I forgot to take out of the oven."

"Don't worry, I'll go pull it out. You two get acquainted."

As soon as Elisabeth disappeared into the kitchen, her mother placed the dish on the table with a thud then turned to him. "Now, I don't know who you are or what you're up to, but my baby girl is my—"

Elisabeth came skipping out of the house holding two bottles of wine. "Do you like red or white?"

He stared at the bottles for a moment then back at her mother.

"Oh, don't worry about Momma—she'll drink either."

As if the previous moment had never happened, her mother said, "Now, the white one's a Pinot Grigio from New York. It's got a *deceptive* aftertaste. However, the red's from the hills of North Carolina. It's a good, smooth southern Merlot. It's got an *honest*, full-bodied flavor you might want to try."

"The red one—definitely the red," he said without hesitation.

Elisabeth poured a glass for each of them. "Here's to family, health, happiness, and new friendships."

For the first thirty minutes, Paul participated in polite small talk with Hanna while focusing his main conversation on Elisabeth and her interests. "What do you want to do when you graduate?"

"I know this sounds ridiculous, but I'd love to take my journal, strap on a backpack, and hike across Europe, capturing all my experiences on paper."

The words sounded like music to him as he envisioned himself by her side, tracking through the French Alps. "I love that idea."

"My baby loves to write, Mr. Talbert, and she's good at it," she said, rubbing her daughter's arm.

"Please, Ms. Mitchell, call me Paul."

"Yeah, Momma, why're you being so formal?"

Not wanting to ruin her daughter's evening, she put her reservations aside. "Okay, Paul. Did Elisabeth tell you she won the coveted Franklin Jennings Award for her collection of short stories?"

"Now that certainly deserves a toast," he said, holding up his glass. "Have you always wanted to write?"

"She's been writing ever since she was a young'n on the—"

"On the where?" he asked.

"On the... uh—the schoolyard. She used to write all the time on the playground or anywhere she could find when she was little."

Elisabeth hung her head.

"Oh, I'm sorry, dear," Hanna said, putting her hand on her shoulder. "I was going to tell—"

"Momma, you don't have to."

"You see," Hanna said, turning to him, "my baby has a certain type of memory issue. Anything beyond the last several years is a blur. Doctors can't explain it." She stroked her daughter's cheek. "It doesn't matter now, does it, baby?"

"No," she said, looking to the side.

Paul placed his knife and fork to the side and leaned forward. "It might help you to know I've got a similar problem."

"Really?" both Hanna and Elisabeth said at the same time.

"My childhood's pretty much a blur too. A few months before I came here, I was hit by a car."

"Is that where you got the scar on your cheek?" Elisabeth asked.

"I don't recall. That's a blur too. In the accident, I hit my head, causing me to experience several days of amnesia. Ever since then, my long-term memories have been a mess. I can only vaguely remember my childhood of going from foster home to foster home and nothing about my parents."

"Where are they? Hanna asked.

"Mother ran off. Father's dead."

"I'm so sorry," Hanna said, placing her hand over her heart.

"I guess the saving grace is not being able to remember those years too well."

"Do you have any brothers or sisters?" she said in a gentle tone.

"None I know of."

"Any relatives?

"No, no relatives either." He stared into his plate for

a moment then snapped his head up. "Say, would you happen to have any rum?"

"We don't have any rum, but we've got plenty of bourbon," Hanna said. "I was going to fix me one. Would you like one too?"

"That'd be great." He smiled as he sensed her warming to him.

Elisabeth looked at her mother. "Momma, don't you—"

"Oh, don't worry, I'm just going to make me a small one."

As she walked to the liquor cabinet, Elisabeth tapped him on the shoulder. "Do you realize how strange this is?"

"Oh, it's strange all right."

"I mean strange in how *similar* we are. Our love of writing, our memories, the plantation, our—"

"What about the plantation?"

Elisabeth gleamed. "This is the surprise I had for you and why I wanted you to meet Momma."

"Why would you want him to meet me?" Hanna said, reappearing with two glasses of the brown liquid.

"Because he's information-hunting about the plantation, and I thought he could ask you about it."

"Baby, I don't think that's a good idea." She handed him the glass.

"Why not?"

"Well, I'm not feeling up to it, to be honest."

"Another migraine?"

She hesitated. "Why don't you just show him the collection instead?"

Elisabeth bounced in her chair. "Would you like to see some pictures from the Willow Creek years?"

"Of course," he said, throwing his napkin onto the table

and standing.

She took him by the hand and led him back into the house and into the hallway. The entire hall, from the kitchen to the front door, was one long corridor of pictures and paintings.

"See this one here," she said, pointing to a grainy black-and-white portrait of a tall, distinguished man on a horse.

Paul's heartbeat quickened. Could this be a distant relative?

"Do you know who he is?" she asked with raised eyebrows.

"No, I don't."

"Neither do we!" she said, laughing. "We bought it at the flea market. We call it *Man on a $5 horse.*"

"That's what you paid for it, isn't it?" he chortled.

"Yep." She pulled him along a few more feet. "Now this one we *do* know," she said, rubbing her finger along the tattered gold-leaf frame. The image was of a dirt street lined with shops with wooden signs hanging off the sides. There were horses and wagons, women in billowing dresses, men in top hats, and some in Confederate uniforms. Other than a few blurry images, the quality was good.

"Ever heard of Mathew Brady?"

"Sounds familiar."

"He was probably *the* most famous photographer during the Civil War. He took this picture of our downtown. Look at this." She pointed to a small narrow building with a line of young men going through the front door. Next to it, a Confederate soldier stood staring at the ground. "That's the recruitment office. See all those boys? They're all enlisting in the army."

"Whoa, that's incredible." He touched the image of the

soldier. "I wonder how many made it home?" He shook his head. "I bet this is some kind of expensive. How'd you get it?"

"Momma bought it at an auction."

"What did you say she did again?"

"I didn't. She works at the hospital."

He turned back to the picture. "How did she know it was by Mathew Brady?"

"It came with a certificate of authenticity like all the rest of these on the walls."

"Holy cow," he said, wandering from picture to picture. "This is like a museum. Are they all of Beaufort?"

"Yep, Momma's got a thing for this ole town."

"How come?"

"Not sure. She should've been a historian instead of a cook—she knows everything about that time period."

His eyebrows raised. "I thought you said she worked at the hospital."

"She does. She's a cook in the cafeteria."

"How can she—I mean, how did she learn so much about it?"

"You'll have to ask her." She pulled him to the last picture hanging next to the front door. The frame was battered, and the glass was cloudy around the edges.

"This one's Momma's favorite."

He stared at it for a minute, taking in every detail. "I think it's mine too," he said. He couldn't help but smile at the group of black and white people with their arms around one another. Something about it resonated with him. In one corner, a huge black man stood proudly by a fire pit with a pig roasting on top. In the back, sitting atop a horse was a distinguished bearded gentleman. Beside his horse was a pretty young girl with long dark hair standing next to a bushy-haired boy with his arm draped over the shoulder of a black boy. Both were obviously competing for the biggest grin as they stretched their lips to the limit.

His eyes darted around the picture. "Do you know where it was taken?"

Elisabeth started to speak until her mother motioned her to halt. "We don't," Hanna said.

"But, Momma, you—"

"Elisabeth—please." Her mother looked at her with a raised eyebrow. "No," she sighed, "I'm afraid this one didn't include a certificate, which usually has the location on it."

"I bet that's a slave owner on the horse," said Paul.

"Probably," Hanna replied.

"But it's strange," he said, rolling his head for a better angle. "Their expressions. They all look… happy… even the slaves look happier than other pictures from that time."

She nodded. "Well, if you'll excuse me, I need to go clean up."

Paul turned to Elisabeth. "I should probably go too."

She followed him out the door. "I have a suggestion. Since Momma wasn't much help tonight, why don't we take a trip to the library tomorrow and do some research of our own?"

"But I've already done so much. I don't believe we'd find anything else." It suddenly occurred to him it wasn't about him finding more on the plantation—it was about spending time with her. "Actually, it might be worth a shot. Yeah, I love the idea."

"Great! How about nine thirty? We'll grab some bagels and be one of the first in the library."

He bowed, his hand stretched out toward his van. "Your green chariot will be awaiting you at precisely nine thirty." He paused. "Seriously, thank you for such a nice time tonight."

She tilted her head down while still looking up at him, her eyes warm and inviting. "I'm glad you were at the Tiki Bar last night," she said softly.

"Me too."

He started to walk away, then turned back for a second, then walked on. Before jumping into his van, he looked back. She was standing behind the screen door, still smiling and waving. It was just a simple moment in time, but one memory he knew he would never forget.

As he drove back to the camping grounds where he'd been spending his nights, he passed the hospital where Elisabeth said her mother worked. He could still picture her gorgeous home with all the luxurious cars lining the roads within the expensive neighborhood. It suddenly came to him that of all the things they talked about, not once was her father mentioned. Tomorrow might not provide anything more about the Willow Creek Plantation, but it would shed light elsewhere.

Chapter 20

At eight thirty the next morning, an annoying buzzing pulled him out of his first good night's sleep in months. He jammed his hand between the backseat cushions and pulled out his cell phone. The screen read "Zoey."

"For heaven's sake, lady, what're you calling me for at eight thirty on a Saturday?"

"Look here, Rip Van Winkle. It's not Saturday, it's Friday—a workday. Why haven't you called me in two days? You were supposed to be back by now. I've been worried."

"Hold on a second," he said, pulling on a T-shirt and rubbing the sleep out of his eyes. "Has it really been two days?"

"Uh, yeah. Are you neglecting your best friend?"

"Well, first of all, you might be my *only* friend, and secondly, are you sure it's been two days?"

"Yes! Pauly, are you drinking already?"

"No. I haven't really felt like it. I mean, I've drunk some, but not much. It's so nice here. The town's beyond charming, the weather's great, the beaches are fantastic with the softest, whitest sand, and the people…" The vision of Elisabeth at the door flashed before him. "The people are so nice and so beautiful."

"Wait a minute. Have-have you met someone?"

"I've met a lot of people," he chuckled.

"You've met someone, haven't you?"

"Welllll, kinda. She's a senior at the local college, and get this—she wants to be a writer. She's pretty good too. But the best part—she loves, loves, loves my van."

"Marry her—now! Paul, that's awesome. How many times have you seen her?"

"Well, we've only known each other two days, and last night was, I guess, what you'd consider a date."

"Okay, you gotta listen to me on this."

"Alright."

"Go slowww. Two days is a blip. You come off too strong, and you'll scare her away. And do *not* be that stalker guy we always see on those cold-case shows."

"Don't worry, I promise. Anyway, I'll keep you posted. So why are you calling me this early?"

"I already told you—I was worried about you. Plus, I had some morning errands to run and was bored. Remember that grey jacket of yours you gave me? I hope you don't mind, but I dropped it off at a consignment shop a friend of mine owns. Man, you were right. That thing was heavy as a Chevy."

"At eight thirty in the morning?"

"That's not early for most people. Besides, it's now eight forty."

"Eight forty! I'm supposed to meet Elisabeth in fifty minutes, and I haven't even showered."

"I like that name. Elisabeth. Very regal."

"Sorry, Zo, gotta run. I'll call you later."

"Toodles."

With two minutes to spare, he arrived at Elisabeth's house. Before he could stop, she was out the front door and skipping her way across the front lawn carrying a bag of bagels.

He rolled the window down. "Don't worry about the door, I fixed it."

She bounced in beside him. "Wow, look at you mister handy man! This is going to be so much fun."

He threw his head back and laughed. "Are you for real?"

"Yep, that's me—certifiably real."

"No, I mean, you actually enjoy research?"

"If I'm going to be any good at my profession, I've gotta do my research, right?" She flashed him a grin while holding up her brown bag. "But first, we have to stop at the coffee shop."

"Yesss. Another reason I knew I liked you."

A few minutes into their bagels and coffee, Paul pulled out a tiny notepad and pen.

"Whatcha writing?"

"Nothing. I'm doodling. I do it when I'm happy or nervous."

"Which is it? Are you happy or nervous?" she asked.

"I-I suppose both." He started to go on, but he remembered Zoey's advice to take it slow.

Oblivious of the time, they chatted the morning away, forgetting their vow to be the first people in the library.

"Would you folks like to order lunch?" a young waitress asked.

Elisabeth looked at her cell phone, confirming the time. "Wow, can you believe it's noon already?"

"I've got an idea," he said.

"I'm in," she said, propping her chin on her palms in anticipation.

"But you don't even know what it is yet."

"Doesn't matter, I'm in."

For the rest of the day, they acted on his idea. Ditching the library, they leisurely strolled about the city, and he listened attentively as she played tourist guide. Then he amused her when he used her own words to describe the city to perfect strangers. He marveled at her light, airy personality and how she brought joy to everyone she met. At every turn there was something familiar about her that was drawing him closer to her.

As the sun dipped over the horizon, they found themselves sitting on the beach, sharing a bottle of wine.

"To the end of a perfect day," he said, raising his glass.

"To the perfect day!" she replied.

He looked down as he placed his hand on top of hers. When he looked up, her eyes told him what he was hoping for. He leaned forward and gently pressed his lips to hers.

"The perfect day," she said softly, kissing him again.

As the last rays of light faded, they snuggled together.

"Since we didn't get that research in today, what do you say we give it a go tomorrow?" she said.

"It's a date—I mean, it's research. It's… uh—"

She put her hand over his mouth and whispered into his ear. "It's okay. You can say it's a date. We've already kissed." She pulled her hand away and gave him a quick peck. "See there? We did it again."

"You'll bring the bagels?"

"Wouldn't be without 'em."

"Then it really is a date," he said and smiled.

At precisely nine thirty the next day, they began as they

had the day before, and like before, they whiled away the morning in the coffee shop, once again neglecting the library.

"Should we at least attempt to do some research today?" Paul asked.

"We probably should." She pursed her lips. "Yeah, let's do it." She jumped up and grabbed him by the hand. "Come on, if we don't go now, we'll end up drinking wine on the beach again."

The next two hours flew by as they romped around the library like a couple of flirty teenagers playing tag in and out of the bookshelves and generally annoying the students and serious researchers.

After being reprimanded by a stern-looking librarian for smooching in the world-history section, Paul suggested maybe they should *actually* do some real investigative work.

"Okay, let's spend the next hour and see who can come up with the most information," he said. "We'll make a contest out of it. Meet you back at this table in one hour, and we'll compare."

"You're on," she said, leaping out of her seat. Before he could stand, she had disappeared into the stacks.

At the end of the hour, he trotted back to their table where he found her with her nose deep into a large picture book. "Wow, look at you."

She scrunched her face. "I didn't find a lot, but I did get a few pieces of data with the help of the librarian. I also found this awesome coffee-table book of Beaufort that has a couple pics I thought you might find interesting. What did you find?"

He handed her a small paperback book, *The Most Influential Female Authors of the Twenty-first Century.* "I thought you'd like to see what company you'll be in one day."

"Aww, how sweet." She held it to her chest. "I'll read it tonight."

"Let's see what you got," he said.

She pulled a sheet of paper from the back of the picture book. "This info is from the Beaufort County tax department. It indicates the Willow Creek Plantation was approximately eleven hundred acres and was owned by a Mr. Braxton Winslow. Its plat shows that Willow Creek did, in fact, run through it, and the center of the land is located where the mall is now." She ran her finger over several lines. "It also states that most of it burnt down in August of 1864. I can't make out this next line. The ink is so faded, but it looks like it says something about Union troops. I guess they're the ones who burnt it."

"Good job. That's a lot more than I got." He sighed. "I just wish I could find some sort of ties with *someone* here—or anywhere, for that matter. It's like I'm floating in space without a lifeline to anyone."

"Can you come to dinner again tonight? I think it's time Momma pitches in."

"What do you mean?"

"I'm sure she knows something about Willow Creek she's not telling us. I wasn't kidding when I told you she was like a historian in this area. She doesn't talk about it with anybody. I mainly hear her rambling about it when's she's been drinking heavily."

"What! Your mother—"

"Binge drinks? Oh yeah. It can get out of hand too,

especially when it comes to Willow Creek. I've tried to help her, but she won't let me in. She won't go to a doctor or any kind of support group either."

"I didn't ask about this earlier because I didn't think it was my place, but what about your dad? Is he around at all?"

"She's never been married. Momma adopted me when I was two."

"Have you ever sought him out, or has he ever been in your life in any way?"

"No, according to her, she's never had contact with either of my biological parents." Her lip quivered. "To be honest, I don't have any feelings or desires to know my birth parents because she's been both a mom and dad. It's just that I have this hole in me…"

He threw his arms around her. "I understand completely. When you can't remember anything, it's like life has cheated you."

"Exactly," she said, hanging her head.

He put a finger under her chin and pulled her head up. "Don't worry. There's so much time to build more memories, and before long, you won't have room for all of them."

She put her head on his shoulder. "So will you come over tonight?"

"Of course."

When he arrived that evening, Hanna answered the door with a bourbon in hand accompanied by a big grin. "Hi, Paul, come on in. Elisabeth's taken on cooking responsibilities tonight, and I'm keeping her company."

"You've raised a talented daughter."

"That I have. Come on back, and we'll keep her company together. Can I get you some rum? I stocked up today, knowing you were coming."

"Thanks, Hanna, but I'm fine with some of your sweet iced tea."

"Suit yourself."

"Hey, you," Elisabeth said, sticking her head out from the kitchen. "Come on back."

"Wow, your mom's being super nice," he whispered.

"'Cause she's getting to know you."

"Here you go," Hanna said, rounding the corner with his tea. "Are you prepared for some of the best lasagna in Beaufort?"

"Yes, ma'am, I'm all about anything Italian, especially lasagna."

"You'll have to come by the cafeteria on Wednesday. That's my special Italian menu for the week. You can compare me against my young prodigy here."

Elisabeth twitched. "You guys hear a buzzing sound?"

"Oh, that's me," he said, pulling his cell phone out of his pocket, the frown on his face matching the disgusted tone of his voice. "Aw shoot, it's my old boss. I believe I'll deny this one."

"Don't you think you should take it? What if it's about your friend Zoey?" Elisabeth said.

"Probably going to get chewed out again, but hey— who cares? I'm already fired." He swiped the answer key. "Hello, this is Paul," he said, walking into the dining room.

Hanna nestled up to Elisabeth like a teenager preparing for a delicious round of gossip. "Why would he be calling after hours when he doesn't even work there anymore?" she whispered.

Elisabeth shrugged as she pulled the lasagna from the oven.

A minute passed in silence as the voice on the other end of the line held him captive. "You're kidding me," Paul blurted. "You can't be serious."

Elisabeth and Hanna's ears perked as the words filtered into the kitchen.

"Are you sure about this?" he said.

Elisabeth and Hanna stood with their heads frozen in the direction of the dining room.

"I mean, I had a blast writing it—especially the Spoon character—but do you think that's a good title? I guess it doesn't matter at this point." He paused. "I'm flabbergasted. And you're sure about this?"

A moment of silence passed when all they could hear was his pacing.

"What? How much did you say? Hang on a minute." He stuck his head around the corner, his hand covering his phone. "You're *not* going to believe this," he whispered toward Elisabeth. Then he disappeared for another minute before reemerging back into the kitchen with a huge grin on his face.

"What was *that* all about?" she asked.

He still had his phone in his hand, staring at it as if he had discovered it possessed magical powers. Transferring his gaze to Elisabeth, he said, "They-they want to publish my manuscript."

"They what?"

He looked back at his phone again. "My friend Zoey, the one I used to work with, gave my old boss a story I'd been working on, and they liked it. In fact, they liked it so much—they want to publish it!"

Elisabeth screamed as she threw her arms around his neck. "That's incredible, and how exciting!" She grabbed him by the hands and danced him in circles. "You truly are an author."

Hanna leaned against the counter with her arms folded, her face expressionless. "Paul, tell me one thing. Who, exactly, is Spoon?"

"He's one of the main characters," he said, continuing to dance with Elisabeth.

"What kind of character?"

"A young slave boy, during the Civil War. He's friends with the plantation owner's son."

She grabbed her bourbon, guzzled it, then immediately refilled it. "Really now? You truly believe that could happen?"

He stopped dancing. "Well, I—"

"Go on, tell me the plot of this here *story*."

"Oh, do tell," Elisabeth said, hopping onto a chair next to him.

"Don't you want to eat before the lasagna gets cold?" he said.

"We can wait," she said, bouncing up and down.

Hanna narrowed her eyes on him. "Yes, we can wait." Her words were monotone and direct.

"Since it's not finished, I'll give you the highlights. I can't believe they liked it enough to pay me an advance to finish it."

"Go on, give us the gist, but no spoilers," Elisabeth said. "I want to wait until I can read it in its entirety."

"It's about a plantation during the Civil War. The plantation owner's son befriends a slave boy named Spoon. Their friendship really takes off after Spoon gives him a diary in which he records everything. In fact, I use the diary to tell a large part of the story."

"Like a narration," Elisabeth chimed in.

"Exactly. Anyway, through a series of tragic events, the slave boy is disgraced and punished to the point of being maimed for life. The plantation owner's son believes he's to blame and runs off to war, leaving the plantation in the hands of a tyrannical uncle. From there, the estate spirals out of control and into poverty and ruin. That's as far as I've gotten."

"Where'd you get this story?" Hanna asked flatly.

"I made it up—it's pure fiction."

"You just made it up? Out of the blue? How does one do that, Paul?"

"Momma, he's a writer. That's what fiction writers do."

"Hanna, they told me I was constantly writing during the days I had amnesia, plus I was on a lot of morphine. I assume the combination is how it all came together. To be honest, I think it was all a dream."

"And you say you're going to finish *this* book?"

"Of course he is," Elisabeth said. "Weren't you listening?"

"I suppose you're looking for us to give you the rest of the story?" Hanna said.

"I'm not sure I understand."

"And this plantation in your book—it has a name?"

"Well, it didn't until recently," Paul said, turning to Elisabeth. "I'm going to call it—Willow Creek Plantation."

Hanna slammed her glass against the kitchen sink, cracking it and slicing her palm open. "By God, you will not!"

"Momma! *What* on earth is wrong with you!" Elisabeth said, jumping out of her chair.

"Did I say something wrong?" he asked.

Hanna slung a dishrag around her hand to stop the bleeding. With the other, she grabbed the bottle of bourbon and poured another glass. "I knew from the first time we met you were up to no good."

"What do you mean the first time you met?" Elisabeth said, helping her secure the makeshift bandage on her hand.

Sloshing her drink out of the glass, Hanna motioned at him. "I met this polecat at Tony's the same night you did. Like an old spider, he was snooping around, asking questions about Willow Creek Plantation, saying he had relatives here." She glared at him. "Tell the truth. You don't have a single descendant in these parts—do you?"

"I-I don't know. That's why I'm here. Honestly, Ms. Mitchell, I came here on a mission to find out some of my past."

"No, sir! You came looking to dig up the past for a fat, juicy New York bestseller, all at the sake of the people who—" She turned away, biting her lip and then swinging back toward him. "I think you need to leave."

"Momma, you're drunk. Please!"

"I may be drunk, but I'm not blind. I can see a snake coilin' up around my daughter's leg. You and your whole memory-loss thing too—saying you had it like my girl, just to get closer."

"I don't understand," he said, approaching her. "I was just—"

Elisabeth grabbed his arm and turned him to the door. "I'm sorry, Paul. Maybe we should leave."

"But I honestly—"

"Please," she whispered in his ear. She quickly led him out the front door, leaving Hanna pacing back and forth in the kitchen.

He clasped his hands together on top of his head. "What on earth just happened?" he said, walking in circles.

"I don't know, but you need to get in the van quickly," she said, pulling him to the curb.

"But I need to explain."

"Trust me, you need to leave *now*," she said, prodding him into the driver's seat.

"But—" He barely got the word out before she turned and ran back into the house.

The image of the beautiful girl behind the screen door was gone.

Chapter 21

Once back at the campground, he called Elisabeth only to be sent straight to her voicemail. After several more tries, he texted her.

Hours passed as he lay in his van, awaiting her call. As midnight approached and sleep began to overtake him, he convinced himself he was bound to wake to an early morning text at a minimum.

Unfortunately, by eight the next morning, he had not received either a call or text. Rationalizing he deserved an answer for being so severely ousted, he headed to her house until he remembered Zoey's advice to take it slow. But this was different. He was clueless as to his downfall and needed to know what he had done wrong. He hadn't lied about anything, and he had been an honorable and complete gentleman to both of them.

Halfway there, he began to realize whatever had caused the turn of events would only be exacerbated by his pursuit for answers. He would be pushing the boundaries of stalking, as Zoey had so adamantly warned him against. Instead, he decided to pull into the coffee shop he and Elisabeth had been frequenting and drown his woes in caffeine.

Although he'd become accustomed to brooding, this time was different. This time it involved the loss of something he had not yet gained. His inner voice perpetuated his self-loathing and his ongoing story that he didn't deserve to be happy. Whatever the reason, he turned inward, convinced now that he had indeed done something wrong.

Placing his phone onto the counter, he stared at it with contempt. Silently, it lay next to a pack of sweetener, taunting him. Unable to take it anymore, he grabbed it and began poking the keypad when two arms wrapped around him from behind. The scent of perfume electrified his senses as he realized he had been found just in time.

"I was praying you'd be here," Elisabeth said, spinning him around in the chair. "I'm so sorry about last night. I was going to call, but my mom hid my phone like I was a twelve-year-old."

"I thought... I—well... I don't know what I thought," he said, squeezing her tighter. "What did I do? Why was your mom so mad at me? Have I—"

"You haven't done anything. It's her," she said, sitting next to him. "For some reason, she believes you're here on some unholy mission."

"Unholy! Who does she think I am—the devil?"

"Remember I told you about how she can go dark when she's been drinking and how it seems to be related to Willow Creek?" She paused, and he nodded. "Well, last night was the perfect storm. She'd been drinking most of the afternoon, and when you brought up the plantation, that's what set her off." She hung her head. "I'm sorry, I never wanted you to see that side of her. She's struggled with this for as long as I can remember."

He put his arm around her. "Don't worry, everyone's got their problems. Lord knows I've got my bag of junk."

"I know," she said, "but sometimes I think she's losing her mind."

"Did she give you any indication of what I did wrong?"

"Not really. She just kept repeating that she thought you were up to no good, and you were going to ruin us."

"How or why would I want to do that? I just met her, and you know I'd never do anything to hurt you."

"And that's what makes it so strange."

"How was she this morning?"

"Still upset, but she didn't want to talk about it because she had a migraine. She actually called in sick."

"Does she have them a lot?"

"Enough to have to take medication."

"Maybe that has something to do with it." He hugged her again. "I'm sorry. I'm just glad you don't think I'm the devil."

"Of course not."

"Not to change the subject, but... I have to go back to New York. My boss said the book deal is contingent upon me working there under his supervision."

"Oh no! Can't you finish it here?"

"Yeah, I could, but—"

"But what?"

"Remember when I said we all have our problems?"

She looked at him sideways.

"Like your mom, I've been prone to drink too much." He put his hands up. "But I really believe I'm getting through that now." He stopped and looked off to the side then back to her. "We've only known each other such a short time, and I understand it's breaking all the rules to unload all my baggage this soon, but you have a right to know how far from perfect I am. I think you can already tell I have a lot of anxiety about my past. I'm not sure how you can cope with not knowing yours, but it's eating away at me—to the point of feeling like I'm going insane. That's why I came here—to find out who I am. It sounds absurd, but I'm just trying to find my way home."

He stopped and began counting the sound of the cheap clock on the wall ticking off the seconds as he waited for her to bolt for the door.

"Paul, I realize you have your issues—just like my mom—like that guy over in the booth talking to himself—like the waitress next to us with tearstains on her cheeks—and like I do." She took both his hands, brought them to her lips, and kissed them. "Everybody is broken in some way." She gazed into his eyes with a gentle intensity full of warmth and understanding. "I can't explain it, but I feel more connected to you in a way I've never experienced with anyone before. I don't know what you've been through and what you've dealt with, but you're right, I can sense your anxieties, and I can certainly appreciate your need to understand your past. I don't know how, but I do." She pulled closer. "But I'm not going to run away from it."

He leaned forward, touching his forehead to hers. "Well, if you're not going to run away from me, would you consider running to me?"

She pulled back. "What exactly are you talking about?"

"Well, I was wondering if you'd consider coming to see me while I finished the manuscript."

"To New York City? I've never been out of South Carolina."

"It'll be so much fun. I promise you'll have a blast.

You can be my muse."

"Who wouldn't want to be a muse to a soon-to-be famous author?" She threw her arms around his neck. "I'd love to come." She pulled away again. "But Momma. She'd never let me go."

"I thought about that. You don't have to come exactly when I leave. Don't you have a school break pretty soon?"

"In a few weeks, we'll have two weeks off."

"Perfect. You could tell her you and your girlfriend are going on a trip then."

"Yeah, that should work." She jumped up, chanting, "New—York—City—New—York—City—New—York—City!"

"I'll show you all around—the Statue of Liberty, the Met, Times Square. You're going to love it. And you'll get to meet Zoey—speaking of which, I need to call her."

She slapped her hand to the side of her head. "I've got so much to do between now and then. Oh, Paul, this is beyond exciting. I can't wait."

"Me neither." He pulled her to him and kissed her. "There's one other request I have. Would you mind watching the van for me?"

"Sure, but how will you get back?"

"They've already booked me a flight. Plus, I'm not sure the green machine would make it anyway."

"When's the flight?"

He frowned. "That's the thing—it's this evening."

"Why so soon? Do they have you on some sort of unrealistic deadline?"

"I think it's some sort of test to see if I'm committed to the project. I had to agree."

"No, I understand. You can't afford to look a gift horse

in the mouth."

"Ahhh, your first cliché," he said, hugging her.

"Ooops, my bad. How about, *Beggars can't be choosers*" she snickered.

He laughed. "How about you take me to the airport, and when you get home, check for flights. You know, *He who hesitates is lost.*"

"Oh my word, that's horrible. It doesn't even apply."

"Yes, it does."

"No, it doesn't."

"Yes, it does."

"Oh, stop it!" she said, playfully swatting his chest.

He grabbed her hand and kissed it. "Come on, let's get out of here. I only have a couple hours before I have to be in the air."

After a quick stroll along the beach, they headed to the airport. As they pulled in front of the terminal, Paul's phone rang.

"It's Zoey. I'll call her back once I'm checked in."

"Does she even know about the book deal?"

"I assume she does since she's the one who gave them the manuscript." He pulled his backpack from behind him and flung it over his shoulder.

Her head lowered.

"Don't worry, your break will be here before you know it," he said, brushing her hair from her eyes. "New York's going to fall in love with you." He kissed her again. "Wish me luck," he said, turning to go inside.

"Call me when you get in." she said waving him goodbye.

After making it through check-in and settling down at the gate, he called Zoey. It only took one ring for her to answer.

"Where've you been? I've been dying to talk to you."

"Why's that?" he said in his best deadpan delivery.

"You know, mister."

"Know what?"

"Your book deal!" she squealed.

"Oh, that."

"Shut up, you. Can you believe it though? I mean honestly—Greg in a deal with a guy he fired. Ain't life rich?"

"Zo, I want to thank you so—"

"Don't you worry, we'll talk royalty splits later. When will you be back?"

"Tonight. In fact, I'm at the airport now. My flight's scheduled to get in at six thirty. Can you come get me?"

"I'll be there with bells on. And Paul—you're not going to believe what I have for you."

"Well, tell me. I've got another twenty minutes before boarding."

"No way. This is too awesome to talk about over the phone. But trust me. This is *the best* present you'll ever get from me."

Chapter 22

Paul laughed out loud as he exited the plane to find Zoey wearing a chauffeur's hat, holding a large piece of cardboard with his name scrawled across it.

"Like my new occupation?" she yelled out, pushing her way through the crowd.

"Perfect. It's so you," he said, hugging her.

"Just test-driving—no pun intended—what it's going to be like having to cart you all over the place once you become a best-selling author."

"A half-written manuscript doesn't bode well for good prophesizing, but I appreciate your enthusiasm. Enough about the book, aren't you glad to see me?"

"I already hugged you," she cackled. "What more do you want?"

He dropped his bag and surprised her with another hug. "What I want is for you to realize how incredible you are, Zoey Antonelli. Everything you've done for me since the accident—helping to keep me sane, taking care of me, pushing me to go to Beaufort—not to mention submitting my book to Greg."

"Uh—okay," she said, not knowing how to respond to

her elevated level of appreciation.

"How about you? How's the job going?"

"I'm fine, and the job is… well, you know—it's a job. But what I want is to know about Miss Dixie Chick."

"Elisabeth?"

"Yes, Elisabeth!" she said, tucking her arm under his. "Tell me everything."

As they dodged in and out of the relentless stream of hurried travelers, he regaled her with his stories of Beaufort. With the exception of his encounters with Hanna, he left nothing out.

When they were in her car, he talked at length about Elisabeth and how his feelings for her had grown. "Zo, you wouldn't believe how much we have in common. But what's so bizarre—and I don't mean that in a weird way, but more in a supernatural way—is she understands me. I can't put my finger on it, but it's—"

"Love?"

"Love? What? Why, I don't—"

"You're in love, Pauly. Admit it."

"But you told me to take it slow. That's what I'm doing."

"Yeah, I said that, but love doesn't always work the same way. Everyone experiences it differently, it doesn't necessarily have to move at the same pace. All I was saying was don't scare her off. If she's into you, then, heck, full steam ahead."

He fidgeted in his seat. "Well, I don't know about all that, but I can't wait for you to meet her."

"You know what's funny? We're almost to your apartment, and you haven't asked me once to stop and get a drink."

"Because I don't feel like it."

"Well, hold on to that thought," she said as they pulled up to his brownstone, "because what you're about to behold is going to make you want to celebrate."

"Ta—da!" she said, flinging his apartment door open.

He dropped his bags. The disastrous mess he had left behind was now all sparkles and sunshine. The clutter was gone. As a result of her organizational skills, his little hovel appeared twice as big as before. All the dishes were clean, nothing was on the floor, and even some of the furniture had been rearranged.

"You did all this?" he said, spreading his arms apart while turning in a circle.

"I couldn't help myself," she squealed. "You like it?"

"I most certainly do. This does call for a celebration."

"Hold on. I'm glad you like it, but this isn't what we need to jump up and down about."

"Ohhh, the book deal."

"Nope—not it either," she said, motioning him to the couch while reaching behind the coffee table. "You need to sit for this."

No sooner was he seated than she was presenting him with a blue-and-tan-plaid flannel shirt, folded neatly into a rectangle with the sleeves wrapped into a stumpy bow.

"Oh... well... okay. I see you found my shirt," he snickered.

"Unfold it." Her eyes were as wide as a child's on Christmas morning. Her whole body was shaking. "Look what's inside."

"Let me guess—a T-shirt."

"Come on, come on," she said, pushing it at him.

"Okay already," he said, sliding a black book out of

the flannel facade.

She bit her lip as she watched him inspect the back and then the spine.

"This looks really old." He pulled it to his nose and inhaled, the musty smell of old leather and aged parchment confirming it.

She monitored his eyes as he inspected the cover.

He flipped to the first page, spending a minute, scanning it top to bottom. "What is this?"

She clapped. "It's a diary!"

"A diary? Where'd it come from?"

"You! It was in your coat."

"What coat?"

"Your old grey coat. The one you gave me that I ended up taking to my friend's consignment shop. It was inside the lining."

"What?"

"Apparently there was a hole in one of the pockets, and it fell inside. My friend was about to clean it and discovered it inside the bottom hem." She twirled around. "How cool is that?"

He continued his inspection, rotating it from side to side.

"Did you see the date on the inside back cover?"

He flipped the back open. "Are you kidding me?" He squinted as he read aloud. "Pettigrew and Jones Publishing, 1845. Holy cow!"

She continued clapping. "Now go to the front and read."

He gingerly pulled the cover open, respecting the artifact's age, his gaze engrossed by the page. Slowly his eyes traced across the first sentence, then faster to the second, then faster still to the third and fourth. In a moment, he was rifling through the pages, devouring every line. His jaw hung open as each word resonated with him. Midway through, he dropped it to his lap and looked up at her, his mouth agape.

She stood motionless, her hands clasped together under her chin.

"Do you realize what this is?"

She nodded.

"This is my book—and more! Everything in my manuscript—*everything*—is here but in more detail."

He turned back to the miracle that lay in his palms and continued reading, transfixed by each word, mesmerized by the phenomenon of how they made it to his manuscript. After thirty minutes, a tap on his shoulder pulled him out of his trance.

"I've gotta go finish an article that's due tomorrow morning. Are you going to be alright?"

He gazed at her as if being awakened from a dream. "Yeah, of course," he said, coming back to the reality that lay outside the diary. "I can't believe this, can you?"

"Pretty incredible."

"I even mention a diary in my manuscript. Do you remember reading that?"

"Yeah. It's kinda spooky."

"It most certainly is," he said, rubbing his chin.

She picked up her purse. "Okay, I really gotta go now. I'll call you tomorrow, okay?"

He continued staring at the book. "Yeah—that'll be good—call tomorrow," he said in a robotic cadence. As soon as the door shut behind her, he grabbed his phone and texted Elisabeth, *Do NOT make plane reservations.*

Everything is fine but I'm on my way back. Paul.

He tossed his phone aside and opened the diary again, marveling at the quality of the paper and thinking about what might have caused each blemish and stain. He tried to imagine how they got there. He daydreamed of the author penning each word. Slowly, he flipped through the pages one by one. Two-thirds of the way through, he came to a hole that had been cut through to the back cover. A small crust of dirt melded them together. He ran his finger around its jagged edges. Why would anyone cut a hole in the pages of a diary? Placing it aside, he fell asleep, dreaming of Beaufort.

Chapter 23

When he spotted his green van coming down the terminal lane with Elisabeth behind the wheel, his heart jumped.

"Hey, stranger!" she said, pulling alongside the curb.

He tossed his backpack onto the rear seat and slid in beside her. "I just couldn't stay away," he said with a smile and lingering kiss. "Thanks for picking me up."

"Of course," she said.

"I know it's crazy that I'm already back, but something's happened."

"Yeah, I'm glad you're back and that you said everything was fine but why the quick turnaround?"

"Everything is actually more than fine. I just need to see Hanna as soon as possible."

"I don't think that's a good idea."

"Seriously, she's going to want to see me." He placed his hand on her knee. "I'll tell you all about it on the way back. One other thing though. I remember there being some antique stores around town, but are there any that carry old books?"

"Yeah, there's one that's pretty reputable. In fact, that's his specialty. He's got some dating back to the Revolutionary War."

"Great. Can we stop by before we go see your mom?"

"Sure. She should be finished with her shift by the time we get back, but Paul, I don't think seeing her right now is wise. She's liable to pull out her pistol if she sees you again—especially since I told her you'd already left."

His eyebrows rose. "Your mom's *packing a gun*?"

"That's why I wanted you to leave so quick the other night."

He leaned over the backseat and grabbed his backpack. "When you see this, you're going to change your mind." He reached in and pulled out a bubble-wrapped package containing the diary.

After peeling the wrapping away, he held it out in front of the steering wheel. "This is why we're going to the bookstore. This black book is also why your mom's going to be more than happy to see me."

The hour-long commute to Beaufort flew by as Paul detailed everything about the diary—how it had been lost, where it was found, and, more importantly, what its contents revealed. She was so enthralled, she almost swerved off the road several times as she tried processing the bizarre tale.

By the time they arrived at the bookstore, she was shaking. "This is too strange." She jumped out of the van and ran to the entrance, waving him in. "Hurry, they close in fifteen minutes."

A tiny bell above the door welcomed them in with a friendly jingle while the smell of musty paperbacks, leather, and incense greeted them. Books of all shapes and sizes occupied every nook and cranny. Five aisles of old wooden bins lined the length of the store, each filled with a specific genre of book along with plaques containing information about their contents.

In the back corner, a little old man in tiny spectacles stood hunched over a large ledger. "May I help you?" he said as he scribbled away.

"Yes, sir," Elisabeth said, motioning Paul toward her. "My friend has a book he'd like you to take a look at."

"What you got, sonny?"

Paul pulled out his diary and placed it on the counter.

The old man looked up from his glasses. "You understand this is a *bookstore*, not a *diary shop*, don't ya?"

"Oh, I just assumed—"

"Ahhh, gotcha," he said, slapping his ledger closed. "Just kidding, young fella, a diary's a book too. Let me take a looky." He picked it up as if holding a relic, then slowly turned it side to side, inspecting every millimeter and paying particular attention to the spine. "Cover's in pretty good shape." He wiped the counter with his sleeve then carefully placed it facedown and opened the back cover. "Hmmm. Interesting." He turned it back over, opened the front cover, and slowly proceeded through the pages. Every so often, he would stop to examine the text with an oversized magnifying glass.

Paul tapped his fingers together. "So, what do you—"

"Patience, young man."

The doorbell jingled as a middle-aged couple entered.

"Sorry, we're closed," he projected his voice through the aisles.

"Do you want us to leave now?" asked Elisabeth.

"Oh no. I'm not finished yet." He continued scrutinizing each page. "It's not often I get to see something like this."

Paul mouthed to Elisabeth, "I told you."

"Well, sir," the old man said, laying his glasses on the counter, "what you have here is a hundred percent authentic. The publishing house was a major player during the Civil War era. In addition to books, they also published a lot of diaries during that time."

"How come?" she asked.

"Boys were going off to war, wives and girlfriends were left at home—they all wanted to put their experiences and emotions on paper." He tapped his finger on the diary. "Like the fellow who owned this one here." He smiled. "Pretty good writer too." He turned it over for one last look at the back cover. "Would you like to sell it?"

"Oh no. I just wanted to see if it was authentic."

"I'm sorry if we wasted your time, sir," Elisabeth said. "Can we pay you for your evaluation?"

"No, no, this is fun for me. I enjoy stepping back in time with pieces like this. Do you at least want to find out how much it's worth?"

Paul pursed his lips. "I know it wouldn't hurt, but I'd rather not. At this point, it's invaluable to me."

"I understand. Sentimental value is priceless. If it weren't for the hole in the back and the bloodstains, it would be worth more than you think."

"What bloodstains?"

The man reopened it and thumbed through the pages, pointing out several blotchy areas. "I can't say for sure, but based on the coloration and research I've done in the past, that's what my guess would be."

"I thought those might be coffee or tea stains."

The old man shrugged. "Could be that too," he chuckled.

Paul shook his hand. "Thank you for your time. We'll

definitely be back."

"And next time," Elisabeth said, as they headed out the door, "I promise we'll buy something."

The drive to Elisabeth's house was a mixed bag of excitement and anxiety. Paul was giddy about the thought of showing Hanna the diary. At the same time, Elisabeth shuddered at the possibility of one of her mother's mood swings.

As the van pulled into the driveway, she leaned over and put her hand on his arm. "I know you're excited, but would you mind if I start the conversation?"

"That's a good idea."

Elisabeth's legs grew weaker as she led him to the front door. "Momma? You home?" she said through the screen door.

"In here, sweetie."

"Remember, I'll start," she whispered as they made their way into the living room.

A broom whisked its way around the corner and into the living room, followed by Hanna, head down, concentrating on the dust bunnies she was pushing into a pile. "This place gets so dusty, I thought I'd do a little spring cleaning." She looked up. "You know a clean house is—" Her eyes flashed past Elisabeth and on to Paul, her chest rising and falling as she prepared for the inevitable confrontation.

"Momma, before you say anything, you need to listen. Paul has—"

The broom fell from Hanna's hand as she dropped to her knees and dug into the coffee table's bottom drawer. "You told me he had left," she snarled.

"Yes, ma'am, I did—but—there's a reason he's back. A good reason." She turned to him. "Tell her."

"Ms. Mitchell, I have something I want to show you that'll help you see I'm not out to do any harm."

"Where is it?" she muttered to herself, flinging things out of the drawer.

"Show her, Paul, before she—"

"I have the diary!" he blurted.

She continued digging.

"Ms. Mitchell," he said, his voice rising, "I—have—the—diary."

She stopped and looked up at him with a blank stare.

"I have *the* diary," he said, holding it out to her as if presenting a gift to a queen.

"The diary? You mean the diary you mentioned in your book?"

"Yes, ma'am." He placed it on the coffee table in front of her. "I hope you'll have an open mind."

She leaned forward, hovering over the book like a bird of prey observing its next meal. "You say this is it?" She slowly ran her finger over the jagged carving of the word *diary* on the cover.

"It is."

She placed one hand over her heart. With the other, she opened the cover.

Minutes passed as she stared at the page, studying every word. She turned and looked up at them without expression then returned to the book, flipping the page, repeating the process again and again.

Paul and Elisabeth watched as her fury smoldered with every new page. Occasionally she would cover her mouth with her hand, repressing a reaction to what she had read.

Most noticeable was how her hand trembled as it traced over each line. The grandfather clock in the hallway slowly ticked away the passing hour as she continued absorbing everything the book offered. When she got to the section of pages with the hole in them, she rolled her shoulders.

"Momma, look at the inside cover."

She flipped over the remaining blank pages, clutching her chest with both hands and sighing as she silently read the inscription.

"Can you believe it, Momma? That diary was printed in 1845"

Hanna wrung her hands. "Where'd you find this, Paul?"

"It was in the lining of the coat I was wearing when the cab hit me."

"Oh my," she said, placing her hand over her forehead, "I feel a migraine coming on. Elisabeth, I'm out of my pills. Can you run to the pharmacy and pick up my prescription?"

"Sure."

"Paul, would you go with her? It's just two blocks away."

"Sure."

The moment they stepped outside, Hanna rushed to her bedroom with the diary in hand. She pulled a box of papers from under her bed and stretched the most tattered one out next to the last page of the diary. She gasped. With one hand on the diary, she scrolled over the inscription *To Mase, yor frend Jeziah C.* With the other hand, she scrolled across the weathered page, comparing each letter to those in the diary. An identical match.

Fifteen minutes later, Elisabeth and Paul returned to

find Hanna standing next to the coffee table.

"Momma, the pharmacist said he just filled your prescription last week. Did you forget?"

"Oh, for heaven sakes, I guess I did. I'm sorry to make you run off like that. I'm feeling better now anyway."

Elisabeth looked at Paul with a raised eyebrow.

"Did you look at the diary anymore?" he said eagerly.

"A little."

"What do you think about the stained pages? The book dealer believes it's blood."

"What? Whose blood?"

"I have no idea."

Hanna twisted her head to him with the same narrowed glare she had given him upon his arrival. "Are you telling me the whole truth? This diary was on you, and you don't know how it got there? And it's got blood on it!" She put her fingers to her temple and rubbed. She turned back to him. "I'm sorry, I don't believe that's possible."

Paul looked at her quizzically. "But doesn't this diary at least point to something? Why would I have it? I mean—I can't explain how I have it or why the notes I made match as they do, but it's got to mean something, right?"

"Something, yes, but it's not adding up to me. I can't wrap my mind around the assumption that just because you have it means you're a relative of the Winslows. It's all too fishy."

"I don't understand, Hanna. The diary aside, I'm just asking for your help. The only reason I'm here is—" He glanced at Elisabeth. "*One* of the reasons, I mean, is to help piece together a part of my past." He hesitated. "It's actually at the request of my doctor and for my sanity. I promise you, I do *not* have any hidden agenda—only that one. Won't you please—"

She threw up her hand. "Stop!" She sighed and closed her eyes, then rubbed the sides of her head with both hands.

"Hanna, please. I get you don't want to—"

"I said, stop," she said in a gravely whisper, her eyes still closed. "I have my reasons. Don't ask me again. Elisabeth, hand me that glass of water off the end table."

Elisabeth handed her the glass.

"I'm sorry, but my migraine has come back. I'm going to take my medicine then lie down." She turned and walked toward her room.

"But, Ms. Mitchell—pleeeease."

Elisabeth shook her head for him to dispense with his pleas.

Hanna stopped at her bedroom door, grimacing from the throbbing pain shooting through her brain, coupled with the growing frustrations of Paul's nagging. "Alright," she said through clenched teeth, "I can tell you this much. You may indeed have one relative here. If you can get him to talk—then by all means, have at him."

"Wait! Who're you talking about?" he called after her.

As she was about to close the door, she said over her shoulder, "Judge Joseph. Elisabeth knows him." The door shut.

Chapter 24

Judge Joseph. The name was beyond vague. Paul started toward Hanna's bedroom until Elisabeth seized him by the arm.

"Let her be."

"But she's throwing out riddles that need answers."

"Please wait. I know who she's talking about."

His attention flashed back to her. "Who is he? Where's he live? What's he do?"

She put her arm under his and led him to the front porch. As soon as they were outside, she locked the door.

"Why'd you do that?"

"Paul, I think my mother is losing it." She tapped her fingers together rapidly. "Seriously, she's declining right before my eyes. She used to be so sweet, but anytime anything about Willow Creek comes up, or she sees you, she becomes unhinged." She began to weep.

He wrapped his arms around her. "Please don't cry. It'll be alright." He brushed her hair back, and his voice softened. "I guess the best thing for me to do is just leave."

"And go where?"

"Back to New York."

"No, please don't say that." She squeezed him tight. "Please don't go."

"But if I'm having this effect on your mother, it's not healthy—not for her and not for you."

"Don't worry about me. I'll be more unhappy if you go. And whatever Momma's going through is going to keep happening anyway. I honestly believe the migraines have something to do with it." She looked down as she processed her thoughts. "I need to take you someplace."

"Where?"

"To see Judge Joseph," she said as she walked to the van. "Come on. We need to head to the Tiki Bar."

"Now we're talking!" he said, jumping behind the wheel.

Twenty minutes later, they pulled into the barren parking lot of the Willow Creek Mall.

"Don't park in the front." She pointed to a far corner guarded by a large trash dumpster. "We need to go behind the building."

The sparsely lit parking lot grew dimmer as the van rounded the dumpster. A single floodlight hung on each corner of the building's backside, illuminating one lane of broken pavement. From the cracked edges of the road to the creek that lay off in the distance, a film of light rolled across two acres of an unkempt field full of weeds, briars, and small saplings.

"Go to the middle of the building and park where there's not much light."

"Does he work here?" he asked as the van came to a stop.

"No. Just follow me," she whispered. "And be quiet. This part of town has gangs, and they hang out around here doing drug deals and whatever else gangs do."

"Hold on," he said, reaching into the backseat and producing a tire wrench.

"Good idea." Taking him by the hand, she led him into the field and toward the creek. The farther they went, the thicker the brush became, and the darker it got. The briars ripped at their clothing, attempting to keep them from passing.

"Hold on a minute. I'm stuck," he said, grappling with a throng of briars wrapped around his legs. "Where exactly are we going?"

She pointed straight ahead. The fraction of light making its way across the field hinted at a small building.

"Is he some sort of hermit?"

"Shhhh. Remember the gangs."

He tightened his grip on the tire wrench.

As they made their way to within thirty yards, she pulled out her cell phone and turned on the flashlight app. The light was strong enough to reveal three partial stone walls surrounded by overgrown bushes, vines, and more briars.

"Is this where he was supposed to be?" he whispered, barely audible over the creek's rushing water.

"No need to whisper anymore," she said.

"Doesn't look like anybody's been here in ages. Are you sure this is where he lived?"

"I'm not sure who lived here. I don't even know what kind of building this was."

"Then why are we—"

"Over here," she said, pushing through the brush to the opposite side of the decrepit structure. "There," she pointed.

A second later, he was standing beside her, following the line of her index finger ten yards ahead of them. He walked past her to a decaying granite obelisk, placing his palm against the top of the chest-high monument then slowly moving it downward until he felt the chiseled etchings identifying the remains of the person who lay beneath. He pulled the ivy away.

As she shined the light over his shoulders, he read the inscriptions aloud. "In Memory of Joseph Tiberius Winslow, August 30, 1804, to April 20, 1863."

"I don't understand. Is this a joke? Why would your mother want to introduce me to a dead guy?"

"Because he's the closest thing to a potential descendant of the plantation that exists. The guy under this rock was the brother of the owner of Willow Creek. According to Momma, the Yankees burnt the plantation and erased everything else they could about the family, which is why you can't find anything out about them. She's convinced this will prove your digging for information is at a dead end, and you'll leave." She wrung her hands.

"What's wrong?"

"She-she told me not to tell you *anything* else."

"But what's to hide?"

"It's just that I promised I wouldn't say anything, and I've never lied to her. But you have a right to know."

"Please, Elisabeth, you of all people understand I need to know as much as I can."

She paced back and forth, then stopped, walked to the gravestone, and placed her hand on it. "Apparently, we're connected to him and the plantation."

The noisy creek stilled. All sound ceased as his focus fell on her. "How?"

"We're descendants of slaves there—that's how."

He stepped back. "That would explain why she knows more about it than what exists publicly. But why is she so hostile to me and offended that I want to learn more? Why won't she help me?"

"The other night after you left—the night she hid my cell phone—we had a huge argument. I told her she needed to tell me exactly why she was treating you the way she was. If she didn't, I was going to leave."

"What did she say?"

"That if you knew what happened at the plantation, you could use it against us. She thinks you're some kind of investigative journalist from the *Chronicle* looking for a salacious true-life story to wrap a book around."

"What about the diary?"

"She believes that's how you got the idea for the book in the first place. She's convinced you found it in a bookstore someplace then did research which led you here. She thinks you're bringing it up now because you found out we're connected to the plantation and can help provide the missing pieces to what went on there. She wouldn't say what it was exactly, but something terrible happened that destroyed the lives of everyone who lived there for generations—even the slaves."

He closed his eyes as he tried putting the pieces of Hanna's paranoia together. "You're telling me your mother believes that, if I write this story, it's going to uncover something on your family that's going to ruin you."

"Yes."

"Elisabeth, I don't want to be invasive, but can you tell me how your mom can afford such a gorgeous house in the most expensive part of the city?"

236

"She says it's the result of good investments."

"In the stock market or where?"

She shrugged. "Just investments, she says."

"I still don't understand why any story could do your family harm. With all due respect to your mom and your ancestors, I've got to keep asking these types of questions."

"I know you do. I just don't think anything else is going to surface. Unless the good Judge resurrects, I'm afraid my mother's right—it's all a dead end—literally."

"Why do you call him Judge?"

"That's what Momma said he was."

Paul rubbed the back of his neck. A moment later he was on his hands and knees, scraping away weeds from the base of the tombstone. He clawed up a handful of dirt and stared at it. Slowly his fingers closed around the soil, squeezing it until his hand shook.

"Are you okay?" she said, wrapping her hands around his fist.

Her touch triggered him to loosen his grip, letting its contents fall back to earth. "I'm fine." He turned back to the grave. "Yeah," he said with a growing smile. "Yeah, I'm good—really good." He put his arm around her. "Come on, let's get out of here."

As they turned and walked back through the field, he shouted over his shoulder, "We'll be seeing you, Judge."

Chapter 25

The following day, Elisabeth went about her regular school schedule, calling Paul between classes just to chat. "You sound out of breath," she said as he answered her last call.

"Just getting in a workout," he grunted.

"Working on your abs? A girl loves some abs."

"Everything," he huffed. "I'm working on parts I've never worked on before."

"Well, don't forget those abs."

"After dinner, will you do something for me?" he asked.

"Depends on those abs."

"Seriously now. Just say you will, and you'll have an open mind about it—please."

"You know I will. But why so mysterious?"

"Let's call it payback for last night's little adventure. I promise it'll be worth it.

"I guess I owe you one."

"Great, I'll pick you up at eight. Oh, and wear something comfortable—jeans and tennis shoes. Hiking boots would be even better."

That evening he treated her to a full-on crab fest at one of Beaufort's famous seafood houses. When they thought no one was watching, they playfully flipped shrimp at one another then dove into a bucket of crabs. With their miniature sledgehammers, they whacked away at the clawed delicacies, laughing all the while as pieces of shells and tender meat bounced off their tiny bibs.

"Now I know why you asked me to dress this way." After several more rounds of crab whacking and shrimp tosses, Elisabeth finished with a toast. "Here's to futures without pasts," she said, raising her glass.

"Great toast. To add to that, in preparation for our evening still ahead, here's to being open-minded."

"Oh no," she feigned, "I have to be open-minded?"

"For tonight to be successful, the answer is a solid yes. Remember the famous Frank Zappa who so eloquently put it, 'A mind is like a parachute. It doesn't work if it's not open'?"

"Oh joy, we're going night skydiving," she giggled.

"No more wine for this one," he said, motioning the waiter for the check.

As they walked to his van, he turned her around and pressed into her with a long, slow kiss. "Elisabeth, I'm not sure what this journey is all about or where it will take us, but I'm glad we're on it together."

She wrapped her arms around his neck, kissed his ear, and ended with the softest of kisses to his lips.

It was everything he could do to simmer himself down for the task ahead. "You ready?" he asked.

"Let's do this—this whatever." She smiled.

As they drove out of the parking lot, she leaned over and put her head on his shoulder. "You're still not going to tell me where we're going?"

"Nope."

She bounced in her seat. "I love surprises."

A few minutes later, they were pulling into the same desolate parking lot as the night before. Elisabeth looked around, wondering if he had inadvertently taken a wrong turn. "Where're we going?"

"Just trust me," he said as they pulled to the back of the mall.

"Paul, seriously, *what* are we doing?"

After stopping in the same spot, he walked around and opened her door. "Last night opened my eyes to what I needed to do." He grabbed her by the hands. "Please, just come with me. I have something to show you."

Shaking her head, she followed him back through the field and to the decaying building. As they rounded the corner to the tombstone, she could barely make out what appeared to be a pile of tools lying next to a tarp that had been spread out in front of the grave.

"What's all this?"

He picked up a small lantern, placed it at the base of the gravestone, and flicked it on. For a moment, it appeared as if they had come across a modern-day grave robbery in progress. On the ground lay a pickax, a shovel, a pair of work gloves, and a heap of empty water bottles.

"Don't tell me what's under that tarp. Tell me you haven't—"

He pulled it away, revealing a six-foot rectangular hole roughly five feet deep.

"Oh, my God. You didn't," she said, covering her mouth. "Paul, how could you?"

"How couldn't I? It's the only way."

"Only way to what? Get thrown in jail?" She stepped back as she prepared to run. "This is what you were doing when I called today?"

"Listen to me," he said, grabbing her. "I realized last night there was only one way I could prove it to your mother. Trust me, Elisabeth, this is it."

"Is what? I don't understand," she said, squirming to break free.

"If I can get a sample of Winslow's remains, I can match them against my DNA. If there's a match, it'll prove I'm a descendant. I'll have my answers and your mother will know I'm not a threat. And how awesome will it be that our pasts are connected in such a way?"

"How's that?" she asked, her voice rising. "My ancestors were slaves to yours! Really, Paul?"

"Oh no, I-I didn't mean it that way," he pleaded. "I'm so sorry." He turned away. "I'm such an idiot," he said, lowering his chin.

She paused for a minute, letting only the sounds of toads and crickets occupy the night. Another minute passed as she paced back and forth, finally stopping in front of him. "Look at me." She placed her palms on his cheeks and lifted his head. "That was a long time ago. Everyone deserves a past. If this helps you find it, then I guess we have to go through with it."

He took her into his arms and whispered into her ear, "I think I'm falling in—"

She pulled back and held him at arm's length, staring at him. "You're falling in—what?"

"I-I mean..." he stammered, wiping his forehead, "I mean, I think I need to fall back into this hole and get the job done. Yeah, I need to get on with this, don't I?"

She lifted an eyebrow. "Well, okay, what do you need me to do?"

He grabbed a shovel, jumped into the hole, then reached up and handed her his cell phone. "Just record me."

"What for? To show the police?"

"To show your mom I didn't stage any of this. Keep an eye out for anybody while you're at it."

Fifteen minutes later, the thrust of his shovel produced a welcomed clink. The sound of metal against metal. He knelt and swiped dirt away from a corroded piece of brass.

"I think we're here!" Paul exclaimed.

"What do you mean?"

"I'm about six feet down, which is where they normally bury folks, and I just found what I think is a buckle. If there's anything left of him it's at this level." He handed it up to her.

"I believe you're right," she said rubbing her hand across its jagged edges. "It's got an indention in the frame where that little prongy thing goes."

"Can you hand me the light. I've got to dig by hand and need to see what's what."

She lowered the lantern to him then sat and crossed her legs patiently waiting while he continued his ghoulish endeavor. As she bided her time, her attention turned out to the field where they had come. Suddenly every sound filled her with dread. Every cricket's chirp, snap of a twig or rustling of leaves conjured images of either the police or worse, a gang member. Twenty minutes passed. She began biting her nails when suddenly Paul jumped up like a jack-in-the-box causing her to tumble backwards.

"I've got it!" he shouted.

"Got what?"

"They didn't decay."

"What didn't?"

"Here, take these," he said handing her six dirty chicklet sized objects. He climbed out of the hole.

"Yuck—Are these his teeth?" she said, rocking back on her heels.

"Yes indeed," he said. "These should be perfect!"

By the time he covered the grave and got all the tools back to the car, it was close to ten o'clock. "Is your mom still awake?"

"She should be. It's her night to watch the TV shows she recorded from the week."

"I'm sure she'll be happy to forego them tonight," he said. "We've got a better show lined up."

On their way back, Elisabeth expressed her concerns about her mother's reaction. "I pray she hasn't been drinking. Lord knows what she'll do when we present this to her."

Stepping out of the van, they could hear the television from inside.

Elisabeth eased her way into the living room. "Hey, Momma," she said sheepishly.

"Hi, honey. You want to watch a show with me? I made a bowl of popcorn."

A second later, Paul entered, carrying Joseph Winslow's teeth wrapped in a dirty bath towel.

Upon seeing him, Hanna's eyes glared red. "You're like a bad boomerang that keeps coming back."

Elisabeth found the remote and turned off the TV. "Momma, you need to hear him out."

Hanna sat stone-faced, arms crossed, and fuming.

Paul's stomach churned. This was one presentation he

knew he had to nail. "Hanna, the first thing I want you to know is that I completely understand. I respect your privacy and would never do anything to harm you or your family. I know I have to prove myself to you, and I realize it sounds absurd when I tell you I think I may have relatives from Willow Creek. In my heart of hearts, though, I honestly believe it may be possible. My hope is you'll allow me to try one more time to convince you of all this." He glanced at Elisabeth, then back to her. "If I can't prove it, I promise I'll go back to New York, I won't finish the book, and I'll never return."

"Paul!" Elisabeth slapped him on the shoulder. "We never talked about that."

He looked at her. His eyes were gentle and warm. "I'm sorry. I would never be able to live with myself if I tore you two apart."

Hanna unfolded her arms and stood. "You'd really do that? You'd sacrifice your feelings for the sake of my family?"

He nodded.

She placed her hands on her hips. "So then, what is it you have to say?"

He shifted his weight while fidgeting with his artifact. "We've been to Joseph Winslow's grave." He paused as he watched her face grow flush. "Now this is where I pray you'll be open-minded. The only way I could think to prove I'm related was through DNA."

Her eyes narrowed.

He lifted the towel. "These teeth are from Joseph Winslow. We dug them up this evening. If they test—"

Hanna stumbled back into her chair, clutching her chest. "You've brought the devil into this house. Get them out!" She pointed to the door. "Get them out!"

"But, Hanna—"

"I said, get—them—out!"

"Take them outside," Elisabeth said, pulling him to the door. "Put them on the front porch."

"Okay, okay." He opened the door and placed them on the front steps. When he returned, Hanna was bent over, wheezing. Elisabeth slapped an inhaler into her palm, instructing her to take a puff immediately.

A minute later, Hanna's breathing had turned to a series of long deep inhales and exhales. She glared up at him. "I know what you're going to ask, and if I agree, this is going to be the end of it. Are we clear?"

"Yes, ma'am."

"You want a DNA match with you and those—those things outside. Is that correct?"

"That's right."

"And you'll abide by what you told me earlier?"

"Yes."

"Well then, Elisabeth, go into my room and get my black bag." She turned to him. "And you go find a box and place those things in it—but do *not* bring it back in here. Put it in the backseat of my car along with the diary. Then both of you meet me in the kitchen."

"But why the diary—"

"No buts. Just do it."

"Yes, ma'am."

Several minutes later, the three stood in the kitchen. Elisabeth pulled out a syringe and an empty vial from the black bag and laid them on the table.

Hanna tapped him on the right forearm. "Roll up your

sleeve."

"Wait, you're not a medical person," he said. "How can you—"

"You want to do this or not?"

"Well, yes," he said, pulling his sleeve above his elbow, "but shouldn't we get someone who knows what they're doing?"

"I've had practice," she said, wrapping an oversized rubber band around his bicep then slapping him on the vein.

"Ouch!" he screeched as the needle penetrated his arm.

Hanna unwrapped the rubber band, releasing the blood into the vial. She grinned at him, obviously delighting in his discomfort. "Hold still, or we'll have to do this again."

"Is it over?" Elisabeth said, peeking through her fingers.

"All done," Hanna smirked. "Can you believe that's my first time?"

"Yes, I can," he said, rubbing his arm. "How are you going to get the test done?"

"Dr. Adams will handle it for me. It should be two or three days."

"Momma used to date Dr. Adams. He's still smitten with her. He'll do anything for her, won't he, Momma?"

"We'll see." Hanna tapped the top of the vial. "Oh, and Paul?" she said with a raised eyebrow. "Dr. Adams is pretty thorough with all his testing, so expect a drug screening to come with it."

Chapter 26

Over the next couple days, Elisabeth continued to see Paul away from her home. Hanna remained suspicious of him, and he was reluctant to venture any more visits until the DNA results came in.

On the third day, he spent the morning in the library, teaching her how to effectively replace weak adverbs with strong verbs and various other writing techniques. After a quick lunch, he dropped her off with the promise to call her later. He hadn't gotten to the end of the block yet when his phone rang.

"Paul, there's something wrong with Momma. Can you come back?"

Within less than a minute, he was meeting her back on the front lawn.

"What's wrong?"

"I don't know. She's just sitting in her room, staring at a picture. I keep calling her name, but she's not responding."

Through the cracked door, he could see she was doing just as Elisabeth had said. Her body was upright and sitting motionless on the edge of the bed. Her head was bent down, gazing into her lap. As they got closer, he could see her eyes were puffy and red, the tracks of dried tears steaked down her cheeks.

"Momma, can you hear me?"

"Should I say something?" he whispered.

Elisabeth nodded.

"Hanna—Ms. Mitchell, it's me—Paul."

Still no response. He leaned forward to see that the picture that held her transfixed was her favorite one from the hallway, the one of black and white people standing with their arms around each other.

He slowly reached over and took the edge of the picture with his thumb and forefinger. "Hanna," he said, pulling it away, "can you hear me?"

She jerked the picture back against her chest, still gazing into her lap.

"Should we call a doctor?" Elisabeth asked.

"I'm not sure," he said, transferring his focus to the small stack of papers that had been underneath it. Across the top, the words *DNA Test Results* jumped off the page. Below it was a paragraph of medical jargon followed by a series of blurry lines running down the left side of the page with another series running down the right side. Both sets of lines had small blobs in the same spots on both sides of the paper. At the bottom of the page, another block of text included the one-word headline *Summary* followed by a single line that caused his legs to weaken.

"Elisabeth, look!" His trembling finger hovered over the line that read *Test subjects—a conclusive match.* "Do you know what this means?" he shouted.

She held her breath, pointing to the same line. "Why, this means—"

"It means you were right." Hanna's voice cracked as she emerged from her trance.

"Momma, are you okay?"

"Yes." The word was flat but clear. She looked up and gazed at him with a sense of wonderment, her eyes surveying every inch of his face. She glanced at Elisabeth then fixated back on him. "Yes—you were right."

Paul stood speechless.

Without warning, she pulled him down next to the bed. He willingly knelt beside her, free of the burden of worrying that she might rebuke him. He followed her eyes back to the DNA results then watched as she pulled out a faded piece of paper with worn edges.

"Is that a page from—"

"Your diary," she said, rubbing her fingers across a muddled brown stain. "And this—this is blood."

Paul flashed a look at Elisabeth. "The bookshop owner *was* right." He looked back at Hanna. "But… how do you know it's blood?"

Her face was tender and warm, with an expression that embodied love. She pulled him closer. "You're not only a descendant of Joseph Winslow—you're also the owner of this diary."

"Of course I am," he said.

"No. This is—your—diary."

"We understand that, Momma."

Hanna shook her head. "You're not hearing what I'm saying. This diary that's in your possession *now* was yours in 1849. That's when it was given to you. It wasn't given to a distant relative who gave it to their son, who gave it to his daughter, who gave it to her daughter, and so on. No. It's not from one of your ancestors." She placed her hand on his shoulder. "It's from—you!"

Paul jumped up, stumbling as he reeled from her revelation.

Elisabeth grabbed him by the waist. "Momma, what on earth are you talking about? You're not making sense. I think you need to lie down." She turned to Paul and whispered in his ear. "Stay with her. I'm going to call Dr. Kinkaid."

"No!" Hanna shouted, and then her voice calmed. "No, child, I'm okay. But it's your turn to listen now."

Elisabeth looked at him.

He nodded, then turned to Hanna. "Okay... what exactly are you saying?"

"I need to show you first." She picked up the page from his diary, its edges quivering as she laid it beside her. She pulled out a second DNA report and placed it on top of the diary page. With her index finger she tapped on it three times. "It's you."

"It's me?" He held his hands out, surrendering to the fact he had no idea what she was talking about. "I'm sorry, Hanna. I'm lost."

Her eyes glistened as she stood and took his face in her palms. "I'm so sorry... had I known..." Her eyes surveyed his hair, eyes, nose, and chin. "I should have looked harder. But I can see you now. I can see you clear as Willow Creek water." She ran her fingers across his cheek. "I can see you with your beard." She took a lock of his hair between her fingers, and tears began to form. "And I can see you with that full mop of hair. Oh, Mase, my precious, precious boy. Will you ever forgive me?"

He pulled away, bewildered by the intense display of affection, along with her plea for forgiveness. He inched back as she reached out to him, tears cascading down her cheeks.

Elisabeth gasped.

"What's wrong?" he said.

Elisabeth stood behind Hanna with one hand over her heart and the other holding the second document. She sat on the bed and began rubbing her eyes as if to alter the contents of the page. "This report. It can't be true."

"But it is," Hanna said.

Elisabeth bit her lip. "This is a different DNA report."

"For what?" he asked.

"It's a comparison between the diary page—and you! It says the blood on the page is a match with the DNA from *your* blood sample."

The room began to turn around him faster and faster as his mind worked to comprehend her statement. All sound faded away. For a moment, time stood still. Hanna was frozen in front of him, smiling, while Elisabeth sat motionless on the bed, her eyes fixed on the report.

From out of the void came a tiny syllable, soft and warm— "Mase." A decibel louder—"Mase." Again, louder—"Mase." The warmth of Hanna's hands on his cheeks pulled him back, all his senses collapsing in on him. "Mase, it's me. I'm here."

He jerked his head back and forth, blinking away the web produced by the thousands of thoughts jarring his brain.

She bent her head to his. "You need to sit before you fall." She pulled him back to the bed and sat him next to Elisabeth, who was still looking for an error in the report. Hanna backed up and clasped her hands together. "If Spoon could see you now."

"Forgive me, but I think I need one of your migraine pills."

She laughed. "My dear Mase—you might just need the entire bottle."

"Why are you calling him 'Mase'?" Elisabeth asked.

"I don't expect you to believe what I'm going to tell you."

"Probably not," she said.

"Well, there's nothing I can do about that." She looked at Paul. "I was open-minded for you. Will you try to be for me?"

"Of course."

She cleared her throat and wiped away her tears. "Now that I know who you are, I can tell you what you've been waiting to hear." She paused and straightened herself. "I'm not sure you'll want to hear everything, but it's yours, and you have a right to it." She looked at Elisabeth. "You're part of this too, honey. I hope you'll understand why I've kept it from you for all these years."

"Before you go any further, can I ask one question?" he said. "Are these reports real?"

"Every one of them are and they've all been certified. And I hope you don't mind that I ripped the page out of your diary, but I had to be sure."

"I'm having a hard time believing they could be."

"Sometimes, things are true even though they can't be explained. You'll just have to listen and decide for yourself." She closed her eyes, and her lips moved as she mouthed a silent prayer. When she finished, she clasped her hands together and calmly began.

"Paul, you were born in 1841 to the owner of the Willow Creek Plantation. Your mother died in childbirth.

Your name was Masen Randolph Winslow, and everyone called you Mase. You had an older sister named Annabelle, and your father was Braxton Winslow. He was a good man. You also had a best friend, a slave boy named Jeziah Campbell. His nickname was Spoon."

"Because he played them?" Paul asked.

"That's right," she said. "And oh, how he could. Mr. Brax, that's what everyone called your daddy, would have him perform at dinner parties and other occasions. You see, he loved Spoon too. Your daddy wasn't like the rest of the slave owners. Don't get me wrong, everyone worked hard on that plantation, but he felt responsible for them all and treated them fairly. Unfortunately, he had a debilitating case of apoplexy." Her voice faltered. She exhaled then began again.

"That year was 1862, and the Civil War was starting to rage. You ended up enlisting. Right before you were set to ship off is when—" She threw her hands over her mouth, squeezing her eyes shut. "I thought this would be easier."

"You don't have to go on," Elisabeth said, tugging on Paul's arm in a subtle indication he should agree with her.

As entertaining as it was, he was beginning to agree that her mother did indeed have an illness. "Yes, Hanna, you can stop now."

"No! I'm okay. Just give me a minute." She paced back and forth, then stopped. "A couple nights before you went off to war is when the devil was set loose on Willow Creek. That night is when your sweet sister was raped. Everyone suspected Spoon, but it was actually a man named Silas." She dug her fingernails into her palms and stumbled backward.

Paul jumped up, catching her before she collapsed. He

sat her in a chair while Elisabeth ran off to the kitchen, bringing her back a glass of water.

When he saw she had regained her composure, he asked, "Is what you're telling us all passed down by your relatives? Are there other diaries or something?"

"No, there're no relatives or diaries."

"So how do you know all these things?"

She put the glass on the table and stared at him for a moment. "Because." Another long moment passed with only the sound of the clock ticking down the hall. "Because," she began again, "I was there too."

Elisabeth sat motionless, convinced her mother had plunged into madness. She turned to Paul. "Can you please call Dr. Kincaid?"

"Hold on, missy. Before you go sending me off to the asylum, there's something else you need to see." She pointed to a small wooden trunk in the corner. "In that box is a large wooden scrapbook. Would you bring it to me, please?" Her voice was steady and calm.

Paul opened the trunk and produced an oversized, oak-covered binder with a leather-looped spine.

She placed it in her lap then flipped to the last page. "Here we are," she said, turning it around to them. "What do you see?"

"It looks like a copy of the picture you were looking at when we came in," he said.

"It does look similar, but it's not the same," she said almost playfully. "Mr. Brax wanted to make sure the photographer got a good picture, so he had him take two. If you'll notice, this one's not as fuzzy in places."

She ran her finger across it to where the blurry image of the lady wearing the kerchief was standing. Unlike the other picture, this face was in focus. The rounded features with the broad smile were undeniable. They belonged to the woman now cradling the wooden binder.

Paul's jaw hung open. "You—that-that's you!"

She ran her finger to the man on the horse. "And that's your daddy." Her finger moved to the pretty brunette girl next to him. "That's your sister, Annabelle, and this little black boy, that's Spoon. See those shiny things coming out of his pockets?"

"Spoons?" he said.

"Yep. And this young fellow with the bushy head of hair next to him, that's—"

"Me?"

"Yes, that's you—Masen Winslow."

He leaned over to within inches, taking in every edge, curve, and nuance of the boy's features.

"Do you see the resemblance?" she asked.

"I-I do! I can't believe this, but I do. Elisabeth look— that's me!"

Hanna turned to her and smiled. "This picture has one exception to it that the other doesn't. It includes one very significant addition."

"Oh, my God!" Elisabeth squealed, pointing beside the big black man next to the pig cooker. "Is that—"

"Yes! That's you, baby girl. That's my Sissy."

"You called me Sissy?"

"I changed your name when the memory stone took us away."

Elisabeth tilted her head, "A stone did what?"

"Paul, would you open the trunk again? Underneath the blankets, there's a small box. Would you bring it to me?"

He pulled himself from the picture and quickly returned, holding a small three-inch-square pine box.

"Thank you," she said, laying it on top of the picture. She looked at Elisabeth then turned to Paul. "Are you two still with me?"

They both nodded in hushed anticipation.

"I realize how strange all this must be for you, but— you have to trust me." She slowly lifted the lid and reached in as if taking a robin's egg from its nest. Wrapped in the straw that protected it lay a stone a tad smaller than the box that held it. A smooth oval, it was a golden-brown color mixed with flecks of grey.

"It looks rather ordinary," he said.

"I can assure you it's anything *but* ordinary. A stone like this is what saved Elisabeth and me. And I'm sure it's like the one that saved you as well."

"From what—and how? It's just a rock."

She shook her head. "I told you, it's not an ordinary rock. It's a *memory stone*."

Paul rubbed the side of his head while Elisabeth sat hanging on her mother's every word.

"I need to tell you the rest of the story," she said, placing the stone back in its box. "Remember I told you everyone thought Spoon raped your sister, but it was really the man named Silas?"

"Yes."

"While Spoon was still suspected of being the one who raped Annabelle, your uncle Joseph had him strung up and was about to shoot him. You stepped in and stopped him. But what you felt you had to do in place of his execution had almost the same results."

"Which was?"

Her voice shifted to a blue monotone. "With a metal rod, you beat him to within an inch of his life."

For the next twenty minutes, Paul struggled through her description of the ordeal of that night. He winced as she explained how the rod ripped the flesh from his friend's ribs and how he contemplated suicide after learning of Spoon's innocence. His heartbeat rose with every gritty detail.

From some unknown place, a wave of remorse washed over him. How could he feel for a person he really didn't know? How could he feel the guilt of inflicting an unjust punishment when he was not that person? Suddenly, the past was more raw and real than he had wanted, and it was tearing away who he had become in the present, revealing the villain he thought himself to be from the past. He looked at her with apologetic eyes. "I can't believe I was such a monster. I was just like every other slave owner."

"No, Paul. You mustn't think that. It wasn't your fault. You didn't know." She placed her hand on his shoulder. "Maybe I should stop."

"No, you warned me. I need to hear everything."

"Elisabeth? This is about you too," she said calmly. "Are you okay?"

"Yes, ma'am."

Hanna took a steady breath and turned back to Paul. "Okay then… A couple days later, you were sent off to serve in the army. For several months, we got reports about your bravery. Your daddy was so proud. During this time, we nursed Spoon back to health as best we could, but no sooner was he on his feet than your uncle sent him off to be a valet for a colonel friend of his." She balled her hand into a fist. "Besides Silas, your uncle was the evilest creature to ever walk this earth."

After taking a minute to compose herself, she continued. "About this time, we received two separate messages that turned things from bad to worse. The first was that the Yankees captured your uncle's colonel friend along with all his staff, including Spoon. The second was that you had deserted. Together, this news sent your daddy's health further down. With no one else to turn to, he had your uncle take over the plantation. Your daddy never knew about them, but there were beatings and whippings all the time. Then that Easter Sunday, after dinner, someone slashed his neck."

"Whose neck?"

"Your uncle's. A few of the slaves ran off, fearing for their lives." She hung her head. "Later that night, someone also…" she squeezed her eyes shut as her voice faltered. "Later that night…" she proceeded slowly, a tear rolled down her cheek, "someone cut the throat of the slave foreman. His name was Cluc." She wiped her eyes. "Fearing for their lives, the rest of the slaves ran off. Only two remained—myself and my girl." She smiled and took Elisabeth by the hand. "Knowing we were probably the next victims, I packed our bags and prepared our escape.

"Just before midnight, we were about to leave our cabin when someone pounded on the door, yelling to let him in or he'd kill us. It was Silas. Why he'd returned, I didn't know, but I wasn't going to stay to find out. When he pounded a second time, I knew the only way to escape was calling upon the memory stones."

"Like the one in the box?" he asked.

She nodded.

"That was the only weapon you had—a rock?"

"No, no. The stone isn't a weapon, Paul. It's a…" She paused, looking upwards in search of the right words. "Before I can tell you about the stones, there's something else you need to know about me."

Elisabeth held her breath, awaiting the next layer of a story that continued to take her breath. Paul leaned forward as she began.

"From generation to generation, certain abilities have been passed down through my family to me, things that allow me to harness the power of nature and use its gifts. One was the use of memory stones in times of trouble.

"Before my mother passed away, she left me five of them. How they came into her possession, she never said, but they weren't from any of our rivers, streams, mountains, or lakes. They were billions of years old but appeared in a place and time almost 2,000 years ago for a purpose that changed the world." A reverence enveloped her, and her eyes brightened as she spoke. "Supposedly these five pieces of hardened earth were from where Christ's disciple Stephen was stoned."

"They were used to kill him?" Elisabeth gasped.

"I don't think the Bible says the stoning killed him," Paul said. "I believe it says he simply fell asleep."

"So you *have* read your Bible." Everything about Hanna was now aglow. "The power they possess is how you, me, and Elisabeth were saved. When Silas came to the cabin that night, I called upon that power to shield us from the ultimate danger."

"Death?" Elisabeth said.

"That's right. When met with a life-or-death situation, you need only cup a stone in your palm and close your eyes. In an instant, time races forward, leaving the danger behind—decades, even centuries in the past. Upon opening your hand, a whole new world is there for you to begin anew."

Paul swallowed. "Are you talking about time travel?"

"I believe I am," she replied. "That night, when Sissy and I were in the cabin, before Silas could break in, we used the stones to escape."

"Momma, why don't I remember any of this and you do?"

"A single stone can be used for two people *if* one is holding it and the other is covering that person's hand with theirs. The person who's actually holding the stone doesn't remember anything."

"You covered mine?"

"I had to, dear. I covered it to protect you. I knew carrying the past would have been too much of a burden for you. I didn't want you to remember anything about the horrors you had seen and the sadness that I knew would follow you. Although it wouldn't matter, I even changed our names simply because if we were going to be starting over, I wanted it to be complete."

Hanna turned to Paul. "This is probably what happened to you as well. You must have been in a life-or-death situation."

"So I had a memory stone?"

"Of course."

"How can you be sure?"

She smiled. "Because I'm the one who gave it to you."

"Wait!" His eyes lit up. "That's the stone mentioned in the diary. I recall reading the entry about how you gave me a stone to remember you by, but there was no mention of its powers."

"It wasn't the time to explain it. You were under too much stress. I'm not sure what happened, but somewhere along the way, someone else who knew its powers must've helped you use it."

"What about my life today?" he said. "You both transported like I did, but things are different for you. You simply appeared with no real connections to today's world whereas I have an actually modern-day past."

"You're right about our not having any connections. We didn't have any descendants and without any lineage there was no way for us to have a *modern-day past* as you call it. It was tough establishing our lives here in the beginning—fake ids, taking crappy jobs that were usually off the books, and studying—oh how we had to study! We had to learn everything about the modern world." She turned to Elisabeth and smiled. "And my poor baby had it even harder. She had all her functioning skills of reading, writing and speaking but because of how I used the memory stone she couldn't remember any of the past. I can't even begin to get into how many lies and schemes I came up with to help her fit in."

Paul shook his head. "But I show up and actually have some connections. I have an identity as Paul, I'm a writer who has a past in the here and now."

Hanna nodded. "That's right. Whoever helped you use the stone also knew how to manipulate it. They evidently saw beyond your physical pain and were able to see the emotional agony you were holding inside. They must've believed the only way for you to survive in the future was by performing a soul chant."

"Performing what?"

"It's an ancient chant that, if done just before the person

travels, causes the stone to seek out the person in the future who's closest to them in appearance and character—oftentimes it's a distant relative."

His face scrunched up. "Like a doppelganger?"

"Doppel what?" said Elisabeth.

"It's someone's double," he said. "Everybody supposedly has one."

Hanna half nodded. "Well, that's a possibility, but in this case, I believe it was the latter. I believe it chose Paul Talbert because he was the closest fit to you and because you were related, which presented an even better chance of him looking like you."

"Ohhh, this is too strange," Elisabeth blurted. "We're talking about Paul Talbert as if he's not you."

"I know, honey," she said with a smile, "but the man with us right now is more Mase Winslow than Paul Talbert. He has Paul's name and memories, but his body and DNA are really Mase's. He doesn't know it, but he's got Mase's memories as well—they're just hidden." She turned back to him. "This is another reason you've struggled so much. Your present life's misfortunes combined with your subconscious past have created the perfect storm of anxiety inside you." She reached out and took him into her arms. "I can't image how much you've suffered."

He pulled back. "What about him? What happened to the Paul that was taken?"

"When the stone finds the perfect match, that person simply vanishes from wherever they are. The traveler appears at the same time—someplace nearby. In your case it was Central Park."

Elisabeth rose and began pacing in a circle. "Okay— okay, this sounds so absurd but it actually makes sense.

This explains why you—the Paul whose place you took—never knew about Willow Creek. Because you were orphaned at such an early age with neither of your parents or any relatives telling you about your past, there was no way you *could* have known about your lineage—especially that far back. You were lucky your friend Zoey helped find enough information that led you to Beaufort."

Paul shook his head. "I-I just don't have the words." He looked intently into Hanna's eyes then turned his gaze to the box. "These stones—their power…"

"I know. Each one is its own miracle."

"Didn't you say there were five?"

"I did, but when they're used, they vanish. Like a river ultimately wears a boulder into nothing, I guess the river of time wears away the memory stone until it's gone."

"Then if mine was used, as was yours, shouldn't you have three left?"

"I should, but when Silas came to the cabin that night, I was in such a panic I left one in the hole under my bed where I had hid them. I stuffed one in my pocket but the other fell to the ground. I didn't have time to pick it up."

Paul was reeling from the barrage of revelations she had heaped upon him, but with each new layer of the surreal came answers. His skepticism faded as his past came into focus. Everything that had not made sense was now perfectly clear to him.

Chapter 27

Paul and Elisabeth spent the majority of the next morning discussing the phenomenon that was their past and the miraculous events that brought them to where they were today. Their lives suddenly had a foundation. Hundreds of questions remained, but at least they were at a place they could continue to build from. Part of that future, Paul said, was to finish his book.

"I'm not sure anyone will believe it but it's a story I have to tell."

"You probably need to talk to Momma since she's a part of all this."

"You're right. I know she has her reservations, but if I rename the plantation and veer everything away from here, maybe she'll be okay with it."

"I'm supposed to meet her to go grocery shopping after her lunch shift, which should be in about thirty minutes. We can talk to her then."

A half hour later, they were in front of Elisabeth's house.

"Shoot. She went on without me."

"How can you tell?"

"There's a note on the front door. She still doesn't like texting. She's so old school."

"Nineteenth-century old school," he chuckled.

"That's almost funny," she said, skipping her way to the front porch. She pulled the note off the screen door. "It's about as funny as—"

"Does it say when she left?"

"No. It's not from Momma." She twisted her head. "Does this look like a prank?" she said, handing him the piece of paper.

Two sentences written with a large magic marker were scrawled across the page. *I know about the legacy and that you know where it's at. Have your man friend leave one bar in the hollow tree trunk next to the Angel statue in Haven Ridge Cemetery at noon tomorrow, and you'll never hear from me again.*

"Yeah. Looks like a joke to me."

"Sorry, kids," Hanna said, walking through the lawn, carrying a bag of groceries. "I got off early so I went ahead and did the shopping."

"Momma, have any of the neighborhood boys played tricks on you before?"

"No, why?" she said, stepping onto the porch.

Elisabeth held out the paper to her. "This note was left on the door."

Hanna covered her mouth, sending the bag of groceries smashing onto the bricks.

"What's wrong, Momma?"

"This is what I feared might happen." She looked back across the yard, then quickly scanned the neighboring houses. "Come inside, quick."

"What about the groceries?"

"Leave them!" she said, locking the door behind them.

"What's going on, Momma? You're breathing hard enough to have a heart attack."

"I may indeed. This note is what I was talking about all along. Someone knows more about Willow Creek than we want them to."

"What else do they want to know?" Paul asked.

"The legacy. They've come looking for it." She peered through the plantation shutters then snapped them shut. "I knew someone would come sooner or later."

"What legacy?"

"Paul, have you shared anything in print or had any conversation about Willow Creek with anyone other than Sissy and me—I mean Elisabeth?"

"No, I promise."

"Momma, *what* legacy?"

Hanna lowered her head and paced back and forth. "I'll bet a dollar to a donut it's the man who's been snooping around for the past month."

"Momma, stop! *What* legacy are you talking about?"

She froze in the middle of the room. "Judge Joseph's legacy."

"Can you explain what it is exactly?" Paul asked.

"It's an old wives' tale, but supposedly, your good ole uncle Joseph stole gold from the Confederate treasury and buried it somewhere on the plantation."

"Then the legacy's a joke?" he said.

"No, it's just a tall tale."

"Hmmm," he said, scratching his chin. "Is there anything else you need to tell us?"

"It's just a story, Paul, and whoever this guy is, he *must* be insane. There's always someone out there looking for gold that isn't there. This is another reason I didn't trust you at first," Hanna said.

"We need to go to the police, Momma."

"No, I don't want this to get out. It'll only draw more treasure hunters."

"I have an idea," said Paul. "We'll do as he says. At noon tomorrow, your man friend—I assume that's me—will carry out his wishes."

"You'll what?"

"Not exactly like he thinks though. What I'll do is put a bogus bar of whatever in the tree trunk tomorrow, pretend to ride off, then hide in the bushes. All the while, I'll be videoing him on my phone. When he comes out, I'll show him he was being recorded. If he doesn't skedaddle, we can then take it to the authorities."

"Okay, that sounds good. Do you want me to go with you?" Hanna asked.

"No, you should stay here with Elisabeth. I'll have the police number programmed into my cell phone just in case."

The next day Paul arrived at the house with a brick covered in gold foil wrapping paper purchased at the dollar store. "I figured he had to be talking about a gold ingot."

"Are you sure about this?" Hanna said. "What if he's got a gun? You should take mine."

"No, no, I'll be fine. Trust me. Once he knows he's been recorded, that'll scare him off for good. Everyone knows how powerful videos are in helping arrest people these days."

Hearing their conversation, Elisabeth came running out of her bedroom. She wrapped her arms around him so tightly he dropped his fake gold bar along with his cell phone. "I've made up my mind. I'm coming with you."

He turned to Hanna. "Can you please ground your daughter for the rest of the day?"

"He's right, honey. You need to stay here," she said, handing him the fake bar along with her 9mm Luger.

"Seriously, I don't need the gun," he said, handing it back to her. "Just my gold will do." As he headed to his van, he looked back and blew Elisabeth a kiss. She was standing behind the screen door waving, looking more beautiful than ever.

For the next few minutes, he reminisced about the first time he left her at that door. He thought about how eager she was to see him just now and how warm her hug was that caused him to drop his fake gold and cell phone. His phone—he hadn't picked it up off the floor. Without it, the plan wouldn't work. He quickly turned the car around and headed back. Within five minutes, he was parked outside her house again. He started across the lawn but stopped within feet of the front door when he heard Hanna screaming.

"Get out of my house!" Her voice was unbalanced yet defiant.

Positioning himself against the wall, Paul craned his neck around the corner. Standing in the middle of the room was a huge man in a trench coat wearing a tattered black cowboy hat pulled down over strands of greasy black hair. In his hand was a knife he held pointed only inches from her face.

"Where is it?" he growled. "You know every inch of that place. If you don't tell me, I swear to the almighty, I'll kill you, same as I done the Judge and Cluc." He rolled his head enough to reveal the charred profile of a burn victim, the flesh folding in irregular red shapes across his cheek. "And I promise I'll kill that girl of yours too—"

In a fury, Paul burst inside, tackling the intruder, sending the knife flying across the floor.

With a groan, the man pulled himself off the floor with Paul clinging to his back, holding him in a headlock.

The man cursed as he thrashed about, trying to free himself from the stranglehold. A second later, he reached over his shoulder, grabbed Paul's jacket, and flung him into the wall. His head slammed against a picture frame, then everything went dark.

"Paul? Paul! Are you okay?" Elisabeth's hands on his face wakened him.

He blinked several times as he groped his way up off the floor. "Where's your mother?" he said, massaging the growing lump on the back of his head.

"Hurry! We can catch him!" Hanna yelled through the screen door.

Still holding the back of his head, he ran onto the front porch. "Where's he at?"

"He's getting into the old red sedan at the end of the block," she said, already jumping into his van.

Elisabeth ran up to them. "Wait, I'm coming too."

"No," Hanna said as she stuffed her pistol into her pocket, "you stay here."

"She's right. It's too dangerous now. Just hang tight— we'll be back."

Life breathed back into his old junker as the tires squealed across the pavement in pursuit of the red sedan.

"Where'd he go?" he said, scanning the intersection ahead.

She pointed to the left. "He's turning on to Davis Street."

The van fishtailed around the corner.

"Slow down. You can't let him know we're following him."

"Hanna, do you know who this guy is?"

"No, I'd remember a face like that."

"What did he mean when he said he'd killed the Judge and Cluc? And he said you knew every inch of that place."

The next two blocks passed with no reply.

"Hanna? Hanna! Did you hear me?"

"No, it couldn't be," she muttered, leaning forward and placing her hand against the windshield. "Speed up, we're losing him." The sudden acceleration threw her back into her seat.

Within fifteen minutes, they were out of the city and winding through Beaufort's backwoods—knee-deep into the sticks as the locals would say.

Hanna remained silent, keeping vigilant eyes on the red sedan, only speaking to tell him to either speed up or slow down. "I don't like how far out we're getting," she finally said.

"Neither do I." He hated to ask, but… "Did you bring—"

"Right here," she said, patting the Luger in her pocket.

In a matter of seconds, the hardpan dirt road transitioned into a minefield of potholes, and the van bounced and rattled its way through a narrow path of live oaks. Suddenly the day turned into night as the red sedan vanished into the darkness of the tunnel created by the moss-covered canopy.

"Dang it. We lost him," Paul said.

"No, look, it's opening up."

As they pulled into the light, he stopped the van. Ahead of them was a secluded stretch of rotting farmland the size of a football field. Gigantic cedars and hemlock trees bordered every side, tucking it away from the rest of the world. At the far end was a sagging barn.

"He must be in there." Paul put the van in reverse and moved it back under the cover of the canopy.

"What're you doing?"

"Let's wait here a minute." He grabbed his cell phone and set it to begin recording. "Sooner or later, he'll come out into the open, and we can make our move."

"Then what?" she said, pulling her gun out.

"I'm not sure." He eyed the weapon in her lap. "We've got him cornered." A moment passed as he contemplated the danger of their strategy. "Why don't we call the police?"

"No. I don't want any more attention drawn to this."

"But it'd be much safer if—"

"No—I said no!"

The rebuke stopped him cold, leaving them with twenty minutes of silence as they watched the barn for signs of movement.

"Do you think he's still in there?" he finally said.

"Where would he go?"

"If he knows we're out here, we could be here until dark, then he could sneak off."

Hanna gripped her pistol. "Come on then," she said, stepping out onto the dirt road.

Paul pushed past her. "Not so fast. We've got to go around by the woods, or else he'll spot us out in the open."

When they were within thirty yards of the barn, they stopped. "Stay here," he said, tiptoeing toward a small crack between two moldy pieces of siding. He cupped his hands around his eyes and peered inside.

A few seconds later, he was running to the back corner, motioning her to follow. The frown on his face indicated they had been duped. "He's gone!"

The back side of the barn was an exit that led straight out into a dirt road hidden by another overgrown passage out to wherever.

The first few minutes back in the van were filled with silence as they fumed over their failed attempt to bring closure.

"I still don't understand why he was asking all those things. He obviously thinks he knows you."

Hanna sat close-lipped, staring ahead.

"You know who he is, don't you?" he said.

She maintained her silence.

Paul pulled the car to the shoulder. "I can tell this is no random treasure seeker. I'm not moving until you tell me what's going on."

"Okay, okay!" she said, slamming her gun onto the dashboard. "You're right, or at least I think you're right. He's not random. I don't know how but I think this is Silas."

"Silas? The guy that raped Annabelle?"

"Yes. I don't know why or how he's here, but he is. I'm sorry I didn't tell you this before. I was only trying to protect my family." Her eyebrows drew together. "It's not an old wives' tale—the myth about the gold. It's true. There *is* gold—lots of it."

His eyes grew large. "Where'd it come from?"

"I was telling the truth when I said the Judge stole it from the Confederates. I helped him bury it. The Judge was so weak he couldn't lift a gunny sack of cotton off the ground. He came to me one night telling me he had some boxes of ammunition he wanted to bury in case the Yankees came and tried to confiscate the plantation's weapons.

"While I was placing the last box in the ground, the lid slid off, revealing four shiny bars of gold. Thank goodness he didn't see it, or else he would've killed me right there."

"What's Elisabeth think about all this?"

"She doesn't know. I couldn't put that burden on her."

"How many boxes were there?"

"Five."

"Holy cow!" He slapped his hand against his cheek. "That's gotta be several million dollars."

"Try seven."

"Seven! Have you used any of it?"

"Child, how do you think we got that house?"

"Hanna, I hope you won't take offense, but you don't seem very happy having all that money."

She lowered her head. "I'm not."

"But you were a slave with nothing. Then, in a second, you're free. And a millionaire to boot."

"It's a worn-out saying, but it's the truth—money doesn't bring happiness. Family, friends, doing the right thing—that's what brings happiness. The life I'm living now is fake. Don't get me wrong, I'm thankful for the blessings of a second chance, but if I could go back, I would in a second."

"But why?"

"Being a slave for anyone anywhere is bad but Willow Creek was better than other plantations. It wasn't Disney World or anything, but it *was* better... that is until your uncle Joseph took control." She looked out the window. "We were making a difference."

"Who was?"

"Your daddy and me."

"How could you?"

Her lip quivered. "Your daddy owned slaves alright, but he wasn't anything like the rest of them—the other plantation owners that is. He inherited over a hundred slaves when your grandfather died. Over the years those numbers decreased as he started to free them. He eventually only kept enough to keep the plantation going and to help keep his leg of the railroad going. I was actually one of the conductors."

"Railroad? Conductor?"

"Paul, Willow Creek was one of the points along the secret route known as the Underground Railroad. Slaves used it to escape to free states and Canada. As a conductor, I was sent on missions, by your father, to bring them to the plantation where we'd hide them before transporting them up the line to another safe house." She threw her hands over her eyes and wept, tears running through her fingers. "I-I left them. I left them all behind."

"I'm sure you did all you could."

"No!" she said, straightening herself and wiping her eyes. "I did *not* do all I could. If it weren't for Satan's henchman, I could have helped free more of them." She turned to him, her eyes full of remorse. "I've always wanted to go back, but I can't. I don't deserve to be here." Her breaths came in sobs.

Without the words to address her sentiments, he could only nod.

Chapter 28

As they drove up to her house, Paul narrowed his eyes on the front porch. "Why's the door off the hinges?"

Hanna jumped out of the van before it came to a stop. "Elisabeth!" She flung open the door and disappeared inside. "Elisabeth!" The word accompanied by the opening and closing of doors reverberated throughout the house and onto the front lawn.

Paul's heartbeat increased with every empty room he searched. It beat the fastest when he entered the kitchen. From the mess, it looked like his earlier altercation had occurred there and not in the living room. The chopping-block table was lying on its side, drawers were pulled out, and pieces of broken plates and glasses were scattered across the tile floor. The most disconcerting item of all was the paring knife, dripping with blood, at the foot of the refrigerator.

A moment later, Hanna came running in, her eyes darting in every direction.

"Did you check behind the gazebo?" he asked.

"Yes!" she said, rubbing the back of her neck while pacing back and forth.

"All the rooms? What about the garage?"

"Everywhere. She's gone—Paul, my baby's gone!"

He picked up the knife and stared at it, his gaze passing over the blade and onto the refrigerator. "What's this?" he said, pulling off a note taped next to the handle.

He placed the knife on the counter. "We have to go,"

"What's it say?"

He grabbed her by the wrist and pulled her outside to the van. "He's got her."

"Where's my baby?" she said, slamming the door behind her.

"He's taken her to the barn we just came from." He slapped the wheel as they sped off. "We took too long. It's all my fault. I should've never pulled over and asked all those questions."

"What else did the note say?"

He pushed the accelerator to the floorboard and tightened his lips. "He said he'll kill her if you don't tell him where the gold is. He wants to meet us. And we better not bring the police."

"Oh, my baby! My baby girl!"

"Hanna, I still think we need to call the cops."

"But he said—"

"I know, but we're not trained for this. I'll explain the situation. They'll know how to handle it." He pushed his phone to her.

She pressed the activation button. Nothing. "Did you leave the recorder on?"

"Oh, come on! Don't tell me it's dead?" He glanced at its blank screen. "What about your gun?"

"It's in my pocket. Fully loaded—all eight rounds."

"Good. We're going to need it."

Minutes later, they were flying over the cratered dirt roads toward the kidnapper's lair. Through the tunnel and across the hidden field, they raced until the van skidded up to the barn, sending a cloud of dust into the air, obscuring the large door.

Hanna was out in front of the van, brandishing her pistol before he could turn off the ignition.

"Hold on now!" He grabbed her around the waist and spun her back toward him.

"Where's my girl?" she yelled loud enough to alert anyone in the vicinity of their presence.

"Wait a second." He pulled her back. "We have to be patient." He calmly placed his hand on her gun and guided it back into her pocket.

A clacking of metal followed by the creaking of rusted hinges turned them around. They watched as the massive door swung its way across the barn's gravel threshold.

Standing in the middle of the entrance was the hulking figure of the man in the trench coat. With his head tilted to the ground, only the top of his weathered Stetson was revealed to them. He studied each of his steps as he approached them.

"You ought not to be pullin' a weapon when you don't know the weapon you be up against." The tip of the hat rose by degrees, revealing, inch by inch, the ghastly beast beneath its brim.

Hanna dug her nails into Paul's arm as she choked back her disgust. The entire left side of the man's face was burnt, with black and red lumps of meat fused together in ghoulish angles. She could almost smell the burning flesh that had been scorched from where his lips had been. Across the right side of his forehead was a freshly opened gash, inflicted by Elisabeth's paring knife. Underneath, with its milky film and misaligned pupil, was the dead eye that had haunted Hanna's dreams so many nights.

As if paying homage to a queen, he pulled his hat off and stretched it out to his side while taking an exaggerated bow. Tossing it aside, he straightened his body in a stiff vertical, then walked toward her, his red eyes boring deeper into her with each step.

Within ten feet, he stopped. The unburnt corner of his mouth contorted upward in a gruesome display of rotting gums and blackened teeth. "Hello, Maudie," he snarled with the same gravel baritone she remembered from their first encounter at Willow Creek.

Her legs gave way, and Paul continued holding her upright as she staggered backward. "My God. It is you," she grimaced.

"M'lady," he said, tilting his head forward.

"H-how did you—"

"I knew all along ya had them rocks. But all I wanted was the gold." Saliva dripped from the edge of his mutilated lips. "Like what ya see? You and yur sweet Sissy done this."

"We didn't do anything! Where's my daughter, you-you demon!" She lurched forward only to be yanked back into Paul's arms.

Silas shook his head slowly. "If ya had just let me in that night, we wouldn't be here. But no! Ya had to use yur voodoo." He ground his fist into his hand. "I had to bust in." His voice cracked as he broke into manic laughter. "And poof—ya was gone! And it weren't but a second before one of them other darkies locked the door and threw a torch to it."

"But we didn't have anything to do with that," she pleaded.

"Shut up!" His chest heaved, and his eyes twitched as the blood pulsated across the veins in his forehead. "If I hadn't found that rock ya left, I'd be dead. That's right, I knew what they was for. I was burnin' alive when I found it, but I found it, and now I'm here, and I want that gold. Ya *owe* me that gold!"

"I'll tell you where it's at—I swear. You can have all of it. Just show me my baby!"

His voice softened to a low rumble. "I'll be glad to show ya the little angel," he said, walking to the other side of the barn.

As they turned the corner, a soft breeze laden with the smell of gasoline filled their nostrils. Hidden behind an overgrown holly bush, mounted by decaying wooden brackets, was a large rusty tank suspended over a dark hole approximately five feet in diameter. A nozzle stuck out of the tank, producing a thin, steady stream of fluid that ran through a steel grate covering the opening.

Hanna gritted her teeth. "Where is she?"

He smiled and motioned to the hole.

In a panic, she ran to it and fell to her knees. "Elisabeth!"

A hand, groping for her mother's touch, suddenly appeared through the crisscrossed metal bars. Hanna grabbed her hand, stroking it. "Momma's here, baby. Everything's going to be alright now."

The duct tape covering her daughter's mouth prevented a reply, but the horror in her eyes communicated everything.

"That there smell, from what's runnin' down and puddlin' up round yur girl—that's what they call pe—tro—le—um." He chuckled as he pulled out a lighter and flicked a flame to life. "*An eye for an eye*, so says the good book."

"No!" Paul held up his hands. "Take me. Let her go, and I'll go into your pit—please—let her go."

"You? I don't need *you*. What I need is Miss Maudie to tell me where that gold is." He held the lighter in front of him and walked to the hole.

Breaking free of his grasp, Hanna pulled her pistol from her pocket.

The blast that followed echoed through the woods. Then everything went silent.

A tug at his leg drew Paul back into the moment. Hanna lay sprawled across the ground, clutching the middle of her chest while holding onto the cuff of his pants.

Her Luger lay next to her hand while Silas's revolver rested firmly in his, smoke drifting from the barrel into the wind.

"She ought not to be dischargin' a firearm toward a tank of pe—tro—le—um."

Paul fell beside her, cupping the back of her head with one hand and covering her wound with the other. The blood oozed through his fingers and onto the ground. "No! You can't go. It's not your time."

Blood gurgled from her mouth as she writhed in pain. "You—you—got to…" She raked her hand across the ground as if searching for a lost object.

"You've got to lie still."

She groaned. "You have to—"

"Please, Hanna," was all Paul knew to say.

She continued running her hand along the ground while her body convulsed uncontrollably.

Silas waved the lighter above her head. "The girl burns if you don't tell me where the gold is."

Paul glared up at him. "Can't you see she's dying, you fool?"

"Then she best be tellin' me where it is before she do."

Paul curled his fingers into a fist only to look down and find Hanna pulling them open again. The corners of her mouth slowly turned upward as a veil of peace fell across her face. He watched as she placed a piece of gravel in his open palm with one hand. With the other, he felt her slide the Luger into his pocket.

"The stone," she whispered.

"What'd she say?" barked Silas.

Paul leaned forward, turning his ear to her mouth.

She squeezed his hand around the tiny rock. "The last stone…" The words barely audible, they faded away with her final breath.

He waited—praying—but there was nothing else. Putting his head to her chest, he confirmed what he already knew.

"Don't tell me she done died."

"You killed her."

Silas's face grew red with rage. "Then say goodbye to the girl."

"Wait! I know where to find it," he said.

"You? She told you?"

"Not exactly."

Silas hovered the lighter over the pit.

"No, wait! She-she has a map of where it is though. It's in her house. I-I can get it for you."

Silas killed the flame, at the same time bringing his revolver to within inches of Paul's nose. "Screw me over, boy, and I'll burn ya both at the same time. You got forty-five minutes. If yur not back by then, I swear I'll light her up. And I best not see nary a law dog sniff'n about. Now get!"

A minute later, Paul was speeding down the road, swerving in and out of traffic. His mind was a tangled knot of frantic thoughts trying to figure out how to produce a bogus map for Silas while freeing Elisabeth. His brain locked up, and his ability to process anything came in starts and stops as an avalanche of guilt crashed in on him.

The girl he was falling in love with was minutes away from a horrific death while her mother's lifeless body lay only feet away from her. Had he stayed in New York, none of this would have happened. He was to blame for it all.

He stared at the piece of gravel Hanna had placed in his hand. What purpose could it possibly have? Why, in her last seconds, would she have wanted him to have it?

Unable to solve the riddle, he threw it against the passenger-side window. The crack of glass jarred his brain—he had it. The answer couldn't be any clearer. The gravel was in place of a stone—a memory stone.

Within twenty minutes, he was plowing through Elisabeth's lawn, up onto her front steps. Two minutes later, he was back behind the wheel with a pen and notepad along with Hanna's pine box containing the memory stone. He glanced at the clock on the dashboard—exactly twenty-three minutes to make it back. He threw the van into reverse and punched it back onto the road. Along the way, he scribbled on the notepad.

With a minute to spare, he was back at the barn where he found Silas flicking cigar ashes to within inches of the pit. He could see Elisabeth's fingers clutching the grate's metal bars. All he had to do now was divert Silas's attention and draw him away from the pit long enough to get the memory stone to Elisabeth. He prayed she would know what it was and remember how Hanna had said to use it.

"I hope you got what I need," Silas said, puffing out a small cloud of smoke.

Paul walked to the pit only to have Silas jump in front of him. "Hold steady, boy. Where's the map?"

Paul pulled out a crumpled piece of paper and handed it to Silas, whose eyebrows rose and fell as he flipped the paper over and back again.

Paul started inching his way around him and had begun to reach for the stone when Silas grabbed him by the collar. With a twist of his thick wrist, the shirt became a noose. In one mighty yank, Paul was flying backward.

"What is this?" Silas said, cramming the paper against Paul's cheek. "I thought you said you was bringin' a map. What's these numbers here?"

Paul pulled back. "It *is* a map. Those are the directions."

The paper shook between the man's thick fingers. "Ain't no map. These is just words jumbled up with numbers," he snarled.

Paul gulped. "It's-it's directions with longitude and latitude."

Silas leaned forward and took a long drag off his cigar, the smoke filtering through the hole in his cheek. He pushed the paper back into Paul's chest. "Numbers don't say nothin'. Put it *all* in words, boy."

Clearing his throat, Paul said, "Basically, what it's saying is from the mall's farthest back corner, walk fifty paces straight north. At the lamp post, turn ninety degrees right and walk forty-five feet. Dig between the cypress tree and large rock."

"Hmmm…" Silas rubbed his hand through his greasy beard then twisted his head, trying to visualize the location.

These few seconds of distraction were all Paul needed. He dodged left then sprinted toward the hole when suddenly a massive arm swept his legs out from beneath him. Silas's size belied his quickness. He stood towering over him—fuming. A swift kick to his stomach flushed the wind from Paul's lungs.

"What kind of fool you take me for? Ain't no gold there! Ain't nothing but pavement! You really thought you could buy time for yur girl? Well, time's up." He turned toward the barn then spun back around, kicking Paul in the ribs.

Doubled over and gasping for air, out of the corner of his eye, he watched his tormentor walk toward the pit. He was holding his cigar out to his side, the glowing tip ready to ignite the darkness where Elisabeth waited helplessly.

Adrenaline sprang him to his feet, but his rage propelled him forward. Silas turned around in time to see Paul dropping his shoulder into his stomach, sending him flying backwards onto the ground. His revolver and cigar skidded across the dirt, the cigar stopping inches from a small river of gasoline leading to the pit.

Before Paul could stand, Silas had him in a headlock and was slamming him into the barn then onto the metal grate next to Elisabeth's outstretched hands. With unrelenting anger, Silas grabbed Paul's feet and pulled him across the steel bars, the jagged edges ripping across his chest and stomach.

"I have a memory stone," he blurted as he was being drug away. "I'll-I'll throw it—"

Before he could finish, a thundering right hook crashed into his chin, driving him unconscious and facedown back onto the grate.

Silas stepped back, admiring the effects of his blow. "Perfect," he said, grinning. "I'll snuff you out together." He whipped off his belt, wrapped it around Paul's left hand and tied it to the grate, then turned and looked for his revolver.

Elisabeth reached through the bars, tugging on Paul's shirt, desperately trying to wake him.

At the same time, Silas paced in a circle, searching for his weapon. Frustrated at his inability to find it, he walked back to the pit, rolling his head, intrigued by her delicate fingers gently stroking her boyfriend's hair. With the full weight of his body, he pounded his boot onto her hand. Her muffled cry and the jarring of the boot against steel resonated through Paul's brain. His eyes fluttered open.

"There's my baby," Silas said, spotting the butt end of his gun sticking out from under the corner of the barn. With the glee of a schoolboy, he pranced his way to it while Paul tried pulling himself to his feet, only to find himself tied to the grate.

Catching a glimmer of Silas's blackened snarl as he wrapped his hand around his revolver, Paul looked down at Elisabeth and smiled, then reached into his pocket and pulled out the memory stone. With his fingers wrapped tightly around it, he passed his hand through the bars down into the darkness. "Everything's going to be alright…"

The memory of the gunshot would travel with him. What would not was the pain of the bullet that penetrated his heart and the sound of the ricochet that sparked the explosion that cost Elisabeth her life that day.

Chapter 29

There were no shadows, silhouettes, or shades of grey as he made the journey—only a solid black void. There was no starting point with no momentum pushing him in any direction. There was no sense of time because there was nothing for time to advance toward.

But then, from out of the silent abyss, came a low roar like the gushing waters of a faraway river, followed by a tug—a magnetic attraction from the core of nothing to something. He suddenly felt as if he were being pulled backward, slowly at first, then faster and faster. The roar grew louder as the darkness faded to deep blues and purples, then brighter shades of green, red, vibrant orange and yellow. Suddenly he was flying through space in a swirling vortex of colors.

Abruptly, it all came to a halt, and black replaced the rainbow of colors again. Only the sounds of the rushing water remained. Seconds passed before the sound of his pulse fell into rhythm with the movement of his chest. The roar drifted into a soft lullaby of wind whisking through leaves.

Instead of the cold steel of the metal grate, he felt the

warmth and comfort of fur beneath him. He hesitated to open his eyes for fear of disrupting the tranquility of the moment, knowing his nemesis was sure to be in striking distance. Slowly he opened them. Where Silas should have been standing was now the outline of the small, hunched figure of a feeble old lady.

"Ohhh, mercy!" The old woman clapped her hands together. "Ya done come back."

He patted his body, confirming he was whole—that he was real. His eyes grew wider as he took in the tiny cabin's candles, bones, straw figurines, and assorted amulets hanging from the walls. The smell of incense brought it all crashing back to him.

"Juana—is that you?"

She walked beside him, to the same fur bed on which he'd been lying when he passed to the future.

"Yes, sir. It's Juana," she said, dancing in circles.

"How'd I get here?"

"Why, da stone brung ya."

He remembered. He never handed it to Elisabeth. As he was about to, Silas fired the shot that killed him. With the memory stone in his possession, he was the one that made the journey through time—not her.

"But-but… I thought it sent you to the future."

"True for da first time. First time it take ya forward. Second time it bring ya back."

"Back?"

"When ya use a stone a second time, ya comes back where ya was—same place, same day, same minute." She looked him over. "Dis time ya come back shined up like a brand-new penny with nary a hair on dat pretty face." She tilted her head. "Anybody else put a hand on da stone when ya come back?"

"No."

"So ya gots all ya memories where ya been?"

He nodded, a wave of sadness washing over him. Hanna was dead, and Elisabeth was sure to follow her. Everything from his future was gone and doomed never to happen. Despair, guilt, and anxiety accompanied his memories of the past, along with those of his future. Images of Spoon's mangled body, his sister's rape, and his perceived selfish enlistment into the army entangled with the tragic events he had just escaped.

"My, my, my... youz hurtin' worse than when ya left."

He turned his head away and closed his eyes. All he wanted was to wake up from the nightmare of being tossed about in time.

"Mr. Mase—Mr. Mase? Ya hear me?" She poked him in the shoulder. "What's ya gonna do now?"

"I don't know. I have no future, and all that's in the here and now is doomed."

"Don't understand 'bout the here and now, but ya gots to be careful 'bout da future. Whatever happened there gonna change if ya ain't careful with what ya does now."

His eyes brightened. "Yes—that's it!" He grabbed her by the elbow. "What day is it?"

"I done told ya. It's da same day."

"Oh—that's right!" He leaped off the bed and headed for the door.

"Wait—ya gonna leave this?"

He turned to find her holding Hanna's Luger.

"Musta fell out ya jacket."

He took the gun and placed it back in his pocket, smiling to himself, remembering the moment she had slipped it there.

"Thank you for saving my life." He stepped back and kissed her on the forehead, then turned and ran out the door.

"Wherez ya going?"

"To help a friend! I hope to see you again," he yelled over his shoulder as he headed into the woods.

"Juana hopes to see Mr. Mase again too."

The name was suddenly comfortable again. Masen Winslow was fully present with an eye on securing the future of his family and himself.

He would just have to change the course of his history to do it.

For the next several hours, he trudged through the woods over the same path he used to get to the hospital when he learned that Spoon had been captured and taken to a place called Pointer's Cove. Shortly before nightfall he stepped out onto the streets of the little town where so many soldiers had been brought to either heal or die from their wounds.

"Excuse me, sir," he said to an elderly man passing by. "Can you tell me which way to Pointer's Cove?"

"Why would you wanna go there, young fella?"

"I have a friend there."

The man gave him a once-over. "Where'd you get them duds you got on? You ain't from around here, are you?" He glared at him. "Your friend a Yank?"

"No, sir, he's from Beaufort, South Carolina. He was captured and—" He stopped as he figured any more details would only draw more suspicion to him.

"Well, you might wanna reconsider," the old man said. "Yanks took it over a week ago. Surprised you ain't heard how bad we was whupped."

"Yes, sir, I know. Can you tell me which direction and how far?"

"Suit yourself." He turned and pointed due north. "Straight ahead. She's a full day's ride into the hill country—she's down in the hollow."

"Much obliged," said Mase. He took one step north and stopped. A day's ride meant two on foot, maybe more depending on how steep the climb was. If he was going to have any chance of achieving his objective, he would have to find a horse, and judging by the old man's reaction, a change of clothes was in order as well. The answer to both came quicker than he'd hoped.

Just outside town, he spotted a Union cavalryman on the side of the road attending to his horse's hooves. A deep ditch ran along the edge of the road that allowed Mase to crawl to within several feet of the unsuspecting soldier. A dead tree branch came to serve a greater purpose. He threw it against the horse's neck, causing him to rear up. The soldier stumbled back. Mase leaped to his feet, grabbed him around the neck, and wrestled him to the ground.

Fifteen minutes later, the soldier was standing naked, strapped to a tree and watching Mase ride off on his horse, wearing his uniform. The man's bloody finger lay at his feet as a reminder he should have provided his name and company's password when asked the first time.

He rode through the night without taking any breaks. A steady incline with several steep turns indicated he was entering the hill country, just as the old man mentioned. Only once did he have to supply the secret word to a roadside sentinel. Gaining entry into the town, let alone the prison, would be a different matter altogether.

As day broke, along with it came a heavy fog obscuring his vision but extending his ability to proceed without hindrance. His horse, however, had had enough and would not budge. He would have to trek the rest of the way on foot.

The sun's rays continued to filter through the mist, creating a haze thick enough to hide an entire regiment. Blindly he trudged on, each step getting harder as the road continued to rise. As he had often done, his thoughts flicked back to his past failures, along with those of his future. He had beaten himself to an emotional pulp throughout time. The farther he walked, the closer he knew he was to either redemption or capture and execution. Regardless of the outcome, he was determined to complete the journey.

Slowly the woods came alive as the mist faded. A covey of quail flushed from their hiding place, and squirrels scampered through the foliage while bluebirds and robins chirped in the new day. Ahead, the road appeared to end at the top of another steep hill, a backdrop of blue sky and white linen clouds stretching beyond it. Although it was beautiful, he regretted the departure of the fog and the protection it provided.

Exhausted, he collapsed onto a large boulder at the top of the hill and examined the lay of the land below. The winding road down into Pointer's Cove led into one long street dividing the tiny town into two sections, a handful of narrow alleys and buildings occupying either side. Based on the number of tents, he estimated there to be only four hundred soldiers encamped on one side of the town. On the other side, squeezed in between the buildings and a railroad track, was a ten-acre makeshift prison holding more than a thousand Confederates.

The undermanned prison itself was only half-complete. The walls facing toward the town and the railroad tracks were constructed of wood while the other two were a mesh of wires awaiting their transformation. With a jittery guard positioned every twenty feet, any plan executed during the day was sure to fail. He would have to wait until nightfall.

The first order of business was to determine if Spoon was even at the camp. If he was, then he would need to create a strong diversion to draw the guards' attention away from their post long enough for him to free Spoon somehow. If that was successful, he would then need to have an escape route as well as transportation back south—ultimately getting back to Willow Creek by Easter to complete the final stage of his plan. Based on his calculations, he had two days to accomplish freeing his friend and three days to make it home.

He bowed his head, mouthed a prayer, then set off to accomplish his first task. Instead of walking straight into camp and risking inquiries at the front guard station, he maneuvered his way around to the part of the surrounding forest closest to the town. As a group of soldiers walked by, he simply fell in behind them. When they passed the quartermaster's office, he broke off. Walking up the steps, he patted the pocket that held his Luger. Eight rounds. With that many shots, he was sure he could handle most situations.

A cloud of smoke engulfed him upon opening the door. A bespectacled officer sat hunched over a desk, scribbling on a ledger while puffing a cigar. Behind him sat a young soldier practicing his knife-throwing skills by flipping his blade into the wooden planks between his feet.

"May I help you, Lieutenant?" The quartermaster said, peering over his glasses.

"Yes, sir. I'd like to inquire about a certain prisoner that may have been brought in last week."

He stopped writing and straightened up in his chair. "May I ask the nature of the inquiry?"

"Yes, sir. The prisoner is believed to be in possession of information that may help the war effort. If he's here, I've been ordered to interrogate him."

"Do you have written orders from Captain Davis?"

Mase struggled to keep steady. "No, sir. I was simply ordered to make the inquiry."

The soldier stopped his knife throwing.

The quartermaster pursed his lips. "The captain always gives his orders in written form. What's your name, Lieutenant?"

"Graham, sir—Lieutenant Benjamin Graham."

The quartermaster pulled off his glasses and turned to the soldier behind him. "Private, would you mind calling in Sergeant Quin?"

"I wouldn't advise that, sir."

The quartermaster held out his hand for the private to remain seated, laid his cigar aside, and leaned forward. "And the reason being?"

"The nature of the request could not be provided in writing." He slowly inched his hand toward his pocket.

"And why not, pray tell?"

Mase's heart raced. "Because it's of a private matter. One that involves... a young lady."

The quartermaster did not move, but the edges of his mouth curled upward. He turned to the private and burst out laughing. "Looks like Devil Davis is at it again."

"Yes, sir. Looks that way," Mase replied.

The quartermaster grabbed a large book from under his desk and flipped it open. "What's the prisoner's name?"

"Jeziah Campbell."

The quartermaster dragged his finger down the page then flipped through the next four pages in the same manner. He shook his head. "No Jeziah Cambell."

"I'm sorry, sir. It's Campbell—with a P in the middle."

The quartermaster huffed as he repeated the process. "We have two Campbells—Frederick and George. Could he have gone by either of those?"

"I'm afraid not."

"I'm sorry then, Lieutenant. We don't have him."

"Could he have been shipped out already?"

"Nope," he said, leaning back in his chair, "we haven't made any shipments yet. Our first one is tomorrow at six thirty in the morning."

Mase's heart sank. "Thank you, sir." He saluted. As he headed for the door, he turned back. "By chance, any negros come through?"

The quartermaster gave a heavy sigh and turned to the private. "Hand me that book behind you with the red cover." He looked back at Mase with a raised eyebrow. "A negro, huh?"

"Yes, sir."

The quartermaster opened the book. "We keep all non-enlisted prisoners separate." He scanned the first page, then the second. "Got 'em—Jeziah Campbell—sector C. You'll need to interrogate him today though. He's due to go out on tomorrow's first transport."

Mase resisted the urge to hug the officer, opting to respond in a deadpan tone. "Thank you, sir. I can do that now if possible."

The quartermaster turned to the private. "Assist the lieutenant to the woodshed, then retrieve the prisoner." He lowered his voice. "And, Private, given the nature of the interrogation, you'll need to remain outside—understood?"

"Yes, sir. Follow me, Lieutenant."

As the private led him past the wire side of the prison to the corner closest to the railroad tracks, Mase couldn't believe how open and vulnerable it was. If there were fewer guards, he was sure his fellow Confederates could easily cross the fifteen-foot deadline and rip their way through the wire with limited casualties.

The woodshed the quartermaster spoke of was a small square structure with no windows and just enough room for a table and two chairs. "Wait here," the private said, ushering him inside.

Mase's knee bobbed repeatedly as he awaited his friend's arrival. Several minutes later, metal rattled outside, and he jumped to his feet. The door swung open with the private bulling his way inside, lugging a length of chain behind him. The man shackled to the other end was frail and sickly. His chin rested on his chest from both fatigue and submission. With one swift yank, the private catapulted the prisoner inside, shoving him into the chair opposite Mase. The chains clanged to the floor. "He's all yours, Lieutenant."

As soon as the door closed, Mase bent down and grabbed him by the shoulders. "Spoon, it's me—Mase!"

Spoon's body swayed back and forth. He lifted his head for a second only to have it drop again. The ravages of imprisonment and the guards' abuse had drained him.

Mase put his hands on the sides of his friend's face and lifted his head, his heart sinking as he watched Spoon struggle to stay alert. His face was a thin wrapping of skin over skull. His right eye drooped from lack of nourishment and sleep while the other remained shut, void of sight from the beating Silas had given him that horrid night.

"Spoon. It's me, Mase."

His one good eye brightened. He coughed several times then sighed. "Mase. Is-is it really you?"

Mase's lip quivered. "Yes—it's me."

He reached up and rubbed Mase's chin. "Where're your whiskers?"

"It's a long story," he chuckled.

Spoon ran a bony hand across Mase's sleeve, stopping on his lieutenant insignia. "You one of them now?"

"No, still a Reb. I stole the uniform to sneak in." He leaned in and whispered, "I'm supposed to be interrogating you."

Spoon shook his head. "You big knucklehead—you're gonna get a whuppin'." His words poured out slow and labored, each one requiring more energy than the one before.

"I've missed you, brother." Mase threw his arms around him, then took him by the shoulders and squared him up, prepping him for what he had waited so long to say. "I'm here to take you home."

Spoon shut his eye and rocked back and forth as tears ran over his hollow cheeks. He coughed again, harder and longer than the first.

"I'm going to need your help to make it happen though. Can you manage it?"

Spoon replied with a shallow nod.

"Good. In the morning, right before sunrise, be as

close as possible to the corner that's outside this wood-shed. Don't go over the deadline or they'll shoot you. Be ready to meet me at that corner when you hear the signal. Got it?"

Spoon began coughing again.

Mase placed his palm against his head. "You've got a fever."

"I'll be alright," he wheezed. "What's that signal you mentioned?"

"Lieutenant—you finished?" came the private's voice from outside.

"One more minute," he yelled back. He turned to Spoon. "We've got to get you feeling better." He reached inside his pocket and pulled out two pieces of hardtack. "Eat these. You need to get some strength back."

"But I ain't hungry," he said between coughs.

Mase shoved them into his pocket. "You can eat them later." He put his hand back on his forehead. "Promise me you'll eat them though?"

Spoon nodded. "What's the signal?" His voice began to trail off.

Mase sighed, realizing his friend's condition was growing graver by the minute. "Just listen for a big bang." He started out the door, then turned and smiled. "Can you believe it? We're going home—you and me—home to Willow Creek."

Chapter 30

Mase spent the remainder of the day dodging in and out of buildings, covertly maneuvering around the prison as he pieced together the strategy for their escape. His uniform allowed him to infiltrate the area better than he could have imagined—even to the point of gaining him access to the armory. It had also enabled him to engage in conversation with several raw recruits that had come in that day. Their eyes opened wide as he told them about the impending attack from the Confederate forces just over the ridge.

"Are you for sure, Lieutenant?"

"Sure I'm sure. Johnny Reb's got a counterattack in the making. You boys hear any gunfire, you need to make for town. That's where our stronghold is."

The recruits stumbled over themselves, thanking him for the military nugget.

"By the way, this is new information, so you might want to pass it on amongst the troops."

Sensing he had pushed his luck as much as he could, he stole away in the fading light to a crawlspace beneath the train station. Cramped with only three feet of head-space, it was the perfect hideaway. He stretched out next to a ventilation hole in the foundation and peered down the northern end of the tracks where the train would be coming in, then he turned south, making sure the handcar he had positioned on the rails was still there. Rickety as it was, it was good enough to transport him and his best friend to freedom.

Exhausted from being awake for more than twenty-four hours, he closed his eyes. Sleep arrived quickly, and with it came a dream of him and Spoon climbing onto the handcar and heading south while a long black train full of Confederates rolled off in the opposite direction. As the dream locomotive faded away, its whistle remained. Instead of growing fainter, it grew louder. Three sharp blasts—each louder than the previous—jolted him awake. He rolled over to the hole in the wall and looked north to see the train barreling toward the station, arriving on time and in the cover of darkness.

He crawled outside and discreetly moved into position behind a large water tank. Two rows of twenty soldiers marched past him to the station platform where another fifty stood ready to begin the transportation of prisoners. He pulled Hanna's Luger from his pocket and aimed it across the street at a bucket sitting on top of a stack of hay bales. He was confident he could make the shot but not sure of the outcome. God willing, a second and third shot would follow—the ones that would make the difference.

He wiped the pistol's handle for a better grip, then flipped the safety off and waited, sweat beading on his forehead. The train continued chugging its way toward the station.

Out of nowhere, a lineman came running alongside the

tracks, waving a lantern over his head. "There's a handcar on the track! Somebody move it down!" The train whistle blared another series of blasts, obscuring his plea.

Mase turned to the southern end of the track and realized the fatality of his mistake to position the car closer to the station. He watched helplessly as the train rolled into it, knocking it off the rails. Although still intact, it might as well have been smashed into a million pieces as there was no way for him to physically put it back.

With no time to think, he continued to act. Wiping the sweat from his eyes, he took aim at the water pail and squeezed the trigger. The bullet's impact into the packed black powder blew the bucket to smithereens, simultaneously catching the hay on fire. A third of the camp's soldiers, along with a handful of townspeople, rushed to the inferno, trying to douse the flames before they could spread.

He tucked the Luger in his pocket and ran undetected through back alleys to the opposite side of town. In a similar fashion, he fired his second shot into another carefully disguised explosive—a mason jar filled with more black powder—he had strategically located next to the telegraph office. Instead of hay, a dozen other jars filled with kerosene provided even more disastrous results.

Within seconds, the entire building and the two beside it were ablaze. Mounted officers tried restraining their panicked horses while yelling orders and dispatching more soldiers to save the building that supported their most important means of communication.

So far, the explosions and fires had helped divide the Federal troops and create the chaos he had hoped for. One final shot remained. He leaned back against the wall and crept back into the shadows.

"Halt! Who goes there?"

Mase turned around to find the private who had escorted him to the woodshed, his musket pointed straight at him.

"Lieutenant? Is that you?"

"It is," he said, raising his hands in the air.

"What are you doing back here?"

"Yes, Lieutenant, what exactly *are* you doing back here?" came a voice from the other end of the alley. A tall soldier walked out of the dark, his sword drawn, his insignia indicating a true lieutenant.

"Sir, I heard the first explosion and then the second. I assumed we were under attack, so I headed to the telegraph office to send out a message. But it was too late."

The soldier raised his sword. "Your name, if you please."

"Lieutenant Benjamin Graham."

A glint of light flashed across the saber's edge as it slashed through the air, suspending an inch from his neck.

"If you don't wish to have your jugular sliced, I suggest you tell me where the real Lieutenant Graham is."

Mase slowly moved his hand nearer his pocket. Muskets and swords were no match for the Luger. He just needed the gun to be lowered and the blade taken from his neck. A split second between the two and he could be done with the matter. *The truth*, he thought, *the truth shall set you free.*

"I was transported here from the future to accomplish a mission that involved my overpowering your Lieutenant Graham, taking his uniform, and—"

"Stop!"

Mase felt the moment about to crest.

The officer stepped back, as if fearing the insanity of

what he just heard might rub off on him. "Private, take this lunatic into custody."

The moment the musket barrel dipped below horizontal, Mase's hand was on his pistol. He fired two rounds, one splitting the lieutenant's sternum, the other blowing off the right side of the private's skull. By the time the bodies hit the ground, he was already halfway down the alley.

A minute later, sweating profusely and feeling like his heart would beat out of his chest, he was back in the shadows and tucked behind an empty watering trough across from the armory. Mayhem swirled about him as soldiers ran through the streets carrying water pails. He suddenly realized transferring prisoners was the least of the Union's worries. To his advantage the process was sure to be delayed.

For a moment, he could breathe and think about an alternative escape plan since the handcar was disabled. He calculated having fired the Luger four times. He would need all four remaining bullets for his revised strategy.

With everyone around him concentrating on extinguishing fires, he was able to focus on his most challenging shot. The distance to the target was twice as far as the others. He could get closer, but the ramifications of being even twenty steps nearer could be deadly in regard to the size of the explosion he anticipated.

His hands shook with fatigue and adrenaline—and the knowledge he could not afford to miss. Fewer remaining bullets meant increasing chances of death. Thankful for the trough's foundation, he grabbed his pistol with both hands and propped it on the corner.

Past the length of the gun barrel, beyond its sight, was the window to the armory's front room, its four panes painted black by the Union to keep its contents secret. On the inside, behind the lower right pane, was a small canister of black powder he had placed as the catalyst to what he prayed would be a chain reaction.

Two short breaths calmed his nerves. He held onto the third to help him center his target, then he squeezed the trigger. The force of the initial blast blew his hat off. The third, fourth, and fifth left him lying on his back with splinters of wood and debris raining down on him. Smaller explosions followed in various sequences intermixed with an increasing number of small-caliber gun blasts. Distinguishing them from ammunitions going off and invading Confederate fire was impossible. His desire to create a diversion proved more than successful.

As troops continued managing fires and searching for phantom invaders, he weaved his way to the stables. After finding a length of rope, he mounted a spirited mare and raced bareback into the streets and to his rendezvous point with Spoon. As he had expected, only a handful of nervous guards remained stationed around the prison. Inside, Confederates paced back and forth like wild beasts sensing the kill, ready to feast.

When he reached the back corner, he was met by an anxious young private assigned to secure its position. "Private, I need you and the next man over to head to the armory. We need more help with the fire. Hurry!" The soldiers darted off without questions, leaving only one soldier manning the fence some fifty yards away.

Mase pushed on one of the fence posts. Much to his delight it moved several inches indicating another of the prison's shoddy construction efforts. Out of the corner of his eye, he saw Spoon hobbling toward him. Using the horse to obstruct his actions, he tied the rope around the fence post then lassoed the other end around the mare's neck. The slap to her rump sent the animal galloping off into the back field, pulling most of the fence with her. The roar of the prisoners drowned out the surrounding anarchy as they rushed through the gaping hole.

A bugle blared out the signal to commence firing, and dozens of men fell with the first volley. Another dozen fell with the second round. Mase pushed his way through the wave of men, trying to find his friend. Trampled by the horde, Spoon lay on the ground fifty yards in front of him, holding his chest and coughing uncontrollably.

"Spoon!" he called and waved at his friend. "I'm coming!" The last thing he remembered was the crunch of a Confederate's fist to the side of his head.

"He ain't no Yankee," were the words he awoke to a moment later. Spoon's arm was wrapped around him, shielding him against more attacks. "You gotta get out of those blues, Mase. They think you're one of 'em." He looked around frantically. "I know—play dead!"

Mase readily obliged.

A few minutes later, Spoon returned, gasping for air and holding a grey jacket and hat. He tilted his head toward a fallen Confederate. "He says it's okay."

Mase quickly made the switch. "Come on, we gotta get to the train."

"But that train's going north."

"Not today she isn't," he said with a grin. "Today, she's headin' south." Mase turned his back to Spoon. "Now jump on."

After several attempts, Spoon pulled himself onto Mase's back, and they were off and running toward the train. Fifty yards from the last boxcar they ducked behind a hedgerow and looked back on where they had been.

The sun peeked over the hillside into the hollow. Its rays of pinks and purples mixed with the smoke of the burning buildings, creating a muddy haze illuminating the hellish spectacle of murder and destruction that raged through the town. Every building was ablaze, every Union soldier was in mortal combat with a man in grey. The only men not engaged in the battle were the handful guarding the train.

Each of the five cars had an armed soldier standing in front of the sliding door. The engine room was an unknown. Mase pulled his Luger from his pocket. "Four bullets, five Yankees," he whispered to himself. "Stay here," he told Spoon.

He crouched down and ran around the back of the train facing out into the woods. Not a Federal in sight. All the guards were on the other side facing the prison, watching and hoping their countrymen would regain order.

He slowly slid the back door open just enough to take aim at the unsuspecting guard on the other side. His shot that took the soldier's life blended with the rest of the explosions, allowing his kill to go unnoticed. On a more noticeable scale was Spoon's declining condition. As he limped toward Mase, his labored breathing and perpetual cough were becoming as worrisome to Mase as any enemy counterattack. Running to meet him, Spoon fell into his arms.

"Let's get you inside." Mase hoisted him onto the edge of the boxcar and laid him on his side.

Spoon rolled over and stretched his hand out to the woods. He tried speaking again but could only grunt.

"Come," was all he could manage to say.

Mase turned around to find two Confederates walking toward him. One was old and scruffy, the other young and fresh-faced. The older one carried a musket. Together they were dragging an unconscious soldier with them, his head matted with blood.

"We seen you heading here," said the older one. "You thinkin' what I think you are?"

"Yes. I could use your help. Is that thing loaded?"

"Yep."

"You any good with it?"

"I'm from Mississippi," he said with a smirk.

"Well, put your man on board then y'all follow me to the next car."

"*That man* is our colonel."

"Okay, then put *your colonel* on board, then follow me."

As they were attending to the soldier, Mase took off his jacket and put it around Spoon's shoulders. He put his hand to his forehead. "Dang, you're burning up something fierce."

Spoon tried to speak but had no energy. All he could do was cough.

Mase patted him on the leg. "I'll be back shortly."

The two soldiers followed him to the adjacent boxcar where he laid out his plan with military efficiency.

"What's your name, son?" said the one with the musket.

"Corporal Masen Winslow."

"Well then, Corporal, let's get at 'em."

At that, the three men split off into different directions, the older heading to the back of the train, the younger to the front. Mase ran to the middle car where he positioned himself underneath the train a few feet away from the soldier stationed in front of it. His heart pounded as he waited.

"Yeeehah! Let the turkey shoot begin, boys!" yelled the younger soldier out in front of the engine. As hoped, all the guards turned his way. A second later, the crack of musket fire from the back of the train dropped the second guard like a sack of potatoes. Simultaneously, Mase silenced the third guard with an easy shot from underneath the train. He rolled out next to the dead body just in time to take aim on the fourth guard running to the aid of his fallen comrade. *Pow.* The soldier fell to his knees, his head slamming into the soft earth, face-first, just inches from him.

The older soldier ran huffing past him toward the engine where the last guard was pulling his bayonet from the young Confederate's stomach. With his head tucked low, the older man rammed into the guard, sending the Yankee's weapon flying out of his hands, then he dropped to his knees beside the young boy.

Behind him, the Union soldier had found a replacement weapon, a large rock, and was standing over his head, preparing to bring it down upon him when Mase's last bullet blew his brainpan from his skull. The locomotive came to life. Steam blasted from the engine, and the wheels squealed into rotation in the direction from which they had come.

Mase ran up to the older soldier as he was caring for his wounded comrade. "We need to get him to one of the cars quick." Together they carried the soldier to the car closest to the engine and placed him inside. "Take care of him. I'll be back."

"But, Corporal, we're headed in the wrong direction."

Mase was already climbing up the side of the car. "I know." He pulled himself onto the roof and crawled toward the engine, peeking over the edge. Only two men were manning it. A slender one was feverishly pushing and pulling levers, and a large, surly one was shoveling coal into the boiler's firebox and cursing. Swinging his feet over the edge, Mase leaped onto the small platform between the engine and the boxcar. "Reverse this train—now!" He swung his empty Luger from one to the other.

The men put their hands in the air. The skinny one's eyes were wide as a fawn's. The bigger one had no expression.

"For God's sake, this isn't a robbery." Mase grabbed his gun with both hands to steady a sudden case of tremors brought on by his lack of ammunition. The only real weapon he had now was the tone of voice. "Put the train in reverse—now!"

The man pulling levers reached up and pulled a handle, causing the wheels to come to a screeching halt. The momentum threw Mase back into the boxcar behind him. He grabbed the platform railing and pulled himself back into the engine's cab.

"Go on!" he ordered, thrusting the gun at the skinny man's control station.

"Ye-ye-yes, sir." He reached across the firebox, grabbed another large metal lever, and thrust it forward. The train jerked into motion as the wheels slowly rotated in the opposite direction.

Mase looked back. To his surprise, a horde of Confederates were climbing into the cars as more ran across the field to do the same. The train continued to gain speed, and the prison gradually faded out of sight. "Does this railway go through South Carolina?" he asked.

"Yes, sir. All the way to Charleston."

"Good. That's where we're going. No stops—understood?"

"Yes, sir."

Exhausted, he sat on a small bench seat at the back of the cab, propped the gun on his knee, and stared into the firebox. The burly man stopped shoveling and turned around, cocking his head as he studied his gun. "Never seen such a fancy pistol. What kind is it?"

"Luger."

"How many bullets it got?" The man moved forward.

Mase stood. "Enough for each of you—two for you if you step a foot closer."

The man snarled and turned back to shoveling his coal.

Mase returned to his seat. The clickity-clack of the metal wheels on the track combined with the whirl of the wind passing through the open cab lulled him into a trance. His heart was on the mend, and his soul was full of hope. He was taking his friend home. If he got him there in time, he could change everything. The future of friends, family, and generations to come was at stake.

His eyes grew heavy, and he began to nod off. The first time his head bobbed, he caught himself, vowing not to allow it to happen again. The second time his chin hit his chest, he jerked himself awake and rubbed his eyes. When he opened them, all he saw was the flat side of a shovel swinging into his forehead.

The next thing he knew, he was waking up beside the tracks, blood streaming from a gash running from his hairline down into his right eye. The train was nowhere in sight. He pounded the ground with his fist. How could he have let this happen when so much was at stake? Suddenly everything was in jeopardy. Was he still in enemy territory? Was he halfway home, a quarter of the way? Tearing a strip of cloth from the bottom of his shirt, he wrapped it around his head and continued on.

An hour of walking brought him to the crossroads of a town smaller than the one he had just left. Only a block away, the train tracks disappeared into a covered bridge that crossed over a large, fast-moving river. Every other direction was flat and barren. Except for a scraggly boy rolling a wheel hoop toward him and an old man napping in a chair outside a barbershop, it was pretty much vacant.

"New in town?" the boy asked.

"Just passing through."

"You a Reb or Yank?"

"Where exactly is this place?"

"Binghamton City," he said.

"How far by train are we from Pointer's Cove?"

"Hmm, by train—I'd say a couple hours. If youz a Reb, you might wanna skedaddle. There's a handful of Yanks still roaming these parts."

"So the town is—"

"Reb by heart, Yankee by the takin'.

"You're a Confederate then?"

"Momma says in these times we need to bend with the wind. But I says we need to stay true to who we is."

"Mordecai, get yur tail over here," yelled the old man, waking from his nap.

"Sorry, mister, gotta go. Unc's callin'."

The old man grabbed the boy's elbow and drug him

squirming around the corner of the barbershop. A moment later, the sounds of boots and clanking hardware resonated from the street they had turned down. Two armed Union soldiers walked around the corner. The moment they spotted him, their pace quickened. He headed in the direction of the bridge, matching their tempo.

"You there—stop!"

He began to run.

"Stop now, or we'll shoot!"

A glance back proved the threat to be real. They had stopped and were taking aim. The crack of the musket sent a minnie ball whizzing past his ear. With not enough energy to outrun them, he knew his only escape was the bridge.

The additional time it took them to take their shot allowed him to pass through the bridge then climb over the side railing, onto the outside of the bridge opposite their view. The river's current looked capable of taking him downstream, but was it deep enough for the jump? As the sound of boots clomped through the bridge, he continued to inch his way to its middle.

"Where'd he go?" echoed a voice from inside, followed by the sound of their boots on their way out into the open.

"There he is."

Clinging to the side, he turned to see the second soldier preparing to shoot. As he was about to pull the trigger, Mase jumped, the force of his fall taking him deeper and harder than he had anticipated. His left foot jammed into the jagged edge of a submerged boulder. *Snap.* The pain shot through his ankle up to his hip. Moments later, he emerged, gasping for air, above the torrent of white water and let out a guttural growl.

After a few minutes, the white water calmed into a

lazy river, and he rolled over and looked back. With the bridge long out of sight, he continued to float on, the cool water and the lack of pressure on his foot easing the pain. The serenity around him ran contrary to his inner anguish. The river had saved him but was now taking him farther away from his destiny. He had to get back to the railroad tracks. It was his only way home. He squeezed his eyes together and asked God to help him out of this.

The sandy shoal he climbed onto was a welcome intermediary to the hard ground of the river's bank. For a moment, there was mild discomfort, but when he stepped onto dry land, putting all his weight on his ankle, the pain almost brought him to his knees. He grimaced as he stepped forward. The second step was slightly better. The third was worse than the first.

So it went for the next hour as he slogged his way back to the tracks. By the time he hobbled up to the railroad's gravel shoulders, he was spent. The gash on his forehead was bleeding again, his head was pounding, and his ankle was on fire. He looked out at the endless miles of steel and crossties ahead of him, took two steps forward, and collapsed facedown into the jagged rocks, blood trickling from his forehead. His breath became shallower as he drifted into unconsciousness.

Chapter 31

"Look yonder, Sarge."

"What?"

"Them buzzards circlin' up ahead. We might be too late."

A few minutes later the soldiers pulled their wagon alongside the lump of flesh the birds of prey had been waiting to feast upon.

A stout, heavily bearded sergeant in his middle years bent down and rolled the body over. "He matches the description, alright." He placed his hand on his neck. "Well, I'll be. Private, this here fella is still alive." He put his arms under Mase's shoulders. "Help me get him in the wagon."

Together they tossed him onto a bed of hay. Climbing onto the bench seat, the sergeant snapped the reins. "Giddup." The wagon jerked into motion, and Mase's eyes fluttered as he faded out of consciousness.

For the next several hours, the two men bantered back and forth about whether their passenger was a deserter. By the time they arrived at their destination, they decided it didn't matter since it was out of their hands.

The closer they got to the train depot, the more skittish the horse became as the sergeant worked the wagon through rows of hundreds of beleaguered soldiers, all waiting to board a train.

"Where's Captain Edwards?" he asked the lead guard as they rolled up to the station platform.

"Straight ahead, sir—in the main office."

"Tell him Sergeant Tatum has Winslow."

Several of the nearby Confederates waiting to board the train began whispering.

"Excuse me, Sergeant. Did we hear correctly? Is that Corporal *Masen Winslow* you got in the back?"

"It is."

"Is he dead?"

"No—and don't go disturbing him."

"No, sir. 'course not." The soldier walked to the wagon and stopped to peer over the side. Another soldier walked up beside him, reached in, and placed his hand on Mase's shoulder.

"Mind yourself back there," the sergeant barked.

A few minutes later, the guarded conversation had spread throughout the station. The line of men waiting to board the train was now queued up in front of the buckboard in which Mase was lying. One by one, they silently walked by, tipping their hats, touching the side of the wagon, or whispering their prayers. All the while, the sergeant and his private held vigil over their passenger.

Three shrill whistles split the air and sent all the men scurrying back to the train. A tall, lean captain walked onto the platform. "All men back in line. Boarding in five minutes."

He stepped to the wagon and looked inside. "Well done," he said to the two soldiers who had brought Mase in. "Take him to the rear car and place him in the back corner next to the negro." He pulled out a small wax-sealed envelope. "Put this in his pocket and tell the negro boy to make sure he knows it's there when he wakes up."

A few minutes later, the two soldiers were back in their wagon, preparing for their next assignment. Before departing, the sergeant turned and saluted the locomotive's last car as it chugged out of sight into the southern horizon.

After a couple hours, Mase stirred and rolled back and forth, trying to get comfortable. No position, not even lying on his back, provided relief. His forehead and ankle were throbbing. Rather than lie in misery, he pulled himself to a sitting position against the back wall. Slumped next to him, crammed into the corner, was the frail figure of a black man, his head wobbling in rhythm with the train. "Spoon, is that you?" He nudged him. "Spoon?"

Spoon's head barely rose. "Mase—you—you—made it," he said, leaning into his shoulder.

Mase wrapped his arms around him "Can you believe it? We're alive—and we're here together." He suddenly pulled back. "Wait! Is this the boxcar I put you in?"

Spoon nodded.

"How'd I get here? Which way are we going?"

"Confederate soldiers brung you in. We're going south."

"Confederates? But—I'm a deserter. They're taking me back to hang me!"

Spoon broke into gravel-filled laughter that immediately morphed into a violent cough. He doubled over, clutching his chest. As the attack subsided, he released a wheezy sigh then slowly moved his head back and forth. "There ain't gonna be no hangin', you knucklehead," he said with a broken laugh.

"But I left and didn't come back—that's desertion!"

"None of that means diddly-squat. You came back. When you came back for me, you came back for all of 'em."

Mase turned around. More than fifty men were packed into the boxcar, and they were all staring at him. An older soldier pushed his way through the crowd, holding his hat with both hands out in front of him. "I'm sorry, Corporal Winslow, for not coming with you."

"You're one of the soldiers who helped me take out the train guards."

"Yes, sir," he said, lowering his head. "I got to the engine room too late. They'd already thrown you off." His tone intensified. "But I let 'em have it something good though. I'm sorry I didn't—"

"It's alright. What's your name?"

"Private Archie Millsap."

"Well, Archie, I'm here now, and that's all that matters."

Spoon tugged at his arm. "All these men are here 'cause of you."

"That's right," the private said. "These and all the ones in the other four boxcars. All told, 298 men, including our Colonel Reynolds."

"You see. You ain't no deserter—you're a hero." Spoon grabbed his chest, staving off another coughing attack.

"Why don't you rest?" Mase urged.

Spoon shook his head and wiped his mouth with his sleeve, leaving a track of blood across it. "No time for that. We got some catchin' up to do." He winked at him with his good eye. "What ya think Maudie and Sissy been doing all this time?"

Mase wanted to dive into the miracle of the memory stones and explain where he had been and what he still needed to do and how little time there was left. There was just too much. More than anything, though, he wanted Spoon to know how sorry he was for the suffering he had caused him. Tears filled his eyes. "The night I took the thunder stick from Uncle Joseph and then—"

"Don't you be going there, Mase."

"I-I didn't know it was Silas. I swear I didn't. On my honor, I didn't know."

"I know. Trust me, I do."

"But I've caused you so much pain. I've caused everyone pain."

"You gotta get that out of your head," Spoon said, grabbing Mase's forearm. "That's the devil telling you those things."

Mase looked at him, his eyes pleading. "Can you ever forgive me?"

Spoon moved his hand to Mase's shoulder and smiled the same as he did on the day he gave him his diary. "Don't you be frettin' none 'bout that," he said, struggling through a high-pitched wheeze. "Ain't nothin' to forgive."

For a brief time, Spoon was able to rest without coughing. Taking the opportunity, they reminisced about their youth—their times playing in the creek, the barbeques, and their most exciting adventures.

"Maybe you and me can snag some crawdads outa the creek when we get back."

"That sounds like a grand idea," Mase said, wincing as

he pulled his boot off. Where his ankle bone should have been visible was a swollen mass of purple and blue flesh. A blister of equal size wrapped around his heel.

"Looks painful," Spoon said, his whole body shaking.

Mase put his hand across his forehead. "Your fever's worse than before." He turned to the rest of the soldiers. "Anyone have a canteen of water?" He had barely spoken the words before three men were offering their canisters to him.

"Thank you, fellas. One'll do fine."

He turned back to find Spoon struggling to tear off a strip of his own shirt as sweat ran down the side of his face. "Ca—can you h—help me?"

"Uh, sure." With a quick yank, two feet of tattered fabric came off in his hand.

"And the wa—wa—water, please."

Mase placed both the fabric and canteen into his trembling hands. Instead of drinking the water, as he hoped he would do, Spoon poured it over Mase's injured foot then dried it with the piece of his shirt. Tears welled up in Mase's eyes, then he took Spoon by the hands, preventing him from finishing his task.

"Don't," he said shaking his head. "I'm okay. Seriously."

Spoon gently removed his hands and proceeded drying Mase's foot. He finished by wrapping the ankle with the strips of fabric from his shirt. "Th—th—there," he said, "all done."

Mase smiled. "Doc Parkin couldn't have done any better."

Spoon patted him on the knee, then closed his eyes. "Oh, happy days," he said as his head fell onto his friend's shoulder. Weary, wounded, and sick, together, they drifted asleep as the other soldiers watched in awe of a bond that, as countrymen, they had been fighting so hard to keep divided.

Morning arrived just as the train pulled into the station. All the soldiers piled out, worn thin and tattered but exuberant as they stepped so deeply into the heart of the Confederacy. Two men remained wedged into the farthest corner of the last car.

"Excuse me, Corporal Winslow, we've arrived."

Sun filled the boxcar, revealing a young officer standing in the entrance. "Proud to have you here in Charleston, sir. Might I assist you in debarking?"

Mase raised his aching head toward the blurry silhouette. Heaving himself up, he hobbled toward him.

"I'd be glad to get you a crutch for the hitch in that leg," the soldier said.

"A crutch would be nice, but can you do me a favor and have some of your men bring a stretcher for my friend? He needs to be seen by a doctor immediately."

No sooner had he clicked his heels and departed than two stout men arrived with the requested items.

"Try not to wake him," Mase said as they lifted Spoon onto the canvas stretcher. "And please make sure a doctor gets to him right away."

Stepping out onto the station platform was like stepping into another world. The mildew and rot of the dank boxcar yielded to a clear blue sky hanging atop a town absent of fires, explosions, and men stabbing, shooting, and choking one another. The only thing remotely disturbing was the annoying young boy hawking newspapers at him.

"Hey, mister, two bits, and you can read all about

yesterday's big escape from Pointer's Cove."

"Sorry, young man. Afraid I haven't any money."

"Sure about that, mister? It's a doozy."

"It's okay. I've already heard about it. Say, can you tell me what day it is?"

"For two bits, I can," he said with a toothy grin. "Just pullin' yur leg. It's Friday."

"Good Friday?"

"Yes, sir."

"Plenty good for you, fellas," joked a nearby soldier.

"For sure," he replied with an obligatory smile. The pun was weak, but the meaning could not have been any more accurate. Celebration would have to wait, however. According to Maudie, Cluc was killed on Easter sometime in the evening. And right before midnight, she and Sissy used the memory stones to escape. If he was to alter these events, he had roughly two and a half days to make it back to Willow Creek by sundown. Given a sturdy horse, he calculated he could easily make it by sometime Sunday morning, leaving him the rest of the day to prepare.

Suddenly feeling dizzy, he seized his crutch with both hands.

A soldier rushed over, took him by the waist, and walked him to a bench. "Are you okay, Corporal?"

"Just a little dizzy."

"When was the last time you ate?"

"I don't recall."

The soldier reached into his pocket and pulled out an apple. "Here—have this."

Mase gripped the fruit with both hands and chomped into it. Within seconds only the core remained.

"Feeling better?"

"Yes, thank you."

"Good, let's go see the doc now."

"Doctor?" said Mase. "I don't have time for that. I've got to—"

"Sorry, sir, Captain's orders," he said, ushering him toward the hospital.

"Can you at least take me to where Spoon is?"

The soldier chuckled. "Now why would you want to go to the mess hall?"

"No, no, Spoon's my friend. I had them take him to the hospital."

"Oh, you mean the negro boy. Yes, of course."

The hospital was crowded with a throng of wounded and sick soldiers, all waiting to be seen by one physician.

"Wait here," the soldier said, returning a minute later and escorting Mase to a small operating room that had recently been used, considering the fresh pools of blood on the metal table and the crimson pile of rags in the corner.

A moment later, the door swung open and in walked a portly man wearing glasses and a white coat covered in blood, his hands outstretched, as if meeting an old friend. "Why, Corporal Winslow," he said, shaking his hand more rapidly than gentlemanly acceptable, "what a pleasure to meet you. I'm Dr. Burns."

"Good morning, Doctor."

"Your exploits are extraordinary. The entire city of Charleston is abuzz with the details. I myself am fascinated by how you commandeered the enemy's locomotive." He chuckled at his choice of the word *commandeered*. "Would you mind regaling me with the—"

"I'm sorry, Doc. I'd like to do that, but unfortunately, I

have another urgent matter I need to address."

The doctor raised his eyebrows. "Ah yes, no rest for the weary, I presume."

"Can I see my friend?"

"Your friend is Spoon—correct?"

"That's right."

The doctor's exuberant tone suddenly turned serious. "Per your request, I saw your friend immediately. Given, as you said, your matter is urgent, I'll get straight to it. Your friend, I'm afraid, has internal bleeding. It's slow, mind you, but… we can't stop it."

Mase hobbled toward the doctor. "What do you mean, you *can't* stop it?"

"The injury, evidently caused by blunt force, is located where we're unable to get to it. It's only a matter of time."

"How much time?"

"Three—maybe four days. Unfortunately, his fever is getting worse, which may expedite it by a day or two. We just can't tell."

Mase's scream reverberated throughout the building. Swinging his crutch over his head, he brought it crashing onto the metal table, breaking it into hundreds of pieces. He slammed his fists against the wall then sat, throwing his head in his hands while the doctor backed himself into the corner.

Eventually, Mase lifted his head. "I'm sorry. Please forgive me. It's just—"

"No need to apologize," the doctor said, inching his way toward the door, ready to run upon another outburst. "I-I understand completely."

"I need to see him."

"You might want him to rest a bit—"

"I said—I need to see him!" Mase commanded.

"Of course, of course. He's across the hall." The doctor hurriedly shuffled his way out the door, leading Mase to an improvised room that was nothing more than a tiny alcove partitioned off by several dirty pieces of linen sewn together.

"I'd like a moment with him."

"Certainly," the doctor replied, following him through the divider.

"Alone," Mase said.

"Oh, certainly," said the doctor, retreating into the hall. "I'm only a few doors down if you need me."

Behind the veil, Spoon lay on what appeared to be two large coffee tables butted together, his head tilted toward a wooden bucket by his side. Hearing Mase enter, he looked up and smiled, his teeth tinged red from the internal injuries.

"Hey, Mase." His voice was thin and weak.

"Hey, knucklehead." Mase squeezed his hand, wanting to tell him everything was going to be alright and he was going to get well, but he had never lied to Spoon before. "Doc says you're pretty banged up."

"Doesn't hurt all that much—just dog tired."

Mase's lip quivered. "Is there anything I can do? You want some water, maybe a blanket?"

"I'm fine," he said. "But I shore would like to hear about your new orders."

"Orders? Why would I be getting orders?"

"I'm sorry. I forgot to tell you." Spoon closed his eyes, summoning more energy. "The two fellas who toted you onto the train put your orders in your jacket's front pocket."

With two fingers, Mase pulled out the small envelope, his blood beginning to boil as he stared down on the wax seal bearing the Confederate monogram. No matter what the orders, he would not be obeying them. Nothing or no one was going to jeopardize his chances of getting Spoon to Willow Creek. A court-martial would simply have to wait.

Mase grabbed it and began to rip it in half when Spoon placed his hand on it. "You at least gotta read it."

"I reckon." Mase sighed as he broke the seal and extracted a one-page document.

His eyebrows rose. "Why, these aren't orders at all." He squinted to make sure he was seeing correctly. "It's a directive granting me an honorable discharge for valor displayed at Pointer's Cove." His jaw dropped. "They're giving me a horse and whatever I need to return home. It's signed 'Colonel Johnathon Reynolds, 103rd Georgia Brigade.' There's a line at the bottom—*Take care of our boy Jeziah.*" He looked at Spoon. "That was the colonel those fellows put on the train, wasn't it?"

Spoon nodded. "I was one of his valets. Colonel John was always lookin' out for me."

Mase stared out the window, his eyes darting here and there as he processed the contents of the paper, the journey ahead, and what he had to do when he reached his destination.

Two young boys were playing a make-do game of cornhole with rocks in place of bags and a circle drawn in the dirt for the target. A corner of his mouth turned up as he watched them attempt to toss the rocks into the dirty ring. His heart took an additional beat as he turned his gaze to his dying friend.

"They won't need the stones," he whispered to himself.

"What'd you say?" Spoon asked.

His face suddenly aglow, Mase took Spoon gently by

the shoulders. "Maudie and Sissy won't need the stones!" He jumped up and started for the door. "Don't worry," he said, pulling the curtain to the side, "I'll be right back."

An hour later, he was back in the hospital discussing his plans with the doctor.

"I don't understand what's so compelling about your getting to Beaufort by Easter, but going by wagon is going to make it tough. You could do it by yourself on horse-back but by *wagon*—I don't think so. Most likely, he'll die along the way."

"I understand, Doc, but I have to."

"It's Good Friday. Why don't you let him pass peacefully here? I promise I'll see to him personally."

"I appreciate your concerns as well as your offer, but I *have* to do this."

"Doesn't make sense to me, but if you're bent on it, then by all means—he's your negro."

"No, sir. He's my friend."

"Suit yourself. I'll have an orderly bring him out."

A few minutes later, Spoon was in a wheelchair being shuttled onto the street and to the back of a wagon where Mase stood leaning on his new crutch.

"What's all this?" Spoon whispered.

"I told you back at Pointer's Cove—we're going home."

"You're something else, you know that?"

"Yep," he said, placing the crutch to the side. "Now, help me get your lazy butt into the wagon." Mase reached under Spoon's arms and began to lift when two strapping soldiers intervened by lifting Spoon out of the chair and laying him across the fresh bed of hay that filled the back.

Mase threw a blanket over him, tucking it in around him just as Maudie had done when he was little. "You ready for ole Percy to take us home?"

"Who's Percy?"

"Why, he's the fella pulling this-here wagon."

"Percy—that's a good horse name."

As they pulled out of town, the city's clock tower chimed twelve times. Southward they headed, hoping and praying for the speedy journey Mase knew they so desperately needed.

Chapter 32

The road out of Charleston was an easy one with fellow travelers passing by about every thirty minutes. The hard-packed earth that wound through vast tracts of wide-open farmland was smooth and comfortable on Percy's hooves, the few bumps making it tolerable for Spoon. The doctor had warned that if Spoon were jostled about too much, it could kill him. The burden of ensuring a stable ride along with keeping a steady pace had Mase on edge. In planning for the latter, he had taken advantage of Colonel Reynolds' generous offer by requesting the wagon be stocked with food and water for them as well as drawn by Percy. In addition, he had been given a fully loaded revolver with holster, a canvas tarp, and a pocket watch, which he placed beside him and referred to every twenty minutes.

If all went well, they would push on until three in the morning, sleep a few hours, then begin again at sunrise for the same schedule on Saturday. With no mishaps, they would be at Willow Creek sometime around noon the following day—Easter Sunday.

For the rest of the afternoon, the skies remained blue-bird clear with white fluffy clouds floating along. Just before dusk, the wind picked up, and the skies turned grey. Claps of thunder from far away grew louder. Trees began to sway, and birds darted about, looking for shelter. Mase wiped away the raindrops that had started to obscure the time on his pocket watch. Seven o'clock. They still had a solid eight hours of travel to stay on schedule. He pulled the horse to a hard stop, reached under the bench seat, and pulled out the tarp. Within minutes he had stretched it over the wagon, wrapping Spoon inside a cocoon of hay and canvas.

For the first few hours, the rain was steady but light enough to allow them to move along at the same pace. By midnight, however, it was coming down in buckets, causing them to creep along at barely more than walking speed. Their only saving grace came when the road took a turn into a long stretch of forest. With the trees helping to shield them from the rain, they were able to get one last hour of travel in before the road opened to a tobacco field.

After tending to Percy, Mase crawled under the tarp. Spoon, who had slept the entire way, awoke just long enough to take some water and eat a piece of jerky. Within a few minutes, he was back asleep. Soaking wet, Mase lay next to him, watching his chest rise and fall and praying for it to continue long enough for them to reach the plantation. A moment later, exhaustion, along with the rain's rhythmic cadence against the canvas, lulled him to sleep.

The next morning, Mase woke from a few hours of fitful slumber. Blurry-eyed, unrested, and with the ever-present burning sensation in his ankle, he wiggled his way out from under the tarp to see a thin layer of pink clouds dissolving into space. Since Spoon was still asleep and they were behind schedule by two or three hours, he hooked Percy to the wagon, and they proceeded on, only to come to a standstill at the edge of the forest. Unlike the patch of road protected by the canopy of leaves, the one leading into the open was just what he had expected—a muddy nightmare that most likely would not be dry until noon. Traversing it was a gamble he had to take.

With a flick of the reins, the horse pulled the wagon into the open. Immediately the wheels began to sink. If he proceeded at the same pace, they would sink even deeper. If he pulled back, they most certainly would be stuck. He had to move forward—and fast. He snapped the reins, and the wagon lurched ahead. Without letting up, he prodded the horse onward, yelling and lashing him until they reached another wooded area where the ground was firm again. Percy neighed and stomped in protest of the forced sprint, but to Mase's surprise and relief, Spoon had not moved.

On they went until noon. Mase repeated the tactic of running his rig at breakneck speed from one section of dry ground to another until the horse refused to move. Under the shade of a pecan tree, he unharnessed his wagon and let the beast rest while he tended to his friend. Spoon's cough had returned, and blood trickled from the corners of his mouth.

Unlike the morning's first run, Spoon had awoken to experience every jarring bump produced by the dozens of sprints Mase was forced to execute. His guilt grew knowing with every mad dash he was moving Spoon one step closer to death.

"I'm sorry. If I didn't keep us moving, we'd have gotten stuck. I promise not to put you through any more of this. We'll wait here for a couple hours until the road dries out."

Spoon raised his hand, as slowly and with as much effort as if it were lead, and placed it on his. It was cold and dry. Mase's heart sank as Spoon inhaled then pushed out each word in three long breaths. "Do—what you—have to."

By noon the road was firm enough to proceed but not enough to move at Friday's pace. Large clumps of earth clung to the wheels, creating a drag on the wagon and forcing the horse to work twice as hard. Already worn down by the series of grueling morning runs, Percy moved forward in starts and stops. At times, Mase had to use his crutch as leverage when dragging him forward by his bridle.

As midnight approached, neither man nor beast could go any farther. They would simply have to rest and get up three hours earlier to make it by dusk. Even then, he wasn't sure of the timing as he had no idea how far away they truly were. All he could do was estimate the hours he thought they had lost. As he calculated the severity of their situation, his optimism of making it to the plantation early began to wane.

Morning came later than he wished. Instead of waking to the pitch-black of the wee hours as he had planned, he awoke six hours later to a brilliant, pale-blue dawn. He leaned back and let loose a loathing growl aimed only at himself. Sleep was not something he could afford, yet his body had indulged in it anyway. Each additional hour behind schedule was another death knell for those he loved. He had no idea how he was going to make up the time. He would figure it out on the road or die trying.

The only positive was that Percy was more rested, and the roads were dry again. After checking on Spoon and hitching the wagon, they were on their way, this time at a quicker pace than Saturday.

A couple hours later, he pulled in behind a man and his wife in a wagon stocked full of young'ns, all dressed in their Sunday-go-to-meeting clothes. Coming alongside them, Mase eyed their two fresh horses with envy. "Good morning, folks."

"Howdy there, stranger," the man chirped.

"Happy Easter," all the children chimed in.

"Happy Easter to y'all as well. By the way, do you happen to know how far Beaufort is?" Mase asked.

"Sure. I rode it straight last week. She's about twelve hours."

"Really!" Twelve hours to Beaufort and another hour to Willow Creek would get them there by nine that night. His mud sprints had gained him time. "Thank you!"

"Sure thing. When you get to town, go east at the town square, and it's dead straight for twelve."

"Wait—twelve straight? Don't you mean it's twelve hours from *here* to Beaufort?"

"No, sir. I'm sorry, I meant to say it's twelve from the center of our town."

"Well, how far is it to town?" He held his breath.

"Three hours."

"Come on, Pa," squealed the oldest child. "We're gonna miss the egg hunt."

Mase suddenly felt dizzy as the revelation of the additional three hours soaked in.

"You okay, mister?" the lady asked.

"Ye—Yes. I'm fine." Mase shook his head, clearing his

mind of the sour news. It would now be close to midnight before they reached the plantation. Sixteen hours with one ragged horse pulling a wagon with a passenger on the verge of death. He wanted to scream but didn't know at who or what. The rain, the mud, his oversleeping—all the delays flashed in his mind as culprits.

"Thank you kindly. You folks have a happy Easter." With a set jaw, he snapped the reins and set Percy begrudgingly back in motion. Somehow, he would have to make up the time.

The town through which they passed was not much more than the intersection of two roads and a handful of buildings. It's only point of interest was the livery stable where he tried to negotiate trading his horse for a fresh one.

"I've got twelve hours ahead of me," Mase said, pointing to the haggard creature hitched to his wagon. "I don't think he'll make it."

"I believe ya on that," the stable owner said.

"If you'll trade him out, I promise to return with ten times the payment."

"I'm sorry, young fella. We got burned with a similar promise a few weeks back. Unfortunately, I can't do a straight trade attached to any kind of promise of sending money."

Walking back to his rig, Mase spotted the wagon owned by the family he had met on the way. When he suggested swapping out one of his mares with his horse, the answer was a resounding no. "Sorry, mister, I gotta get 'em back to the farm fresh so I can plow under my bottom forty."

For a second, Mase thought of circling back and stealing a horse from the stable, but the idea quickly died as he realized how lucky he had been to not be shot as a deserter. Horse thieving would not be tolerated nor forgiven, even for the hero of Pointer's Cove. He decided then that he would make it home with his soul intact... no matter the consequences.

The afternoon was a slow burn of growing anxiety and fear as he continued to monitor the strength of both Percy and Spoon. Both continued to fade with each mile, requiring him to stop every hour to let them rest. His own condition waned as well. The pain in his ankle now shot up to his hip, and the gash on his forehead had begun to throb.

With no landmarks to help gauge his distance, he had to rely on input from the occasional farmers or slaves tending their fields alongside the road. At seven o'clock he made his last inquiry of the day with a pig farmer who confirmed Beaufort to still be four hours away. With the additional hour to the plantation, he could not afford any more breaks. He stomped the floorboard and proceeded onward at the same grueling pace.

The remaining miles stretched on forever as pain and fatigue took their toll. Percy, soaked in sweat, began biting at his bit and rearing up occasionally in attempts to free himself of the wagon while Spoon lay curled inside, rocking in agony. Mase continued to fight through his exhaustion and his own pains while battling his demons of guilt and despair.

At 10:33 that evening, the wagon rolled into the vacant streets of downtown Beaufort, the flickering oil lamps along

Bay Street highlighting remnants of the day's festivities. Broken colored eggshells lay strewn across the wood-plank sidewalks, and pastel streamers tumbled along, drifting into the air whenever the breeze kicked up. Past the recruitment office was Franklin's Blacksmith Shop, the site of his and Spoon's legendary potato battle. He pulled the wagon up to it and got out to check on Spoon under the streetlamp.

"Wh-wh-who is it?" came a voice from behind the building.

"Just checking my load," Mase said, looking under the tarp.

A little man carrying a pitchfork appeared around the corner. "W-w-well, we're c-closed."

"Levi Johnston? Is that you?"

"Th-that's me. Who's askin'?"

"It's me. Mase Winslow."

"M-Mase?" He cocked his head. "You look different. Where's your b-beard?"

"Long story. You work here?"

He puffed his chest. "Yep."

"Can you do me a favor? I've got to get to Willow Creek before midnight."

"Th-that's an hour's hard ride."

"I know, I know. Can you loan me a fresh horse?"

"Wish I c-could, but we ain't boardin' any right now."

Mase slapped his hand against his thigh, paced back and forth, then frantically unharnessed Percy from the wagon. "Can you stow my rig in the stable for the night?"

"Why sure," he said. "Least I can do f-for the hero of P-P-Pointer's C-Cove."

Mase took the revolver from under the seat, strapped it

around his waist, then led Levi to the back of the wagon. "Now, don't panic." He pulled up the edge of the tarp.

"Wh-what in t-tarnation? That fella don't look so good."

"It's Spoon. He's part of Willow Creek. If you would, keep the tarp over him and leave the stable door unlatched so I can get in. I'll be back before sunup." He grabbed Percy's mane and pulled himself onto his back.

"D-don't you want a s-saddle?"

"No time." Mase kicked his heels into the animal's sides. With the wagon no longer a burden, Percy bolted forward, hitting full gallop within seconds. To gain as much speed as possible, he leaned forward as far as he could, his cheek rubbing against the horse's sweaty neck.

For ten minutes, the beleaguered animal huffed down the narrow road toward the plantation with Mase whipping the reins across his sides. With time running out and every second ticking off quicker than the one before, the hoofbeats pounded into the dirt like an executioner's drum roll.

Suddenly the steed's newfound energy faltered as his gallop's smooth, rhythmic motion turned jerky. He dipped as his massive engine began to sputter.

In the distance, Mase could hear the swishing waters of his beloved Willow Creek. When they finally reached its banks, Percy's gait was beyond unsteady. Slowly they waded in. Halfway across, Percy lost his footing and the seventeen-hundred-pound beast collapsed into the water with Mase clinging to his mane. The poor animal lay kicking and neighing in high-pitched tones as it tried desperately to stand.

With all his might, Mase tried prodding the pitiful animal up by tugging on his reins. All Percy could do was lie there panting, saliva dripping from his mouth. The broken bone protruding from below his left-front knee made it impossible for him to do anything but suffer. The only course of action was to put him out of his misery.

He reached to his holster, but the revolver was gone. He plunged his hand into the water and ran it along the bottom until finally finding the weapon wedged between two rocks. Dripping wet, he placed the barrel at the top of the horse's mane and began to pull the trigger, then stopped. He could not risk the shot. With Silas lurking nearby, he could not chance alerting him to his presence. Mase shoved the gun back into his holster. The element of surprise had to be maintained. Percy would have to continue to struggle in the current until Mase could return to put him out of his misery.

Chapter 33

Mase's familiarity with the path from the creek to the plantation enabled him to move along swiftly while hope and adrenaline helped him overcome the pain in his ankle. As he moved, he played out his plan in his head until—halfway into the woods—a sound stopped him cold. In front of him, leaves rustled, then twigs snapped underfoot. They were the same sounds that preceded the sniper's shot that had landed him in Juana's cabin. He inched his revolver to his chest.

A light floated through the trees—bobbing and weaving in and out of sight, closer and closer until—

"Who's that?" came a voice from behind the tiny flame.

He clicked the revolver into firing position.

"Go on. Ain't nothin'," whispered another voice farther behind.

Mase stretched the gun in the direction of the light and held a sweaty finger on the trigger. He waited. The ground crunched and crackled as two figures emerged from the brush. "Don't—move," Mase said.

The figures continued toward him.

"I said, do—not—move." His voice was slow, deliberate,

and filled with intent.

"Yes, sir. We stayin' put," the lead figure said, throwing his hands in the air.

"Who's behind you?"

"That's Benjamin, sir."

"And who might you be?"

"Angus Walker."

Recognizing the voice and name to be one of the Willow Creek slaves, he lowered his revolver. "Angus, it's me, Mase." He walked up to him and put his hand out.

"That really you, Mr. Mase?" Angus whispered as he raised the candle for a better look.

"Sho'nuff," said the other man, appearing from behind. "Mr. Mase, it's me, Benjamin Douglas." He reached past Angus and grabbed Mase's hand.

"What're you men doing out here?" he asked.

"Oh, uh… well, uh… we—"

"You don't have to tell me. I know you're running."

They both looked to the ground.

"Don't worry, I understand."

They looked at one another. "You do?"

"Yes. And I'm back to make it right."

"Mr. Mase, it's been bad since you went off to war. We all been beat like dogs. They been doing unspeakable things. Jus' this evenin'—"

"No need to go on. Run if you want, nobody's going to come after you. You've got my word on it. Right now, I *have* to find Maudie and Sissy. Do you know where they are?"

"No, sir. After we found Cluc, we knew we had to run, so we took off."

"What time is it?"

"Coming up on midnight, I suppose. I don't rightly—"

"That's okay." Mase patted both on the shoulders then turned back onto the path. "You boys be safe now," he said, disappearing into the forest.

Moments later, he reappeared at the edge of the woods where the path ran in front of the row of slave cabins. On most nights, there would be a half-dozen candles burning in the windows along with two or three torches lighting the dirty trail to the big house. But not tonight. Tonight, all light had been extinguished to aid the mass exodus that was to come.

Thankful for the cover of darkness, he snuck around the back of the cabins to avoid being detected. If Silas saw him, it would jeopardize his plan. All he had to do was get to Maudie's undetected before she and Sissy arrived. Once there, they would wait inside until Silas came pounding on the door. Mase would open it and more than gratefully unload his revolver. He prayed he would make it in time.

He was too late. From five cabins away, he heard feet pattering along the path from the pond toward her cabin. All he could make out were their silhouettes, the larger one pulling the other by the hand. As they got closer, he could hear their panicked breathing.

He started to shout that he was there to protect them, but he had to remain quiet. Knowing Silas was right behind, he would have to alter his plan and wait to catch him by surprise. Maudie said he had banged on the door two separate times and that the second time, when he yelled to let him in, they used the stones. As long as Mase took Silas down before then, his plan would work.

By the time they closed the door behind them, he

had made it to the neighboring cabin. Silas would be there any second. Mase pulled his revolver and waited in the shadows, listening to the blood thumping through his temples. His hands shook remembering the bear-like strength the man possessed.

From out of the woods, like an enraged bull released from its holding pin, barreled the dark figure of the man he was sent back in time to kill. Silas bounded toward the door, grunting, ready to beat his way through. When he was only a few yards away, Mase stepped from the shadows, the revolver stretched out before him, gripped in both hands.

Silas froze, his eyes narrowing as the corner of his lip curled up like a snake climbing his cheek.

Mase took two steps closer. "Remember me?"

"Well, I'll be. If it ain't the deserter—back from hell."

"Which is exactly where you're going." Mase yanked the trigger.

There was no clap of thunder. No flash of lightning. Only the click of the firing hammer against wet metal. He stared at the weapon the river's water had rendered useless. He pulled the trigger again—still nothing.

Before he could react, Silas was digging his shoulder into Mase's stomach, running him into the ground. His fists, like meaty sledgehammers, slammed into one side of Mase's face then the other, again and again. In an instant, Silas was straddling him, holding the revolver in one hand while still beating him with the other. The taste of gunmetal mingled with Mase's blood as Silas jammed the pistol into his mouth.

"Like how it feels, little man?" Silas said, thrusting it farther into his throat as his eyes bulged, wild with rage. He leaned next to Mase's ear and pulled the trigger. "Bang!" he yelped. He pulled it again—click, and again—click, and again—click. "She should dry out any second now," Silas howled.

Mase flailed helplessly, grasping at the gun, choking on its barrel.

"Forget this!" Silas jerked the weapon from Mase's mouth and threw it away. Ready to end the battle, he reached behind him and pulled a six-inch knife from his boot. Leveraging his massive frame, he leaned back, holding it with both hands above his head, preparing to drive it into Mase's heart. Mase closed his eyes, waiting for the final blow.

Phwop! Silas' head lurched forward with the rest of his body following. The full weight of his torso landed across Mase's chest, his beard scraping Mase's cheek as his head collided, face-first, with the dirt.

Mase's eyes fluttered as he faded into unconsciousness. From above, a blurry figure rammed a shoe into the beast's side, sending the mountain of flesh rolling over.

Mase sucked wind back into his lungs.

"Oh, dear child!"

The words floated over him like a warm blanket. "Maudie?" he said, struggling to bring her into focus.

She dropped the rock used to topple the goliath and pulled him to his feet. "My dear, dear boy," she said, cupping his face in her hands.

Two arms wrapped around him from behind. "You came back!" His heartbeat quickened. The voice... so soft, sweet, and familiar. The girl he had fallen in love with from the future—the one he could not save—was embracing him once again.

He staggered around to her. "Sissy... it *is* you." His eyes and cheeks were swollen, a gash split his left eyebrow, but his bloodstained smile drew her into him. Squeezing him tighter, she pressed her head against his chest as her tears flowed onto his shirt.

"It's alright—you're safe now," he muttered. With a stroke of her hair, the last of his strength left his body. His legs wobbled, and he began to fall.

"We got you," Maudie said, reaching around them both. Together they stood holding him steady as he faded into unconsciousness.

"Si—las!" From out in the darkness, a high-pitched voice split the night air with the two razor-sharp syllables.

Spinning around, they watched as the beast regained his senses and stood, knife in hand, ready to finish them all. His greasy hair and the fresh blood oozing down his neck glistened in the moonlight as he glanced over his shoulder in the direction from which his name had come, then back to them.

"I'll gut each of ya," he growled, "slow and dull until ya tell me whar that gold is."

"Move and die!" The voice came again.

Unable to find the source of the command, he dug his heels into the ground, lowered his head and charged. The ignition of both barrels sent a lethal round of buckshot into his back. With a colossal thud, he collapsed at their feet. Maudie and Sissy opened their eyes, watching as his life drained into a puddle of blood around them.

A cloud of smoke lingered beside the cabin, encircling the phantom responsible for sending their enemy to answer for his sins. The weapon remained aloft, shaking, still in a firing position in case the demon resurrected again. As the smoke faded, the figure of a tall, dark-haired girl emerged, and the barrel eased downward. Her features had weathered. She was thinner now. The bags under her eyes showed the stress of where she had been and the bittersweetness of her return. Annabelle Winslow had come home.

Maudie eased Mase to the ground. "Go fetch Jim and Samuel," she instructed Sissy. "Tell 'em to bring a wagon. And tell the rest there's no need to run." Then she turned and walked toward the corner of the cabin where Annabelle still stood, shaking and clutching the gun.

"Annabelle—honey." Her voice was tender and warm. "It's okay now. You're home."

Annabelle continued to stare blankly at Silas's corpse as tears welled in her eyes and her lip quivered.

"Maudie's here, dear." She placed her hand onto Annabelle's cheek. "You're home, honey. You're safe. Ain't nobody—ever—gonna hurt you again."

Annabelle turned to her, wanting nothing more now than to wrap her arms around the woman who had cared for her since birth. She fell into Maudie's arms, and together they wept.

Candles began flickering in the windows throughout the slaves' quarters. Several torches popped up along the path, illuminating the night as slaves crept out of their cabins and down to Maudie and Annabelle. Sissy stood next to them, tending to Mase as he lay unconscious in a wagon. The gathering of slaves encircled them, half laying hands on Annabelle, the other half on Mase. Some prayed silently, some in whispers. The soft, reverent murmuring faded into a hushed version of "Swing Low, Sweet Chariot."

As the body of souls swayed in unison, holding hands,

looking toward the heavens, the line slowly parted as Dr. Parkin wheeled Braxton Winslow to his daughter's side. Still shaking, she fell to her knees beside his chair, hugging and kissing him. Unable to form a sentence anymore, he drew a tear-stained heart on his chalkboard and held it out to her. The slaves sang on, mindful of this glorious Easter day.

With Maudie and Sissy's help, they all climbed into the wagon with Mase. Annabelle was still holding the shotgun with which she had killed Silas. Braxton put his hands on hers, slowly shaking his head. Gently he pulled it from her and handed it to Dr. Parkin, who laid it next to him in the front seat.

As they passed the pond, Doc stopped the rig and turned to the back of the wagon. "Brax. What would you like me to do with it?"

His arm stretched out to the pond was Braxton's reply.

The doctor nodded, then picked up the shotgun and walked to the water's edge. With both hands, he grabbed it at the end of the barrel, just above the custom engraving that read *ThunderStick*. With as much strength as he could muster, he flung it out into the water.

Mase's eyes fluttered open to a hazy, sun-filled room. The scent of jasmine floated through the open window as a golden hue cast into every corner, revealing objects from his past. He smiled at the dings on the bedside table, all incurred during glorious battles fought with toy soldiers. His riding boots, given to him when he was six, still stood in the corner. A bracelet made of braided strips of leather given to him by Sissy on his fifteenth birthday hung on the doorknob. If not for the throbbing pain in his head, he would have believed he was in heaven.

With a groan, he pulled back the blanket and swung his legs to the floor, the shift to vertical sending the room spinning. Like a wounded sloth, he pulled himself up by the bedpost.

"My word," Maudie said, carrying a bowl of broth through the door, her face beaming. "Child, you need to lay down before you fall over."

"Maudie!" he said, reaching out to her.

In a second, she was hugging him tighter than she had ever done before, and then she took his face in her hands. "It took you long enough to get back to us."

"You wouldn't believe just how far away I was."

"You're here now—that's all that matters." She pulled back. "But you do need to get back in bed. You didn't pass out for nothing." She pulled a tiny hand mirror from the bedside table and held it out to him.

The reflection resembled a patched-up rag doll more than a young man in his prime. His face was gaunt. His left eye was still swollen shut, and his nose and cheek were black and blue. The only thing on the mend was the cut across his eyebrow, which Dr. Parkin had sewn shut that night.

"Hmmm, not too shabby," he said.

"Mister funny bones, you'd best be getting back in bed before you fall apart."

He leaned past her toward the window. "Say—that wagon in the front lawn. It looks like the one Spoon and I came in on."

She turned to follow his gaze out the window to the tarp-covered wagon next to the front porch. Her voice suddenly turned somber. "Mase, you need to lay back down."

"I'm sorry," he said, wobbling toward the door. "I have to go get Spoon. I left him in town. I have to—"

"He's *not* in town."

His eyes brightened. "He's here?"

"Will you sit for me a minute? Please?" She pulled a chair from the corner and helped him into it. "Spoon *was* here."

"What do you mean *was*? Where's he now?"

She looked out the window then to the ceiling before closing her eyes, her lips moving in silent prayer. Turning back to him, she balled her hands together, pressing them against her chin. "I need to finish a story I started with you in this room before you left to go fight."

"Can't you tell me where Spoon is first?"

"Patience. Just listen."

He loosened his grip on the armrest and sat back.

"The night before you left, I started to tell you about the stone I had given you. Do you remember it—the one you put in your diary?"

"Of course."

"And remember, I said it was more than it appeared and that it possessed a special power?"

"Yes."

"That stone has the ability to change lives. It can—"

"I know, Maudie," he said, beaming. "I know *every-thing* about the memory stone."

She tucked her chin. "But how?"

"Because *you* told me everything."

"What? I don't think so. Our conversation was interrupted before I could go any further."

"I remember that too," he said. "You told me later."

She closed her eyes, shaking her head. "I'm sure I never got to explain it all."

"But you did." He paused. "I believe it's *me* who needs to tell *you* a story."

She pulled a chair next to him. "Maybe so," she said, folding her hands in her lap.

For the next hour, he walked her through every twist and turn of his journey. He described how she had explained its powers and how one stone had taken him into the future and another had brought him back. She chuckled as he explained how she thought he was out to sabotage them, tears filled her eyes as he told her how he and Sissy had fallen in love, and her blood boiled as he described Silas's murderous attempts on all their lives.

When he finished, she sat shaking her head, holding her hand over her heart. "My, oh my. Most folks would've hightailed it out of here after hearing that story." A long moment passed. "Plain to see, isn't it?"

"What is?"

"How much good they can do." She took his hand into her lap. "Mase, I had to do something."

"What?"

"I had to use the stones again."

"Again?"

She patted his hand. "Honey, Levi Johnston brought Spoon back early this morning. He knew he was dying and thought we'd want him here when he passed."

"Please tell me he's not—"

She silenced him with a lift of her finger. "Doc Parkin confirmed he only had an hour or two left. I had to act fast. I met with your daddy and told him everything."

The slapping of chalk against slate turned their heads.

Sitting in his wheelchair at the doorway was Mr. Winslow, holding the chalkboard. The jagged lettering read, *I didn't believe her.*

"Dad!" Mase said, pushing himself up.

Braxton waved him to stay seated. His paralysis still very much a part of his life, he wheeled himself to the edge of the bed and nodded for Maudie to continue.

"No, sir," she said, smiling back at him, "Mr. Brax wouldn't have *any of it*—at first—but I told him every-thing about the stones, same as I did with you."

"What happened?"

Her voice melted into a loving tone. "As Spoon lay in the wagon dying, I placed one of the stones in his hand. Mr. Brax and Annabelle were by his side. As we waited, Annabelle began to cry. I knew she was crying for him but also for herself. She still hadn't let go of what happened that night, and it was easy to see she was never going to. Killing Silas hadn't healed her heart.

"Somehow our Spoon knew her pain." She paused as tears fell. "Even in his death, he could sense it. With his last breaths, he asked if she would hold his hand. As she reached down, I saw him open his palm with the stone in it. She laid hers over it. Just before he passed, he placed his other hand on top and wrapped his fingers around hers. A second later—they were gone."

No one moved. The wind whisked through the open window into the room. A dove landed on the windowsill, its cooing breaking the silence.

Braxton pointed Mase to his chalkboard.

He smiled as he watched him write, *They have new lives.*

Putting his arms around his father, Mase whispered in

his ear, "They most certainly do."

Over the next several weeks Mase's wounds healed as did the plantation's. There were no more beatings or intimidating threats from overbearing foremen. No one ran away. Even those that had run came back.

As life settled back into place, Mase explained his odyssey through time to his father. Braxton's eyes grew large, and he sat listening with rapt attention as Mase painted the picture of how different the world would be and how the plantation's future generations were in jeopardy.

When he finished, Braxton sat, staring at the ground. Although his body was failing him, he was as mentally sharp as he had always been, so Mase was not surprised that his father wanted to explore the opportunities his travels had presented. As if every second counted, he grabbed his chalkboard and scribbled, *Can we change things?*

It was a question Mase had anticipated, and his face lit up. "Yes," he said, clasping his hands together, "and I have a plan."

Two hours later, Mase was wheeling his father onto the front porch. The faint sound of gospel songs seasoned with the scent of honeysuckle floated across the lawn. Both their faces were beaming from their discussion. Braxton's face brightened even more as he watched Sissy bound her way up the steps to steal his son away for a stroll around the pond.

As he watched them walking hand in hand, Braxton thought about the consequences of the relationship Mase had developed in a time that was more understanding. If they were to share a life together now it would be fraught with danger. All he wanted to do was protect them, then he smiled realizing that he was seeing the future and what could be.

Chapter 34
(Today)

Zoey fiddled with the pink strip of hair that bisected her black locks, twirling and twisting it into an entangled rat's nest, while thumping her pencil against a coffee mug in rhythm with the headbanging tunes pounding through her earphones. It was her most used go-to tactic of coping with her tyrannical boss and the ever-growing pressures of her job.

"How bad is this one?" squeaked a petite young girl, placing a small stack of envelopes on her desk.

"Hi Petra," she said, laying the headphones to the side.

"Is it a bad assignment?"

Zoey rolled her eyes. "Not as bad as some. I have to interview a bunch of people who give money to charities. I'm supposed to find out how they got their money, what prompted them to turn do-gooder, and then how much moola they're doling out."

"What's wrong with that? Sounds pretty noble to me."

"Oh man, don't I sound like the Wicked Witch of the West? I'm sorry, I'm a little tainted. I had a bad experience last year with an article that opened my eyes to the fact that some of these guys are just about the tax breaks and public perception." She paused. "Hmmm, I bet Greg would love an article that put the rotten ones in the hot seat."

"You mean exposing these guys for what they are?"

"Yeah," she said. "He loves anything edgy."

"Sounds like a Pulitzer Prize in the making. Well, I gotta finish delivering the mail. Holler if you need anything."

Zoey placed her earphones back on and resumed pencil tapping as she dove into a three-inch stack of papers on her potential philanthropic targets. The dullness of the assignment suddenly glistened with righteousness. Exposing a fake shining knight would be more beneficial to an *NYC Chronicle* reader than any sugarcoated flimflam story.

From her list of ten prospects, she circled three: Jameson McDougle, Ectro Corp, San Francisco, California; Frances Schwartz, Mingle and Manners Inc. Houston, Texas; and Raymond and Belle Lanier, WCP Org., Charleston, South Carolina. Next to the latter, she wrote, *trust-fund baby.*

The next afternoon as she prepared for her cross-country trips, Greg stepped into her office. "Ready for the crusade?" he asked.

"Getting there," she said, shoving her laptop into a satchel.

"What's the plan? It's already Tuesday, and I need the draft by next Wednesday."

She continued stuffing manila folders and notepads into another bag. "Relax. They've all agreed to meet with me for a half day. I'm going to start with McDougle in San Fran then Schwartz in Houston and finish with the Laniers in Charleston. With travel time, I should be back by Wednesday."

He wagged an authoritative finger at her. "Make sure you do. And don't forget, these guys are among the top-five charitable contributors in the US. Don't screw this up, Antonelli. We can't afford the liability or court costs of going head-to-head with gazillionaires."

"Don't worry, boss. I'll play it safe."

"Safe? Don't fold on me right out of the shoot though. I still need you to pit bull this one. I'm footing the bill on these trips based on *your* concept. Just don't screw it up and get us sued."

"Right, right—don't screw it up." She grabbed her satchel and slung her bag over her shoulder. "Gotta run," she said, rushing out the door, pretending to be late for her flight. "I'll keep you updated."

Her promotion to a full-fledged editor—handed to her on a silver platter by Paul Talbert—had been bittersweet. It had catapulted her into the position she had always wanted, but the price was having to deal with Greg's constant tirades and thumbscrew tactics.

It had been ten years since Paul's disappearance, and without him as a sounding board and confidant, the job had grown tiresome. More than anything, she still couldn't get over the idea she hadn't done enough to help him, and she was haunted by the thought of him taking his own life in some remote place with no one around. Besides that, she missed everything about him and wished she had expressed her true feelings when she had the chance.

By the end of the week, she had met with the first two individuals on her list and come away with nothing other than they were solid businesspeople with hearts for helping others. Jameson McDougle was a former Eagle Scout and missionary who had built a company out of his grandparents' garage and Francis Schwartz was an orphan who had created her business through hiring former foster kids and fellow orphans.

There was no cooking of the books, and all contributions were legit, according to the *Chronicle*'s lawyers. As much as she tried to uncover dirt and give Greg what he wanted, she was also relieved to discover there were still good people in the world.

With the weekend ahead and nothing to show for her efforts, she decided to do something she had wanted to do since Paul vanished. Having already visited Charleston numerous times, she decided to venture out. She would rent a car and take the short hour-and-a-half drive to Beaufort and spend a couple days exploring the town he had grown so fond of. If it didn't live up to his description, she would simply turn around and head back.

Her midnight arrival into the city left her just enough time to check into one of the oceanside hotels. Without the slightest thought of unpacking, she opened the windows to the warm sea breeze and promptly fell asleep to the sounds of the waves lapping onto the shore.

Seagulls, sun, and the scent of bacon emanating from the hotel's outdoor grill woke her the next morning. Still fully clothed, she quickly changed and headed in the direction of the savory aroma.

"Hey, miss," said a pleasant-looking gentleman in a chef's hat, carrying a plate of biscuits down the hall. "Are you looking for the best breakfast in Beaufort?"

"I am," she said, stifling a yawn.

"Well, follow me."

A moment later, she was sitting poolside, watching the sun bedazzle the horizon while being served a hearty portion of shrimp and grits.

"Didn't I tell ya we had the best breakfast in town?" the chef said.

"You were sooo right," she gushed, her mouth still half-full.

"Where you from?" he asked.

"New York City."

"Ahhh, I actually studied cooking there several years ago. Amazing how much energy there is in that town. Are you sightseeing, here on business, a wedding or something?"

"You might say I'm on a business detour. A friend of mine fell in love with the place, so I'm checking it out before heading back to Charleston on Monday."

"What's your agenda?"

"Maybe a buggy tour and a visit to the lighthouse. I also heard the shops along Bay Street are nice. Oh—and I also wanted to go by the Willow Creek Mall."

"Sounds like a fun day. All those are great ideas. Not sure about the Willow Creek Mall though."

"What do you mean?"

"Never heard of it."

"Really? It's supposed to be in a shady part of town."

"I know the Willow Creek Plantation area, but there's no mall there and it's *far* from shady."

"You're sure there's not a mall there?"

"Positive. The main things in that area are a bunch of huge houses and an awesome estate where the plantation used to be. It's a 500-acre spread where kids go for help."

Suddenly her desire to experience the rest of the town was on the back burner.

Within the hour, she was in her car, winding her way through the streets of the Willow Creek Plantation section of Beaufort. She rolled the windows down and drove below the speed limit, taking in the genteel splendor of the antebellum mansions and Victorian homes with their finely manicured lawns, iron-fenced courtyards, and well-maintained window boxes. Mothers meandered through the community gardens, pushing their babies in lace-covered strollers. Children chased butterflies and played kickball and tag.

A soccer ball suddenly jetted into her path from out of nowhere. She brought the car to an abrupt halt as a little girl with pigtails ran out in front to retrieve it. Scurrying back to the roadside, she stopped next to a large wooden sign at the entrance to a cobblestone road leading into a canopy of moss-covered oaks. The sign read *Bellehaven Ranch*.

Zoey backed up, then pulled forward onto the cobblestone. The little girl ran beside her and yelled, "You here to get your kid, ma'am?"

Zoey stopped and leaned out the window. "No, just visiting. Do you go to camp here?"

"Ain't a camp, ma'am. It's a horse place for kids. Jake, he's my stepbrother, he comes here. You ought to bring your kid here. It's real pretty, and the folks who run it are really, really nice too."

"Why, thanks, young lady. I think I'll take a look right now." She gave the accelerator a nudge and crept the car into the tunnel of Spanish moss. After several minutes the cobblestone turned to asphalt, and the trees thinned out, revealing two hundred yards of road that gradually rose through plush, rolling hills.

On the left side, white fences stretched off into the distance, framing the property all the way to a creek lined with willow trees. Horses of various sizes, colors, and breeds grazed on the lush grass as children and adults walked alongside them, some petting them, some feeding them apples. All were smiling.

On the right side was a large pond with huge shade trees spread around a stunning, Victorian-style gazebo. As the road reached its zenith, the house that sat on top sent her heart fluttering. Amid century-old hickories and live oaks was a majestic, two-story antebellum mansion. Pristine white with massive columns and wrap-around porches on both levels, it was the centerpiece to a dreamscape known as Bellehaven Ranch.

As she pulled into a parking space in the front lawn marked "Guest," a young lady in a khaki shirt and shorts walked out to meet her. "Welcome to Bellehaven," she said, halfway to the car.

"Hi, I'm Zoey Antonelli."

"Pleased to meet you, Zoey," she said, holding out her hand. "I'm Nancy Sanders—outreach director."

"Wow, this is such a magnificent property."

"That it is," she said. "Do you have a child with you, or are you just checking us out?"

"Just checking you out." Zoey paused. "Actually, I don't know anything about what you do. I'm here because a friend told me about you—or rather about a mall that was *supposed* to be here." She looked off to the side and laughed. "I know I'm not making any sense. To be honest,

I didn't think you even existed."

Nancy motioned her to follow. "Come on," she said, leading her to the pasture side of the road. "Let's take a walk, and I'll explain what we're all about. In a nutshell, we help kids who are hurting by connecting them with our rescue horses. By 'rescue,' I mean we get them from places that either don't want them anymore or that they've been abused." They walked to the fence. "See that little boy brushing the copper mare?"

"Yes."

"The horse's name is Lindey. She's blind. The little boy—he's blind in one eye. We have kids that have experienced all types of trauma—the kinds that come from physical or emotional abuse, including sexual. We have ones that have been neglected, have an illness, or lost someone from a death. The concept is that kids need elements of a healthy relationship, especially safety and trust. They connect with the horses and their stories of rescue and restoration. Establishing a safe, caring relationship with these special animals can help them begin the healing process."

"Oh my gosh. What a great story and an incredible cause."

"It truly is."

"What does it cost?"

Her face glowed. "Not a thing. It's all privately funded."

"By who?"

"WCP."

Zoey's jaw dropped. "Of course, Willow Creek Plantation Organization!"

"You know about WCP?"

"Not much at the moment, but I hope to soon. I'm doing an investigative report for the *NYC Chronicle*, and they're on my list to interview. In fact, I'm supposed to meet with Raymond and Belle Lanier in Charleston on Monday."

"Oh, how great. You'll love them."

"Yeah, I can't wait," Zoey said, her lip curling into a question mark.

"Is there something else you'd like to ask?"

"I'm sure this'll sound strange, but when I said I didn't think you existed, it's because a friend of mine told me, about ten years ago, there was a mall located here."

"Hmmm, not sure where they would've come up with that. We started Bellehaven about ten years ago. The whole property, which used to be the Willow Creek Plantation, has been here since before the Civil War." She paused. "Let's go back to the house, and I'll give you some brochures on us. It may help with your meeting with Ray and Belle."

As they walked back to the house, a white van pulled in next to Zoey's car. A black man jumped out, ran to the back, and pulled out several large foil-covered trays.

"Getting an early start on today's picnic?" Nancy said.

He turned and flashed a smile their way. "Morning, Miss Nancy." His voice was warm and welcoming with an infectious cheerfulness. "Kids gonna love what we got for 'em today." He looked directly at Zoey. "Will you be joining us, ma'am? We got plenty."

"Oh, no. I'm afraid I won't be able to."

"Well, if ya change your mind or wanna take some with ya, let me know. Y'all have a blessed day!" He turned and trotted off around the corner of the house.

"How often do you have picnics?" Zoey asked.

"Every day—compliments of that gentleman and his soup kitchen." She tilted her head to the front of the house.

"Come on in. I'll get you those brochures."

The house was full of light. A joyful air floated throughout as children, parents, and staff members darted between
rooms. Screen doors squeaked open and smacked shut as
staffers bounced in and out, preparing for their noonday
feast.

Zoey turned in a circle as she followed her guide
through the foyer to a living room that had been converted
into a welcome center. "Wow, there must be a thousand
pictures on these walls."

"Never counted, but that sounds about right. We take
pics of all our kids," she said, pulling a brochure and several flyers from a desk drawer.

"Everybody looks so happy."

"Probably because they are," Nancy said, handing the
information to her. "Look these over while I take care of
something in the kitchen. I'll only be a minute."

Sitting on a small wooden bench next to an open
window, Zoey spread out the information and began
reading. The sounds of laughter and merriment resonated
through the open house, filling the space with a tangible
sense of peace and harmony.

When Nancy returned, she found Zoey staring out the
window. "Did you get a chance to read any of the material?"

"Oh yes. I finished everything."

"Excellent. Do you have any questions?"

"None about what you do per se. However, I am curious
about the history of the plantation itself—how it survived
and got where it is today. And the money behind it all. I
didn't see any of that covered in the literature."

"I do get that question fairly often. At the request of WCP, we don't include that information because the program's two trustees don't care to be in the spotlight. As far as the background of the plantation, I'd be glad to tell you what I know."

"That'd be great," Zoey said, pulling out a pen and notepad. "You mind if I take some notes?"

"Not at all. So, where would you like me to begin?"

"How about the history of the plantation?"

"Sure." Nancy locked her fingers in front of her as she began her practiced speech. "The actual plantation dates back to the early eighteen hundreds. It was approximately eleven hundred acres. Its main source of income was cotton, corn, soybeans, and cattle. The original owner was Kendall Winslow. He initially had about a hundred slaves, but that dwindled after he passed away because..." she paused, a gleam in her eye, "the son he passed it to was *actually* a Union sympathizer who opposed slavery. In fact, his plantation was part of the Underground Railroad! Do you know about the Underground Railroad?"

"It was a network of secret routes and safe houses that helped slaves escape into Free States and Canada. What was the plantation owner's name?"

"His name was Braxton Winslow. And let me tell you—that was one brave man. If he'd been caught, he'd have been lynched, drawn and quartered and whatever else."

Zoey twisted her mouth. "With fewer slaves doing the work, couldn't that break a plantation back then?"

"Absolutely. But he just happened to have one heck of a son—a young man by the name of Masen. Not only was he a war hero, but he was also an incredibly savvy businessman. The story has it, he could predict the future.

During the war, he seemed to know the South was going to lose, so he prepared himself by secretly investing in various industries that did extremely well. No one knows where the money for the investments came from though. Considering the ravages of the war and the lack of slaves to work the plantation, they were going broke. People believe he had access to some sort of hidden reserve. There's even an old wives' tale that he dipped into some gold that was stolen from the Confederacy."

"What did he put his money into?"

"I never can get the timing right, but, as I recall, his investments included reinforced concrete, kerosene refineries, then a little thing called the telephone. Oh—and these always tickle me—but around 1870 it was paper clips, clothes hangers, and barbed wire.

"What's even more interesting is his ability to invest appeared to have passed down in the Winslow DNA. Every generation after him has invested in the most profitable new technologies and inventions of their time. It's as if they had a road map of when and where to put their money—hence the billions that have accrued over these many years."

"You said Bellehaven started ten years ago."

"That's right."

"Can you tell me how the transition came about?"

"I'm sorry, that's something the Laniers will have to help you out with."

"I understand. I can't thank you enough for all your time. This is going to be a tremendous help for my Monday meeting. And your organization is simply marvelous. I wish I had something like this when—"

Nancy waited for her to continue then wrapped her arms around her with a knowing hug. "You tell Ray and

Belle hello for me, would you? It was a pleasure meeting you."

"I will." Zoey thanked her again, then turned and headed out the door and back to her hotel.

Chapter 35

By the time Monday morning arrived, Zoey was more than eager to get back to Charleston. She understood why Paul had fallen in love with Beaufort but was aching to learn more about the ranch from the Laniers. She had already made up her mind that they were good people, and no skeletons would be lurking in their corporate closets.

The building the WCP Organization occupied was the most unassuming of all those on Meeting Street. Wedged between two historic Georgian-style offices, its one-story, plain brick façade was a pockmark on the outstanding architecture Charleston was known for. The interior, however, stood in stark contrast to the exterior. Crown molding, plush chairs, and warm tones, along with hundreds of pictures of happy kids from Bellehaven more than made up for its exterior's shortcomings.

"Hello. You must be the one and only Zoey Antonelli," said the spunky, young receptionist upon her arrival.

Zoey couldn't help but chuckle, comparing this greeting with the stoic ones delivered by the *Chronicle*'s receptionists. "Why, yes. I am. How could you tell?"

"Sign told me," she grinned, pointing to an LED display on the wall featuring an actual picture of her along with her name and company in scrolling letters.

"Oh my gosh. I love it," Zoey said.

"If you'll have a seat, Ray and Belle will be out in—"

"A flash!" said a chiseled, middle-aged man, bounding down the hall. Halfway through the doorway, he was holding out his hand. "Hi, Zoey, I'm Ray. We're thrilled to have you with us today."

"I'm thrilled to be here," she said. "I'm just thankful for your and Mrs. Lanier's time."

"Please, call me Ray," he said, ushering her into a conference room that resembled a Victorian parlor more than a meeting space. The large monitor on the wall was the only giveaway that it was a place of doing business.

The receptionist brought in a tray stacked with donuts, bagels, coffee, tea, and water. "Can I get you anything else, Zoey?"

"No, I'm fine, thank you," she said, admiring the incredible spread.

"Sorry I'm late."

Zoey turned to find a tall, statuesque brunette woman walking through the door.

"Hi, honey," she said, bending over to give her husband a kiss before reaching out her hand to Zoey. "Hi, I'm Belle." An air of grace followed her around the table and a Southern charm exuded from each syllable of her introduction. "We're so pleased to meet you. I hope you've been enjoying the city."

"Actually, I've been in Beaufort for the past two days. I even went by Bellehaven Ranch."

"Oh my, then you've seen a piece of heaven," she said.

"I believe I have. By the way, Nancy Sanders said to tell you hello."

"We just love Nancy."

"She was extremely helpful," Zoey said, putting her hand to her chest. "What you're doing there, Mrs. Lanier, is so inspiring. And to be honest, it's really what I wanted to talk to you about."

"Wonderful," Mrs. Lanier said with a smile.

"But before we get into it, I have some other questions I wanted to ask regarding your finances and charitable contributions. As I mentioned on the phone, the piece is about your philanthropic giving."

"What would you like to know, dear?" Mrs. Lanier asked while her husband reached under the table and pulled out a large box labeled "Taxes/Financials/Charities."

Placing it in front of Zoey, he said, "These are copies of all our financials and charitable giving."

Zoey clapped her hands. "I'm so impressed. Nobody else has been this prepared."

"It's that military training." Mrs. Lanier turned to her husband. "Thank you, Captain Lanier," she said in an over-the-top Southern accent.

"Oorah," he replied.

"Can I take it back with me, Captain Lanier?" Zoey blushed. "Is that correct? Do I call you 'Captain'?"

He laughed. "You can just call me Ray and you can take the entire box and whatever else you think you need."

"Thank you sooo much. This saves us from a lot of boring questions. But I do have a few I'd like to ask, if that's alright."

"Shoot," he said.

"I was able to glean from Nancy the vast majority of

your wealth has come from investments, is that correct?"

"Correct."

"And from my preliminary research, it looks like most of your money is from trusts that have worked their way down over seven generations."

"Actually, it's been eight."

"And it appears there're two trusts valued at a total of $1.25 billion."

Just then the door opened, and the receptionist peeked her head around the corner. "I'm sorry, Ray, but I have your son on the line. There's nothing wrong, but he'd like to speak with you."

As he walked out, Belle picked up a remote and pointed it to the monitor. "While he's gone," she said, fiddling with the buttons, "why don't we watch our Bellehaven video."

"Oh, I'd love that!" Zoey said, straightening in her chair.

In a moment, the Bellehaven Ranch logo popped on-screen with an aerial shot of the property fading in from behind. The narrator's warm voice began with a high-level description of the organization and its purpose, followed by statistics on the thousands of children that had participated in its programs.

"Excuse me," Belle said. "Let me go check on Ray just to make sure everything's alright."

"Oh, sure," Zoey replied, continuing to watch picture after picture of kids and parents flashing across the screen. Moments later Nancy Sanders appeared, talking about the importance of the outreach program. As the narrator took over for the last segment, soothing music faded in as images of their daily picnics scrolled across the monitor.

Zoey leaned forward as the camera zoomed in on the image of the nice man she had met from the soup kitchen.

"Sorry about that," Belle said, stepping back into the room.

Zoey paused the video, leaving the smiling man's face framed in the center of the screen.

"Did you like the video?"

"I loved it. It's incredibly professional."

"Why, thank you. So where'd we leave off?"

"The trusts. I was confirming there're two that are valued at $1.25 billion and that one's in your name and the other's in your husband's. Is that correct?"

"Not exactly."

Zoey blinked. "I'm sorry, what part did I get wrong?"

The corners of Belle's mouth turned up slightly. "Lots of people think Ray and I are the two trustees."

"I'm confused. You and Ray *aren't* the trustees?"

"I am but not Ray." She shuffled through the box on the table and pulled out a multipage document. She flipped a couple pages then handed it to Zoey. "This is the section of the trust that indicates whose name it's in."

Zoey ran her finger across the legal jargon then stopped and read the bold print that said, "*Name of Trustee— Annabelle H. Winslow.*" She tilted her head. "Annabelle?"

"Everybody calls me Belle, but Annabelle is my given name."

"So you're a direct descendant?"

"I am, but this is where it gets confusing—and one of the reasons we don't like to share too much." She hesitated. "It's all in the box Ray has for you, but I'll try to explain it here. You see, it was hard to prove my lineage with the Winslows because I didn't have any direct living relatives, and the other, distant relatives I did have had never met me. It was as if I had just dropped out of the sky.

"To complicate matters further, when I was young, I had a form of amnesia that wiped out all my memories before the age of twenty-one. That's why you'll also find a lot of DNA records in the box along with a string of finely crafted stipulations of how the trust money was to flow from generation to generation until finally reaching us. The way Masen Winslow had it written, every generation was fully aware that one day the money would end up with me—the girl from out of nowhere."

"You said 'us' in a previous sentence. I thought it was in *your* name."

"That's because there is another trustee."

"Who?"

She turned to the monitor, her face glowing. "Him."

Zoey dropped her pen. "The man who caters your picnics? I met him."

"Then you've also met an angel, my dear." Belle walked to the monitor. "The man in this picture," she said, placing her fingers to his pixelated image, "is the man that cared for me until I met Ray. He provided me with a roof over my head, food to eat, and he comforted me when others teased and shunned me for being the misfit with no memory. I was orphaned into this world, and he was there, providing me with unconditional love." She teared up. "And he's done the same for so many others."

"But how did he become a trustee? He's not a family member, is he?"

She shook her head. "No, we're not related. The stipulation in my trust indicated I would have a man in my life who would take care of me. There's a whole section that goes into detail about his physical features along with his moral character. It stipulates I was to give him whatever portion of the trust I deemed appropriate."

"But how can you verify he's the one?"

"By virtue of this," she said, revealing a black box from underneath the table. "You see, Masen Winslow loved to write." She opened the box and lifted out a plain leather-bound book about three inches deep. "This is one of his journals. It was locked in a safety deposit box with instructions to give it to me when my trust had been granted. Its pages chronicle a story of redemption and faith. It describes an extraordinary journey of how love transcends time. It describes the man you see on the screen in perfect detail. I knew without a doubt that this man," she turned back to the monitor, "Jeziah Campbell, was the second recipient of the trust."

Zoey shook her head. "Never in my life have I heard of such stipulations to a trust. How much did you give him?"

"Half."

"You mean he's worth $625 million!"

"He was. That's changed now based on what he's given away."

"Which is?"

She beamed. "Everything."

"Oh my gosh!" Zoey said, placing her hand over her mouth. "I... well, I-I've never—"

"I know," Belle said. "Not something you see happening too often."

Zoey rubbed her temples, trying to reconcile the magnitude of such generosity. "Is what he's given away public knowledge?"

"Oh no," Belle said, shaking her head.

"Why?"

"Simple. He doesn't want it to be. Will you please promise to keep it to yourself?"

"Oh yes, by all means." Zoey eyed the journal. "But how many people know about that?"

"Just three."

"Can you tell me who they are?"

"Certainly. Myself, my husband, and now—you."

"Me? Why am I the only other person?"

Belle's eyes sparkled as she placed her hand on her shoulder. "Because you, my dear, are part of its pages. Masen Winslow has written you would know him as Paul Talbert, and one day we should seek you out. That's why we were over the moon when you contacted us." She paused. "I'm sorry so many years have passed. We should have looked for you sooner."

All sensation left Zoey's body as she sat thunderstruck. She tried to speak, but all she could do was sit there, trying to put the pieces together—the diary he was basing a book on, her discovery the plantation existed, and now the journal. The room spun faster and faster.

"Zoey." Her name came from a faraway place. Then louder. "Zoey—are you okay?"

She blinked, clearing away the puzzle pieces cluttering her mind. "I-I guess," she said, looking up to find Ray standing beside her. Belle was stroking her hair.

"Have a drink of water," Belle said, reaching for the tray.

With both hands, Zoey grabbed the glass and gulped. A moment passed. "This is all so surreal." Her heart was pounding. "It doesn't make any sense, but then again... it-it makes perfect sense. I *did* know Paul. He *had* a diary and was writing a book from it. He described the plantation, but then he couldn't find it, but then there it was—just as it was in his diary—and then..." She looked squarely into Belle's eyes. "Then there was—you."

"Amazing, isn't it?"

Zoey looked out the window, placing her hand on her chest. No one spoke. Finally, she turned back to them. "This isn't a joke, is it?"

"No," Ray said.

"And I'm not dreaming?" she said softly, not wanting to break the spell.

"No. It's not a dream." Belle patted her hand. "*Your* Paul Talbert was *our* Mase Winslow."

Zoey chuckled to herself. "My sweet, sweet Pauly— spinning a tale through time."

As she sat staring at the journal, Belle slowly pushed it toward her. "Now it's your turn," she said.

"I'm not sure what you mean."

"Zoey, on the last page are instructions that you are to take ownership of it." Belle flipped to the back, pointed to the last entry, and read aloud. "Upon finding Zoey Antonelli, please pass ownership of this journal to her. She will have all the pieces to finish the story." Belle paused at the next line. "Do you know why he'd sign it, 'Your literary Sasquatch'?"

Zoey burst into tears and laughter. All she could do was nod.

"There's one other thing," Belle said, pulling a small envelope out of the box. "This is for you."

"What is it?"

"We don't know," Ray said. "We were just instructed to give it to you along with the journal. Since it's got a wax seal on it, we didn't think it appropriate to open. Whatever it is, there's something with some weight inside."

"Do you mind if I open it now? The seal looks like it's going to fall off any minute anyway."

"If you don't mind me looking on."

"Not at all."

Just as she had anticipated, the slightest swipe of her fingernail popped the seal. As she turned it up, a thin, flat key clinked onto the table.

"Is that it?" Belle asked.

"No, there's a paper of some sort." With the tips of her fingers, Zoey carefully pulled out a folded sheet of paper then gently flattened it out next to the key.

"It's a key to a safety deposit box, Zoey! That's your documentation to use it. Where's it located?" exclaimed Belle.

"Wouldn't you know it?" Zoey chuckled. "It's at the Low Country Savings and Loan, Beaufort, South Carolina. They probably aren't even in business anymore."

"Oh, yes they are!" Belle clapped.

"That's who we work with at Bellehaven," Ray said.

After several minutes of marveling at her new treasures, Zoey stood and thanked them for their time.

Belle took her by the hand, and together they walked out into the hustle and bustle of downtown Charleston. The warm salt air and the sound of seagulls helped confirm her time with the Laniers was not a dream.

"When are you heading back to New York?" Belle asked.

Zoey pressed her lips together as she thought. "Probably tomorrow afternoon. Since I'm down here, I suppose I should go back to Beaufort and see about a certain safety deposit box. But to be honest, I want to go back to Bellehaven more than anything."

Belle put her hands on her shoulders. "Why, I think that's a grand idea." She hugged her, then watched her walk to her car. "Make sure you tell everyone Belle and Ray say hi," she shouted after her. "Oh! And please stay in touch."

That evening Zoey pulled into the same oceanside hotel she had stayed at the night before. After placing a quick room-service order, she rushed a shower then flopped onto the bed where she dove into Mase's journal. For the next four hours she sat riveted to the pages, each turn of the parchment bringing a new revelation more surreal than the one before.

Chapter 36

The next morning Zoey woke with the journal laid out on her chest—the spot she envisioned it would end up many times in the future.

After finishing breakfast, she hopped in her car, turned on the radio, and leaned her head back for her leisurely ride to the ranch. The sun brightened as the rumpling sounds of tires over the cobblestone entrance changed to the smooth whirring of rubber on the asphalt road leading up to the great house on the hill.

Because it was such a well-run ship, a staff member spotted her vehicle and dispatched a khaki-clad welcoming committee of one to meet her. Before she could turn off the ignition, a young man was at her window, ready and eager to make her feel at home. "Hi, I'm Mike Brown."

"Hi, Mike, I'm Zoey Antonelli."

"Are you a parent, guardian, or just visiting?"

"Just visiting. This is my second time out. I was here the day before and met with Nancy. Is she around, by chance?"

"I'm afraid she's off today. Is there something I can help you with?"

"Sure. To be honest, it's not Nancy I was here to see anyway."

"Oh. Who did you want to see?"

"Jeziah Campbell. I realize I'm probably early since he comes in around noon to cater your picnics."

The young man chuckled. "No, ma'am. JC lives here."

"Oh, of course he does," she said, trying not to sound foolish.

He pointed to a wall of greenery a hundred yards past the house. "He's right behind that big row of cedars."

"You mean he doesn't live in the big house?"

"Oh no, ma'am," he said with a grin. "Just follow the path. His place is the first one on the other side. You want me to take you?"

"No thanks, I can manage."

The path, made up of beautifully laid flagstones bordered by daisies, was a pleasant walk. The left side was open to the back of the big house, along with the pastures where the rescued horses romped about while unleashing their healing powers. To the right was a wall of flora rich with goldenrod contrasting against a backdrop of purple wisteria cascading from the trees that ran along a small brook.

As she approached the corner, just to the edge of the cedars, she stopped. Wiping her palms dry, she prepared herself for an encounter with the closest thing to a ghost she would ever have. She released a long, deep breath.

The difference between the plantation's main house and the three tiny cabins on the other side of the tree line was stark in both elegance and size. She could tell they had been refurbished with modern appliances, electricity, and plumbing. Other than that, she knew by their diminutive size, they most likely were former slave quarters. She looked back at the big house and wondered if the khaki-uniformed staffer had played a joke on her. Could a millionaire, even a former one, truly reside in such a space?

"Can I help you, miss?" came a voice from behind.

She spun around to find a black man holding a large bucket of potatoes. "Are you Jeziah Campbell?"

He smiled the same ear-to-ear grin from two days earlier. "Yes, ma'am, that's me."

At that moment she noticed something a tad out of symmetry with his face. His left eye was slightly out of line and a tad brighter. It was glass. Somehow it added to the warmth of all his natural features.

"And you'd be Ms. Antonelli."

"Why, yes. How did you know?"

"Been expecting you." He tilted his bucket to the first cabin. "Mind if I put these taters down?" he said almost apologetically.

"Oh, sure."

He trotted to his cabin, laid them on the front step, then hurried back. He brushed his palms across the sides of his overalls then reached out his hand. "Pleased to official-ly meet you, Ms. Antonelli," he said, bending in a slight bowing motion. "Is it okay if I call you Zoey?"

"By all means," she said, bemused by the sincerity of his politeness. "Sorry, I'm from New York. Southern hos-pitality is a little foreign to me."

He laughed. "Oh, I'm sure New Yorkers got manners too—probably just comes out in different ways. So glad you came back to see us."

"Yes, sir. I met with Ray and Belle Lanier yesterday and—"

"Don't you love them two?"

"Yes. Anyway, I met with them, and it was great and all, and well, I... uh—"

"It's okay," he said, pausing to give her a moment to feel more comfortable with her obvious question. "Don't be afraid. You can ask me anything."

"How'd you know I wanted to ask you something?"

He leaned toward her with half a grin. "Well, you didn't drop in ta peel taters, now did ya?"

She laughed. "No. But I promise to help if you'll answer my question."

"Deal. Is it okay if we do a walk-and-talk though? I need to be headin' back to the big house. Gotta get ready for the picnic."

"Of course. I almost forgot about your picnics."

He pulled a green apple from his pocket and began shining it as they strolled back up the path.

She cleared her throat. "According to Belle, you were part of a trust amounting to $625 million and you gave..." she paused, "all of it to charity." She stopped and turned to him. "Is that right?"

He continued rubbing the apple. "Yep."

Her lips parted, but no words followed.

"I take it you don't cotton to such a thing."

"Oh no, it's not that. I mean, it's an incredibly noble gesture but—*all* of it? Surely you wanted to keep some." She looked back at the tiny cabin. "Don't you need to hold on to a little bit?"

He looked at his apple. "This here's a Granny Smith. I like 'em better than the red ones." He detoured off the path over to the pasture. "Would you like one?"

"No, thank you."

He continued toward the fence with her stumbling after

him through the tall grass.

"Mr. Campbell—"

"Jeziah," he said over his shoulder.

"I'm sorry—I mean, Jeziah—that's so much money. It doesn't make sense."

As they reached the fence line, a mangy brown mare galloped up, her mane half-gone, the contour of every rib showing through her thin hide. Dozens of crude branding marks and other burns covered her neck and shoulders.

He held out the apple, which she promptly chomped down.

"Oh my gosh. What happened to her?" she said.

"This here's Grace. She came to us 'bout two months ago from a farm that didn't want her." He pointed to a long streak of grey hair running across her back leg. "See that-there odd colorin' on her hindquarters? Breeders don't much like those kinds of things. 'Cause she wasn't pretty like the other fillies, she got the bum end of an angry owner. Horses don't need brandin' no more, but Grace got thirteen plus another seven burns." He stroked the side of her neck. "But she's got a heart of gold. Still a little skittish but sweet as can be."

He turned back to her. "All that money you mentioned me giving away? None of it was mine anyhow. To be honest, I didn't want it, but Belle wouldn't take no for an answer. I gots all I need right here. Got my cabin, my friends up yonder at the big house, girls like Grace here, and a heap of love comin' and going. Best thing for me was to give that money to those that needed it." He paused. "We ain't on this earth to keep things for ourselves anyhow."

He reached into his pocket and brought out another

apple. "Wanna give it a try?"

"Sure," she whispered. When she took the fruit and stretched it across the fence to the disfigured mare, her shirt sleeve pulled up, revealing a tattoo of a butterfly designed to cover an ugly whelp on her inner wrist. Grace chomped away at the Granny Smith, and Zoey laughed as the horse nuzzled up to her in appreciation.

"She likes you," he said with a pat on her shoulder. Then Jeziah turned to her and smiled. "Will you do something for me?"

"Sure," said Zoey.

He held his palm open to her, tilting his head toward his hand. "Will you trust me?" he said warmly. "I just need ya to see something."

She nodded.

He pulled his shirttail out, then led her hand underneath. She stopped and took a deep breath. "It's alright," he said, guiding it to the center of his back. She fidgeted. "Don't worry," he reassured her in a whisper. Then he gently moved her fingers over the scars he still bore from so long ago.

She jerked back. "Oh my God—what happened?"

"It's okay," he said softly. Then he took her hand again and slowly pushed back her sleeve, revealing more tattoos—all covering the scars of so many cigarette burns. With his other hand, he rubbed the inside of her wrist, stopping on top of the butterfly. "All of us been hurt, Ms. Zoey."

Her eyes glistened with tears.

"Ain't no need in thinkin' we're alone."

She stood in silence.

"You know you're not alone, don't ya?"

She slowly nodded as tears rolled down her cheeks, then

she threw her arms around his neck, her breath coming in sobs. "H-how did you—"

"Ain't important." He pulled back and looked her in the eyes, tenderness and love radiating in his words. "We just forgive—we move on—and we care for those that need it."

Hand in hand, they walked back to the big house.

Before they reached her car, a group of children came running around the other side of the house. "There he is!" they yelled.

"Oops, I forgot," he said. "Afraid I gotta say goodbye here."

The children swarmed around him, tugging and pulling him through the lawn up onto the front porch.

"Sorry, Miss Zoey," he yelled over his shoulder. "Gotta tend to something for the chillins." He blew her a kiss, then plopped down on the top step while the eager youngsters gathered on the steps below.

"Did you get what you needed?" said the young man in khaki walking across the lawn.

She looked over the green pastures and saw Grace running carefree, ready to share the miracle she was. "Yes," she replied, "I got everything."

The young man opened the car door for her. She started to step in, then stopped and looked back at the porch where Jeziah sat chatting with the children as they patiently waited for the performance he had been summoned for. As he reached into his pocket, they squealed with delight.

Suddenly his hands were in motion—up and down his legs, across his chest, back and forth between his knees and under his arms. All the while, the staccato sounds of metal against metal filled the air. The children bounced around, stomping their feet and clapping in rhythm with every clickity-clack produced by the sterling-silver instruments.

She looked on in amazement. "I don't believe I've ever seen anything quite like that."

"It's a dying art for sure," the young man said.

"What is it he's doing?"

"Spoons, ma'am. He's playing the spoons."

As she pulled out of the parking lot, she rolled down her windows, leaving behind the sounds of children laughing over the clickety-clacking rhythms of her new friend. One more stop and she would be on her way back to New York and the sounds of sirens, horns, and people shouting at one another.

"Welcome to Low Country Savings and Loan," said the young bank clerk. "How may I help you?"

"I have a safety deposit box key along with this document. Is there someone who can help me access it?"

"Hmmm. Ms. Antonelli, I'm afraid this document isn't quite enough to get you access. You'll need to—"

"Excuse me," said a handsome man in a suit, "did you say Antonelli?"

"Yes."

"Zoey Antonelli?"

"Yes."

"Hi, I'm Bart Kennedy, branch manager. If you'll follow me, I think we can take care of you." He turned back to the counter. "Jen, can you bring an inventory sheet?"

"Thank you so much," Zoey said, following him down

the hall, through a maze of metal doors and gates that lead to a small room lined with safety deposit boxes.

"May I have the key?" he said, holding out his hand.

"Here you go."

"You must be pretty special," he said as he inserted it into the box.

"How's that?"

"The Laniers called yesterday to tell me you'd be coming." He slid out the box and laid it on the table. "Ready to see what's inside?"

"I don't know if it can top what I got yesterday, but sure, open away."

He turned the latch and flipped up the lid. "What in the—" He tilted his head. "How interesting. Jen, please note on the inventory sheet that there's only one item in the box. The contents—a stone."

The young clerk scribbled the findings onto the page with a muffled snicker.

"I'm sorry, Ms. Antonelli," he said placing his hand on her shoulder, "you never know what's in these things, especially those that've been here this long. Jen, would you enter next to the item a value of zero."

"No wait," Zoey said. She gazed down into the box for a long moment, her smile growing bigger. "No—please mark it—priceless."

A Personal Note From The Author

If you read *The Memory Stones* I would like to say a heartfelt thank you for sharing your time with me. If you enjoyed it and have time to post an honest review, I would greatly appreciate it. And if you'd like to contact me directly, feel free to email me through my website below. I love making new friends!

For more info visit:
LewisPennington.com

About The Author

Lewis Pennington graduated from East Carolina University in Greenville, North Carolina with a degree in Graphic Design and Marketing. Upon graduation, he moved to New York City where he began his career with the now defunct Science Fiction Magazine *Omni Magazine.* After decades of navigating through the corporate marketing maze he is now focusing on his next chapter in life—providing readers with inspirational fiction. Lewis and his family live in Asheville, North Carolina.

Made in the USA
Monee, IL
11 April 2022

94453726R00225